ACCLAIM FOR THE NOVELS OF JILLIAN MEDOFF

I COULDN'T LOVE YOU MORE

"The incredibly talented Jillian Medoff is one of those authors whose storytelling is so honest it feels more like truth than like fiction. Funny, wrenching, suspenseful, and smart, *I Couldn't Love You More* is one of those books that stays with you long after you've finished the last page."

—Lauren Grodstein, author of *A Friend of the Family*

"*I Couldn't Love You More* hits the universal truths, the deepest search for identity, family, and belonging. This captivating page-turner draws readers right into the intricacies of the human heart."

—Diana Abu-Jaber, author of *Birds of Paradise* and *Crescent*

"The witty and (sometimes) wise heroine of *I Couldn't Love You More* is an unmarried wife, a mother, a step-mother, a daughter, a sister, a would-be lover, and she is approaching middle age. Need I say more? Jillian Medoff has written an honest and comic novel that is unflinching and tremendous with love."

—Binnie Kirshenbaum, author of *The Scenic Route*

"Incisive, poignant, witty . . . How can a book be so harrowing and so acidly funny at the same time? I closed this addictive novel with a satisfied sigh."

—Jancee Dunn, author of *Why Is My Mother Getting A Tattoo? And Other Questions I Wish I Never Had to Ask*

"A thoroughly involving and intimately real portrait of a blended family in crisis. Jillian Medoff takes you inside the mind of a narrator undergoing life-changing events, and the voice in her head could be yours."

—Janice Erlbaum, author of *Girlbomb* and *Have You Found Her*

"Every woman has one: the guy who got away. So what happens when he walks into your life again? If you were happy before—can you still make that claim? The choices we make—and the ones we don't make—form the backbone of Jillian Medoff's wonderful novel. These are characters you know, or might even have been, and their trials and tribulations are by turn devastating, hilarious, and painfully familiar."

—Jodi Picoult, *New York Times* bestselling author of
Sing You Home and *House Rules*

"Unflinching in its honesty, *I Couldn't Love You More* is an intimate story of contemporary family love—with all its maddening and miraculous complexities. Jillian Medoff's writing dazzles the brain, cracks up the funny bone, and breaks open the heart. Her characters are so realistically layered, you'll sometimes want to hug them and sometimes want to shout at them, but you'll never want to forget them."

—Seré Prince Halverson, author of *The Underside of Joy*

HUNGER POINT

"[A] wonderfully obsessive novel . . . bitterly funny."
—*Vanity Fair*

"[A] semi-picaresque odyssey from self-loathing to self-acceptance and sanity . . . as recklessly candid as only a first novel can be."
—*New York Times*

"In this affecting first novel, Medoff captures the angst of female gen Xers . . . a funny novel that confronts the terrors of anorexia and other modern ills with empathy and understanding."
—*People*

"[An] unusually honest, painfully funny novel about a tight-knit family's struggle."
—*Entertainment Weekly*

"*Hunger Point* delivers one of the most fully realized narrators to come along in years—a sultry, suburban Holden Caulfield."
—*Paper* magazine

"Seamless . . . Frannie's voice is bright, wry, vulgar, and brilliantly contemporary . . . The novel succeeds in working through dark, profound topics in a tone that is surprisingly entertaining, often funny . . . Her personal grace, strength, and warmth embody the power and ultimate success of *Hunger Point*."
—*Cleveland Plain Dealer*

"Uproariously funny . . . raw-boned . . . promising and revealing and tailor-made for readers fighting memories of . . . stolen self-esteem."
—*Newsday*

"Jillian Medoff writes with bone-scraping clarity, pitiless insight and . . . vast, almost shameless, humor . . . *Hunger Point* is no low-calorie, no-salt novel; instead it is rich with sweetness and depth in intermingling flavors more satisfying even than Belgian chocolate."
—*Atlanta Journal-Constitution*

"At once heartbreaking and funny, a debut novel on death and renewal that is strong and honest . . . an exuberant meditation on life, family, and the hard-won satisfactions of personal change."
—*Kirkus Reviews*

"I devoured *Hunger Point*. I read it compulsively, savoring the bittersweet story . . . an edgy, contemporary bildungsroman . . . should be shrink-wrapped with the latest diet gospels as a necessary corrective.
—Gregory Maguire, author of *Wicked:
The Life and Times of the Wicked Witch of the West*

"Frannie is a wry, witty heroine who manages to be both sarcastic and poignant . . . Medoff skillfully captures Frannie's impotence in the face of food and her parents' well-meaning but destructive love [and has] accomplished a rare feat: capturing the delicate emotional nuances of bulimia and anorexia."

—*Boston Herald*

"A good read with a main character you'll be sure to identify with, and it will also remind you that, most often, being self-centered is no way to be centered at all."

—*BUST* magazine

"[A] wonderfully written chronicle of a lost woman's relationship with her mother, father, sister, and food. In Medoff's well-formed characters, each of us can see a friend, a family member, perhaps ourselves . . . Relish this book."

—*Austin American-Statesman*

"A novel that is so powerful, painful, and shocking that the memory of her message will last much longer than it would in a non-fiction format . . . Her heroine, Frannie, is more than a fictional device. She's a remarkable feat of writing skills . . . There's humor without comedy; there is sadness without pathos. So the messages come across without effort."

—*Oklahoman*

"Medoff tells this tale with irreverence and a wicked sense of humor . . . [she] shines a spotlight on the messages society sends young women in confused times."

—*Milwaukee Journal Sentinel*

GOOD GIRLS GONE BAD

"A black comedy version of *Sex and the City*."

—*Glamour*

"Acerbic wit and pathos distinguish Medoff's accomplished second novel . . . Medoff beautifully balances the women's diverting quirkiness with Janey's own sincere struggle in choosing life over death. Another success, combining genuine psychological depth with humor and irony."

—*Kirkus Reviews*

"*Good Girls Gone Bad* starts with a comic bang . . . As with life, the novel takes the good with the bad, and Medoff ensures that Janey faces all of it with charmingly self-abasing humor and consistently spot-on timing."

—*Houston Chronicle*

"Jillian Medoff takes an intriguing premise, turns it upside down, and sends it careening ahead, trailing delight and debauchery in its wake."

—Maggie Estep, author of *Alice Fantastic*

"Funny, surprising, and deftly written, *Good Girls Gone Bad* is a rich, witty, heartfelt second novel from Medoff. Fans of *Hunger Point* will welcome this addition."

—*Tampa Tribune*

"Fans will enjoy this well-written look at what happens when group therapy members bond a little too well . . . recommended for all collections of contemporary women's fiction."

—*Library Journal*

"*Good Girls Gone Bad* is a light in the tunnel that is single women's fiction. These women long for true love and male companionship, but their existence doesn't depend on it. *Good Girls* is more about friendship and personal reconciliation. While the characters are undoubtedly crazy, their friendship keeps them sane."

—*Charlotte Observer*

"It boasts snappy one-liners, a well-dressed Pekingese, an outlandishly funny plot during the first two-thirds of the book, and a hairpin turn toward tragedy."

—*Booklist*

"Every woman needs two copies of *Good Girls Gone Bad*. One to laugh with and cry to. The other to give to whatever man has broken her heart.

—J. D. Landis, author of *Lying in Bed* and *Longing*

I Couldn't Love You More

A NOVEL

Jillian Medoff

five
spot

Copyright © 2012 by Jillian Medoff

5 Spot
Hachette Book Group
237 Park Avenue
New York, NY 10017

www.5-spot.com

5 Spot is an imprint of Grand Central Publishing.
The 5 Spot name and logo are trademarks of Hachette Book Group, Inc.

The publisher is not responsible for websites (or their content) that are not owned by the publisher.

Printed in the United States of America

First Edition: May 2012
10 9 8 7 6

Library of Congress Cataloging-in-Publication Data

Medoff, Jillian.
I couldn't love you more / Jillian Medoff.—1st ed.
   p. cm.
ISBN 978-0-446-58462-3
1. Life change events—Fiction. I. Title.
PS3563.E26I3 2012
813'.54—dc22
                    2011008634

For Keith and all my girls

Author's Note

This novel, once abandoned, exists only because Jennifer Gates and Rachel Sussman believed it could. Together, we dismantled a 450-page manuscript and then reconstructed it, brand new. That they read every word of this book, multiple times, over the course of two (*two!*) years is a testament to their patience, tenacity, and foresight. That they did this even as I stood on the far side of advantage is nothing short of miraculous.

To Jen and Rachel, and all of Zachary Shuster Harmsworth Literary: my deepest gratitude, awe, true love.

February 27, 2011
Brooklyn, N.Y.

I Couldn't
Love You More

Once Upon a Time

AT THE BEGINNING of my daughter's princess party, right before Cinderella is scheduled to arrive, my sister Sylvia announces, apropos of nothing, that she is going blind.

Alarmed, I look up. "What do you mean by 'blind'?"

"I mean I'm having trouble seeing out of my eyes."

We're standing side by side in my foyer, where I'm trying to corral ten pint-sized princesses into the adjacent living room. Sylvia is studying her eyes in the mirror, and I want to give her my full attention, but Cinderella is due any minute, and the girls are running wild.

"Did this just happen?" I ask, catching a petite Snow White before she clips a corner. "Careful, princess, careful."

"No, it's been gradual." Still staring at her reflection, Sylvia grimaces. "Last week, when I was reviewing a deposition, I noticed the words were blurry and kind of dark. But it was midnight, so I figured I was just tired. Now, though, I can barely see my hand in front of my face." To prove her point, she holds up her hand at arm's length and then squints, as if pretending to count her fingers.

She had me until the demonstration. I believed her vision was blurry. The deposition made perfect sense. I could even accept that she'd been at her office until midnight. But once she started with the fluttering fingers and the fixed zombie eyes, I knew exactly what was happening. My thirty-six-year-old sister was about to snatch the spotlight from her

four-year-old niece—on the kid's birthday, no less—and it was up to me
to stop her.

"Please, Sylvia," I say delicately. "Can't this wait?" But I don't hear
her response because there's a loud crash in my kitchen, followed by
screeches of laughter. As bands of roving girls stampede by, I spy my
daughter's curly red hair among the swishing ponytails.

"Hailey! Let's settle down, okay?" I reach out to grab her, but she's
moving too fast.

"In a second, Mommy!" she promises as she dashes away.

Sylvia is petulant. "Something's wrong, Eliot. Please take a look."

"I'm not an ophthalmologist," I remind her, which of course makes
no difference—when she tilts her head forward, I (ever-dutifully) lean
in to examine her eyes. But before I offer my expert opinion, I scout
around for our little sister, Maggie, who has once again wandered off.

I spot her across the room. "Maggie! What are you doing?" We
refer to Maggie as "little," but she's actually thirty-three, although you
wouldn't know it from the way she's crouched underneath my dining
room table. "Cinderella will be here any minute. You said you were setting up the living room."

She crawls out from between two chairs. "I decided to build a fort
instead," she says as she stands up and brushes herself off. Her jeans are
covered with crumbs, which tells me that I didn't vacuum as well as
I'd thought. "What if the princesses need to hide from the dragon?"
Maggie pauses. "Wait a second. I think I'm mixing up my fairy tales."

Sylvia nods. "It happens. They're highly complex narratives." Beside
us, she's blinking rapidly, as if signaling Morse code to a distant ally.

"What's wrong with her?" Maggie asks.

"She said she's having trouble with her eyes."

"I'm *blind*, Eliot," Sylvia corrects me.

"Again?" Maggie sighs. "Didn't you 'go blind' when we took Hailey
to that Chihuahua movie? You were so bored you raced out of the theater yelling, *'Oh God, my eyes,'* and then went down the street and got
your nails done."

"I wasn't *bored*, Maggie. It was a *corneal abrasion*. I almost had to wear an *eye patch*." Sylvia turns to me. "How can you just stand there? Do you not even care? This is serious, Eliot."

"Of course I care," I reply, but Hailey's back and tugging on my hand.

"Cinderella's coming! Mommy, we have to get ready. I love her so, so much."

I need to make a move, but seized with sudden indecision, I just stand there for a second, watching the door and praying that my daughter's favorite princess shows up soon.

Cinderella is the centerpiece of Hailey's birthday party. I'd hired her from All Star Atlanta, a troupe of actors who perform at children's parties around town. Although the cost gave me pause, once her booker described the two-hour interactive floor show, which featured a selection of preapproved princess activities, including a princess sing-along, I was sold.

"Let's go, princesses!" I call out weakly. I feel self-conscious shouting at the girls while their mothers stand by, idly watching, but once my own mother steps in, we're able to sweep all ten children into the living room. The adults follow behind, even Sylvia, although her eye affliction forces her to move very slowly.

My sister's drama isn't unusual, but it is inconvenient, especially today. Hailey recently changed nursery schools, so this party is a chance for her to spend time with her new pals outside of class. If I had more space, I would've also invited their mothers, but my house is far too small for so many people. As it turned out, two of the mothers did ask to stay, although they both offered, graciously, to lend a hand with the kids. And while I was anxious to make a good impression, I can see now that my husband, Grant, had a point when he said I was overthinking the event.

"It's a birthday party," he reminded me during my decorating frenzy. "She's only four."

"I know, I know. I'm done, I'm done. Okay"—I held out my arms— "what do you think?"

We both looked around. Our house was buckling under the weight of pink streamers, pink balloons, pink Mardi Gras beads, and pink feather boas. My kitchen table was set for a tea party that could rival any held at Versailles, and there was a banner suspended from the ceiling that read *Welcome to the Ball* in gold glitter script. But when I started to pull down the streamers, conceding that, yes, it probably was a bit much, Grant shook his head. "Absolutely not. It's perfect—like we're inside a big pink piñata!" He squeezed my shoulders. "Hailey will love it, Eliot—you did a great job."

Hailey is the youngest of three girls. Because she is so often denied the same privileges we grant her elder sisters—later bedtimes, certain TV shows, pricey Game Boys—I wanted her birthday to be special. So along with the princess theme and decorations, we asked her guests to dress up as their best-loved fairy-tale heroines, which is how we ended up with five Cinderellas, two Snow Whites, and three Sleeping Beauties. Each girl is wearing a miniature ball gown, bejeweled tiara, and plastic high heels, and they're all giddy at the prospect of meeting the real-life Cinderella.

I was a little nervous about hosting nine kids we don't know, but so far they've all been very sweet to Hailey, if a bit wound up. And it's to the mothers' credit that despite never having met my sister before, the two women are listening to Sylvia with genuine concern.

"This isn't a joke, Eliot," she says, feeling around for a chair. "I really can't see." She sighs heavily. "I guess it's true: fertility drugs *can* have a terrible effect on your vision."

Phoebe, the alpha mother, reaches out to guide her into a chair. "Are you taking Clomid? My friend took Clomid, and she had the same problem. In fact, her vision got so bad she had to stop driving…" Trailing off, she notices a bevy of girls using my brand-new couch as a trampoline. One of them realized that by launching herself off the arm of the neighboring (equally new) recliner, she could practically fly, and the others are clamoring behind her, demanding a turn. "Careful with your dresses!" Phoebe shouts. This, it occurs to me, is what she meant by "lending a hand" with the kids.

"Did you know Sylvia was taking fertility drugs?" I ask Maggie.

"I didn't even know she wanted children," Maggie replies, and we both turn to Sylvia, but she's focused on Phoebe.

"My God!" she exclaims. "Your hair is *gorgeous* and looks so *soft*. May I touch it? Please? Just one quick pat?"

Phoebe has very short, frosted blond hair that hugs her scalp like a swim cap. Although it's nicer than, say, my hair, which is a mousy auburn shag cut to hide my thinning part, it's no more gorgeous than anyone else's. But Sylvia has the uncanny ability to zero in on a perfect stranger's hidden vanity, and soon she's petting the woman's head as they discuss deep-cleansing shampoos and the benefits of learning Braille. Meanwhile, Phoebe's daughter has taken off her ball gown and is doing belly flops in her underwear onto my expensive leather sofa.

"Mommy!" I hear my own daughter shout. "Where's the special guest?" Hailey is standing on the arm of the recliner, tottering in her plastic heels. "We've been waiting so long."

"Careful, princess," Maggie says, racing to grab Hailey before she topples over.

"Catch me, Aunt Maggie!" Arms outstretched, Hailey flings herself at my sister, who catches her easily and then dances her around the room. Maggie is agile, with an athlete's grace, and their impromptu waltz is surprisingly elegant.

"What a stunning girl," Phoebe says to her companion, unconsciously fingering her own cropped hair. "What I wouldn't give for curls like that." Given the way Phoebe stares, I know intuitively that she's referring to my sister's long, reddish-gold ringlets, not my daughter's messy red mop.

"That's Maggie," Sylvia tells the mothers, as if addressing the studio audience. "She's the pretty sister. Eliot's the good one." She grins. "I'm the bad sister, the one with all the *issues*."

Chuckling, Phoebe smooths her knee-length skirt. "Well, I'm a bad girl myself—reformed, of course." She touches Sylvia's shoulder. "You should probably relax if you're feeling unwell."

"I probably should," Sylvia agrees. She offers the woman her arm. "If it's all the same to you, Ellie, I think I'll lie down on the couch. Could you ask the kids to clear out for a while?"

"Sylvia," I plead, trying to tamp down my frustration, "please don't do this now. Cinderella will be here any minute, and we need the living room. Why don't you go upstairs?"

"And miss Hailey's birthday party?" Sylvia replies sweetly. "No way."

Phoebe turns to her friend. "Can you give me a hand here?"

And so it happens that my perfectly healthy, eagle-eyed sister gets two complete strangers to help her traverse my tiny living room floor. One offers her aspirin; the other, a cup of tea.

"Get ready, girls!" I cry out, clapping maniacally. "Cinderella's coming!"

"News flash," my mother says, walking in. "Cinderella isn't coming." She spots Sylvia lying on the couch. "Oh, my God, Eliot—is she okay?"

"Cinderella's not coming?" Hailey shrieks. She's back up on the recliner, stomping her plastic high heels into the rich brown leather. "That's not fair!"

Several of the princesses start to cry; the rest fall, keening and moaning, to their knees. Watching this, I get a sense of what Graceland was like the day Elvis died, and I blink back sudden tears of my own. Three weeks of preparation, and in less than two minutes, Hailey's party has fallen apart. Adding insult to injury are my two guests misguidedly ministering to my sister.

"Apparently," my mother says, "Cinderella slipped a disk doing a gymnastics routine somewhere in Dunwoody. Call the guy back. He'll tell you the whole story."

This makes the princesses cry harder. "I want gymnastics!" Hailey shouts, and her friends rally to her cause, yelling, "Gymnastics, gymnastics!" over and over until Sylvia bolts up from her sickbed to shush them.

"So, Eliot, what's your backup plan?" asks Phoebe, who along with the other adults is waiting for me to take action.

I can barely hear her over the princesses' wailing. "Backup plan?" I say blankly.

"You don't have a backup plan?" She's incredulous. "I hate to tell you this, dear, but if Cinderella really is laid up in Dunwoody, you have a long afternoon ahead of you."

⌒

As it turns out, Phoebe is right. Cinderella's aborted appearance dampens everyone's mood. Had Grant been here, he would have told jokes— or juggled, even—and added some much-needed levity. But earlier he received an emergency call from his teenage daughter, Charlotte, my elder stepdaughter, and had to run out. So with Grant gone, Sylvia (thankfully) resting upstairs, and Maggie disappeared (again), it falls to me to entertain the princesses alone.

For the next two hours, I try everything: freeze dance, musical chairs, pin-the-crown-on-the-queen, a tea party, even a princess parade. But nothing cheers the girls up. All they want is Cinderella, which I understand. Despite my brave face, I'm crushed she's not here, especially when I spot a heartbroken Hailey peeking out the front window, searching for the missing princess.

Eventually, Maggie wanders over. "I want cake," she says, pulling me up off the floor, where I'm overseeing a lackluster game of hot potato. We retreat to the dining room to join my guests, who are sitting with my mother, sipping decaf and nibbling Cheddar Goldfish. I'm about to admit defeat and send everyone home when I see Gail, my seven-year-old stepdaughter, organizing a game of duck, duck, goose. That's my girl, I think, watching with pride as she tries to salvage her little sister's birthday. She won't give up without a fight, either.

Unfortunately, news from the front isn't good.

"Hailey's friends are bored," Gail tells me, walking over. "They said this is the worst party ever."

"The worst princess party in the history of all princess parties?"

Smiling, I hold her fingers and twirl her around and around. In honor of her sister's birthday, Gail is wearing a miniskirt I found in a vintage store on Peachtree. As she spins on her toes, the skirt flares up. Underneath, she has on a pair of camouflage-print shorts. "Well, I appreciate your help. Hailey is lucky to have you for a sister."

"Which is more than we can say about your aunt Sylvia," Maggie observes. "Considering she lied about taking fertility drugs so she could sleep all afternoon."

"Maybe she really doesn't feel well," I say. "Let's give her the benefit of the doubt."

Maggie snorts. "And you guys call me the dumb one." She turns away, flicking her long hair in my face. Sylvia doesn't always lie; Maggie really is the prettiest of us, although her cool beauty—luminous blue eyes, straight white teeth, perfect lips—belies a lovable loopiness, which you can feel in the warmth of her smile. When my sister smiles, it's like seeing the sun come out.

I check my watch. "It's time for cake. Gail, please round up the princesses. I'll go upstairs and find Sylvia." But as I get up from my seat, my mother stops me.

"Let Sylvia be. She's not feeling well." For some reason, this cracks her up.

"What's so funny?"

"Nothing," she says, then laughs even harder. "Eliot, you stay here. I'll get the cake."

A few minutes later, I'm down on my knees, helping Hailey rebuckle her plastic shoes, when the princesses start to yell. My mother must have brought out the cake, I think, but when I look up, I see it's not the cake they're cheering—it's the person holding it. Dressed in a sequined cocktail dress, a platinum wig, heaps of plastic bracelets, and (my) diamond stud earrings, Sylvia steps into the dining room, balancing the cake in a pair of gloved hands. Her dress is gaudy, her wig askew, both gloves have holes, and her lipstick is smeared, but my sister has never looked more dazzling.

"Hello, ladies," she says. "I'm Princess Petunia. Cinderella couldn't make it today, so she sent me."

The ten princesses swoon. "Are you a real princess?" they all want to know.

"Of course I'm a real princess. Why else would I be here?" Sylvia holds out the enormous cake, which I take from her hands. "It's me," she whispers.

"I know," I whisper back. "You look amazing."

Hailey is overjoyed. "You're not a princess. You're Aunt Sylvia!"

"No, I'm Princess Petunia, and I'm here to make your wishes come true." Then, from out of nowhere, Sylvia produces a handful of necklaces—one more glittery than the next. She goes around the table, drapes a necklace over each guest's head, and kisses her cheek. "You are so beautiful," she says solemnly. "Thank you for coming."

Shrieking with pleasure, Hailey tosses her necklace into the air. The other princesses see this, and nine more go flying. And suddenly my ordinary little house has sparkling jewels raining down from the ceiling.

"*Mommy,*" I hear. "*Mommy, Mommy, Mommy*—this is the best party *ever!*"

⌒

"You saved the day, Sylvia," I say. "Princess Petunia saved the day."

It's later, much later, after all the princesses have gone home, after Hailey and Gail have opened all the presents and misplaced all the cards, after we've vacuumed up the glitter and runaway beads and dried frosting, after Charlotte and Grant have finally walked in. A half hour ago, Grant went upstairs with the girls, so I'm left with my mother and sisters to do the party postmortem.

Sylvia beams. "I did save the day, didn't I? That party was a disaster until I showed up. Thank God for me."

My mother is hiding a smile, and I can tell she has a secret. "What?" I ask her.

"Sylvia has something important she wants to share."

"Don't say it, Dolores," Sylvia warns. "It's *my* news, not yours." But she's smiling, too, and a beat later, she and my mother are laughing hysterically.

Watching them, it strikes me that when Sylvia is my mother's age (seventy-eight), she will look just like her. Sylvia has the same shoulder-length, fiery red hair my mother had when we were kids, although my mother's is silver now and cut in a sleek bob. They also share a perpetually bemused expression, as if they know something you don't. Sylvia, Maggie, and I don't resemble one another—or our mother—but you can tell we're related. We all have the same fair skin, light eyes, and freckles. And, of course, there's the red hair, which we also share in one shade or another.

"Come on," Maggie says. "Tell us your news already. Oh, I know: *you've gone blind*."

"Don't be dramatic, Maggie," Sylvia says. "It's so unbecoming." She looks at my mother, and for a second they say nothing. Then they both speak at the same time.

"I saw Finn!" Sylvia shouts. "Finn Montgomery—remember Finn, from Emory?"

She saw Finn? *My* Finn? Hearing this, I freeze. But wait, there's more.

"Your sister's pregnant!" my mother blurts out. "She's due next May!"

Maggie throws her arms around my neck. "You're pregnant? Eliot, that's so great!"

"*I'm* the one who's pregnant, you dope," Sylvia says, then turns to my mother. "I *told* you I wanted to wait, Dolores. *Roger* doesn't even know yet."

"Hold on." Maggie is confused. "So that stuff about fertility drugs was *true*?"

I'm still reeling. "You saw Finn? He's back in Atlanta?"

My mother is unconvinced. "Oh, Sylvia, you're always seeing *someone*. Two months ago you were convinced you saw Yasir Arafat. I told you: the man's been dead for *years*."

But Sylvia has moved on. "So remember I had those stabbing pains in my stomach, and I was *sure* I had abdominal cancer? Well, I called an oncologist, but the same day—*the! same! exact! day!*—I missed my period. Guess what?" She sits up. "It's not cancer."

"You're really pregnant?" Maggie sounds concerned. For the record: Sylvia once toted an infant Hailey through the mall in a puppy cargo bag because the BabyBjörn "compromised her spine." "She can breathe just fine in there," she snapped when the security guard in Victoria's Secret threatened to call the police. (I heard this story only after the fact, but it was the first—and last—time Sylvia babysat.)

"I planned to tell you earlier," she continues, "but I felt so sick all day. And those kids—*Jesus Christ*, Eliot, are they always so freaking loud?"

"You're really pregnant?" Maggie repeats.

"Stop saying that, Maggie! When it was Eliot, you were like 'You're *pregnant?*' but since it's me you're like '*You're* pregnant?' Why can't you just be happy for me?"

"We *are* happy for you," Maggie and I say in unison. But unable to help myself, I add, "So where did you see Finn? Was he alone?"

Sylvia rolls her eyes. "God, could you be more self-involved, Eliot? We're discussing *my unborn child* here. But no, he wasn't alone. I saw him at the movies, sitting with some blonde." She barks with laughter. "Oh, my God, he got so *fat*. The theater was *packed*, but you couldn't miss him. The guy's, like, *huge*."

Finn fat? Impossible. I exhale in relief. "I doubt Finn got fat, Sylvia." It's weird to say *fat*, even weirder than saying *Finn*. We don't allow the word *fat* in our house. I'd rather have Hailey tell someone to *fuck off* than call her *fat*. "It could've been anyone."

"Oh, so now you don't believe me? You think I lied about that, too?"

"I didn't say you *lied*. But you only met him once. And if the place was packed..." I shrug.

"Eliot, do you really think I'm so *insensitive* that I would *make up* a story about seeing *Finn*, a guy it took you *years* to get over? What kind of person do you think I am?"

"That's not what she said," Maggie points out.

Sylvia whips around. "Why are you two ganging up on me?"

"We're not," Maggie says, but it's too late. Sylvia is on a tear, ranting about how *selfish* and *jealous* we are, how *thoughtless* and *rude*; how she's finally *pregnant* after all these years, but the only thing we can focus on is *Eliot* and her *fat* ex-boyfriend.

"This was supposed to be *my* moment," she sniffs, glaring at me. "You *always* do this."

Although this signals the end of the evening, it's not the end of the story. Princess parties are over when the clock strikes twelve, but families go on forever, which is why I'm not all that worried about Sylvia being angry. Still, I do feel awful when she storms off, especially since there was something so magical about the party. In a single afternoon, I saw her transformed from a sister into a princess, from a princess into an expectant mother, and from a mother back to herself. And the truth is, sometimes my sisters and I do get jealous, and sometimes we do say things to—and about—one another that are thoughtless and rude. We don't mean them, though. It's just whenever we're together, we slip into our old familiar roles. As the eldest, I'm in charge, Maggie is the one we look after, and Sylvia is caught in the middle. Despite our best efforts to transcend them, these roles are ingrained and immutable; and because of this, we behave accordingly, even against our better judgment.

I'm sure most people think it shouldn't matter at this point who among us is the prettiest or smartest since we're all adults now, each with lives of our own. But it does matter—it will always matter. I mean, if you don't know your place in the family, how can you possibly know your place in the world?

Book One

There are only two or three human stories, and they go on repeating themselves as fiercely as if they had never happened before.

— Willa Cather, *O Pioneers!*, 1913

Chapter One

I'M A LIGHT SLEEPER, which means I'm usually awake before everyone else. Today is no exception, although I'm lost in thought when the alarm goes off, so the buzzing startles me. Groaning dramatically, Grant shuts it off, then leans over to kiss me good morning, but I'm already getting out of bed.

"Hey, wait a second," he says, pulling me back. "What's the big rush?"

I shrug. "No rush...although it is five thirty. One of us should get in the shower."

I refer to Grant as my husband, although we're not really married. We've been together five years, though, and we're raising three girls: Hailey, who turned four yesterday, is our daughter, and Charlotte and Gail, who are fourteen and seven, are from his first marriage.

"That so?" Lying on his side, Grant grins at me, creating tiny creases in the corners of his eyes. He's forty, two years older than me, and has started to show his age in interesting and not unattractive ways. "Okay, Eliot, let's hear it. What's bothering you?"

"Nothing's bothering me." But then I smile, unable to help myself. Like my mother, I'm a lousy liar and an even worse secret keeper.

"In other words, you're still annoyed at me for yesterday."

"Annoyed?" I reply, wide-eyed. "What could I *possibly* be annoyed about?"

I can't stand confrontation, so I shy away from arguments, even

when—like now—I not only am irritated but also happen to be justified. My sisters may tease me about being a goody-goody, but they're
not altogether wrong. I'm always opening doors for strangers, giving
up my seat, helping them with their bags when I can barely manage
my own. As with many good girls, anger is my Achilles' heel—my
kryptonite, if you will—that is, the fear that if I get angry at Grant, if
I get angry at anyone I care about, I'll drive them away.

Grant sighs. "Eliot, I thought we resolved this last night. Charlotte
waited for over an hour, but Beth never showed up. So, what was I supposed to do? Leave her there?"

"Of course not, but why didn't you insist she come back here?
Wasn't that the original plan—Beth would pick up Charlotte and bring
her home?"

When Grant got divorced, he and his ex-wife, Beth (whom Sylvia instantly christened "the Sculptress"), decided he would retain custody of
their two daughters, so Charlotte and Gail live with us full-time. Beth
is supposed to have them on alternating weekends, but she often makes
other plans or forgets about them entirely. Yesterday, when Charlotte
called Grant, frantic, from her art class, she was convinced her mother
had been in a terrible accident and was lying in a ditch somewhere. But
the Sculptress was merely out with a friend, sipping a midafternoon
tea that turned into a late afternoon drink. When Charlotte found this
out, she demanded that Grant stop by the restaurant and make sure her
mother was okay. The Sculptress was fine, of course, but Grant, who is
loath to refuse his girls anything, agreed.

"I'm just surprised it took you so long, that's all," I say.

"See!" Grant exclaims. "I *knew* you were mad."

Despite his insistence, I'm really not mad. How can I be mad? Grant
Delaney is a man who rescued his daughter when she was stranded at
art school. He's a man who shouldered the entire burden of raising his
two young children when his wife walked out. Unlike my own father,
unlike most men, Grant is a man who stepped up.

I sigh. "I'm not mad. But come on, Grant—it took you three hours to make a forty-minute trip. You did the same thing during Gail's slumber party. You went out for ice at eight, and didn't come back until eleven thirty. It's"—I search for the precise word—"*inconsiderate*. Did it ever occur to you that I might need a hand?"

"Eliot, your mother and your sisters came over to help you. Did you really need me and Charlotte, too?"

"Grant, you know my family wasn't here to help."

"What about all the other kids' mothers?"

"There were only two, and both of them turned out to be Gluckmans."

When I was young, we lived next door to Sol and Greta Gluckman, a couple who argued with the windows open. "I'm a sexy girl, Solly," the three-hundred-pound Greta used to shout. "And I deserve nice things. So get off your fat ass and find a fucking job." After that, *Gluckman* became our family's code word for indolent divas that live off someone else's hard work. My estranged father, Barney Gordon (né Giordano), is a Gluckman. So is Beth, an unemployed painter whose art is distinguished by large-scale renderings of human genitalia and whom Grant continues to support, even though they divorced more than six years ago.

"What about Sylvia?" Grant asks. "Last night you told me she dressed up like a princess; that she saved the day."

"For ten minutes. I also told you she announced she was blind, collapsed on the couch, and then hid upstairs for the next two hours." Despite myself, I have to laugh.

Grant laughs, too. "Your sister is going to milk this pregnancy for all it's worth. Poor Roger...Sylvia is such a pain in the ass." But he also sounds amused. Grant likes Sylvia a lot. He likes Maggie, too, but feels indebted to Sylvia. After all, she's the one who introduced us.

Grant is an art director at an advertising agency that was sued a few years ago for fraud or breach of contract—I don't remember now, or maybe I never knew. Sylvia's firm handled their defense ("*successfully* handled their defense," she likes to remind me). Afterward, when both teams went out for a celebratory lunch, Sylvia sat next to Grant, who, she found out, was funny and available. Describing him, she said he was more appropriate for me, which meant she'd already considered dating him herself but then decided against it. "Trust me, Eliot," she swore. "He's awesome—handsome, smart, *and* divorced."

"Since when is being divorced a good thing, Sylvia?"

"Don't be dense. *Everyone* knows divorced men make the *best* husbands. Why would you marry a guy who hasn't been broken in first? It's like riding a wild horse. *Trust me,*" she repeated. "It'll be love at first sight."

I can't say that I loved Grant at first sight, but I did love looking at him. His appeal is more rugged than pretty: dark, seductive eyes; black, curly hair threaded with silver; and the faintest hint of a five o'clock shadow. Although he's not a tall man, whatever Grant lacks in height, he makes up in strength. He's well built, with broad shoulders and muscular arms, so he's good at opening jars and shrink-wrap packaging. He's also got a strong character, which, unlike biceps, doesn't soften with age.

I used to believe in love at first sight. I went to college at Emory, where I fell desperately, achingly, in love with Finn Montgomery, and my world turned upside down. When we graduated, Finn moved to New York City, and I haven't seen or spoken to him since. So now that I'm thirty-eight and have some perspective, I believe in lust at first sight and love that grows over time.

When Sylvia suggested I meet Grant, I was almost thirty-three. I'd dated several guys on and off over the years but hadn't had a life-changing love affair since Finn and I split up ten years before. At thirty-three—at any age, I suppose—ten years felt like forever. So I was ready to meet someone—just not someone who'd been rejected twice, first by his wife and then by my sister.

"Thanks, Sylvia," I told her. "But no."

"Eliot, don't be an idiot. Grant is *perfect* for you. I'll come along, and"—she paused—"we'll meet him at his country club."

This, she knew, would sway me, not because he might have money,

but because I love to swim. In the
though I have total control over
to swim. Maggie and Sylvia, in
hundred-meter breaststroke;
my mother insisted go to a
recently paid off.) Althou
sumed that by mentioning Gra
that he loved to swim, too.

Grant's "club," however, turned out to be a
with a dilapidated game room. There was a pool, but
and surrounded by clusters of families.

This is it? I looked around. Where are the lap lanes and divin
boards?

"That's him." Sylvia pointed to a guy wearing swim trunks walking
toward the shallow end. "That's Grant."

The guy's back was turned, so I couldn't see his face. What I could
see, though, was his naked upper body, which formed a perfect V, his
lean, powerful legs, and the confident way he moved. *That's* Grant?"

"I *told* you he was handsome, Eliot," Sylvia said, watching me watch
him. "You *always* doubt me."

"I don't *always* doubt you." Studying Grant, I started to get excited.
It had been a long time since the curve of a man's back made me giddy,
yet there I was, my legs a little loose, my head a little light. What an
unexpected twist, I thought as a great laugh bubbled up inside me.
That's Grant! He was about to step into the water when he turned
slightly, and I realized he was holding a baby. "Hey, Sylvia," I asked,
confused. "Whose baby is that?"

"What baby?" my sister replied. And just like that, I knew we had a
problem.

"The baby he's *cradling in his arms*."

"It's his. How *great* is that? See, I *told* you he was perfect."

"He has a kid?"

"He has two. The older one is on the diving board."

saw a girl, about nine or ten, standing at the end of
mplating a jump. "Come on, Charlotte!" I heard Grant
an do it."

toward him, Sylvia waved. "Hey, Grant, you big
his is my sister Eliot—the one who used to eat dog food! Re-
er I told you about her?"

opened my mouth to protest, but Sylvia had already slipped off her
ndals and was dunking her feet in the water. "Here, Eliot." She patted
the ground. "Come on, girl. Sit, Eliot, sit."

I never ate dog food. Once, when I was ten and Sylvia was eight, she
dared me to bite a Milk-Bone dog biscuit. It was no big deal, but our
mother, a semi-successful author, later referenced the incident in her
two memoirs that chronicled her turbulent marriage to—and messy divorce from—our father, Barney. The whole thing would've been long
forgotten had she not changed my single bite of a Milk-Bone to an entire bowl of kibble, a detail that the press picked up and blew out of
proportion. What everyone failed to realize, however, was that the only
reason my mother included the story at all was to make some convo-
luted point about my father's lack of parenting skills.

I glanced at Grant again, but this time with disappointment. Sylvia
hadn't said anything about children; and not only did this guy have two
(*two!*) girls, but one was still in diapers! I loved kids, but this was too
much, too soon. Tired of being duped by my sister yet again, I stormed
out of the pool area but then realized I couldn't leave because she had
the car keys. Frustrated, I went into the game room, where I watched
Sylvia through the window. I could see her talking to Grant, who was
bobbing around in the water with his baby. He appeared to be laughing
at something Sylvia was saying. They looked natural together, like close
friends, which only made me feel worse. So what if I wasn't interested
in this sad, wifeless man and his two motherless children? He was still
my date, not hers.

Inside the game room, I was suffocating; my T-shirt was soaked with
perspiration. Outside the window, I could see the pool, cool and invit-

ing. So with nothing better to do and nothing to lose, I stripped off my clothing, ran out the door, and dove into the clear blue water.

⌐

The backup alarm buzzes. This time, when Grant reaches over to shut it off, he purposefully grazes my breasts. "Let's blow off work. We can stay in bed and have sex all day."

"With each other?"

"Ha ha. Aren't you witty this morning?" Pinning me to the bed, Grant hovers above my face, then releases his arms and flops on top of me. His skin feels warm against mine.

By now it's ten to six, and Grant needs to get showered, dressed, and out the door by ten after, or it won't pay for him to leave until nine. We live thirty miles north of Atlanta, and getting anywhere in less than an hour requires mastering the city's unrelenting traffic patterns. Grant's office isn't far mileage-wise, but he supervises five designers and likes to get in before they do. My office is all the way downtown, but I have a flexible schedule, so I can work wherever I want as long as I meet my deadlines.

I'm a business writing specialist for Oliver Morgan Consulting, which means I help companies repackage their communications to make bad news sound pleasant. Although it's not a dream job or a calling, I'm surprisingly good at it.

Are You 65 or Older and Ready to Retire?
Do Your Finances Say Otherwise?

Don't despair! You're in great company. In a recent survey, eighty percent (80%) of age-challenged Americans cited "credit card debt," "foolish investments," and "parasitic children" as the Top Three reasons why they're unable to retire. If this sounds familiar, read on. We've put together some of our favorite tips and tools to help make another decade at the office more fun than a day at the beach!

I'm bent over the side of the bed, retrieving my reading glasses, when Grant moves behind me and presses his penis against my ass. He's as hard as a rock. "I want to mow so badly."

In our private bedroom parlance, to "mow"—long "o"—is to have sex. We also "do it," "have relations," and, on occasion, "fuck." Mowing came about when Gail overheard Grant say he wanted to "do it all day." "Do what, Daddy?" she asked, to which a rattled Grant blurted out, "Mow the lawn." These days, we don't mow as often as we'd like, but neither do we let the grass grow too high, if you know what I mean.

Grant wraps his legs around mine and runs his hands, palms down, back and forth over my nipples. "Charlotte was stranded," he whispers. "Please don't be mad at me."

"We're gonna be late." But I close my eyes and sink into the bed. How can I be mad at him? Even with five years and three kids between us, Grant Delaney is a man who still makes me weak.

"You threw Hailey a great party. And you're absolutely right, I was *inconsiderate*. I should've brought Charlotte straight home, but she asked me if she could see her mother..." He runs his fingers down my stomach and along my inner thighs.

"And you didn't want to be stuck here with all those kids—"

"And yes, the princess thing was a bit much. So after we saw Beth, Charlotte and I *may* have stopped for a snack—"

"Hoping to miss the whole party..." I moan softly.

"Not the *whole* party..." With his thumb, he rubs my skin in light circles, making me shiver. The feeling is so good, I almost can't bear it.

"So you admit you abandoned me..." I trail off, no longer caring about the party, about the time, about anything. The house could burn down around us, but as long as Grant keeps touching me in precisely that way, it won't make one bit of difference.

Grant kisses me, openmouthed, a loving kiss of apology. "Yes, I admit it. But there was so much pink in this house, Eliot." He pauses. "I'm sorry I bailed on the party."

Kissing him back, I'm aware of nothing but his mouth on my mouth, the rhythm of his long fingers moving inside me. Suddenly, he pulls away.

"So now that I've admitted to poor judgment," he says, "will you also admit you were angry at me?"

When I don't respond, he pushes me onto my back, bends my knees, and then starts to lick me, very gently, between my legs.

Despite Sylvia's assurances, Grant had no idea that she and I were coming to his club that afternoon. Her grand plan was to parent-trap us together: two bruised, bumbling losers who couldn't see the potential romance that was right in front of them if she hadn't pointed it out so selflessly. (Like many children of divorce, *The Parent Trap* is the Gordon sisters' all-time favorite movie, so much so that Hayley Mills, the original star, inspired my own Hailey's name.) And parent-trap us is exactly what Sylvia did. She called Grant up, found out where he was, and convinced me to ride shotgun.

At first it didn't work. Although perfectly nice, Grant was not someone with whom I saw much of a future. I was polite, certainly, but also relieved when he took his girls home. The younger one was cranky and squirming. The older one needed sunscreen, and then a snack, and then she had to call her mother two, three, four times. What was Sylvia thinking? After all the years I spent crying over Finn, why would I want a man with two children; a man with—okay—an impeccable body, but also an ex-wife, a peeling nose, and what was guaranteed to be a long and pitiful history?

"You haven't even heard his story yet," Sylvia said on the drive home. "All you need to know is that he's devoted to those two gorgeous children. And I have eyes, Eliot. I saw the way you looked at him."

"So what?" I said, breaking my vow not to discuss it with her. "How many times did the older one call her mother? Four? Five?"

"Her name is Charlotte. And the little one is Gail."

"They're *both* little, Sylvia."

"And the reason she calls her mother so often," she continued, ignoring me, "is because she can't get an answer. The Sculptress isn't *there*, Eliot. She's not *interested*, which is where you come in. After a few months with you, those kids will forget all about her, then *bam*—who's the mother now? But you do what you want. All I'm saying is he's a nice guy."

"So why don't you go out with him?"

"Why the hell would I want to raise someone else's kids?"

To be fair, I didn't make it difficult for Grant. He called a few days later, and I agreed to have dinner, which was a surprisingly pleasant experience. As the weeks went on, Grant continued to ask me out, and I continued to go. Why not? I figured. He was gracious and complimentary, called when he said he would, and showed up on time. He told me he'd never dated a green-eyed redhead before and referred to me as a "bonnie Irish lass," or he'd suddenly shout, *"Erin go Bragh!"* like some kind of mating call, which was totally random but also pretty funny considering my mother is a Jew from the Bronx and my dad an Italian Catholic from New Jersey. It was nice to be with a man who thought I was pretty and told me so in a way that felt honest. Eventually, I spent time with Charlotte and Gail, who, it turned out, weren't so bad, either. "They adore you and so do I," Grant told me. "We're so much happier when you're around."

It felt great to be wanted, to have a purpose again, so I began to reconsider. Then one night Grant told me something very personal—something, in fact, that changed my entire perception of him. And after that, our fate was sealed.

We were sitting at dinner, reminiscing about the day we first met. "It's ironic that I was at the pool that afternoon," he said. "I...uh...don't really like the water. Beth had promised to take the kids swimming, but she flaked out at the last minute, so I took them instead."

"Well, you looked like you were having fun. At least you did when Sylvia and I got there."

"To be honest, I don't remember you and Sylvia showing up at all. I remember holding Gail and then wading into the pool—"

"Well, *I* remember." I laughed. "I was watching you through the window. You were having a grand old time, playing with Gail in the water and flirting with Sylvia. God, I was *so annoyed* at her. All I wanted to do was go home, but at the last minute, I just said 'Fuck it' and jumped in. I really didn't expect to see you again."

But the moment I dove in, Grant said, was critical for him. "Eliot, here's the thing: I wasn't flirting with Sylvia. I wasn't even aware that Sylvia was there. Nor was I having a 'grand old time' with Gail. I was actually having a—I don't know what to call it—an out-of-body experience, I guess."

"What do you mean? Like a panic attack?"

"Worse."

Grant, it turned out, has an Achilles' heel, too. But unlike my own fear of anger, his kryptonite is a pathological fear of the water. It's a genuine phobia. When he steps into a pool or lake or, God forbid, the ocean, his arms and legs stiffen and his breathing gets labored. A little bit deeper, panic sets in and then disorientation. Even if the water comes up only to his knees, if he has nothing to grab hold of, his throat closes, his chest constricts, and he'll gasp for air until he blacks out. Supposedly, when Grant was three, his father tossed him into a lake to teach him how to swim. He jumped in right after, and Grant was perfectly safe, but Grant says he can still remember the terror, the way he was flailing, and then—*boom*—he was under.

Can you imagine hurling a toddler into a lake? When he was alive, Fred Delaney was a military man with old-fashioned ideas about parenting, so I can definitely picture it happening. Given Grant's profound hydrophobia, then, he never should have gone into the water, but it was so hot out, and Gail was so miserable.

He shrugged. "What could I do? She needed to cool off."

As soon as he waded in, though, he realized his mistake. Afraid he was going to pass out, he rushed to the side. Then he heard someone shout,

"That's Eliot!" And when he looked up, he was shocked to see Sylvia standing by the pool, pointing to the deep end. "That's my sister!"

"You were like a mirage," Grant said. "There I was, waist-deep in the water, when I lifted my head and saw you dive in. Sunlight ricocheted off the window at the same exact second I touched the wall. Then, *ta da*, my heartbeat slowed down, my breathing evened out, and my panic receded. I felt like you and I had an instant connection, like we were meant for each other. It was love at first sight," he added. "Well, for me, anyway."

Grant is a dreamer, a genuine, true blue romantic; he honestly believes in magical moments and everlasting devotion. It's one of the reasons we're so compatible: like Grant, I believe in true love. Take Finn, for instance. He may not be in my life anymore, but I've never thought that our love wasn't true. It was just of a particular time and place. When we graduated, Finn was offered a job in Manhattan, but I didn't go with him. For years afterward, I was convinced I had made a terrible decision, even though it was like most of my decisions, which are less decisions than default options— that is, months of hemming and hawing until something has to give one way or the other. Case in point: One week after Finn got the offer, he was speeding up I-95 with all his belongings. I, on the other hand, was still dragging my feet back in Atlanta, rereading *Let's Go: New York City*. By the time I was ready to discuss the possibility of moving, Finn was already ensconced in a new life. Had he and I gone up to New York together, we might have salvaged our relationship, but because of my nondecision decision, Finn went alone and never came back. But that's only the first half of the story.

The second half is that I met Grant. It may not have been love at first sight (for me), but it didn't matter. Once he told me about his fear of water, Grant bloomed into a whole person, complete with myriad dimensions. It was like looking through a prism and seeing an entire spectrum of colors where there once was only white. I no longer saw a rejected sad sack. Suddenly, I saw a brave, wifeless man slogging through the pool, protecting his fragile, motherless daughter. Suddenly Grant was heroic: a committed, loving father who could be—who *wanted* to be—depended on.

Thank God, I realized. Thank God I didn't go with Finn to New York. Three months later, he asked me to move in. Six months after that, I was pregnant. And now, at five years and counting, our relationship is solid, and we're both happier than we ever thought possible.

By this point, Grant is determined to get an answer. "It's okay to be angry," he says, raising his face from between my knees. His lips are shiny. Abashed, I avert my eyes. "Everyone gets angry."

I look down. My entire body is pulsating. "You're stopping?"

"Stopping?" Grant wipes his mouth. "Tell you what. Admit you were mad at me, and I'll do anything you want." Raising his eyebrows, he smiles. "Anything..."

I roll my eyes, but I'm smiling, too.

"People get angry," he continues. "People make mistakes. Hopefully, they're forgiven. It's called being human. You, Eliot Gordon, are human. If you get angry, I promise the world as we know it won't end."

He's touching me again, working his way over my coarse hair, then reaching deeply inside me. I gasp but don't move, and Grant works harder. His fingers get slick. I'm sprawled against the pillows. One hand dangles off my knee, and I use it to pull him closer.

"I'm sorry," Grant says, "about the party."

"I was"—I gasp again—"*annoyed* you didn't come straight home."

We both laugh, and then we kiss and kiss, and he sucks on my tongue until I'm moaning beneath him, telling him, "It's okay; it's okay. Come on, Grant, come on."

He's up on his knees, and I'm lying beneath him. He arches his broad, beautiful back, then shifts his weight, and just as he's about to thrust inside me, there's a soft tap, tap, tap on the door.

"Daddy?"

Together, Grant and I hear this through our rock-hard haze; and together, we groan.

There's another tap. "Daddy, it's Gail. My stomach really hurts. Can I come in?"

Chapter Two

"HAILEY! CHARLOTTE! It's time to wake up."

A half hour later, showered and dressed, I walk down the hall, calling out to the kids. Our house is a nondescript, two-story A-frame, with the kitchen, dining room, and den on the first floor and three bedrooms and two bathrooms on the second. Charlotte has her own room, and Hailey and Gail share. Although the house is a rental and cramped for five people, it has a partially finished basement and a small backyard with a deck.

"Come on, guys! I can't be late today. I have an important meeting this afternoon."

Gail is asleep in my bed, so I peek into the hall bathroom, looking for her sisters.

"Oh, hi," I say to Charlotte, who's studying her face in the mirror as she applies another coat of black eyeliner. "You're up."

Charlotte is petite like her parents, and standing on her sisters' step-stool, she looks younger than fourteen. But then she opens her mouth. "I've been up," she says tersely, not to me but to her reflection.

Unlike Gail, who at seven speaks as if everything has just dawned on her, Charlotte is measured and controlled. Although my conversations with Gail are often confusing, they can be highly entertaining, which is more than I can say for her big sister. Charlotte is polite but distant, which for a stepmother is a sign that you're failing as a parent. A child will tell you she hates you only if she feels secure in your love and confident you'll never leave. (Or, I suppose, if she really does hate you.) That Charlotte barely addresses me by my name after five years of living together reveals how little faith she has in our relationship.

I move behind her, hoping my presence will persuade her to lighten up on the eyeliner. "Would you like a waffle?" I ask, transfixed by how painstakingly she works. Never in my life, not even when I had an existential crisis in my mid-twenties and foolishly took the LSATs, have I been able to harness that degree of concentration.

Charlotte has her father's dark eyes and olive skin. In a few more years, once her features sharpen and her acne clears up, she'll be a knockout. Both my stepdaughters will, which I feel comfortable saying only because their good looks can't be attributed to me. I could be pretty myself if I made an effort, but upkeep is a constant battle for a woman nearing forty, and I laid down my weapons a long time ago.

I study our reflections. Charlotte radiates youth—chocolate-brown eyes, glossy black hair, red, red lips—whereas my own pale face barely registers. It strikes me that this is just the beginning, that over time I'll grow fainter and fainter until I'm nothing more than a ghostlike shadow on the glass. This is what it means to lose your looks, I guess. You retain your same features, but they get stripped of their color.

"Excuse me, Eliot," Charlotte says. "Do you need to get in here?"

Glancing up, I realize my head is blocking her view. "Oh. Sorry"— I step sideways—"I thought I saw a crack in the mirror." I speak to her reflection, which now crowds out mine. "So, how about a waffle?"

"I don't have time, but thanks." She blinks a few times, then starts to outline her other eye.

It's only six thirty, but Charlotte is already up and dressed, and because of this, I say nothing about the thick black eyeliner or bloodred lipstick. Nor do I comment on the ripped fishnet stockings, floorlength skirt (is it a towel? a bedspread?), or silver skull dangling between her breasts. I also notice a single streak of blue dye, like a skunk's stripe, in her hair. Still, I say nothing. I don't even suggest that she put on a bra. I do, however, ask again if I can make her a waffle. This

time I squeeze her shoulders, not in a needy way, but like an affectionate gal-pal. My hands are on Charlotte's arms, and I exert just enough
pressure to say, *I know you'd rather be at your mom's house, but you're here
now and I'm making waffles, so why don't you have one? It's only a waffle; it
doesn't mean you love me.* Or words to that effect.

"Like I said, Eliot, I'm not hungry. And just so you know? Mom's
show is at eight, so we need to get there by seven forty-five. We can't
be late, okay?"

Charlotte is referring to her mother's art opening, which is Thursday
night at a gallery downtown. Both she and Gail are going and then
spending the night at the Sculptress's apartment. The girls are so excited, they haven't talked about anything else for weeks.

Still looking at herself, Charlotte piles her hair on top of her head.
"I told Gail I'd give her a French braid," she muses. "Maybe I'll wear
mine up, too." Both girls are obsessed with their hair. They play with
it nonstop—brushing, braiding, curling, clipping. It's enough to drive
you mad, their fingers always tangled up in their scalps, clumps of lost
strands in the sink, the tub, the floor, the sheets. In my worst moments,
I imagine the clumps growing, untamed and unyielding, until they
take over our living room, like the endless jungle of Georgia kudzu that
blankets the trees along the highway.

"That'll be nice," I tell her, stifling the urge to brush her bangs out
of her eyes. No need to invade the kid's personal space so early in the
morning.

"Although long and totally straight, like *ironed*, would make more
sense. I mean, it *is* an art exhibit, so a cool retro style would be good.
Anyway," she adds, "it's really important to Mom that Gail and I are
both on time and dressed up."

"Sure." But I'm momentarily confused. "The show is Thursday,
right? Not tonight?"

"Yes, Eliot. It's *Thursday*."

I understand that from Charlotte's perspective to love me is to betray
her mother. I also understand, probably better than most, that when

your parents split up, you have to choose between them. My sisters and I survived our parents' divorce only because the choice was made for us, although it did make sense that if my mother was the victim, then my father was her persecutor. Like Charlotte, I was too young to understand that human beings are complex creatures and function not in black and white but in shades of gray. Now that I'm an adult, however, and have experienced divorce from Grant's perspective, I know Barney must have had a separate yet equally valid point of view; but back then it was too confusing to sympathize with him or even to remain neutral. As it was, it took all my energy just to hate him. Charlotte doesn't hate Grant, but she does think he's an asshole. Rather, the Sculptress thinks Grant's an asshole and communicates this through Charlotte. This makes me an asshole, too, by association.

I point to her lips. "What color is that?"

"Sex Me Up Red. It's Mom's favorite." Charlotte puckers. "Like it?"

"Love it," I say, and give her one more supportive pat before walking away.

When Grant and I enrolled Hailey at her new school, Riverside Country Day, Charlotte got shafted, not in a big way, but in a way I worry she may resent. I used to drive her to school in the morning, but Riverside is all the way downtown, so now I drive Hailey, which means Charlotte has to get up an hour earlier to catch the bus. Because I feel guilty about this, I let a lot go, raccoon eyeliner and Sex Me Up Red being the least of it. In general, though, I rarely criticize Charlotte and make it a point to celebrate her every accomplishment, no matter how minor ("You folded the laundry? That's amazing! Grant, Charlotte sorted our socks all by herself!"), if only to ensure that her future therapist will be unable to track any latent feelings of low self-esteem back to me.

Grant tells me this is crazy, that when she's in my house, Charlotte is my child, and these dispensations I give her serve only to create, not diminish, a second-class status. "You wouldn't let Hailey walk around like a vampire, and you shouldn't let Charlotte. Set limits, Eliot. For all we know, this is gateway behavior. Next, she'll be cutting school and getting stoned."

"*Gateway* behavior?" I squinted at him. "You're high right now, aren't you?"

Grant is a nervous Nelly about his children and compounds his anxiety by reading far too many magazine articles about good girls gone bad, all of which confirm his fear that Charlotte will end up not just pregnant but also strung out on crack. The only reason he doesn't confine the poor kid to a thirty-foot tower is that I'm here to remind him that his soon-to-be junkie still carries Mr. Nibbles, her childhood bunny, around in her backpack. What I don't tell him is that Charlotte has a website, complete with daily blog and homemade videos, which I discovered when I overheard her talking to the Sculptress. I have mixed feelings about this site, just as I have mixed feelings about anyone, stepdaughter or not, sharing her private issues in public forums. So far, though, the only questionable material I've seen are some nasty posts about her dad and a picture of herself wearing her mother's T-shirt, the one that says Pussy Power in raised red letters. Until Charlotte does something dangerous, I don't plan on telling her I know about the site, and even then I may not tell Grant, although that's more to protect him than to protect her.

The truth is, Grant has no idea how I should raise Charlotte and Gail simply because he's their real (excuse me, *biological*) father. It's altogether different for me, being both their stepmother and their sister's real (ahem, *biological*) mother. If the Sculptress were dead, I could be everyone's mother. But she's not. Beth is alive and absent, so it's much more complex. Charlotte and Gail don't understand why their mother doesn't want them around, a question that fills them with acute anxiety that can be allayed only by more of her, which is something she refuses to give. But what I can do, because I'm here and because I have firsthand knowledge of just how awful this refusal feels, is offer more of myself to compensate. In theory, this is more understanding, more compassion, more time; but in practice, it often translates into more Sex

Me Up Red, more raccoon eyeliner, more blue hair dye. Not to mention that everything I give must balance out equally in all three girls' ledger books, the ones I carry around in my head.

Perhaps I'm trying to solve a problem that doesn't exist, but I don't know how to live otherwise; I don't know how to be. Does giving more make me a good person? Does balancing the books make me a good mother? Will I ever be a good enough mother for Beth's children? A better mother to Hailey? These are not trick questions. I really don't have the answers, so rather than consult a *Dummies* book for stepmothers, I've decided to do it all, just in case. Even if my girls see me as nothing more than some woman who serves up breakfast, ferries them to school, and pulls hair clumps out of the drain, I still want them to know that to me, they're more than one of mine and two of hers. To me, they're three sisters and three daughters. I want each to feel as special as the other and, most important, as beloved as Hailey. And if what I have to offer, if what I can give, is a toasted waffle with sugar-free syrup and a ride to their mother's show, then they might as well take it.

Standing in the doorway of Hailey and Gail's bedroom, I watch my four-year-old sleep. Hailey has bright red hair like her aunt Sylvia and grandmother. Sylvia's original red has faded (her current color is courtesy of a guy down on Peachtree), and my mother's is gone, but Hailey is a pure, unadulterated, shock-to-the-system redhead. My daughter, truth be told, is a quirky-looking child and less classically beautiful than, say, her sisters. With her flame-colored hair, corkscrew curls, and silly freckles, she has a Bozo-like quality—give her a big nose and floppy shoes, and welcome to the Big Top. But she's my quirky clown child, and seeing her curled up on her side, her hands tented prayerlike beneath her chin, leaves me limp with devotion.

"Hailey," I say softly, walking over to the bed. "It's time to wake up."

Rather than rouse her, I slip into her bottom bunk wearing my skirt, jacket, and loafers, then ease her into my arms and hug her against me. Hailey's breathing is restful but quiet, and as I lie with her, I adjust my own breathing so that we inhale in unison, our chests rising and falling as though we share one set of lungs, a single beating heart.

I'm about to doze off when Gail suddenly appears at the door. She leaps into bed with us, her long brown hair flying behind her.

"Oh, my God, Eliot," she yelps, throwing off the blanket. "You're totally dressed."

"Oh, my God, Gail! You're totally not."

Gail wedges her body between me and Hailey, and together we make a three-girl sandwich, with Gail as the salami and Hailey and me as the bread.

"I'm still sleeping," Hailey whines. "Stop talking, you guys."

"I'm still sleeping," Gail mimics. "Stop talking, you guys."

"Well, you seem to be feeling better," I say. "Sleeping in my bed must agree with you."

She shrugs. "Maybe I should stay home today, just to be sure."

"Sounds great," I say brightly.

"Really?"

"Sure, I'd love to have someone do the laundry, go food shopping, and cook for the week while I'm at work. We can also call Daddy, who I'm sure has his own list of chores."

"Forget it." Gail rolls her eyes. "I'd rather go to school."

Gail and I are great buddies. She was only a toddler when I came into her life, and unlike Charlotte, who was eight when her parents split up, Gail claims to have no memories of the time before I arrived. Gail is easygoing and playful. We can have fun in ways that I can't have with Charlotte because we're too distant or with Hailey because we're too close.

Parents aren't supposed to have favorites, but I suppose many of us do. In fact, Grant once told me that because Charlotte has Beth and Hailey has me, Gail belongs to him. "She's no one's favorite," he said proudly. "She's the cheese; she stands alone." This shocked me—not that he felt this way, but that he said it out loud. I always thought having a favorite child was a shameful secret, one you never admit. Nor is a favorite something you choose; it's a feeling, an instinct, that catches you unawares. Grant is an only child, so he doesn't understand that being favored isn't a gift. On the contrary, the weight of a parent's love can be an impossible burden, which is why I sometimes feel compelled to protect Gail from her father's good intentions.

"Eliot, did you know that my mother is a sister-goddess?" Gail says. "She and her friends take sister-goddess classes."

"What are sister-goddess classes?"

"Pleasure classes, like how to get your heart's desire. Anyway, all her sister-goddesses will be at her show on Thursday. And you know what else? Charlotte said she'd fix my hair, maybe in a French braid, because it's such a special occasion."

"She told me. I think that's a great idea." I look at my watch. "We need to get going, or else you'll be late for school."

I try to get up, but Gail won't let me. "Two minutes, Eliot. You're so warm and cozy."

Seeing this, Hailey snaps awake. "No, Gail, stop that! She's my mom, not yours."

"Hailey," I admonish her, "I don't like that at all. Tell your sister you're sorry."

Although I may be overly sensitive, Hailey's possessiveness does concern me. It's hard to distinguish between typical four-year-old behavior and genuine resentment. It also makes me worry that there may be real bitterness between them someday and what I can do—what I should've done already—to prevent it.

But if Gail is bothered, she doesn't show it. "Relax, Hailey. We're just laying here."

"Now it's really time to go." Before we get up, though, I give Gail a tight squeeze, as if I can validate my maternity by sheer strength alone. "Love you," I whisper.

"Love you, too. But I really want to stay home today. *Please*, Eliot?"

Grant has already left, so it's up to me to feed the girls breakfast, walk Gail to school, drive Hailey to Riverside, and get to my office.

At the end of the day, I do the same, just in reverse. Although Grant pitches in when I ask (and I do ask), our life is a well-oiled machine, and I'm chief engineer. Sure, it annoys me when he takes advantage, but he doesn't do it often and, like this morning, apologizes afterward. Ultimately, we both want the same thing: for the girls to remain children as long as possible. This means they need consistent schedules and clearly delineated boundaries. And it's our job, as parents, to enforce them.

It's true that I always try to do the right thing—the good thing—for myself and my children. But this isn't because I think I have all the answers or because I'm so righteous. On the contrary—it's because I learned at a young age that the world is a vast and unforgiving place. Anything can happen: fathers walk out, mothers' careers flounder, money dries up, grandparents drop dead. So amid all the chaos, following the rules makes me feel safe.

My mother was forty when I was born, forty-two when she had Sylvia, and forty-five when she had Maggie. This may not be unusual now, but back then it was very unconventional—as was her writing career. By the time I was born, she'd already published three novels, and although she hadn't planned on having children, my father, an only child, wanted a big family—four kids, at least—and eventually wore her down. They settled on two (Maggie wasn't planned), but neither of them had the temperament for kids. Overwhelmed and depressed, my mother retreated to her work. Or, lonely for company, she'd bitch to me about my father, confiding cringe-worthy details about their marriage as if I were her friend, not her daughter. Similarly, my father quickly realized that big families were loud, messy, and exhausting—nothing at all the way he'd imagined. He was an insurance salesman and started spending more and more time on the road. So with both parents disengaged from our day-to-day lives, my sisters and I were raised like feral animals, with no set schedule for bedtime or meals. We ate Apple Jacks for dinner while watching TV and showed up at school wearing yesterday's clothes, which were the same clothes we'd slept in. We were untrained in basic hygiene (I had no idea, for instance, that you washed your hands after you peed) and walked around with dirty teeth and knotted hair. My mother wasn't unclean, but she was inconsistent and preoccupied with more worldly activities than child care. Her writing was her first—and often only—priority. So, depending on how it was going, she was either cold and detached or far too needy, which left me constantly bewildered as to where I stood: was I her burden or buoy, the child or parent?

Growing up, I wanted the same rules and restrictions that other kids were rebelling against, which is why I make sure my children have clean clothes, fresh milk, and napkins. It's why I tell Gail to help Hailey get dressed but stick around to button her shirt and put her shoes on the right feet, why I make waffles with sugar-free syrup and fresh strawberries for breakfast. It's also why I make a waffle for Charlotte, who claims she doesn't want one but peeks into the toaster just the same.

"It's an extra," I say, handing it to her as she runs out to the bus stop.

The screen door slams. As I watch through the kitchen window, I see the wind lift up her cropped top and expose her smooth, tan belly. It's why seeing this irritates me, why I want to march her upstairs and make her put on a sweater despite the warm September morning. But it's also why, when she wolfs down the waffle in three bites and turns around to wave, I smile big and wave back.

"Have a good day, Charlotte!" I call out, adding, "I love you!" even though she's already gone. Because every kid wants a mom to see her off to school, just like every kid—whether she's yours or someone else's— wants a mom to call out, "I love you!" behind her, even if she pretends not to hear it.

Chapter Three

ATLANTA, GEORGIA, is a sprawling metropolis with a colorful history. In town, you'll find stately old neighborhoods boasting glorious dogwoods, plantation-style mansions, and good ol' boys in seersucker suits and white leather bucks. It's a gorgeous city, leafy and green, and God knows if I had any money, I'd live in it. But my house is miles and miles outside Atlanta proper, way past the double-looped highways and beyond the endless suburban strip malls and half-finished housing developments. We're north of Alpharetta, all the way up in Sandy Oaks, which is like any exurb you'll find outside Denver, Chicago, or Miami. We have everything you can find in town—schools, gyms, nail salons, Target—except for a real city's distinctive charm and character.

Hailey's new school, Riverside Country Day, is in the heart of real Atlanta. I spent my teen years in a nearby neighborhood after we moved down from New Jersey and then spent another four years at Emory. So even though Riverside is a long trek from Sandy Oaks, driving Hailey back and forth every day connects me to my past. It also gets me closer to my sisters and mother, all of whom live within a ten-mile radius. Grant and I have discussed moving down here, but real Atlanta has become too expensive for us, even with our combined salaries.

Hailey and I are on the highway, heading down to school, when my phone rings.

"Hello, Eliot? Are you there?" It's Sylvia. "You are *not* going to *believe* this!"

"Sylvia, I'm here. What's wrong?"

"Nothing's *wrong*, Eliot. I shouldn't even speak to you after your *rude* behavior at Hailey's party, but guess who I'm behind *right now*! *Right at this very minute!*"

"Who, Sylvia?" I ask, although I already know.

"*Finn—Finn Montgomery*—I *told* you he was back in town!"

For a second, I'm stunned. What's Finn doing in Atlanta?

"Hello?...Eliot? Are you there?" I hear her smack her phone. "Fuck this phone!"

"Where are you?" I ask, squeak actually. Hearing her say *Finn* has caused a weight to press down on my windpipe.

"On 85-South, near Georgia Tech. Finn is *three cars away*. Can you believe it?"

"You're *driving*?" She's *driving*? Is this some kind of joke?

"Of course I'm *driving*. How else would I get to work? Oh, my God, Eliot—he looks *good*, too." She thinks for a second. "So who was the fat guy I saw at the movies? It wasn't Finn unless he dropped fifty pounds since last Thursday. That's not impossible, you know."

Now I'm annoyed. "Stop it, Sylvia. You didn't see Finn—at the movies or on the highway. It could be anyone in that car, and you know it."

"I'm telling you, Eliot. *It's him.* He even has an Emory sticker on his back window. Hold on...he's changing lanes...wait...wait...He's getting off! Should I follow him? Holy shit, I am *such* a good sister."

"Sylvia, we're almost at Hailey's school. I'll call you later."

"*Who cares about Hailey's school?* Did you not hear me? I saw *Finn*! And you're like, *whatever*? Eliot, Finn is *here*, on this *highway*, in this *city*, *right now*. It's not *whatever*." And with that, she hangs up.

I turn to Hailey, who's in her car seat behind me. "You okay back there?" I ask, but my phone rings again. "Please don't hang up on me, Sylvia."

"I didn't." It's Maggie, and she's very excited. "Sylvia just saw Finn, and this time she was *right next* to him, like practically touching him! She also said he's not fat! Isn't that *great*?"

I sigh. "Sylvia was driving on the highway. It could've been anyone, Maggie."

"It wasn't him?" Maggie is crushed. "But he had an Emory sticker on his back window."

"Think about it: How many people in Atlanta have Emory stickers?"

She thinks about it. "A lot?" she asks.

This conversation is absurd, even for my sisters. And I'm mad at myself for getting sucked into Sylvia's nonsense. I haven't seen or spoken to Finn in fifteen years, so I don't care if he's in Atlanta, and I certainly don't care if he's fat.

I change the subject. "So, Maggie, guess what I heard. Mom told me Dylan stuck a love letter on your windshield. Is that true?"

"Maybe." But when she starts to laugh, I have my answer.

Maggie works for Unbound Vision, a company that produces industrial films for CNN. She's never had any interest in making movies, so no one is sure how she fell into this job, nor do we know what she does all day. She says she helps run the office and is "sort of involved in postproduction, but not really," and for all her talk of being so busy, she seems to have a lot of free time. She talks on the phone and goes to cocktail parties, although she has a wide circle of friends, so who knows how many of these parties, if any, are business related. Unbound Vision is small, so my guess is that she does a bit of everything— secretarial, fund-raising, marketing—but she's not paid very much and lives with two roommates. Still, my mother loves to tell people about her daughter's career in the entertainment industry, even though the only movie we've seen—a grainy video describing quality control procedures at a poultry-processing plant—had us swearing off Chick-fil-A for six months.

Maggie met Dylan Warner six years ago when Unbound Vision was working on a film about elementary school education. Dylan, who teaches third grade at Riverside Country Day, is a friend of the guy who directed it and was brought in as a technical adviser. Although Dylan didn't get paid for his two-day stint, he did meet Maggie, and they've been dating ever since. I think it's interesting that although our parents' marriage was tumultuous, Maggie, Sylvia, and I have each maintained fairly stable relationships—or at least Maggie's seemed stable. Three weeks ago, Dylan got down on one knee and took her hand. "I love you, Maggie," he told her. "I want to spend the rest of my life with you." But my sister, who is plagued by my same lack of decision-making skills, has yet to agree. "We're only thirty-three," she keeps saying. "How are we supposed to know what we want for the rest of our lives? I can't even decide between tuna or turkey for lunch."

"So," I ask now, "do you plan to write Dylan back?" Spotting the exit for Hailey's school, I merge to the right.

"I thought about it, but he said he doesn't want to see me until I've made a decision. How am I supposed to get a letter to him?"

"I don't know, Maggie. *Mail it?*"

I have a real soft spot for Dylan. Not only does he clearly adore my sister, but he also has a mischievous snakes-and-snails quality that reminds me of Finn, now that I think of it. He's good for Maggie: he grounds her in reality but appreciates her flakiness. He's smart, too. It was Dylan, in fact, who encouraged us to send Hailey to Riverside. His classroom is housed in the same building as Hailey's pre-K, so I've seen him a few times since he and Maggie went on this hiatus. Despite their current status, he is always friendly and never fails to ask after Hailey.

"Listen, Maggie," I say, "I'm five minutes from school. Why don't I stop by his room and see him?"

"And say what?"

"That you miss him, that you love him, that you can't live without him. I mean, the guy proposed. Don't you think it's unfair to make him wait? It's been six years already."

"Eliot, he hasn't been waiting *six years*. He only asked me to marry him three weeks ago." She pauses and then starts to hum, signaling that she's about to say something annoying. "I was thinking this might be a good time to call Barney."

"Come on, Maggie. That's ridiculous."

"It is not! Just because you pretend the guy doesn't exist doesn't mean I have to go along with it." Her voice drops. "He's our *father*, Eliot."

"That doesn't make him any less a stranger."

"And you don't think it's weird that he's just, like, out there but we never speak to him? I mean, does he ever think about us? Don't you wonder about that?"

I don't answer.

"Well, I do, and I'm tired of you and Sylvia calling me an idiot every time I bring him up. He's our father," she repeats. "And I think we should contact him. I'm *going to* contact him—and you can't stop me, so don't even try."

I sigh. This is what Sylvia and I mean when we say Maggie doesn't think things through. She was just a baby the first time Barney left, but she's somehow convinced that her life would be perfect if only he'd stuck around. When she's upset, especially about men, she threatens to track Barney down, as if he's the one who can solve all her problems. It kills me to tell her this (although I often do), but if the man wanted to be in our lives, he would be.

"Listen, Maggie," I say sternly. "Don't call Barney. He can't do anything for you."

"How do you know?"

"Unlike you, I wasn't a toddler when he lived with us. We had a *relationship*, so I think I'm more than qualified to assess what he can and can't do." That I was seven years old during this supposed relationship is immaterial. I'm five years older than Maggie, and as the eldest sister, my worldview is broader and more mature simply because I've been alive longer. "Barney will only disappoint you," I add, softening. "If you're going to call anyone, it should be Dylan. He's the one waiting to hear from you. He's the one who loves you."

She doesn't answer right away. She's going to lose him, I think.

"Don't be an idiot, Maggie. Just pick up the fucking phone and tell him you love him too."

"Don't call me an idiot," is my sister's reply.

⌒

Nestled deep in the woods, Riverside Country Day sits on a hundred acres of prime Atlanta real estate. Throughout its vaulted history, the school has educated hundreds of well-bred southern children, including (as of two weeks ago) Hailey Harper Delaney.

"When are we being there, Mommy?" she asks from the back. "Cars are so boring."

"We're here, sweet pea. All we have to do is drive up the hill and park the car."

Riverside is enormous. The campus is lush and green, with rows of tall trees that hang over the main road, creating a natural canopy. There's also a working farm where students grow a variety of esoteric lettuce strains; a barn with real hay; and a pasture, tack room, and stable where students stall their own quarter horses. The only drawback for us is the hour-long commute each way in Atlanta's relentless traffic.

I glance at Hailey in my rearview mirror. In her plaid skirt, white blouse, and black Mary Jane sneakers, with her wild red hair and wraparound sunglasses, she looks so cute, so Sister Agnes Aloysius meets Madonna, I want to eat her up. Catching my eye, she waves from her car seat.

Oh, my God! Did I just say the only drawback is its location? It's actually the cost. Riverside is so outrageously expensive, I assume—foolishly, I realize—that the cost is a burden for everyone. Along with the tuition, Grant and I pay for horticulture services, stable maintenance, and Hailey's uniforms. There's also a development fund, orientation fees, and countless candy sales and book drives. All told, Riverside's price tag is equivalent to twice our rent, but who am I to complain? After fourteen years here, she'll be able to grow her own arugula.

"Look, Hailey—horses!" Outside the car, three ponies gallop through the pasture. This isn't a school; this is Metro-Goldwyn-Mayer circa 1944, and we're driving past the set of *National Velvet*. "Have you learned anything about horses yet?"

"They poop in big piles, Mommy." Hailey cracks herself up. "Big fat piles of poop."

And here I was thinking all that money isn't worth it.

There's no point, however, in cataloging Riverside's virtues. It's like any private school that caters to wealthy families, which we are not. But Grant was insistent we enroll Hailey here, and adman that he is, he waged a persuasive campaign. "Look at this place," he prodded, waving the glossy brochures in my face. "Their college placement statistics are on a par with the best prep schools in the country. They have two pools—you *love* to swim, Eliot—and horses! They have *actual horses that Hailey can ride.*"

He lobbied for my mother's and sisters' support, and they all jumped in full force. Sylvia had one of her law partners write a recommendation for Hailey, and Maggie asked Dylan to fast-track her application. Not that we needed their help: Grant wasn't above presenting Hailey as a scion of literary royalty who was already exhibiting her grandmother's literary genius. (Indeed, just last week, Hailey pointed out that "the name Beff starts with 'F.' Right, Mommy?")

Getting in, though, was easy. Grant's biggest hurdle, it turned out, was me.

"No way," was the first thing I said. "It's too much money. Maybe later, when she's in high school, but why should we spend twenty-five grand on crayons and glitter glue?"

"It'll be tight," Grant conceded.

"Public school is just as good, and the money we save will send her to college, or beauty school, if it turns out I'm wrong."

"I don't disagree."

"That's your argument?"

"I want this for her," he said quietly.

"You want it for yourself," I said, and again he didn't disagree. But Grant's attitude toward money differs from mine. Maybe it's because his parents were wealthy, but where I'm vigilant about saving, Grant can be . . . not reckless, necessarily, but not careful, either. He's certainly less uptight than I am. In fact, when we met, he said he didn't care about money at all. *Well, you should,* I wanted to say. *According to Sylvia, you're twenty thousand dollars in debt.*

Like me, though, Grant doesn't like to say no. It's one of the reasons why, when he and the Sculptress were married and struggling to make ends meet, he didn't encourage her to find a job. It's also why he continues to pay a not insignificant portion of her monthly expenses, even though she's a fully functioning adult who could, ostensibly, take care of herself. But as much as I wanted to agree to Riverside, I also thought it was foolish to spend that kind of money. Seeing Grant's excitement, though, I knew I had to let him down easy.

"Let me put it another way, Grant," I said gently. "It's *fucking insane.* Besides, we have three kids. How can we send one to a fancy private school and the other two to public?"

"First of all, we make a lot more money than I did when Charlotte and Gail were Hailey's age. Second, if either of them wanted to go, I'd find a way. And third—and most important—they're happy where they are." He paused. "Do you really want to deny Hailey a life-shaping opportunity simply because her sisters don't have it, too? We work hard, Eliot. Why should Hailey suffer because Beth chooses not to earn a living wage?"

Grant kept at it and eventually I gave in, although once I toured the school, I saw his point. How could I not? The grounds are unbelievable, particularly the library and, as Grant pointed out, the dappled palominos. But what really clinched it for me was that parents are welcome anytime in the student dining center. "Grant, look at this!" I yelped. "They have six flavors of frozen yogurt and twelve different toppings!"

Hailey's pre-K and Dylan's third-grade class are housed in the lower school. After pulling into the parking lot, I find a spot and shut off the car. "We're here, Hailey!"

"I hate school. I want to go home."

"We don't use the word *hate*, Hailey. Besides, you *love* school. You have nice teachers, new friends, and lots to do. And when you graduate, statistics indicate that you're more likely to go to a better college, have a profitable career, and a satisfying retirement. This is the path to Emerald City, sweet pea. You remember *The Wizard of Oz*, don't you?"

"It stinks here like horse poop. Don't make me go, Mommy. Please don't leave me!"

And then, to really kick off the day—which at twenty-five grand a year is costing me, roughly, $24 per hour, not including after school—my flame-haired money pit bursts into tears.

⌒

Despite my initial misgivings, I've come to love Riverside. In fact, every time I set foot on campus now, I'm filled with a profound sense of well-being. Once I pass through the gates and travel up the long, winding hill to the classrooms, the air seems crisper, colors and sounds that much brighter. Everything I see—the towering trees, topiary gardens, and castlelike chapel—is grand and imposing, but also familiar, as if part of a dream I once had or a picture book I read when I was very young.

By this point, Hailey has flung herself to the ground and is refusing to walk. "It's not fair!" she shrieks. "I *hate* this place, Mommy. This place is *fat*. It's, like, the *fattest place that ever lived*!"

"Hailey, listen," I say calmly. "If you stop screaming and go to class nicely, I'll bring you M&M's later." After ten minutes of yelling, cajoling, demanding, and pleading, this—bribery—is all I have left.

She pauses. "I can eat them before dinner, right?"

My cell phone rings. It's Grant.

"Fine, Hailey," I say, to which she picks herself up, dusts herself off, and runs into her classroom. Sacrifices and compromises, I remind myself. It's the key to good parenting.

Grant's voice is clipped. "Gail's school called. She's sick. The nurse said she threw up her entire breakfast. Did she eat anything weird this morning?"

"Just a waffle, and she didn't even finish it. Maybe she has the flu. When she came into our room, she said she had a stomachache."

"Well, whatever it is, someone has to go get her."

Neither of us speaks as we each wait for the other to offer. Holding the phone to my ear, I walk into Hailey's classroom, still waiting. Although I'm concerned about Gail, I have a client meeting at noon, and it would make more sense if Grant—whose office is much closer—could pick her up. On the other end, I hear Grant breathing. He's waiting, too.

"Mommy," Hailey calls out, "the baby chicks hatched! Come and see!"

She pulls me over to the incubator. Inside, a cluster of chicks that were in eggs just last Friday have emerged from their shells. They really did hatch! Not one to regularly commune with nature, I'm as excited as Hailey. "Grant, we've got the miracle of life here. I have to call you back."

"What about Gail?"

Again, we're silent.

"Someone has to get her," he repeats. "And I've got two guys in from Tokyo to see my Nike ad."

"Mommy! Look at the chicks! I love them so much. But why are their eyes closed?"

I tap on the glass, but the chicks don't move. "Wake up, guys." Still nothing. "Little chickadees," I sing, "up, up, up!" I flick the glass harder, but they just lie there very, very still.

Oh, my God, I think. All the baby chicks are dead.

"Don't *touch*!" a little boy yelps. "Miss Lulu? Hailey's mommy is touching the glass!"

But something's wrong with the incubator! The baby chicks are dead! "Stand back kids," I call out. "Step away from the chickens."

Holding up my arms, I pirouette around, forcing the children to scatter. "Come on, pea, let's go see the frogs." I reach for Hailey's hand, but she refuses to move.

"But I love the chicks, Mommy. I love them so much."

"Eliot?" Grant is still on the phone. "What about Gail?"

"Can't Beth pick her up, just this once?" Spotting the head teacher, I hurry in her direction. "Miss Lulu?" I call out. "Miss Lulu, I believe we have a *situation* in the *incubator*."

"I already tried Beth, but she's not answering her cell phone. Eliot, Gail is very sick."

From the corner of my eye, I see Hailey climb on a chair and try to unlatch the incubator, first with her fingers and then with her teeth. "Open your eyes, chicks!" She starts to cry. "I love you. Get up, please!"

By now, the entire class has erupted into hysterics. Mothers are holding their children in their arms, trying to shield them from the dead chicks.

"What the hell is going on there?" Grant asks.

My throat catches. "I think Farmer Frank screwed up the incubator. It looks like all the baby chicks suffocated." I spot Phoebe, the frosted blond alpha mom from Hailey's party, steering her daughter away from the incubator. When she sees me, I lift a limp hand in greeting, like a flag at half-mast, out of respect for the dead poultry.

"Eliot, are you crying?" Grant is straining to be kind.

"Of course not." Wiping my eyes, I try to compose myself. What's happened to me? I've always been sentimental, but once Hailey was born, every living creature became another mother's child, and I must weep for them all. "I'm sorry, Grant," I say, sniffling. "But I have to go."

"Eliot, I wouldn't think of asking on any other day, and I realize it's an imposition—"

Poor Gail. I get all choked up for my little Gail bird, whose mother is missing, and for those sweet newborn chicks, all dead. The poor kid really was sick this morning. How did I miss it? I should never have let her go to school.

"I can get her," I tell him. "I'll just reschedule my meeting. The client is a good guy. I'm sure he'll understand."

"You're the best, Eliot. Thank you so much. I owe you one."

"Also, Grant? This morning, both girls reminded me again about their mother's art thing. It's Thursday night, and I promised we'd take them, but please confirm the time with Beth."

"Absolutely," he says, and we both hang up.

Thankfully, the class has quieted down and all the kids are in their seats, ready to start the day. I kneel beside Hailey's chair.

"I'm leaving, sweet pea. Gail doesn't feel well, so I have to pick her up from school."

She doesn't look up from her drawing. "Okay, Mommy," she mumbles.

"Are you still sad about the chicks?"

"Why would I be sad? The chicks aren't dead."

"They're not?" At first I'm skeptical, but then I see Miss Lulu cradling two of the chicks in her arms. The rest are inside the incubator, each one perfectly alive and well.

"They were just sleepy. They needed time to open their eyes."

"Oh," I say, feeling foolish. "Okay, then." I study the chicks again. Eliot Gordon, I tell myself, you are as crazy as your sisters. "Well, have a good day." I kiss her good-bye.

"You too, Mommy," she says, and waves me away.

Outside, in the parking lot, I meet up with Phoebe and her best friend, Grace, who was also at Hailey's party. The two women live as far away from Riverside as I do, but they carpool, a fact they both mentioned.

"If it makes you feel any better, Eliot," Grace says, "I thought the chicks were dead, too."

Phoebe nods. "I was *sure* we'd have to call in a grief counselor. What a *scene* that would've been. By the way, thank you for the lovely party. Sylvia was just a *riot* in that gown, wasn't she, Grace?"

"Absolutely," Grace agrees. "How is she? Is she feeling better?"

"We *adored* her," Phoebe adds. "Please have her call me. You'll do that, won't you?"

Phoebe and Grace are a study in contrasts. Phoebe is a polished Talbots preppy who favors velvet headbands and conservative skirts, whereas Grace is a rocker mom with a nest of brown curls and a sensational body, which she shows off in tight leather pants. Each has a daughter—Phoebe has Ava, and Grace has Josie—and although Hailey has said she'd like to play with Josie, I don't know if, like their mothers, the girls come only as a mismatched set.

"Sylvia is doing fine," I tell them. "And I appreciate you both lending a hand with the party. Hailey had a great time." Pausing, I work up the nerve to invite myself to join their car pool. "So, Phoebe? Didn't you say you and Grace were looking for a third driver? We're up in Sandy Oaks, so it's easy for me to swing by and pick up Ava and Josie... I mean, if you're still interested..."

I hate asking for things, even if they've already been offered. Luckily, Phoebe perks right up. "We're definitely interested. The drive down from Sandy Oaks is a *nightmare*, isn't it? In fact, I wouldn't even be here today, but I'm on the grounds committee, and we're discussing chapel renovations—"

"But we could definitely use a third," Grace cuts in.

Phoebe puts a hand on her slim hip. "That's *not* what I was about to say, *Grace*. You could at least let me finish my *thought*—"

"You know we need a *third*, Phoebe. We were *just* discussing how long it takes to get here—"

"You're renovating the chapel?" I interrupt. "What's wrong with it?"

The Riverside chapel is the most impressive building on campus. In addition to a tall, turreted tower, the chapel has endlessly high ceilings, a medieval-style pulpit, and stained-glass windows that toss off brilliant rainbow prisms when the sun hits it just the right way.

"The roof needs work," Phoebe explains. "And we're painting a mural on the exterior."

A mural? Really? "You're painting a mural? Like RIP, 2Pac?"

"She's not painting the mural *herself*, Eliot," Grace points out.

Phoebe rolls her eyes. "*Obviously*, Grace. I *doubt* that's what she meant." She turns to me to explain. "The chapel was built from high-grade adobe that's weathered in some spots. It's cheaper to paint over the rough patches than to replace the original material."

We both check our watches. "Sorry," I say, "but I really have to—"

"Run," Phoebe interrupts. "I know. Me too. I'm interviewing artists all morning."

She takes Grace's arm, and the two women turn to leave.

"What about the car pool?" I call out after them.

"I'll call you . . . ," Grace says, but Phoebe glares at her.

"*I'll* call her, Grace," she says. "How many times have we discussed this? Car pool is *my* jurisdiction." She waves cheerfully. "Bye, Eliot! Don't forget to tell Sylvia I said hi."

Chapter Four

Memo To: All Barnett Technology Colleagues
From: Lawrence Barnett, CEO
Re: Colorful Protection for a Rainy Day!

Barnett Technologies is more than a corporation; we're a family. And like most families, we "weather" financial challenges together. Due to ever-increasing costs, we're making minor changes to the Barnett Healthcare Plans. Effective immediately, your medical, dental, and prescription drug coverage will no longer be subsidized by the Company. Instead, we're asking you to pay the full cost of this coverage. To help offset these payments, Barnett Technologies is pleased to provide you and your eligible dependents with a *free* Totes umbrella! Available in three colors (red, black, or Barnett blue), these umbrellas are embossed with the Barnett~~-Avery~~ logo as a reminder that *Barnett's always got you covered.* (Note: Supplies are limited.) Be on the lookout for more details in forthcoming communications.

⌣

"Larry? It's Eliot, Eliot Gordon. Thank you so much for rescheduling this meeting. I'm sorry I couldn't make it yesterday, but I had a last-minute emergency." Speaking of my emergency, Gail just spent the past twenty-four hours in bed with a high fever. Although she was better this morning, she didn't feel well enough to go to school today, and since Grant's Tokyo clients are still here, I'm working from home again.

"That's fine, Ellie. *No problema.* I wanted to talk about the health care memo you wrote."

"Perfect. I'm looking at it right now. Let me grab a pen, and we can get started."

My office is a tiny utility closet adjacent to the kitchen. On top of my desk, next to my laptop, there are two naked Polly Pockets and the Polly Pocket dune buggy. The dune buggy has a broken wheel and a roll of Scotch Tape wedged into its moonroof.

As Larry talks, I scramble to find something to write with. From an old Elmo mug that doubles as a pencil cup, I pull out a lip liner, a broken crayon, a dried-out marker, a straw, and finally a pen.

"My problem, Ellie, is with the Barnett-Avery umbrellas. Do we really want to remind people that the Avery deal tanked? I'm personally inclined to go with balloons. On the other hand, we bought ten thousand of those fuckers—excuse my French—and I don't have the storage space, quite frankly, so we may as well unload them sooner rather than later."

Larry Barnett is the CEO of a small technology company. He's an older man—early seventies, with a young trophy wife—so he's been around a long time. Although he's usually reasonable and sensitive to his employees' needs, as with many of my clients these days, lousy market conditions are crippling his business. Ironically, it's these same conditions—recession, depression, all-out economic apocalypse—that are a boon to mine. Positive spin is vital for an organization to function, and you'd be shocked by how much executives will pay for it. But I don't only translate their corporate messages into readable English; I also have to reel them back in when they try to go too far.

"Come on, Larry," I say. "Do you honestly think that after telling people they have to spend thousands of dollars for health care coverage—coverage they used to get for free—they'll be happy with a *balloon*? I mean, an umbrella is bad enough."

Larry is a chucklehead, and he laughs as if I'm a chucklehead, too. "Of course not—that's why I hired you. When it comes to words, Ellie, you can make shit-on-a-stick taste like a Popsicle. Speaking of which, read me your announcement letter."

Larry hired my firm to communicate the details of his company's failed merger with Avery Electronics. The deal was Larry's attempt to raise much-needed capital, but it fell through at the last minute, so now he has to cut his employees' benefits, increase sales goals to offset revenue losses, and lay off staff. "Make it cheerful," he said when we first discussed the assignment. "Make it fun."

I clear my throat. "'In light of this unexpected outcome, Barnett Technologies is reviewing several cost-cutting strategies, which may include staff reductions. We hope—'"

"Whoa, whoa, wait a second. I hear way too much doom and gloom. Where are my Care Bears and cupcakes? My people are scared for their *jobs*, Ellie. They want to know they can support their *families*. We need to bring on the warm and fuzzy. Also? Let's use Barnett *Tech*. It's got *punch*; I like *punch*. And what if we say *windfall* instead of *outcome*?"

"Windfall? Larry, I thought it was a disaster."

"Depends how you look at it, Ellie. Are we talking long- or short-term? Before or after taxes? Employee or shareholder? We can't have employees thinking this Avery bullshit will take us down. *Windfall* is a confidence builder. So is *robust*; it's got *punch* like *Tech*. *Ro-bust, ro-bustly, ro-bustification.* Let's work it in, shall we?"

"I'll try." I make some notes. "Okay, what about this: 'Due to a change in strategic direction, Barnett Tech has decided not to partner with Avery Electronics. However, we perceive this as an unexpected windfall—' Larry, you can't use windfall; it makes no sense."

"Keep going."

"'An unexpected windfall, that, over time, will bring about several areas of opportunity, including more robust sales objectives, deeper revenue streams, and a revitalized workforce.'"

Larry is silent, and I fear it's too positive, if not delusional. I'm about to try again when I hear him whisper, "That is beautiful, Ellie. Sheer poetry, quite frankly. You are a fucking magician, excuse my French."

An hour later, I'm talking to Sylvia. Actually, let me rephrase: Sylvia is refusing to hang up until I concede that the man she saw driving down 85-South is my old college boyfriend who left town after college and hasn't been heard from since.

"Why must you *always* doubt me?" she whines.

"I don't *always* doubt you. I just think it's unlikely you saw Finn on the highway."

"But you have no evidence it *wasn't* him. So agree with me, and I'll drop the whole thing. Just say, 'Yes, the man you saw could have been Finn. And yes, you're amazing, and yes, I totally lucked out having you for a sister.'"

"You know what, Sylvia? At this point, I don't care. If you say it was him, it was him."

"I sense a lack of conviction, Eliot. I need to know you *truly believe* it was him. Otherwise, what you say has no significance for me."

As we talk, I Google "Finnegan Montgomery" but find nothing about him living in Atlanta. I do confirm, however, that he's married, which I already knew from prior research, and has some important job in marketing, which I also knew. What's weird, though, is that he's still at the same company that hired him right out of school (the one that moved him to New York in the first place). Fifteen years at the same place? That doesn't sound like Finn...

Okay, I admit it: I'm curious about him and occasionally check online ("on-the-line," as my mother says) to see what he's up to. He was my first boyfriend, and when we met, I was an innocent virgin—well, maybe not innocent, but certainly guileless as well as inexperienced with boys—and my feelings for him overwhelmed me. It took a long time to get over Finn, but I did, and I grew up a lot in the process. So

even if I do get nostalgic when I hear his name, or feel a frisson of something—excitement? anxiety?—that period of my life was so long ago,
it's as if our relationship happened to another girl entirely.

"So what kind of car was he driving?" I ask as I search for a recent
picture.

"Since you don't care, it was a white Lexus. And also since you don't
care, I plan to prove it was him. I never liked that guy, Eliot, but look
at me, offering to hunt him down. I wish *I* had myself for a sister. But
why are we always talking about you? I'm the one who's pregnant. Or
do you not care about that, either?" Without waiting for my response,
she launches into a ten-minute lament of all her ailments, during which
I work on a PowerPoint presentation.

"Anyway," Sylvia concludes, "I am *so nauseous* it's like I'm on a
boat. No joke, Eliot. *I. Am. So. Seasick. I. Could. Die.*" She pauses. "So,
listen...you're driving Dolores to the airport tomorrow, right?"

"Yeah, why? Her flight's at ten. Did she change it again?"

"I don't know. But she keeps asking me when we're coming. Maggie
and I can go in three weeks. Are you in?"

Our mother is retired (which is a fancy way of saying she hasn't sold
any books in a long time), but she still writes every day. Tomorrow, she's
flying to Wyatt Island, a beach resort in South Carolina, where she's
renting a house for two months to work on a new novel. She keeps referring to this trip as a working getaway, but none of us are sure what
she's getting away from. Nor do we understand why she has to shell out
$5,000 to sit and write in a stranger's house there when she can sit and
write for free in her own house here. She claims the beach relaxes her,
but this makes no sense since she can't stand the sun, the sand, or the
water.

I glance at my calendar. "What are the dates again?"

"Thursday, September twenty-seventh, through Monday, October first."

"Okay, I'll talk to Grant tonight. It might be hard for me to get away."

"And it's so easy for me? E-l-l-l-l-i-o-t..." Sylvia's sigh is so heavy, I
can practically feel her breath through the receiver. "I'm a *trial lawyer*.

Do you have any idea what I do all day? I'm saving lives here. And by the way, why did you tell Maggie that she should call Barney?"

"I did not!"

"Well, she said you did, and I believe her because you can't say no to anyone. The man is a buffoon, Eliot. Why are you encouraging her? What does she think, anyway? That he'll fly down from New Jersey and take her out for ice cream? I know she's my sister, but sometimes that girl has no fucking sense. Am I the only one with a brain in this family?"

Is this rhetorical? I don't know, nor can I ponder the question because someone is tapping on my door. "Sylvia, I have to go. I'll call you later." I turn to see Gail standing behind me with a blanket wrapped around her shoulders.

"Hey, you." I get up from my chair and kiss her forehead. "How do you feel?"

She shrugs. "Okay, I guess. Did my mom call? I left her a couple of messages."

"Not yet, but I'm sure she will." I glance at my watch. It's three o'clock, and in addition to the PowerPoint, I have an executive speech due at five. "Can I get you anything? Some soup, maybe?"

The phone rings. Gail watches hopefully as I check the caller ID. "Is it Mom?"

"No, it's Aunt Maggie. I'll call her back later." As I put down the phone, a typo on my computer screen catches my eye: "financial outlook" should be capitalized. "Damn. I thought I caught that." I sit down to fix it. "One second, Gail," I say, as I scroll through the document, double-checking for other mistakes. "I just need to make sure there's nothing else here..."

"No big deal." But she's sniffling, and when I turn around, I can see she has tears in her eyes.

"Oh Gail, I'm so sorry. I shouldn't be doing two things at once."

"I'm not crying, if that's what you think. My nose is just stuffed up."

Unlike her sisters, Gail is a difficult child to read. I can always tell when something is bothering Charlotte and Hailey, but Gail is my "go along to get along" girl, which means she's always accommodating and easy to parent. But her affability makes it hard to know if she's genuinely okay or just trying not to make waves. Sometimes, too, given Charlotte's moodiness and Hailey's whining, Gail can get lost in the shuffle, so I feel even worse for not giving her my full attention.

I always swore that when I had children, I'd never do to them what my mother did to me and my sisters. My father may have been the one who walked out, but my mother abandoned us, too, although she didn't slink off in the middle of the night the way he did. She left us the way writers leave their children, which is out in the open and in broad daylight. Her life revolved around only two activities: working and going to work. From as far back as I can remember, she was either working on her books or working at a job—teaching, copyediting, anything to pay the bills—so she could make enough money to free herself up to work even more.

I've retained one distinct image from my childhood: my mother's glorious red hair, which she pulled into a high ponytail that brushed the top of her spine. I have no recollection of how she wore her hair in front—side part or center, long bangs or short—because I rarely saw her face. Hunched over her desk, she had literally turned her back on me, and all I remember is that curly red ponytail swinging back and forth as she typed.

I wasn't allowed to interrupt her, but if I did, our interactions went like this:

"Mom?"

Silence.

"Mom?"

"Uh-huh."

"Mom?"

"What?"

Mom! Mom! Mom!

Finally, she'd blink a few times, as if rousing herself from a deep sleep. Then she'd turn and ask me what I wanted. Although she would look in my direction, it was clear she didn't see me, which was as disorienting as it was terrifying.

"I don't know," I'd say, feeling childish, as if I were demanding something outrageous to which I wasn't entitled. "Nothing, I guess. Sorry to bother you."

Her response never varied: "It's okay. You're not bothering me." But she would continue to stare at her typewriter (then later, her computer), and wait, immobile and unreachable, until I finally left the room, and she could begin working again.

I take Gail's hand. "Let's go have soup. And then we'll get into my bed and watch TV."

She points to my computer. "But aren't you working?"

I shrug. "I can work anytime. I'd much rather hang out with you."

A few hours later, the whole family is assembled at the dinner table. Gail's here, too, and although she looks exhausted, she assures me she feels fine.

Our kitchen, like our living and dining rooms, is small (read: cramped) and plain (read: drab), but I've tried to add touches like lace curtains and pictures of the kids to give it some character. Trust me, I'm no decorator, but the house was starting to depress me, particularly the first floor, where the woodwork is dark. So six months ago, we repainted the walls a pale yellow and hung a few mirrors, which immediately brightened everything up and made the rooms seem larger. We also bought new furniture, all of which—from the leather couch in the living room to the glass-topped kitchen table—is comfortable as well as easy to clean. We didn't do much, but looking around, I'm pleased by how much better this place looks.

Gail, I notice, is picking listlessly at her hot dog. She took a nap earlier, which revived her a little, but now she seems to be faltering. "Are you sure you're okay?"

She nods. "I'm not very hungry, though. I'll just eat the mashed potatoes."

"That's fine. Eat what you want."

"I'm not hungry, either," Hailey declares. "I'll just eat the mashed potatoes, too."

Grant points at her with his fork. "Oh no, pickle." He shakes his head. "We're not going through this again. You have to eat everything on your plate."

"How about I eat the hot dog and the mashed potatoes?"

"How about you eat the salad, too?"

As Hailey groans, I remind Grant that I'm driving my mother to the airport in the morning.

"Where's she going?" he asks, distracted. He's helping Hailey cut up her hot dog.

"I told you. She's going to Wyatt Island for two months. And I don't know how much luggage she'll have, but I'd appreciate your taking your computers out of my trunk."

"I'll do it after dinner, I swear. By the way, did we get our money back from the Cinderella people? And did we ever find out why she never showed up?"

"I told you that too. She suffered a work-related injury, so they credited my Amex card."

"Cinderella hurt herself doing gymnastics," Hailey corrects me. "I *love* gymnastics. I wish we had gymnastics at my party."

"Didn't you have fun?" I ask.

She nods. "It was fun, but kind of boring."

Hearing this, Grant jumps up from the table. "You girls need some cocktail party skills." He opens the refrigerator and pulls out four tangerines. "Not only will they serve you well in college, but if you're ever in a situation like Sunday, where your entertainment fails—"

I cut him off. "Oh, so now my party was a failure?"

"How would I know?" He smiles. "I wasn't here, remember?"

He tries to kiss me, but I wriggle away. "Don't push your luck, Grant. Every time I think about Sunday, I get annoyed all over again."

He grabs me in a bear hug. "Forgive me, Eliot. *Please, please* forgive me. It was the party of the century. How could I have missed it?"

"Mommy, it was the best party *ever*," Hailey assures me, licking potatoes off her fingers. "Just kind of boring, too."

"That's so *gross*, Hailey," Charlotte says. "Use a spoon. Have some manners, *please*."

Chastened, Hailey looks to me for comfort.

"Your sister's right," I tell her, although I don't add that Charlotte, who keeps glancing at the phone she's hidden under her napkin, is being equally rude.

"All I'm saying," Grant continues, gently squeezing Hailey's shoulder, "is that everyone should know three good jokes and"—he holds up the tangerines—"how to juggle."

Hailey brightens. "I already know how, Daddy." She climbs down from her booster seat. "Here, let me show you." She takes two tangerines, throws them both in the air, and watches them fall to the floor.

Gail rolls her eyes. "The idea is to *catch* them, dopey."

"I *know*, Gail," Hailey says. "Why is everyone so mean to me?"

"We're not mean," Charlotte tells her. "We just want you to grow up."

Grant interrupts them. "That's enough. Now pay attention. I'm about to amaze you." After retrieving the tangerines, he tosses them up, juggling two, then three, then four.

Although they've seen this routine before, the girls are mesmerized as Grant spins the fruit in the air over and over. Even Charlotte stops fingering her phone long enough to watch.

"The trick is to toss the ball—or in this case, the fruit—from one hand to the other, back and forth." Grant lunges to catch a wayward tangerine.

"Daddy," Hailey says breathlessly, "it's like magic. How did you learn that?"

"I used to be in the circus." His hands continue to fly. "Didn't I tell you? I traveled from city to city, doing my juggling act. Then one day, I saw your mother in the crowd, and *bam*! It was love at first sight. And just like that, my circus days were over."

Hailey looks skeptical. "Really?"

I shake my head. "He's just teasing. Your father watches too many Lifetime movies."

"It takes a strong man to watch Lifetime, Eliot." Grant stops to catch his breath. "But it *was* love at first sight. That part is absolutely true. Okay, who wants to go first?"

"Me!" Hailey shouts. "I do, Daddy—pick me!" But just as she holds out her hands, Grant's cell phone rings in the next room.

"That's my office," he says, racing out. "Sorry, but I have to take this."

After he leaves, I start to clear the table. "Whose turn is it to help?"

"Mine," Gail says. "But I don't feel so good. I'll do extra tomorrow night, I promise."

"I have homework," Charlotte says, already heading toward the stairs.

Like her sisters, Hailey is anxious to go. So when Grant returns to the kitchen, he's surprised to find me alone. "Weren't we having a juggling lesson? Where is everyone?"

"Bed, homework, *Dora*. Sorry." I look at his face. "What's wrong?"

"Stupid client. It's nothing." But he grimaces, rolling his lips inside his mouth until they disappear, which could mean anything from *I have an early meeting* to *They're letting me go*. Normally I give him a wide berth when he's in a bad mood, but tonight he seems really distraught.

"Come on, Grant. Tell me what happened."

"It's so stupid I can't even say it out loud." He sighs. "I can't get the art approved for my Nike ad. This is a really big account, and we can't screw it up. The Tokyo guys want to come all the way back from Japan to see a new color palette, along with all new photography. They'll be here in three weeks, which fucks up the whole production schedule."

"Three weeks?" I blurt out, which I instantly regret. I turn to the table, pick up the platters of uneaten food, and bring them to the counter.

"Why?" Grant asks. He grabs a hot dog with his fingers and gulps it down. "What's happening in three weeks?"

"Hot dogs are a choking hazard, Grant."

"For a toddler, Eliot. What's happening in three weeks?"

"Nothing." I put ketchup and salad dressing back into the refrigerator and stack glasses and silverware in the dishwasher. "It's no big deal, Grant—honestly."

"But . . ."

"My mother asked me to visit her at the beach. It's just a few days—Thursday to Monday. Nothing's been decided yet. Sylvia mentioned it today and I said I'd talk to you."

"Thursday to Monday is *five days*, Eliot. That's like *a whole week*. And the timing is terrible. I don't know if I can do my presentation, entertain the Tokyo guys, and make sure all three kids are where they're supposed to be. What about the week after?"

"Both Maggie and Sylvia can go on the twenty-seventh. We're driving together."

From the look on his face, I can tell Grant's conflicted. He wants to make this happen, but work is work. And this will be the first time I've been gone for more than a night since Hailey was born, which is daunting for us both.

"If it's just a question of timing," I say, "why don't I take Hailey with me? This way, you'll only have to worry about Charlotte and Gail, who can pretty much fend for themselves."

He thinks about this. "If I can shoot the bulk of the photography in the next two weeks, then that might be okay. I'll have to work overtime, but it's an option. Do we have to decide now, though? I just heard about the Tokyo guys tonight."

See, this is why I love Grant. Even though my relationship with my mother and sisters is fraught with drama and makes absolutely no sense to him, he'll go out of his way to make sure I see them. In general, though, we both try to find reasonable compromises to our complicated lives, which is why we don't argue very often. There is one issue, though, that we can never settle, and that's whether or not to get married. I don't see why it matters, but it bothers Grant that we're not, although (in my defense) he hasn't actually come out and asked me. Sure, he throws the idea around, but that's as far as it goes, largely because (in his defense), he knows I'd say no. It's not that I don't love him enough—on the contrary, I love him so much I'm afraid to jeopardize what we have. He and I make the choice every day to be together, which is safer than marriage, because we're not locked into an arrangement we're forever obliged to maintain. By remaining unmarried, I can be with Grant because I choose to, not because I have to. To me, making promises about forever is dangerous. It's tempting fate, like flipping off the gods when their backs are turned, and I'm too superstitious to do that.

Grant claims this is all an excuse, that the real reason I won't marry him is that I can't break away from my mother and sisters. But this isn't true. I just don't think marriage guarantees a relationship's success. Look at Grant. His first marriage was a disaster, and now he's entwined with the Sculptress for the rest of his life. Look at my parents. They thought they could beat the odds by waiting until their late thirties to get married but ended up separating and reuniting two (or three) times before finally divorcing.

For years, my sisters and I watched from the sidelines as they fought and made up, fought and made up. The first time Barney left, I was eight. He didn't go far—three exits south on the Garden State Parkway—and he did visit, but only on occasion and never for long. After that, he came and went a few more times, but the summer after my last year of junior high we moved to Atlanta to be closer to my mother's sister, Barbara, who had health issues, and he stayed behind in New Jersey. At first we saw him every six months, but soon the trips, then the calls, and then the cards tapered off before they stopped for good. The last time I spoke to my father was when I was graduating from college. Momentarily confused, he called me "Barbara," which might not have stung so much if my aunt hadn't just died a few months before.

Grant, I realize, is asking me a question. "Why don't I just call Beth? Maybe Charlotte and Gail can stay with her that week."

"That's a brilliant idea!" I say, and we both crack up. It hadn't occurred to us to ask the Sculptress to watch her own children, although given her track record, why would we? "I'll still take Hailey with me," I add. "Oh, and when you speak to Beth, don't forget to remind her about the show on Thursday. Charlotte said she and Gail are supposed to be there by seven forty-five, but I need you to confirm that. Also, they're planning to sleep at Beth's apartment that night, so please make sure she remembers because she has to take them to school on Friday. She should probably write it down—but don't tell her I said that. Oh, and the computers—please don't forget those, either, okay? I'm leaving really early to pick up my mother tomorrow morning."

Grant just stares at me.

"What?"

"Anything else?" he asks, and even though I know he's joking, I hand him the Fantastik and a wad of paper towels.

"Sure!" I say brightly, steering him toward the table. "How about wiping everything down?"

Chapter Five

IN THE PAST few years, my mother has become preoccupied with three things: other people's money, her own mortality, and rain. But she doesn't call it "rain." She calls it "weather," as in "They're expecting weather on the South Carolina coast throughout September. Those gigantic houses on the beach will be *demolished*, which makes me feel better about not being able to afford one."

When Hailey and I arrive at her house the next morning, this is the first thing she says to me. The second: "They're also predicting hurricane activity near South America." She motions to the TV. As usual, the Weather Channel is on. "It's a level three now, but they expect it to grow *exponentially*. *Exponentially*, by the way, is their word, not mine."

"You'll be fine," I tell her, grabbing her luggage. As I begin to drag it outside, she clicks off the TV and follows me out to my car, where I pop open the trunk. Leaning inside, I shift things around to make room. "Wyatt Island is a thousand miles away from South America."

"You really have no idea how weather systems work, do you, Eliot?" she asks, then launches into a discussion of southerly winds, cold subsurface waters, instability in jet stream flow off Argentina, and the flaws in Doppler technology. As she talks, I lift up Grant's computers—which (*thanks, Grant*) he forgot to remove—and take them out of my trunk, then shove my mother's four bags inside. If her sole agenda for this trip is to sit and write—which to my mind requires a pair of jeans, a T-shirt, and a pencil—then why is she packed for a European Grand Tour?

"I rented an oceanfront property," my mother concludes. "Do you think I'll have a problem?"

"You're asking if a storm in Buenos Aires will demolish a beach house in South Carolina?" I shake my head. "How the hell should I know?"

Hailey likes this phrase. "How the hell should I know?" she echoes from her car seat. This cracks my mother up, so Hailey repeats it.

My mother leans over to give her a wet kiss. "I'll miss you, kid. Will you write to me?"

"You know I can't write, Grandma."

"But you can read!"

In her quest to cultivate her granddaughter's superior intellect, my mother has been teaching Hailey how to read. She tells me it's going *extremely* well, that Hailey is an *exceptional* student, and although I don't doubt my mother's enthusiasm, the last time I saw my daughter holding a book, she was gnawing on it as she sat mesmerized by Big Bird on TV.

"So where are you going, anyway?" Hailey asks my mother.

"I told you, Hailey," I say. "Grandma's going to the beach."

"I love the beach. I love the beach so much. Why can't I go too?"

"Actually..." I look at my mother. "We're going to visit Grandma in a few weeks."

"Hailey's coming too?" My mother is intrigued. She loves having Hailey around—that is, as long as I feed, bathe, wipe, and entertain her.

"Grant has clients coming in from Tokyo that week, so I said I'd take Hailey."

"What about Charlotte and Gail?"

"He's going to ask the Sculptress—uh, Beth—if they can stay with her."

"Which makes sense," my mother notes. "Since they are, after all, her children." She kisses Hailey again, leaving a lipstick imprint on her cheek. "Well, I'm very happy you're coming. I want to spend lots of time together, so if this hurricane blows me out to sea, you'll always remember me."

"And then you'll be dead?"

My mother laughs. "Yes, Hailey, and then I'll be dead."

Both my mother and my daughter are obsessed with death, although for different reasons. To Hailey, death is a long, deep sleep from which she'll wake up with the perfect man's kiss, whereas to my mom, it's an opportunity for posthumous publication and the only way she'll ever escape her staggering Amex bill.

"Mom, don't talk like that. You'll only confuse her." I smile at Hailey. "Are we ready to go?"

She smiles, too. "How the hell should I know?"

My front seat has enough room for two adults, two cups of coffee, and two small purses. Here's what my mother has on her person for our brief ride to the airport: her keys, a cup of decaf (tongue-scalding, no lid), her purse (overstuffed, open), a tote bag, a bottle of water, the "Arts & Leisure" section of *The New York Times*, buttered toast, a Chanel lipstick, a perfume atomizer, a tissue, and a yellow Post-it note with her scribbled flight information, which she's squinting at.

"Oh, shit. I thought my flight was at ten, but this says nine thirty." She looks up. "We'll make it, right?"

At this moment, frankly, I have my own problems. Gail is still sick and needs to see a doctor, but I can't be with her because I have to be here, ferrying my mother and all of her liquids across town. ("Open this water, will you, Eliot?") Grant is with Gail but has a meeting at two, so we agreed to split the day, which is fine except I also have to trek to my office, which is another forty minutes away.

As I calculate exactly how many hours I'll be stuck in my car, my mother makes an observation. "Sylvia is right. You *are* a lousy driver. You don't worry about accidents with Hailey back there?"

"If I'm such a lousy driver, why didn't you have Sylvia or Maggie take you to the airport?"

"Apparently, Sylvia won't operate heavy machinery because she, quote, has a human being growing inside her, and furthermore, the shape of the front seat may put undue stress on her spine, unquote." My mother snorts. "Where she comes up with this stuff, I'll never know. But the real reason is that neither of them offered. That's how they are sometimes, your sisters."

This isn't true, but I don't challenge her. Nor do I respond ten minutes later when she says she would understand if I decided to leave Grant.

"I'm serious," she says, speaking louder in case I didn't hear her. "If living with Grant and the girls is too much, you and Hailey are welcome to move in with me."

"What are you talking about?" I exclaim, glancing to see if Hailey overheard. I lower my voice. "Where do you get these ideas? Why would I leave Grant?"

"It's terrible that he's making you take Hailey to the beach—not that I don't want her there, of course. But I don't think he realizes how much you do. It's a lot to juggle, Eliot—a job, three kids, that house so far away in the middle of nowhere." She pauses. "*I know!* Why don't you tell him that I'm not feeling well? You can say you're coming to Wyatt to take care of me, so neither of us will be able to spend quality time with Hailey. This way, she can stay with him, and you can have a real vacation."

"I'm not going to *lie*, Mom. Be serious."

"Don't be so dramatic, Eliot. It's not a lie. I'm almost eighty years old. I *never* feel well. And don't you think you deserve some time off? Not only do you run around like a crazy person, but you have no help. I mean, look at how Grant *deserted* you during Hailey's birthday party!" My mother shakes her head. "It's just not right." She hands me her water bottle. "Open this again, would you, Eliot? My *God*, I am *parched*."

Breathing deeply, I renew my vow not to get annoyed, regardless of what she says. "Mom, we've been through this already. Charlotte was stranded at her art class. What was Grant supposed to do, leave her there? And he's not *making* me take Hailey to the beach—it was my idea."

"Fine, Charlotte was stranded. Okay, but to be gone for three hours? Eliot, it kills me to see you doing *everything*. I had the same problem with your father. He wasn't interested in being a parent. It's why he didn't fight me for custody—"

"But Grant did fight for custody. And now he's the one raising the kids—"

"And then to refuse you one lousy weekend alone?"

"Grant didn't *refuse* me, Mom, nor do I do *everything*. As a matter of fact, he's missing a major client meeting this morning to take Gail to the doctor. Why? Because *he's her father* and *he loves her*."

She considers this. "Well, if the client is such a big deal, better he should be in the office, no? If he loses his job, what will he do about health insurance? You're not married, you know. Private insurance is *astronomical*. No one can afford it but the very wealthy."

I smile at Hailey, who's staring out the window. "I'm bored, Mommy."

"Me too, Hailey."

My mother twists my rearview mirror to reapply her lipstick. "I guess these days they have *domestic partnerships*. What are you, anyway?"

"What am I what?"

"Are you and Grant domestic partners? Or common-law husband and wife? Or do you call yourselves something else?" She smacks her lips. "What do you think of this color?"

Although my mother likes Grant a lot, it infuriates her that he lets the Sculptress walk all over him. She especially resents that he and I pay Beth's bills while she struggles to sell her "art." You'd think that my mother, who is herself a writer, would empathize with another mother who's also a working artist, but because she can't stand how the Sculptress treats Charlotte and Gail—and because I'm the one who picks up the slack—my mother feels nothing but disgust for her. ("What kind of mother doesn't take her kids to the dentist?" she says. "I may have been busy, but I never neglected your teeth.") I also think she finds the idea of sharing me, or worse, losing me—even to a man I love—hard to accept, and she adopts this dismissive attitude toward Grant to hide how lonely she is. I'm not making excuses for her, but at seventy-eight, she's not going to change. Dealing with an aging mother is like dealing with kids: it's a war of attrition, so pick your battles carefully.

"So," she says, settling in her seat. "Sylvia said she saw Finn Montgomery—and this time it really was him. Has he called you yet?"

"She didn't *see* Finn, Mom. She caught a glimpse of a man who looked like Finn driving down the highway. She couldn't verify it, though, because he was *three cars ahead* of her."

"Still, it would be interesting to have a drink with him, no? Find out what he's up to? I bet he made a lot of money over the years. He was always so ambitious."

"Actually, no, it wouldn't be interesting." I glance at Hailey again, but she's not paying attention to us. "Mom, stop it. I love Grant. I love my life—exactly as it is. And I certainly don't give a shit how much money Finn has, where he lives, or how fat he got!"

"*Finn got fat?*" She gasps in horror. "But he was always so trim."

Years ago, when Grant and I started seeing each other, my mother was concerned. She took me aside and reminded me that I was still young. "Grant is not your only option," she said. "Why take on someone else's headaches?" By "headaches" she meant Charlotte and Gail. And even though she adores the girls now and indulges them—and ignores them—as often as she indulges and ignores Hailey, she still wishes I had an easier life. I also think she's afraid I'll end up like her, compromising too much and then regretting my choices.

My mother is the daughter of immigrants, and her dream was to break away from her outsider's roots by writing great fiction. Early on, she wrote political dramas set in foreign countries—Africa, Israel, Southeast Asia—war-torn regions far away from her own hometown. Although she had no connections in the book industry, through a mystical combination of hard work, talent, and luck, she managed to publish three novels before her late thirties. Those early books got terrific reviews, but they were fairly intellectual and appealed to a narrow audience. As a result, all three novels sold only a few thousand copies combined, and in the years that followed, she couldn't find a publisher willing to purchase her fiction. At one point, her agent was in discussions with a small press about a fourth novel that, along with a story collection, might have broadened my mother's audience and established her as a writer of significance, but an actual contract never materialized.

What my mother could sell, however, were painfully intimate memoirs and a series of autobiographical essays that recounted her histrionic relationships with her parents, husband, and daughters. It's been twenty-five years since those memoirs came out, but my mother is still recognized as a writer who'll say anything, no matter how random, private, or shocking, just to see her name in print.

If you've read my mother's work, for instance, you know that Barney Gordon couldn't hold down a job, refused to go down on her, and neglected his teeth, which resulted in recurring halitosis ("broccoli breath," she called it). You also know that she never wanted to be a mother. Indeed, she can't stand children, and if she had it to do all over again, she would've married Lionel Margolis, the renowned poet laureate (of the Bronx).

"Lionel was my real destiny," she wrote, "my true road not taken."

What you don't know is that Lionel Margolis fucked my mother once in the backseat of his Ford Taurus and muttered, "Oh God, sweet Anita," when he came. He also sent her a series of cease-and-desist letters threatening legal action if she didn't stop publicly discussing their nonexistent relationship. You also may not know that my mother writes under the pseudonym Simone Starr, but her real name is Dolores Schneider, which she considered too ethnic and had legally changed in her twenties. Unfortunately for her, Sylvia learned about this when she was Gail's age and has been calling my mother Dolores or the Big D ever since.

As far as my mother was concerned, her memoirs and essays were nothing more than a means to an end, just a way to make money until the market shifted and honest-to-God literary novelists were once again revered. Sadly, though, her time had passed; and in the last twenty-odd years, she's sold only one other novel that, like her first three, was barely noticed and immediately forgotten.

My mother doesn't talk about her work anymore, nor does she speculate aloud as to why her once auspicious career flatlined. However, I do know she regrets publishing such personal (and prurient) material. True, she made money, but not enough to raise three kids or to retire in comfort. More devastating, though, was that its net effect negated what little traction she'd gained as a novelist. The events she described in her memoirs (even if they hadn't happened) and the persona she created (even if it wasn't real) were so indelible that readers couldn't separate the author from the art, and every subsequent novel had the taint of the nonfiction that preceded it. (It turned out it was difficult for people to read a story about a poverty-stricken family in the Sudan without being reminded that the author had a daughter who ate dog food.)

My sisters and I were raised in the shadow of the career failures of Dolores Schneider—the mother. Her literary pretensions informed our childhood. Each of us is named for her most beloved writers: George Eliot, Sylvia Plath, and Margaret Atwood. (In that same tradition, Hailey Harper Delaney is named for Harper Lee.) And each of us, in different moments and in different ways, bore witness to her private shame and desperation. At the same time, Simone Starr—the writer— is a role model of perseverance and purpose. More than anything else I feel for my mother—devotion, frustration, pity—that she continues to write every day, despite the years and years of rejection, simply fills me with awe.

The airport is fifteen minutes away, and I'm already misty-eyed. Neither of us likes to bicker, but for some reason that's what we do when it's time to say good-bye. In airports and bus terminals, outside train stations and parking garages, my mother and sisters are always leaving one another in the midst of an argument. And every good-bye is worse when they're driving me crazy. I can't wait for them to leave, and then I'm stunned by their absence. Here's your hat, the saying goes, what's your hurry?

As we ride together in silence, I think of all the things I want to tell her: that I'll do my best to visit; that I have faith in her; that she can't give up; that I love her so much.

Suddenly, she grabs my hand. *"Oy vey!"* Holding her stomach, she grits her teeth. *"Oy Goten met."*

"What's the matter?" Alarmed, I break out in a cold sweat. When my mother panics, she tosses off ancient Yiddish expressions. Although her thick, guttural noises make her sound like an über-Jew from the shtetl, in fact as a family we barely celebrated Hanukkah. Still, she's scaring the hell out of me. "Mom, what's wrong?"

"Stop the car, Eliot! *Stop the goddamn car!*" As she shifts in her seat, her purse flips over, and the contents are flung all over the floor.

"Mom, I can't stop at this moment, but I'll pull over as soon as I can." I work hard to stay calm. I keep my eyes on the road, my hands on the wheel. In the back, Hailey starts to cry, frightened by the grown-ups up front who are losing control.

"Oy vey." Beside me, my mother is davening like a dusty old rabbi. *"Oy vey, oy vey."*

"It's okay, Hailey. We're all okay." Slowing down, I maneuver the car into the right-hand lane. One mile to the next exit, then we'll get help, easy, easy. Everybody just needs to relax. "What's the matter, Mom?" I ask softly. Heart attack, stroke, seizure—any one, she'll go fast, but at least she won't suffer. *"Mom, tell me what's wrong."*

"Eliot." She closes her eyes. "I have to pee. *Oy gevalt.* I have to pee so badly, I won't make it to the airport." Still squeezing my hand, she lowers her voice. "Eliot, I think I might go in my pants."

Chapter Six

Memo To: All Barnett Tech Colleagues
From: Lawrence Barnett, CEO
Re: Do the Math: Fewer Benefits + Fewer Decisions = Good News for YOU!

If you're like most people, you have too many choices and too little time. According to a recent survey of the Barnett Tech workforce,* 90.3% of our colleagues feel "overwhelmed" when selecting their benefits, and a staggering 97.6% wish they had "fewer demands placed on them." So, after careful analysis, we've found a way to solve both issues, and free you up to enjoy all that life has to offer.

During the next few months, Barnett Tech will be streamlining your Barnett Benefits Program. Instead of asking you to pay the full cost of your medical benefits, we will no longer provide these, or any other, benefits at all.[†] That's right! Not only will you save money you would've otherwise spent on your Barnett benefits, you'll also save the time you would've lost trying to decipher our benefits materials. And that means more robust savings for YOU!

Due to popular demand, we will continue to offer our four-dollar parking deck subsidy. So now, rather than making multiple decisions about a wide range of plans (plans 93.5% of our colleagues "have never heard of" and another 98.5% "don't understand"), you only have to make one: *Do I want a four-dollar parking deck subsidy or not?*

As a special, one-time promotion, Barnett Tech is pleased to provide you and your eligible dependents with a *free* Totes umbrella! Available in three colors (red, black, or Barnett blue), these umbrellas are embossed with the Barnett-Avery logo as a reminder that *Barnett's always got you covered.* (Note: Supplies are limited.)

* This survey was conducted in the break room and had nine participants (give or take). Results may not be statistically significant.

† Other benefits include but are not limited to Dental, Prescription Drug, Vision, Life Insurance, Short-/Long-Term Disability, AD&D, Retirement Plans, Flexible Spending Accounts, and Paid Time Off.

⌒

By Thursday morning, Gail's fever has broken. Although she claims she feels better, I'm reluctant to let her go to her mother's art opening. On the other hand, I tell Grant as he heads out to work, she'll never forgive us if we make her stay home.

"What do you think?" I ask. "Do we chance it?"

He doesn't see the big deal. "You're overthinking this, Eliot. She had the flu, now she's fine. Besides, it's a two-hour event, if that."

"Grant, she was out of commission all week. And I know the opening will be short, but it still feels like it's too soon for her to be running around, especially at night, and especially when she has school tomorrow. It would be different if she was sleeping here—we could have her in bed by nine. But if she stays at her mother's, she'll be up until midnight."

"Let's decide later," Grant suggests. "If she's okay at school, then she can go; if not, she'll stay home." He kisses me good-bye. "It's not life or death, Eliot. She'll be fine."

"I know. You're absolutely right. We'll decide later." I promise to drop it but then obsess for the rest of the day. I ask my mother, who says Gail should go to the show, but the weather on Wyatt Island is lousy; Maggie, who says Gail should stay home, and she still plans to call Barney so stop trying to talk her out of it; and Sylvia, who says she doesn't give a shit what I decide. "*I'm* the one who's pregnant, Eliot," she snaps. "Why don't you poll the nation about whether or not I should go to the office?"

I also talk to my co-workers about it, including my boss, Jared, who says Gail should go to the show but sleep in her own bed. "Split the difference," he suggests, and then informs me that Barnett Tech hasn't paid their bill for two months. "Call Larry Barnett *today*, Eliot. Find out where the check is—and while you're at it, ask him to please stop sending us those ridiculous umbrellas."

By the time I get home from work, I still haven't made up my mind. But when seven o'clock rolls around, Charlotte and Gail race downstairs to put on their jackets, and the evening is set in motion.

Still, I give it one last shot. "Gail, are you sure you're up to going out tonight?" I lean over and kiss her forehead. Thankfully, she's cool.

"I'm fine." She smiles weakly. "I can't miss Mom's show."

"The sitter's on her way," Grant reminds me.

"Mom's *expecting* us, Eliot," Charlotte interjects. "We can't just *change our plans*."

"No one's suggesting that, Charlotte," I reply calmly. "Sweet pea! Come say good night."

Then again, I tell myself, it could end up being a satisfying evening all around. Hailey will eat candy with the babysitter in front of the TV. Grant and I will enjoy a rare dinner out, alone. And the girls will spend quality time with their mother. Besides, how can I deny them? They've been looking forward to this for weeks. Charlotte kept her promise to French-braid Gail's hair, and Gail is so proud, she keeps swiveling her head to show it off. As for Charlotte, she's all dolled up with frosted blue shadow (Pan Am stewardess, circa 1975) and dark red lipstick. She's so animated that I don't say a word about her wobbly stilettos or her T-shirt, which is emblazoned with the slogan GOT MILK? across her breasts.

In the car, Gail seems tired. She rests her head against the seat and closes her eyes. Charlotte slumps beside her, texting someone, presumably the Sculptress, on her cell phone.

"You told Beth that Gail's been sick, right?" I murmur to Grant.

"I left her three messages." He sighs. "Stop, Eliot. It's enough already."

Beth Delaney isn't a malicious person. I do think that deep down she means well, but—and I don't mean this critically—the woman is a mental case. Some people may be charmed by her self-absorption, but to me, she seems reckless and out of control, as though at any second she could dart into traffic—or worse, her kids will, and instead of grabbing them, she'll clap her hands and praise their spontaneity.

When Grant and I first moved in together, I went out of my way to be friendly and accommodating, but I must have been an easy mark because the Sculptress took advantage of me from the start. If I bought the girls winter coats, she expected boots, gloves, scarves, and hats. If I bought them tickets to a play, she asked to come along—and oh, would I mind getting tickets for her friend Jacinda and Jacinda's lover, McGregor? Then there was the time Charlotte and I bumped into Beth at the art store. "Do you mind covering me, dear?" she asked, gesturing to her cart, which held two cans of paint, two tins of gesso, and a studio easel. "Just deduct it from Grant's check."

I was truly at a loss. It was still early in my relationship with Grant; what did I know about dealing with ex-wives and stepchildren? Yes, I did mind covering her—I minded very much, frankly—but I also didn't want to say no and risk embarrassing her in front of Charlotte, who was standing there, watching. Everything seemed so complicated, with the Sculptress starving for her art, Grant subsidizing her career, and me with my well-paying, chucklehead job. What should I do?

What could I do? I handed over my credit card and told the cashier to ring everything up.

"I'm sorry, Eliot," Grant said when he found out. "That kind of behavior is why we split up. I know it's frustrating, but she's still the mother of my children. Next time, just say no."

Actually, I wanted to say, *the reason you split up was that she was sleeping with someone else,* but I understood his point. Now, though, as he and I stand on the sidewalk outside a packed storefront gallery, unable to gain entry because the crowd inside is violating the building's fire code, I once again curse my need to accommodate everyone.

Sylvia is right, I chastise myself. I am a doormat. Gail should be at home in bed, not standing in the gutter like some kind of street urchin. Next time, *just say no.*

Clutching her father's hand, my poor Gail bird is feverish again and trembling as she scans the crowd for the Sculptress. "Daddy, we have to get in there! We have to find her!"

"I'm sorry, Gail, but we'll never make it through that door." Grant turns to Charlotte, who is trying to hide her own distress by focusing on her phone. "What time did your mother tell you to be here, Charlotte?"

"I *told* you five *times,*" she snaps as her thumbs work the keyboard. "The show starts at *eight.* How was I supposed to know it would be so crowded? I'm texting Mom *right now.*"

"But is she meeting you inside the gallery or out on the street?"

Charlotte doesn't know and Grant doesn't press her, since it's suddenly clear to us both that Beth has failed to make any sort of plan with her daughters.

Grant is furious. "This always happens," he mutters to me. "I called her three times, Eliot—*three fucking times*—to set this up, but she never called back." He shakes his head. "These are her children out here. How can she do this?"

I touch his arm. "Maybe we should just go," I whisper.

Just then Gail screeches, "There she is! There's Mommy!" and bounds toward the door.

As I watch Gail rush off, I catch a glimpse of the Sculptress inside the gallery, addressing a clutch of women and gesturing to a large canvas. She's wearing a shapeless jumper and clogs, which wouldn't look so strange if she hadn't paired them with elbow-length opera gloves. In her hand, she's holding a plastic cup of wine and, from where I'm standing, what looks like a long cigarette holder. Either that or she's puffing on a chopstick.

The Sculptress, although pretentious and kooky, is not unattractive, but she's rough around the edges, like a once grand house that's fallen into disrepair. Pocket-sized and whippet-thin with wild, salt-and-pepper hair, she has a tired, bohemian look. But her features are surprisingly delicate, like her eyes, which are round and doelike with impossibly long lashes. She also has a vulnerable quality that, years ago, was apparently a big draw for men.

Spotting Gail through the window, the Sculptress waves, then picks her way through the crowd and out the door. As soon as she steps on the sidewalk, she lunges at her daughters, grabbing Gail first, then Charlotte, and hugging them tight.

"You came!" she keeps saying as if greeting unexpected acquaintances. "I'm so happy you made it." Although clearly delighted to see the girls, she's distracted and keeps glancing at the crowded door.

"Beth!" a frizzy-haired woman calls out. "Vinita is ready for you. She only has a half hour, though."

The Sculptress holds up a finger. "I'll be there straightaway, Jacinda!" she calls back, using the faux British accent she often adopts in public. "Give me two minutes, love. My girls stopped by to see me!"

After nodding briefly at me, she turns to Grant. "I'm working." Her words are clipped. "A Web reporter's here. She's doing an Internet feature about the show. Can you take the girls inside? Grab a pint, maybe? I'll try to catch up with you later." Before Grant can answer, she grabs Charlotte's and Gail's hands. "I wish I could spend the evening with you, my dears, but I have to meet with a *very important journalist*. She's writing an article about me, which will help me sell lots and lots of paintings. Then I can buy you both lots and lots of presents! Isn't that *amazing*?"

Wait; what? The Sculptress honestly believes someone will pay money for her art? With all due respect, the last painting I saw was a ten-foot rendering of a candy-pink vagina. True, the vagina was designed to raise awareness for the Women's Caucus on Cervical Cancer, but who would want it hanging in their living room?

Gail doesn't care about her mother's paintings. "But we came to be with you. We want to sleep over at your house. *You said we could.*" Twirling around, she tries to show off her braid. "Look!" She starts to tear up. "Please look, Mommy. Look at the way Charlotte did my hair. It's French. You love French things."

Speaking not to Gail but to Grant, the Sculptress shakes her head. "I'm sorry, baby. Tonight won't work. Next week. I promise, cross my heart." She gives Grant a helpless look, one I suspect he's seen many times before.

"But Mommy—"

Grant steps forward. "Gail," he says gently, "your mother has to work now, okay?" Anticipating a meltdown, he swings Gail up into his arms. At seven, she's a little too bulky to be picked up, but Grant holds her tight and whispers in her ear, and soon she starts to nod. She doesn't look happy, but at least she's not crying.

"Speaking of work, Grant," Beth adds, "I have to go to Italy at the end of September, so it doesn't look like I'll be able to take the girls while Eliot is away. I got this *once-in-a-lifetime* apprenticeship in *Roma*." Trilling her tongue, she turns to me. "You're going on vacation, I hear. Wyatt Island is *divine* this time of year."

"I'm spending a few days with my mother. It's not exactly a vacation." I give a small laugh to hide how annoyed I am. "But she'll be there for two months, so I can reschedule."

"Well, I wish I could help." The Sculptress starts to move toward the door, but Charlotte grabs her arm.

"*Mom*, we had *plans* tonight. You *said* we could *sleep over*. We *talked about it*."

Beth brushes a lock of hair out of Charlotte's eyes. "I know, baby, but this interview is *really* important. Besides, Daddy said you had the flu." She kisses her daughter's forehead. "You *do* feel a little warm." She wags a playful finger at Grant. "What were you thinking, mister? You don't bring a sick child out in the cold. She should be *home* in *bed*." Then with a big laugh, a quick hug, and a long smooch, the Sculptress scurries back inside the gallery.

"I'm not the one who was sick!" Charlotte shouts. "It was *Gail*!" But her mother has already disappeared into the crowd.

I catch Charlotte's eye and give her a sympathetic smile. "You okay?"

She doesn't smile back. Instead she says, "Of course I'm okay. Why wouldn't I be? And how great is it that Mom's gonna sell off all her work? She's been working on this series for, like, six months!" But her voice, pinched and hollow, betrays her. "I didn't want to stay at her house tonight anyway," she adds. "I'm really tired."

"Me too," Gail echoes. No longer in Grant's arms, she scrambles next to Charlotte on the sidewalk and grabs her big sister's fingers. "I'm really tired too."

They're both quiet on the drive home, and when I ask, again, if they're okay, they both nod, but they're sitting on opposite ends of the backseat and staring out the window. Later, when they're brushing their teeth, I want to say something comforting, something to take the sting out of the evening, but all that comes to mind is, "Good night."

"Good night," both girls parrot back, neither offering a kiss. Then Charlotte takes Gail's hand, and silently the two sisters go upstairs to bed.

⌒

That night, very late, Gail wakes up sobbing. I can hear her in her room, calling for her father, shouting and mewling at the same time, "Daddy, Daddy! Please come!"

Beside me, Grant is in a dead sleep. "Grant?" I shake his shoulder but get no response.

"Daddy, Daddy, Daddy!"

"I'll go," I say stupidly, getting out of bed.

I find my way down the dim hallway and climb the ladder up to Gail's bunk. In her own bed below, Hailey is splayed like a corpse, undisturbed by her sister's wailing.

"Gail?" I whisper at the top. "Are you okay?"

Seeing me, she cries harder. "I wasn't calling *you*. I was calling *Daddy*."

"I know," I say quietly, nudging her over. "But Daddy's asleep." She's warm like an animal, and I curl against her to absorb her heat. "Why are you crying?"

She doesn't reply at first but then says, "I shouldn't even be here. I was supposed to stay at my mom's."

"I'm sorry." I hug her tight. "I know you were looking forward to it."

"My *own mother* doesn't have time to be with me. I miss her so much." Gail sounds just like her four-year-old sister.

"I know what you mean, Gail. Sometimes my mom is the only person who can make me feel better."

"You're not *listening*, Eliot. She doesn't make me feel better. She cares about her art a million times more than she cares about me. And now she's going away for a long time."

As Gail says this, I remember my mother's swinging red ponytail from my childhood and the way she clutched my hands at the airport yesterday, reluctant to say good-bye. "I'm sorry," she said. Her eyes were wet. "I don't know why I say such stupid things. Grant is a good man; I know you love each other. I'm just going to miss you, that's all. Promise me you'll visit, please, Eliot?"

"I promise," I told her, forgiving her all over again for forcing me to find a bathroom in the middle of rush-hour traffic. She was frightened, I realize now. The Big D was facing two long months of solitude, and panic was settling in. Crazy fears fester in her mind when no one else is around, but she's an old woman whose career is dead, whose parents are dead, whose beloved sister is dead, and who hasn't had a man around in years and years. And at the core of her craziness is one simple wish: not to die without me and my sisters nearby.

Oh, Gail, I think. I miss my mother, too.

I peer at her in the dark. "I *am* listening to you, Gail. I heard every word. I also know how you feel. My mother and your mother were a lot alike. When I was growing up, it was very hard to get her attention."

"Grandma Simone? That's weird. She's not that way to me."

"Well, sometimes grandmas are different with grandkids. But you know how most mothers say the happiest day of their life is the day their kids were born? Well, my mom's happiest day was when she sold her first book. I wasn't even there."

"She told you that?"

I nod. "And her second happiest day was when she sold her second novel. I wasn't there that day, either. My mother always put her work first, and I missed her all the time. It's hard when the most important person in your life has a passion." I choose my words carefully. No matter how much I despise the way Beth treats her children, she's still their mother; the first one, the real one. "But there's no way she loves her art more than you, no way in the world."

"Really?"

Don't be ridiculous, Gail. Of course she does—not because she wants to, but because she can't help it. You can't choose what you love any more than you can choose who. And the longer you keep waiting for her to change, the unhappier you'll be. So I suggest you find a way now to accept her as she is if you want to have any sort of relationship with her.

"Really, Gail," I say quietly. "She couldn't love you more."

I stay with her for a long time, stroking her head as she falls asleep. Her French braid is undone, and her long dark hair fans out on the pillow. "Gail?" I say eventually. "You up?"

She doesn't answer. Her breathing is even and restful.

"You're safe with me," I say, feeling safe myself. Her bunk bed is like our own private nest up in the air. I think about the chicks in Hailey's class and how they weren't dead, just sleeping. Gail isn't motherless, not all the time. "I know you love your mom, but remember I love you, too." I pause. "I love you forever."

I always feel greedy telling Gail and Charlotte that I love them. It's a sort of thievery, isn't it? Like I'm stealing from Beth something to which I have no claim, disrespecting her position in some way. It's why I feel funny referring to all three girls as *mine*, because only one really is; the other two are on loan. Know, though, that I love Gail and Charlotte very deeply; know too that this love is the same as, just different from, the way I love Hailey.

"Eliot?" Gail says, startling me. "I just want to say good night."

"Good night." I am the one, I think. I am the one who understands you, who knows what you need. "Sleep tight."

Chapter Seven

As IT TURNS out, Sylvia was right: it was Finn in that car on the highway.

"I *told* you!" she gloats. "Now you can never doubt me again." Not only did she find him, she adds, but she can verify her information with physical evidence.

"What kind of evidence?" Cradling the phone in my neck, I whip eggs in a bowl. It's Saturday, and I'm making cheese omelets for lunch. "DNA? Carpet fibers? Fingerprints?"

"For your information, nasty girl, Maggie and I are in front of his house *right now*—"

"You're at Finn's *house*?" The egg bowl falls from my hand and cracks on the counter.

"Yup, and there's a *white Lexus* in the driveway with an *Emory sticker* in the back window. It's the *same exact car* I saw on the highway. And I'm about to take a picture with my phone, which—pressing send, there we go—you'll get in one second. Isn't technology amazing?"

I'm still trying to believe that she's at Finn's house. "Maggie's there too? How did you get his address? Have you seen him? Oh, my God, Sylvia—did *he* see *you*?"

"What's with all the questions? First you don't believe me, and now it's, like, an interrogation session at Guantánamo Bay. Give me a chance to present my findings, Officer, and we'll have a Q and A at the end of the hour. Yes, I'm here at his *house*, and so is my trusty sidekick."

I hear Maggie moan, "Why am I always the sidekick? Why can't I be the main person?"

"Maggie, please. So, Eliot, listen to this: Finn has an eight-year-old daughter. Try and guess the capital K Krazy name he gave her." Sylvia pauses. "Oh, forget it, you'll never guess. It's *Humphrey*! What kind of idiot names a girl *Humphrey*? Do they call her *Hump* for short?"

"It's probably a family name," Maggie says, taking the phone. "Hey, Eliot, can you believe Sylvia found Finn, and we're at his house right now?"

"He's got a big-ass house, too," Sylvia says. "It's even bigger than mine. What do you think of that?...Eliot?...Hello? Are you there?"

"What's wrong?" Maggie calls out. "Are you upset?"

"Is it because I said his house is big?" Sylvia asks. "Your house is nice, too. It's cozy, like a little hut." She gets annoyed. "Eliot, why aren't you speaking?"

I'm shocked. All this time I assumed Finn was in New York, but he's actually here, in Atlanta, with me. It bothers me he didn't call—not even once—to say hello. At the same time, it bothers me that this bothers me. *Stop it,* I tell myself. I don't want to care about Finn—I *don't* care about Finn.

I haven't seen nor spoken to Finnegan Montgomery in a very long time. We met in our freshman year at Emory, on the first day of Introductory Spanish. I got to class early and was already situated by the time he slid into the seat behind me. The professor was ten minutes into his lecture, and I was trying to pay attention.

Finn leaned forward to whisper in my ear, "I think I'm in the wrong room. Is this Introduction to the Language and Peoples of New Guinea?"

Pathologically earnest, I didn't realize he was kidding. "No, it's Spanish," I whispered politely over my shoulder. I expected him to leave, but he stayed where he was, then proceeded to talk to the back of my head for the next ninety minutes.

So, that's how it began: *Montgomery, Finnegan,* sat behind *Gordon,*

Eliot, and didn't stop talking all semester. Our relationship was as random as it was unlikely. My first impression of Finn was that he was effeminate and immature. He spoke with a girly pitch and never shut up. I tried to catch a glimpse of his face but couldn't twist far enough around in my seat, so I had no idea what he looked like. From his shrill, nonstop rambling, though, I suspected he had the skittish eyes and underdeveloped body of a boy whose only friends were imaginary. On the other hand, I thought, he was kind of amusing.

Unlike most professors who did no actual teaching on the first day of class, this one planned to use up his entire ninety minutes by reading in Spanish from an ancient textbook. But while everyone else sat in stupefying boredom, I listened—and laughed—as the funny guy behind me hummed "I'm a Frito Bandito" over and over. He also did a series of celebrity impressions and performed dramatic readings from the Emory Student Handbook, including the table of contents and emergency phone numbers. ("The Emory Mental Health Center," Finn intoned, "Four-oh-four-five-five-five-six-one-eight-seven.")

I was an awkward eighteen-year-old. And because I felt so uncharismatic myself, I was captivated by funny people, particularly funny boys. He told me he was from upstate New York and had never traveled south of Baltimore, except for Florida. "What about you?" he asked. "Have you been to Atlanta before?"

Turning my head to the right, I spoke softly. "I'm from here."

"A southern Irish girl. Weird."

"I'm not Irish. Most people think I am—it's the red hair and freckles—but I'm actually half-Jewish and half-Italian."

"I like red hair. You don't see it very often. I like unique things, although I'm not unique myself."

This, I would learn, wasn't true. Finn was a poor kid, a scrapper like me, whose family life had been equally troubled. His problems growing up were different from mine, but he ended up just as insecure, although in college—in life—he was far more successful than I was at fitting in. Despite being a lousy student, Finn was very smart—too smart sometimes. He read a lot and tested well (which was how he maintained a scholarship to Emory), but he also had a cocky side that bordered on obnoxious. Still, he became my best friend, then eventually my boyfriend. He was my first true love, the one boy—the only boy—whose pull I could never resist.

All this came later, though. At that moment, Spanish class had ended, and I was anxious to see if this funny boy was as goofy looking as he sounded.

When I turned around, he was waiting for me, his right hand extended. "Finn Montgomery. Nice to meet you."

Staring at him, I opened my mouth to speak, but nothing came out. *Finn Montgomery. Finn Montgomery. Finn Montgomery.* I sang his name silently, over and over, until the music was all I could hear.

He tried again: "Hi, I'm Finn..." And again: "Hey, red-haired girl, are you okay?"

I closed my eyes, feeling as though I'd stepped off a ledge. *This* was the boy talking to me? This was the boy talking to *me?* This boy had a thatch of wild blond hair; his green eyes were iridescent and shrewd; his smile was brilliant. I was falling faster and faster. I knew, instinctively, I would not survive. *Finn Montgomery, you are the most beautiful boy I have ever seen.*

"*Eliot!*" Sylvia is yelling at me. "*Are you there?* You have a fine little hut. Don't be so fucking sensitive."

"When did Finn get back from New York?" I ask quietly.

"I'm not *Serpico*, for God's sake. I can't find out *everything.*"

"Are you going to call him?" Maggie asks.

"Of course not," Sylvia interrupts. "Why the hell would she call him? Eliot, let me tell you something else about your fake friend Finn. His house is *atrocious.* It's as big as Tara, and his lawn is filled with those idiotic garden gnomes. I mean, one gnome is cute—ironically, of course. But this guy has an entire gnome *population.* It's like a *Lilliputian crop circle.*" This cracks her up. "You know, that's funny, Eliot."

I'm in no mood to laugh. "His house is like *Tara?*" Why does this make me so sad? I look around at my own house, which suddenly seems small and shabby, particularly the stupid yellow walls that show every speck of dirt. The faux wood on my cabinets is warped, my dishwasher doesn't close properly, and you can see the seams in the floor where the tiles are buckling. And because of my earlier carelessness, raw egg is splattered all over the counters. "Sylvia, is it really a mansion?"

"Would you call this place a mansion?" Sylvia asks Maggie.

"What makes a house a mansion? Is it a square footage thing? Or, like, how much it costs?" Maggie pauses. "What? Why are you rolling your eyes? How should I know if it's a mansion or not? I've never built a house before. What do I know about square feet?"

Sylvia sighs. "A simple 'no' would've sufficed. Eliot, listen to me. This place is *so not* a mansion. It's a regular house—just like yours—but oversized and vulgar. The guy probably stumbled into money and had to show off. And I'm not joking about the gnomes. They're hidden all over the grass, like IEDs."

"I have to go," I say abruptly.

"So go," Sylvia says, then reconsiders. "You're going to call him, aren't you? Don't you dare, Eliot. I'm serious." But before I have a chance to defend myself, she hangs up. I don't, though. Instead I stand there, still holding the phone, and debate what to do next.

⌐

Eliot, I think the following is good to go, but please review and give me your comments. Thanks, Larry

Memo To: Barnett Tech Colleagues
From: Lawrence Barnett, CEO
Re: Robust News from Your CEO!

Dear Colleagues,
   As the tides return, eternally, to shore, so does prosperity at

Barnett Tech. Last week, in the aftermath of our failed merger windfall, we saw our stock price tumble down like children tumbling down the hill. But like a phoenix that rises from the ashes, this week the price has shot up like a rocket soaring up to the heavens, whatever heaven you may—or may not—believe in. Barnett Tech is an equal-opportunity employer and does not discriminate against race, religion, creed, or women who feel compelled to lactate in what is supposed to be a place of business.

At Barnett Tech, we realize that the Company's success is a reflection of your "dedication." To reward your "hard work," we are authorizing the return of trash can liners to all employee cubicles. Going forward, from now on, you are no longer required to transport your wet rubbish to the common cafeteria. Instead, you may now dispose of your wet rubbish right in your very own office-ette!

Like that rising phoenix referenced in the aforementioned paragraph, we trust you will enjoy this resurrected employee "perk." Thank you, most sincerely, for your continued "hard work" and "dedication."

⌒

I don't call Finn, and I feel good about that. Even if he does have a mansion like Tara and a white Lexus, he also has lawn gnomes and a daughter named Hump. Besides, I have things, too: I have Grant and Hailey and Charlotte and Gail, and I'm proud of our cobbled-together, waffle-eating family. Look at me, Finn, I keep saying. I didn't collapse when you left. I found someone else, someone better, to love as much as—no, more than—I once loved you. Look at me, Finn: I'm happy.

I feel close to Grant all weekend. Without being asked, he calls a guy to fix the dishwasher, takes Hailey to the park, makes brunch on Sunday, and even cleans up afterward.

"Why are you being so nice to me?" I ask.

It's late Sunday afternoon, and we're upstairs in our room. I'm sitting on the bed, folding laundry, while Grant lies beside me, flipping through the TV channels, searching for something to watch.

"I'm always nice to you," he replies, staring at the screen.

"Sure, you're nice, but not *this* nice. Something else is going on."

"Why can't I just be nice?" Grant tosses aside the remote, then crawls toward me, knocking over my piles of clean clothes. "Why are you so suspicious?" He's grinning, and I know what's coming.

"Grant, wait! All this laundry is clean." Laughing, I try to move away, but he's already on top of me, kissing my cheek, my ear, my head . . . small pecks meant to arouse me. Bunches of clothes lie scattered all over the bed and the floor.

He slips his hands under my T-shirt. "You doubted my motives, and now you must pay."

"Grant, stop." I nudge him with my elbow. "The girls could walk in any second."

"Who cares? It's good for kids to see their parents being affectionate. They should know that their father loves to fondle their mother's luscious breasts."

As soon as he says the word *breasts*, Charlotte appears in the doorway. "Eliot? Hailey needs help in the bathroom." She looks at us closely. "Hey, what are you doing?"

"We're folding the laundry," Grant replies, craning his neck to see her. "What does it look like?"

"Like you're making a big mess."

"Laundry is a very complicated process, Charlotte. Go help your sister, please. Eliot and I have to finish our chores."

"Um, I don't think so, Dad. Hailey's on the *toilet*. She needs help *wiping herself*."

"You may not realize this, Charlotte, but I find poop as gross as you do."

"That's okay," I tell them. "I'll go." I try to get up, but Grant won't let me. "This isn't funny anymore, Grant. Please move your arm."

He groans. "Charlotte, go help Hailey. Just grab some toilet paper and get it done. Please? We're very busy here." He gives me a passionate kiss, which I indulge even though Charlotte is standing there.

"*Dad!*" She giggles as she walks away. "Hailey! Your mother's being *naughty*."

"Grant, that's enough." I pat his arm. "Let me go."

"What's wrong?"

"Nothing's wrong. I have to go wipe your daughter's ass." As I rise from the bed, I toss underwear and socks back into the laundry basket. "We'll pick this up again later, okay?"

"Fine, walk out, Eliot, but mark my words: When I drop dead, the only thing you'll regret is not having sex with me every chance you could." He's on his side, head propped up, watching me. "You should go," he says suddenly.

"Go where?" He doesn't answer, so I repeat myself. This time, I'm annoyed. "Go where, Grant?"

"To Wyatt Island with your mother and sisters."

I lean out into the hall. "*Hailey!* Why don't you try wiping yourself for a change?"

"Will you give me a few M&M's?" she calls back.

"I thought you said you had clients coming in that week."

"I do, but that's my problem, not yours. The other night when Beth told us she was going to Italy—"

"*Roma,*" I interrupt, trilling my tongue.

Grant sneers. "Yeah, *Roma*—and you offered to reschedule your trip, I felt awful—"

"I didn't say it to make you feel awful."

"I know. I felt awful because even though you were nice about it, I could tell you were disappointed. And that's wrong. You shouldn't have to change your plans just because my ex-wife is a nut who refuses to accept responsibility for her children. I also know that when you first told me about the trip, I wasn't very encouraging. That's because . . . I don't know . . . because I'm a dick sometimes. Work has been a nightmare, Eliot. This Nike account is kicking my ass, but I realize, however belatedly, that you have a life too. I was selfish, and I'm sorry. I really am. So go to Wyatt—see your mom, hang out with your sisters. Hell, even have a little fun. I won't complain at all. Well, I probably will complain, but just ignore me."

I study his face. "You're serious? Just you and the kids? Without me?"

"I'm totally serious."

"And you'll get the girls to school, give them dinner, check their homework, etc., etc.?"

"Mommy?" Hailey calls again. "Just one M&M if I try?"

Grant nods. "I'll deal with all of it." He looks pleased with himself. "You're a great mother, stepmother, and wife—girlfriend, partner, whatever—but you're also a great daughter. You should be with your mom if she needs you. Even if she doesn't need you, you still deserve to go to the beach…" He stops.

"What?"

"Nothing." Sheepish, he stares at his hands.

"Just say it, Grant."

"Sometimes I get jealous. I never had brothers or sisters—nor did I have a good relationship with my parents—so when you're with your family, I feel…I don't know…left out, I guess. I know it's wrong—"

"It's not wrong to feel jealous, Grant."

"No, I mean, I know it's my problem, not yours. You're lucky to have them and vice versa, and even though they're totally bizarre—and they *are*, Eliot, even you have to admit that—being with them makes you happy. So I genuinely want you to go and I genuinely want you to have a good time."

"That's so nice." I walk over to the bed and give him a long, wet, meaningful kiss.

Down the hall, we hear Hailey calling, *"Mommy, Mommy, Mommy! Come wipe me, please. I'm all poopy."*

Grant looks at me. "You're taking Hailey, though, right?"

Chapter Eight

As THRILLED AS I am to be going to Wyatt Island, I'm also concerned about Charlotte, who's been holed up in her room since the gallery incident last Thursday. She's obsessed with a boy named Jeremy Jacoby, which I know because I discovered her new Tumblr account and read all her long, mournful posts about him. She also posted angry rants about Grant and me, which was confusing at first since it was the Sculptress who blew her off last week. But after scanning her blog entries, which date back several months, and which are, by turns, nonsensical, narcissistic, insightful, and hilarious, I realized that Charlotte is inconsistent, unstable, and troubled—just like every other fourteen-year-old girl in the world.

When I was fourteen, we had just moved to Atlanta, and I was miserable. This was before the Internet, though, so I never shared my misery with anyone else. Not that I would have back then, either. The idea of people knowing my innermost secrets horrified me; to willingly blog about these secrets to strangers would've been inconceivable. Even now I have trouble with the way people willingly offer up personal details about themselves and their families. Maybe I would feel differently if I had grown up with the Internet, but I doubt it. I've always lived inside my head, and while I'm more forthcoming now than when I was a teenager, I still believe there should be strict boundaries between the public and the private, if only as a means of self-preservation.

Although much about the world has changed, some things haven't, including a teenager's self-loathing. When I was fourteen, everything humiliated me: my body (too fat), my hair (too thin), my skin (too pale), my fingers (too short), my boobs (deformed)—the list went on. Far more comfortable with books than with people, I rarely had many friends. And forget about relationships—with two sisters and no man around, boys were a complete mystery. I'd barely kissed anyone before I met Finn, who was the first boy I slept with. And I've slept with only three others since, including Grant. I wasn't selective as much as awkward, and until Grant came along, I found relationships in general, and sex in particular, to be so fraught with issues that it seemed less stressful to just be alone.

When I look at old pictures of myself, I see a normal, healthy teenager. I wasn't classically beautiful like Maggie, but I was perfectly lovely, with wavy auburn hair, a voluptuous body, and a generous smile. In my mind, though, I was dumpy and ungainly, and my self-consciousness was compounded when my mother's memoirs came out, first when I was thirteen and then at fifteen. Around this time, too, she was writing personal essays that were published in anthologies and various women's magazines. I wasn't popular in high school, but I did become well-known, largely because my mother, though not a household name, was the only published author anyone knew. And while I was happy to see her finally getting recognition, it was a strange and often mortifying experience to be her daughter. For the most part, I felt lost and lonely, yet also exposed, which is an odd paradox.

When your mother is a writer, you are more than just a daughter—you're an endless source of material. The time you were three and announced during a dinner party that your mom has a hairy vagina? That anecdote will be recounted not only during family gatherings, but also in an essay collection devoted to her most embarrassing moments.

At first, you'll feel proud to be immortalized this way; after all, not only do you know where her stories come from, but without you, her stories wouldn't exist. Over time, though, as your adolescent anxieties intensify, it will dawn on you that your mother is revealing your personal life without asking, which is the same thing as reading your diary to strangers. And you'll start to rage. What kind of *parent* does this? you want to know. What kind of *person*? But when you raise the issue, she'll just wave you away. "Don't be so dramatic," she'll say. "Don't be so sensitive." And you'll swallow it, and keep swallowing it. Because when your mother is a writer, everything, anything, is fair game. The bed-wetting travails you should've grown out of? The *one time* you nibbled on a dog biscuit? Your clandestine cookie binges? Your struggles with your weight? All of this will be remembered, recorded, and offered up as Art. Nothing you say, nothing you do, will be private or sacred or even your own. And even though you understand intellectually that few people you know actually read her books, you'll never shake the feeling that everyone is watching. It's primal, this shame. It cuts right to the core. So you'll work that much harder to win people over, to be sweet and accommodating, to be nothing at all like the girl on the page.

It's been twenty-five years since my mother's memoirs came out. Although she and I never sat down and discussed them—not at length, anyway—I have since moved on. During my late twenties and early thirties, I spent time in therapy, where I learned how to forgive her. It was a long process, but my only other option was to stay Peter Panned at fourteen—bitter, silent, burning with humiliation. Although I'm still self-conscious, I'm no longer a mortified teenager. Nor do I resent my mother's career, especially when I see her now: seventy-eight years old, used up and alone, uncelebrated and unacknowledged. And while her passion is one I neither share nor fully understand, it's something I've come to accept. I do forgive my mother her mistakes; I only hope that someday, Charlotte, Gail, and Hailey forgive mine.

Having my own career and my own children has helped me to realize that it's difficult, if not impossible, to choose between your family's needs and your own and to balance all the demands on your time. These days, I'm far too busy to worry about my body, my sexual hang-ups, or the number of men I did or didn't sleep with. Now that I'm a mother, my concern is for my children and how I can spare them the agony of self-loathing, enlighten them about sex, and make sure the number of men they eventually sleep with never exceeds, say, one.

"Two," is what I tell Charlotte. "I've slept with two people. You asked me directly, so I'm answering, but it's a personal question, and boundaries are very important, even among family members."

It's Monday night. Charlotte is at her desk, doing her homework and watching TV. During dinner, she asked some wildly inappropriate questions about my past, which I agreed to discuss with her later. By later, I meant when she was going through menopause. But she wouldn't let up, which is how I came to be sitting on her fluffy pink bedspread, lying about my sexual history.

"Mom doesn't think sex is so personal. She says parents and kids should tell each other everything. That's what makes a family close. She had sex with thirteen guys—including Daddy. Do you think that's a lot?"

"I'm not sure, Charlotte," I say, stalling. "What do you mean by *a lot*?"

"Is thirteen normal or, like, *a lot*?"

I falter, "Sure...it's normal...I guess. I mean, of course it's normal. It's *absolutely* normal. But what's normal for your mother isn't necessarily normal for you."

"But we're not talking about me, Eliot. We're talking about Mom."

Although I wasn't raised with religion, I feel a sudden urge to speak to God. *Please,* I think, looking skyward. *Please help me find a way to end this conversation.*

"Well," I say eventually, "I think the most important thing is that you respect yourself. When I was your age, I didn't like my body, so I wore baggy clothes. And while it's *so great*, Charlotte, that you're proud of yours—because you do have a lovely body—wearing a T-shirt that says GOT MILK? or PUSSY POWER or—what's the other one? MAN TRAINER—calls unnecessary attention to your..." We should paint this room, I think, looking around. It's kind of drab. "To your..."

"Tits?" she asks.

"Yeah, sure." I nod vigorously. "Your tits."

Although this chat we're having is excruciating, I have to press on. As the mother-in-residence, it's my responsibility to discuss safe sex, "just say no," and all the other after-school specials I thought Charlotte's other mother would cover. My dilemma is this: Because the Sculptress is so lenient with Charlotte, I have to be overly strict, but I don't want to sound like a moralist and a prude, both of which (let's be honest) I clearly am. Nor do I want Charlotte to think I'm overriding or judging her mother, although I definitely want to do both—that is, override and judge her.

"There's nothing wrong with a Pussy Power shirt per se," I continue, "and of course I believe in freedom of speech. But I don't like you calling attention to your . . . your breasts."

"It's Mom's shirt," is her reply. "She says I look cute in it."

"You do look cute in that shirt. It's just that men, or rather, boys, guys—although men, too, at this point—will already be looking at you, at your breasts, I mean. Why do you want to give them more of a reason?"

"Mom says that the pussy is powerful, and that women need to stay together."

How can she just say *pussy* like that? It's like any other word to her, like *apple* or *exam*. "Charlotte, I really don't like the word *pussy*. It's not—"

"Cooch?"

"No, it's not the word, Charlotte—"

"Clam? Hoo-hah? I know, like, *hundreds*. Knish? Cooze—"

"*Charlotte, stop it!* The word itself is fine, just not on a T-shirt. A T-shirt that says Pussy Power is actually *repressive*."

"I totally disagree, Eliot." She glances at the TV, then jots something down in her notebook. "I feel really strong when I wear that shirt. So does Mom," she adds, writing and talking at the same time.

"Charlotte, listen. You know how people can twist a concept to suit their own needs? For instance, my family uses the term *Gluckman* to describe people who think they're entitled to whatever they want."

Her eyes dart back to the TV. "Like kids who get cars and computers for no reason?"

"Kind of... Well, sometimes these people are the first to need 'me' time even though they have 'me' time all day. A PUSSY POWER shirt is the same thing. When you wear it, you objectify yourself—you give away your power. Sure, in some contexts, 'pussy power' suggests women rising up against the Man, but on a T-shirt, it has an effect that's contrary to its intent; it's ridiculous, frankly. When I see a woman wearing a PUSSY POWER T-shirt, I don't think 'empowered person,' and most men don't, either. They see a blatant invitation to stare at her... um... breasts."

She looks at me blankly. "So you think Mom is ridiculous?"

"Of course not."

"Then why are you saying she has no power?"

"I'm not. You're intentionally not getting it... Charlotte?"

She's engrossed in something on the screen. "Huh?"

I pick up the remote and snap off the TV. "Don't you have home-work?"

Exasperated, she snaps it back on. "This *is* my homework, Eliot. We're supposed to watch *Star Wars* for science class."

"Are you serious?" They're watching *Star Wars* for science? At Hailey's school, ninth graders are collaborating with NASA engineers to build scaled models of the *Challenger*, reenact the explosion, and then analyze the data using advanced logarithms. "Charlotte, all I want is for you to respect your body... For Christ's sake, Charlotte, look at me!"

When she turns, she has an expression that reminds me of the Sculptress, an expression, disdainful and condescending, that says: *How dare you interrupt my vital* Star Wars *watching?*

"I don't like that T-shirt," I tell her, "and you can't wear it anymore. I suggest you keep it at your mother's house, or else I'm going to throw it out."

"Fine." She presses her red lips together so tight, they lose their color. "Whatever, Eliot."

You're the one who's ridiculous, Eliot, her expression says. *Look at you, so righteous with your waffles and nine-to-five job. You're so* average, *so* ordinary. *My mother is a* painter; *she has* passion. *If you had* passion, *you wouldn't be so* repressed, *you'd be able to say* pussy; *you might even get laid more often.*

"And another thing, Charlotte—I know you have a new blog, and I've read all your posts."

When she gasps, I admit I feel powerful.

"You can keep it—for now—but I don't want to see any more pictures of you half-naked or posts about your sexual fantasies. Nor do I think it's a good idea to call your world history teacher—or your father, for that matter—a 'fucking dick.' The Internet is *not* your secret diary. To expose yourself and your family like that is dangerous and destructive, and I forbid it."

"You can't *forbid* the Internet," Charlotte snaps. "It belongs to, like, the whole world."

"I don't forbid the *Internet*, I forbid you from posting *personal information* on a website that strangers can see."

"My friends love it. *Everyone* loves it, including *Mom*."

"Well, I don't."

She continues to stare at the TV, so I snap it off, then toss the remote in the garbage, where it hits the bottom of the can with a loud clunk. Although this should indicate the end of our discussion, Charlotte isn't finished. This time, though, she takes a different approach.

"Please don't make me take down the blog, Eliot. Do you not want me to have friends?"

This is a hard question—not if I want her to have friends, but how much latitude to give her to communicate with them. More than anything else, I need to protect her, even if it's only from herself. By revealing too much, Charlotte relinquishes her inner life, and she's still just a kid. As a parent, as *her* parent, I can't let that happen.

"I want you to be careful," I tell her. "And that means you can't give out personal information to just anyone."

"You're not *listening*. Those people aren't just anyone; they're my *friends*."

"*You're* not listening, Charlotte: *private things should stay private.*"

She shrugs, which annoys me. And when she asks if we're done, I snap at her, "No, Charlotte. We're not done. This is important."

"Okay, okay. Listen, the blog doesn't mean anything, it's just...I don't know...whatever." She lays her head on her desk and closes her eyes. "I'm really tired. Let's finish our talk tomorrow, okay?"

This really pisses me off. I'm tired of her attitude, tired, too, of letting her run the show. I don't care what kind of lousy behavior her mother allows—or indulges in herself—at her own house; when Charlotte is here she has to follow our rules. And that means she can't act so goddamn disrespectful! "*No, Charlotte!*" I snap. "It's not *whatever*; so *sit up and look at me*! It's like this: If I *ever* go back on that site and see another *goddamn* picture of your stomach, your breasts, or any part of your body, I will rip that computer out of the wall. I will shut you down so fast you won't know what hit you. And stop saying *pussy*. It's not an appropriate word for a fourteen-year-old girl. Ninth graders don't talk about *pussies* or what a *dick* their father is. They show respect for the people who work hard to feed and clothe them. Do you understand?"

I pause, but she's too startled to answer.

"*Now*, Charlotte. I want an answer *right now. Do You Understand Me?*"

"Yes," she says quietly. Her sweet brown eyes fill with tears. "I understand."

"Okay, then. That's good." I'm teary, too, and for a second the two of us sit together, sniffling. Then I stand up and pat her shoulder. "It's getting late. Why don't you finish your homework and get to bed?"

"Okay," she whispers.

"Okay." I breathe deeply. "Okay." And then I go to bed myself.

⌐

At breakfast the next morning, Charlotte is considerably more pleasant. That I actually shouted at her was a first for us, and it's all I can do not to apologize.

"You're right about wearing less makeup, Eliot," she says, batting her lashes. "It does make my eyes seem wider. Don't you think?" She bites into her waffle. "This is so great! I really love waffles."

But when I say, "Charlotte, you can take it down a notch," she gets right to the point.

"Do you plan on telling Daddy about...you know...the whole Tumblr thing?"

"Just be careful, that's all." I point to the clock. "You should go. The bus is coming."

She picks up her backpack and starts to leave but then turns to hug me. Her big bag gets caught between us, making our embrace clumsy, but I wrap my arms around her and squeeze her tight.

"Bye, Eliot," she says, grabbing another waffle from the toaster. As she rushes out, the screen door slams behind her.

I watch her through the window. "Have a good day," I call. When she turns to wave, I add, "I love you!" in relief, then race upstairs to hurry her sisters.

Phoebe finally called with a formal invitation to join her car pool. Grace drove the girls yesterday, which gave me two extra hours in the morning and again in the afternoon. Not only was I able to take a leisurely shower, but I also spent seven straight hours in my actual office. For the first time in weeks, maybe months, I felt organized and relaxed.

Today it's my turn to drive, so this morning is a little different. After Charlotte leaves, I pull my unwashed hair into a ponytail, put on one of Grant's baseball caps, grab my computer, rush Gail to school, stash Hailey in the car, and then head first to Ava's house and then to Josie's. My plan is to drop off the girls at Riverside, then plant myself at the Emory library for a few hours before going back to Riverside to pick them up. I'm sure the library will be crowded, so I doubt I'll get much done, but it's better than having to drive all the way up to my house and back in the middle of the day. Luckily, Phoebe set up a rotating schedule, so I'll have car pool duty only once or twice a week.

A half hour later, I'm barreling down the highway with Hailey, Ava, and Josie chattering behind me. Harnessed side by side into their car seats, with their sunglasses and matching uniforms, the three little girls look like miniature prep school warlords.

"Why can you wear flip-flops but I can't?" Hailey asks me. "That's not fair."

"Because you're the kid and you're going to school, and I'm the mom and I'm going to the library."

"We want to go to the library, too, Mommy. Will you take us with you?"

The other girls chime in, and I glance behind me. Ava and Josie are pint-sized replicas of their mothers. Although only four, Ava already looks like a well-heeled suburban matron. She has Phoebe's same cropped blond hair, upturned nose, and perfectly pressed clothing. Josie, by contrast, is much more . . . earthy. Her uniform is always wrinkled or stained (or both), her book bag overflows with unread notices, and on this particular morning, tiny pieces of scrambled eggs dust her curly brown hair. She also has a smudge on her cheek that, from where I'm sitting, looks like raspberry jelly, however it could very well be blood.

"Why don't you bring us a treat, then?" Hailey suggests. "I'm hungry."

"Bring me plain M&M's," Ava says coolly. "I don't like peanuts or peanut butter or peanut anything."

"Bring me the Molly American Girl doll," says Josie. "Grace won't buy me another one."

"If you're hungry," I say to Hailey, "you should've eaten your breakfast. Here"—I reach backward —"finish your waffle."

"I hate waffles," Hailey says, refusing to take it.

"I hate waffles, too," Josie says. "Grace makes me eat them—"

"Does your mother really let you call her 'Grace'?" I ask.

"I have to throw up," is Josie's reply.

Luckily, she doesn't need the plastic bag I give her, and fifteen minutes later, we reach the school gates. "We're here!" I sing with relief. "We're here, thank God, we're here!"

Clutching sweaters, backpacks, lunch boxes, and anything else I can carry, I help each girl out of her car seat and hustle them all into class. I hang up their gear in the cubbies, kiss them good-bye, then hike up four flights of stairs to find Dylan's third-grade classroom, where I'm supposed to deliver a letter.

Maggie hasn't said whether or not she's spoken to him, but she did beg me to do this one favor. Her bright idea was for me to stick the letter on his windshield, but as I explained, I don't have time to search the entire Riverside parking lot for her boyfriend's car.

"How many cars could there be?" she said. "It's not like all those kids drive, Eliot. Most of them are little."

"You're right, Maggie. Most of them don't drive. But you know who does? The teachers, custodians, librarians—along with everyone else who works there. So why don't I just hand the letter to him, and you just thank me?"

Morning chimes haven't rung yet, but the door to Dylan's classroom is closed. Several children sit on the floor in the hallway, waiting to be let in. Most of them are flipping through folders or writing in notebooks. It's eerily quiet.

"Have you seen Mr. Dylan?" I ask one of the boys.

He doesn't reply, so I stand on my tiptoes to peek in the small window. I can't see what's going on, but just as I turn away, the door swings open. A sleek, well-coiffed woman in designer jeans and high heels stands facing me.

"Yes?" She gives me a chilly once-over, taking in my grungy sweatpants, cutoff T-shirt, drugstore flip-flops, and ball cap. "Can I help you?"

It occurs to me that I'm still holding Hailey's half-eaten waffle. Without thinking, I stuff it into my mouth. Why I don't put it in my gym bag or, better, the garbage remains unclear.

The icy blonde watches me chew. "We're finishing up a parents' meeting." She speaks loudly and slowly, as if I'm a foreigner. "Do you understand English?"

This makes me laugh. "Of course." I swallow. "I have a...um...a delivery for Dylan Warner. This is his classroom, isn't it?"

"It is, but can't this wait?"

The other parents are curious. "Who's there?" I hear Dylan call out.

The woman focuses on my feet, and I curse my unmanicured toes. "I believe it's someone from housekeeping," she calls back. "She has a package she says is urgent."

"No," I say, mortified. "I'm a mother."

She looks at me blankly.

"I mean, I'm a *parent*. My daughter goes to school here. My sister is dating—*was* dating—Dylan. She sent him a letter...I mean, I have a letter she wrote—for him."

Now she looks mortified. "Oh, my God, I'm so sorry. It's just you said you had a delivery. I thought you were from the office. Please excuse me..." She turns away quickly.

Thankfully, Dylan comes to the door. "Eliot? What are you doing here?"

"I'm on my way to work—"

"Dressed like that?"

"Dylan, I'm in a rush, okay? Maggie wanted me to give you this." After thrusting the letter into his hand, I turn to go. "Sorry to interrupt your meeting."

"Wait! I have something for Maggie, too. Can you stay one more second?" He gives me a woeful smile. "Please?"

"Okay, but make it fast."

Like Maggie, Dylan is in his early thirties but looks much younger. Although he's more mature than my sister, he does have boyish qualities—hanging shirttails, perpetual bed head—that I find charming, especially the way he calls his students "little dudes."

He returns a few minutes later. As the parents file out of his classroom, he says his good-byes while handing me an envelope. "You'll make sure she gets this, won't you?"

"Cross my heart." I put it into my bag. "But you two should

really check out the postal service. Their mail carrier program is truly revolutionary."

Dylan studies his hands. "So how is Maggie, anyway?"

How is Maggie? Miserable and missing him? Or adjusting wonderfully and already dating someone else? "Still the prettiest," is my response. "She'd love to hear from you," I add, moving away.

He nods. "Well, thanks again. I guess I'll see you...I don't know...soon, maybe. Say hi to Hailey for me. And Maggie, too," he adds quickly. "Of course say hi to Maggie."

"I will!" By this point I'm halfway down the hall, but just as I reach the stairs, I feel a tap, tap, on my shoulder. I turn, half expecting to see Dylan with more pony express mail, but am surprised to find myself face-to-face with the icy blonde from before.

"Yes?" I ask. "May I help you?"

She gives me a vacant look. Then I hear a familiar voice, one that makes my stomach flip. "She didn't tap you, Eliot. I did."

Finn? I think, whipping around. *Is that you?*

"Yeah," he says aloud, grinning. "It's me."

Chapter Nine

MY FIRST IMPULSE is to call Sylvia, but I'm too shocked to do anything but stand there, shouting, *"Oh, my God,* Finn! *It's you!* You're *here,"* as though he's my long-lost son, back from his voyage to the New World and not dead after all.

"Eliot," he says calmly, drawing out the word.

It's you, I think. *You're here.* I'm so agitated, I feel myself shaking.

"Eliot Gordon." Finn gives me a self-satisfied grin. "Nice outfit," he says, pointing.

"I'm on my way to the library...I mean, work...I work at the library, but I'm not, like, a librarian or anything. I just do work there; it's not library related. Why is everyone so concerned with what I'm wearing?" Finn's actual, physical presence is too much to take in. But when I close my eyes, I'm haunted by an old familiar melody: *Finn Montgomery. Finn Montgomery. Finn Montgomery. It's you, it's you, it's you.*

"Eliot Gordon," he repeats. His voice sounds different, I realize. It's deeper than I remember, more mature. But when I look at him again, I see the guy I once knew, albeit a man now and wearing a tie.

"Look at you, Finn. You're all dressed up." In the hundreds of times I've imagined this moment, I was always dignified and contained. Never once had I failed to take a shower. "Have I ever seen you in a suit before? Well, maybe at graduation. You must have a good job—an important job, rather. So, are you rich?" Of all things to ask, I groan, why that?

He's still grinning, which makes me stop talking—thank God—and grin, too. And there we are, after all these years, grinning.

Finn is tall and sandy haired and impossibly Finn. He has the same perfectly straight teeth, and now they're even whiter against his fading "boys of summer" tan. He's wearing black sunglasses that conceal his eyes and give him a movie star quality that's out of place in the third-grade hallway. *Really, Finn? Sunglasses inside? You're expecting paparazzi?* Still, Finn is blindingly beautiful, although his face is weathered now and fuller around the cheeks and jowls. He also has a small belly that folds over his trousers, which reminds me of Sylvia and how she'll *howl* when I get her on the phone. But she's right: he looks good. If anything, the belly makes him seem ... I don't know ... more real, more Finn-like, more ... Finn-ish.

I have a sudden urge to touch him. Instead, I compliment him. "You. Look. So. Great," I say breathlessly, as if to overcompensate for his pooch. Does he care he got a little pudgy? I'd care, but that's me. Still, always better to err on the side of flattery. "You. Really. Do."

"You look great, too," he replies, which makes me swoon but then has me wondering if he's overcompensating for me, too.

I have so many questions. But first: "How long have you been in Atlanta?"

"Four years." No longer grinning, Finn simply stares.

Four years? Four *years*? Where was I? Four years ago, if I remember correctly, I was trying to mold a family out of a still shell-shocked Grant, two young stepdaughters, and a newborn Hailey. Four years ago, I was pretty shell-shocked myself. Domestic life, it turned out, was grueling. I hadn't foreseen the monotony, the exhaustion, the low-grade depression. Had Finn called me then, anything could've happened. I think about Grant, lying on his side, his head propped up on his muscular arms. "You should go," he'd said. "You deserve a vacation." Four years ago, I was vulnerable. But now? No way.

"So what are you doing here?" I ask.

Finn waves toward Dylan's classroom. "My daughter."

He isn't giving me much, so I fill in the blanks. "You have a daughter? And she goes to Riverside? And Dylan Warner is her teacher? How *weird*! Not that you have a daughter—although that is kind of weird, actually it's *very* weird—but Maggie *dates* Dylan. Remember my sister Maggie? She and Dylan are in love, although they just broke up. You know how that goes, right?"

Finn doesn't reply.

What's with the silent treatment? I want to ask. *You used to be the one who never shut up.* "I had a baby!" I blurt out, rattled by this composed, self-assured man. "Like, from my loins."

Finn continues to stand there, watching me—or at least I think he's watching. Who can tell what he's doing behind those stupid sunglasses?

"Four years ago," I add. "I mean, Hailey is four. But can you believe *I* have a child who goes here, too? Isn't that *ironic*? Both of us in Atlanta, sending our kids to private school—*the irony*, right? Although you have money, so it makes sense. Still, it's pretty *ironic*. Or is it? I mean, is it *ironic* or *coincidental*?"

"Yes," Finn says tartly. "Ironic."

Now I'm annoyed. Why is he so fake and uptight? "She's four," I say again, wanting to crack that puppet smile on his pretty, puffy face. "We call her *Der Führer*." I trill my tongue. "Get it? Because she's so bossy? *Der Führer?*"

Another flash of those white teeth and then a bona fide laugh. "Got it," he says, and I feel him relax. "You're still the same, Eliot," he adds, and this time there's warmth; this time there's Finn. The two of us lock eyes, and I lose track of myself. *It's you,* I think. *You're here.*

It's me, he agrees.

The icy blonde clears her throat.

Finn turns. "Oh," he says, as if surprised to see her still standing there. Then he gently pushes her forward, so that she fills the empty space between us. "This is Parker," he murmurs, touching her again, this time to show ownership. "My wife."

"Der Führer," I repeat mindlessly, not even realizing I said the words until they are already out. "Like Hitler."

⌒

Similar to many suburban colleges, Emory has grand old buildings and leafy quads set close to, but apart from, low-rent bars and cheap pizzerias. There's always construction going on and, with it, endless traffic that backs up along the surrounding streets. But Emory is convenient to Riverside, and my alumni pass gets me into the library, so I occasionally work here between Hailey's drop-offs and pickups instead of hiking all the way across town to my office.

Normally, I don't think twice about being back here, but after my unexpected conversation with Finn, it feels disconcerting to stroll through campus. People and places that have never been related—Finn, Emory, Hailey, Riverside—are all converging at once, and I have the sensation that time is speeding up and careening beyond my control. I feel both dreamy and jittery all morning, as though I'm nursing a hangover with too much coffee. It's impossible to do any work, so I just sit at my computer, click through the Internet, and try to slow myself down.

Around noon, I call Maggie and give her a blow-by-blow of the morning. I tell her about Dylan and the letter but leave out seeing Finn. I also speak to my mother and Sylvia, both of whom accuse me of sounding strange. "Did something happen?" Sylvia demands to know.

"Like what?"

"I don't know, Eliot. You're the one with the strange voice. What's going on?"

For some reason, this strikes me as funny. "Why does everyone keep asking that?"

"Don't play games, Eliot. I'm your sister."

"Nothing's going on. I'm working at the library and then I have to pick up Hailey at school. I'm driving car pool today, but other than that, it's a regular Tuesday morning."

"I don't believe you," she says, which cracks me up even more.

Why don't I tell them about Finn? He's still arrogant, still has the same know-it-all grin, and now he wears sunglasses inside, like a wannabe rock star. So why don't I just say that? Then we could all have a big laugh at his expense, and I'd be able to shake off any lingering preoccupation. But the truth is I'm not ready to give him up yet, or even share him, not until I see what happens next.

As it turns out, Finn calls at one thirty. This surprises me—not just that he calls, but that he does it so soon. Given the strain of our conversation this morning, I didn't think I'd hear from him for a long time, if ever. Nor, frankly, did I relish the idea of repeating the experience. After we finished the introductions, discussed our respective children, and were preparing to leave, Finn had made an offhand comment to his wife about how he and I met.

"I told you about Eliot," he said. "She and I went to Emory together."

That's it? That's how he remembered me? He was my first male friend, my first boyfriend, my first everything. *We were madly in love.* "That's right." I turned to Parker and nodded. "Finn and I met in Spanish. We were *dos amigos.*"

Parker was still distraught over her earlier gaffe. Long-legged and slender, but soft in all the right places, she reminded me of the girls Finn dated before we got together—aspirational packages, every one of them. "I'm sorry," she kept repeating, reddening each time. "It's just you said you had a delivery..."

Under normal circumstances, I would have found her embarrassment endearing; I would've overlooked the rich, highlighted hair, the glossy leather bag, maybe even shared a gaffe of my own. But she was too familiar to me in all the wrong ways.

Still, I forced a smile. "Parker, please. I didn't think twice about it." I felt increasingly diminished by her moneyed good looks, which was compounded by Finn's cool reserve. The brief laugh we'd shared had since passed, and now he refused to even glance in my direction.

I shifted my backpack on my shoulder. Finn adjusted his sunglasses. Parker checked her watch. The tension was lethal.

"So, Eliot, do you keep up with anyone else from Emory?" Parker asked, trying to play hostess. I appreciated the attempt, but I was lording information over her that, had she known, would've probably made her feel a lot less generous. *He was crazy about me, Parker, once.*

"Not really. I wish I had, but with three kids and a full-time job..."

"It's a lot." Parker nodded.

Finn interrupted. "I'm sorry. I have a meeting." He turned to me. "I hate to run..." I sensed he wanted to say more—had expected to say more—but what could he do? "It was great seeing you, Eliot."

As for me, there were still so many questions. He had to go, I understood that—I had to go, too—but to see him again after all this time and not be able to sit down and talk? *Just a few minutes, Finn, please? It's been so long.* And yet—

"It's fine," I told him. "I should go too."

We said our good-byes. Buzzing inside, I lagged behind Finn and Parker, trying to hold myself together until I reached my car. I felt a mix of expectation and sadness, of time rushed and prolonged. *Finn!* I shouted. *Don't go. Not yet.*

Suddenly, as if remembering something, Finn turned around. "We should really get your number, Eliot," he said casually, effortlessly, as if he were pulling off socks.

Although this was clearly a courtesy, I was impressed by how sincere he sounded. Then I remembered that Finn always had a knack for bullshit.

"Sure." I tried to appear equally casual, but my fingers trembled as I scribbled down my number on the back of a deposit slip. And when I gave it to him, our hands brushed, which sent me spinning all over again.

"I'll call you," he promised, tucking the slip in his pocket and taking Parker's arm.

I watched them walk down the hall together. "I'll be here!" I shouted, this time out loud, and then kicked myself. *I'll be here?* It was such an old-Eliot thing to say. *Sure, Finn. You go ahead, live your life. I'll be here, waiting.* Fifteen years ago, we had this exact same exchange, but he never did call—not once—which is why it's so fucking absurd that he's calling me now.

"Eliot?" he's saying. "I'm glad I caught you."

Once again, he plays it cool—*I'm glad I caught you, Eliot*—as if he called every day, as if our entire twenties and most of our thirties hadn't just passed us by.

"Finn? Is that you?" I'm equally cool, although the phone is sweaty in my hand. "I didn't recognize your number, so I almost didn't pick up. But then I was afraid you might be a client."

"No, no client. Just your old friend Finn, checking in."

He's still too smooth, which irritates me. It's the same old Finn, the same hubris, the same sense of entitlement. Look at him, back in town for four whole years and only first calling me now. What does he think? That I have no life of my own? That I'm still sitting by the phone? That I would be so glad, so grateful, to finally hear from him, I would fall all over myself?

"Well, that's nice," I say, just as smooth, as if this call wasn't on my mind as I'd watched him steer Parker down four flights of stairs, outside the building, and into their car; as if I wasn't hoping he would lift his hands from their ten-two position, grab the phone in his jacket, and yell out my name. As if I hadn't been biding my time all these hours alone, touching the soft part of my palm where our hands touched, clutching my phone, waiting, *just waiting* for the damn thing to ring.

"That's nice," I say again, this time adding an easy, breezy laugh, ha ha ha. "I wondered if I would hear from you."

⌒

After so many lost years, I was afraid it would be an ordeal to talk to him again, but it's surprisingly effortless. It's only the two of us, so that makes it easier. And to his credit, Finn is much warmer than he was this morning—warmer, in fact, than I can ever remember. Once we get past "Hi, how are you?" and "Fine, how are you?" he explains why he called, which helps breaks the ice and enables us to pick up our old, familiar rhythm.

"The reason I'm calling...," Finn starts. "Well, actually, there's more than one reason..." He clears his throat, and it occurs to me he's nervous, too. Of course, I tell myself. Of course he's nervous. "It just seemed too abrupt, bumping into you earlier. Nor did it feel right to end it like that, with me rushing off so quickly. I felt badly about it, and wanted to tell you...uh...that."

"Well, that's shockingly mature," I blurt out, only half-kidding. Realizing he's uneasy gives me confidence, although I bite my tongue to keep from adding, *What about the way it ended at Emory? How come you never called to explain that?*

Finn laughs, and I hear him loosening up. "Mature? I wish someone would inform Parker. She says I'm the biggest baby she's ever met."

"So she knows you pretty well, then."

"Oh, I get it now, Eliot. So, this is how it's gonna be..."

We keep things light and upbeat, him focusing primarily on all the ways he's changed, me focusing on all the ways I've changed, and both of us in disbelief over how different we are now from the way we were then. We talk mainly about Hailey and Humphrey ("family name," he confirms) and how funny, *how ironic,* it is that both our kids are at Riverside. The one subject we don't broach is what happened between us, which charges our conversation with long-standing electricity.

"You really do look great," Finn tells me just before we hang up. "I almost didn't recognize you."

"Finn, please." I'm standing in the ladies' room, watching myself in the mirror. Does he mean it? Probably not, but look at the dopey smile on my face! "I didn't look *great.* I was wearing *sweatpants* and *flip-flops. Your wife* thought I was the *janitor.*"

"Not the *janitor,* Eliot. An office worker. And she felt terrible about it. You still can't take a compliment, can you? I said you look great. Now, what do you say?"

"Thank you, Finn. That's very nice of you."

"Believe it or not, I really have changed."

"You have," I agree. "You barely looked at me this morning, much less spoke—hardly the same guy who once serenaded me with 'Frito Bandito.' I kept wondering who the uptight man in the suit was and what he had done with my old friend Finn."

There's a pause, and I fear I've overstepped. But then he asks, "I was that bad?"

"Just a little stiff. And honestly? I thought it was me."

"No, you were fine." He sighs. "And here I was, congratulating myself for not being a total blundering fool..."

"Just a little stiff, Finn," I repeat. "No need for a shame spiral."

He gets serious. "Hey," he says softly. "It's been a long time, Eliot. I've missed you."

"Me too," I whisper. *Oh, Finn. You have no idea.*

Chapter Ten

UNLIKE GRANT, who is oblivious to his looks, Finn has always been aware of his effect on women. This may not have mitigated his insecurity in other areas, but it certainly served him well socially. At seventeen, his hair was blonder and boyishly long, and he had a mischievous grin that suggested endless boozy nights and all sorts of questionable behavior. Finn was, still is, irresistible, the kind of boy whose dangerous good looks could charm you right out of your underwear; the kind of boy who—let's face it—would never be interested in me. Yet every Monday, Wednesday, and Friday from nine o'clock to ten thirty, Finn sat behind me in Introductory Spanish and told me the story of his life. And every Monday, Wednesday, and Friday from nine o'clock to ten thirty, I sat ahead of him in exquisite agony and absorbed every word.

"You're such a good listener," he'd say. "You really do get me."

I wanted to point out that I was a captive audience but didn't want to break the spell of his voice. How either of us passed that class, I'll never know. I was lost in some wistful dream where princely boys with golden hair kissed chubby redheaded girls and loved them forever. As for Finn, he was reprimanded countless times, then eventually forced to move. That was a whole other agony, stuck for an hour and a half without his voice in my ear, his warm breath on my neck.

Finn wanted to see Atlanta, so we drove around a few times, but traffic was unbearable even then, so we moved to the library, where we could talk (and talk and talk) without interruption. It was uncanny how much we had in common: our fathers walked out, our mothers struggled financially, and we both grew up feeling shamed by forces beyond our control.

I used to think Finn and I were drawn to each other because we were more damaged than our classmates. Few of them, it seemed, came from families where children worried about groceries. In retrospect, I'm sure most of them were as troubled as we were, but Finn and I were too caught up in ourselves to notice or care. I talked to Finn in a way I had never talked to anyone before. It was as if a leak had been sprung, and the words gushed out like dirty water. To tell secrets is to surrender, and I gave up everything—the miserable marriage, the father I never spoke to, the mother who exploited her family to advance her career, the memoirs (oh Christ, those memoirs, I talked about those memoirs for *hours*)—and it felt awful, just awful, until it didn't anymore and I could finally exhale. Finn's own dirty water also rose to the surface. He told me stories of his father's debauchery; how the man gambled away the family's savings and then skipped out for good, leaving behind a wife, three little boys, and a mountain of debt. Like me, Finn grew up too fast and raised his two brothers as well as himself. He was also similarly determined not to repeat his parents' mistakes. He wanted to get filthy rich, while I craved a house, a husband, and a nuclear family, but our mutual surrender bound us together. Like POWs, I thought. For life.

Outside the library, we weren't as close. I was a private girl with few close friends, and I was anxious to stay anonymous. Finn, by contrast, was the life of the party. He played Frisbee in the grass, drank beer, and went out with girl after girl after girl. He never dated anyone for longer than a month or two, but soon he winnowed them down to a senior named Dahlia, whom he claimed to be crazy about. Although I was disappointed, it did make sense: Finn, the gorgeous rock star with a long-legged girlfriend, and me, the loner, on my own. But we were still best friends; we just didn't see each other as often. I believed that

I mattered to Finn, that he told me things he never told anyone. I even believed that he loved me—differently, of course, from how he loved Dahlia, but also a little the same.

Sometimes when we talked, Finn would lean in very close. "I'm glad we're friends," he'd say. "You're such an awesome person. Why haven't you met anyone yet?"

I have, I wanted to say, but never did. Instead, I acted uninterested. "I have a lot of work, Finn," I'd tell him. "Not all of us are boy geniuses like you." But I savored these moments, holding them tight in my hand, each one a rare treasure to unlock later and study. He had to know I had a crush on him—how could he not? But I pretended I didn't, and he pretended I didn't, and all that pretending helped to sustain us. Everywhere we looked, boys and girls were becoming friends, sleeping together, then fighting and breaking up. But Finn and I endured, and it was because the deepest part of our relationship—the most gripping—was inside our silences, coded among all the words left unsaid. Or maybe I just told myself this because I loved him and was desperate for him to love me back.

Over time, Finn became bolder. "You know you're pretty, right, Eliot?"

"I don't know. I hadn't really thought about it."

"Well, you are. And you could have so many boyfriends if you went out more. Guys would love you if they knew you."

He'd lean in closer and then closer—just to tell me something funny or give me a hug, it turned out—and I'd start to ache. *Lean closer,* I'd think, willing him to kiss me, just once, just to see how it felt. *Please, Finn; one more inch.* The closer he came, the faster my heart beat; the faster my heart beat, the louder my head roared. Soon, all I could hear was the blood in my ears and my silent pleas for him to *kiss me, Finn. For God's sake, just kiss me already!*

When I remember these moments, I cringe in embarrassment. But I'm not without compassion for that girl, so young and naïve. I also wonder if this was Finn's way of baiting me, of getting me to admit how I felt—not that there's any way I would have. Just because I was able to talk about high school or my family didn't mean I could tell him I loved him. Finn set the course of our relationship. I only followed his lead, which meant he had to act so that I could react.

Someday, I told myself, he'll realize I'm here. Someday he'll see me the same way he sees me now, but also totally different.

So I waited. I waited while he dated Dahlia. I waited when they broke up after four months and he went out with other girls—all stunning, all rich, all nothing like me. For almost three years, until the end of our junior year, I waited. And while I waited, I scrutinized his every move, searching for signs of his secret desire. Then, in the months before summer, something shifted. I got the flu, an ordinary event that for me had extraordinary consequences. I lost weight—not much, maybe ten pounds, but enough to feel good about, enough to make me wonder if I was foolish for waiting. I started to wear makeup, to dress better—again, nothing dramatic, but, as I said, enough to get noticed.

"You seem different," Finn said one night.

"I'm not." Although I felt different even as I denied it.

We were in Finn's room, and I was telling him a story about a guy I liked, Perry, who seemed to like me. This was new, too, that it was me talking to Finn about romance and not the other way around.

"Maybe I am a little different," I admitted.

For the first time in my life, I felt good about myself. Not only was I thinner, but Perry had asked me out. "To study," I told Finn. "Does this mean 'study' or"—I made quote marks—'*study*'?"

Finn laughed. "You're so funny, Eliot. But if you want my opinion, I don't think you want to go out with this guy. To me, he sounds like a loser."

"That's the thing, Finn," I said, my mood instantly punctured. "I didn't ask for your opinion. You don't know me as well as you think you do. Nor are you the only one who's allowed to be happy." I started to leave, but he grabbed my hand.

"Sit still," he said softly. "Stop talking."

Why was he whispering? And why was he looking at me with that hangdog expression? Something wasn't right. Something was very, very different.

"That was a shitty thing to say. I'm sure this guy Perry is perfectly fine." Finn's voice was so quiet, I had to lean in very close. "But I do know you. And I know you don't like him."

"I don't?" Suddenly, the room was very warm. The light was too bright. "I don't like him," I repeated, but this time it was a statement of fact. "I don't...like...him..." I stammered at first but then found my words, which I blurted out in a single gasp: "Because I love you."

Did he say it back? It didn't matter because that's when he kissed me. Finnegan Montgomery kissed Eliot Gordon, and nothing about me has been the same since.

⌣

"Mommy," Hailey asks from the backseat, "why are you wearing tall shoes? And makeup too?"

It's Friday morning, my second time driving car pool, so along with Hailey, Josie and Ava are in the car.

"I have a meeting in my office. It feels good to dress up once in a while."

"Are there gonna be boys at this meeting?"

"What do *you* know about *boys*, Miss Hailey Harper Delaney? You're four years old!"

I raise my eyebrows in the rearview mirror, which cracks her up. Catching a glimpse of my face, I laugh, too. I look different today, different from how I looked yesterday but also from how I look normally. My eyes are a sparkling green, my cheeks are flushed, and my lips are a deep red. Although Lancôme can take credit for the color, the glow is all Grant. For the past three nights, he and I have been staying up late, *mowing the lawn*, as it were; and now I'm consumed with the memory of his mouth on my mouth, his skin on my skin.

"Jesus," Grant said last night as we lay naked and touching. "Where is this coming from?"

"This" was my sudden and insatiable desire, which started when I tried to seduce him over the phone on Tuesday afternoon. "I can't stop thinking about you," I had murmured. "I really want to fuck you."

"Who the hell is this?"

"I really want to *fuck you*," I repeated, rolling the nasty words over my tongue as if they were small, hard candies. "I really want to *fuck you*, Grant." Saying his name made them taste even more delicious.

"*Eliot?* Is this a joke? Because I'll blow off work and meet you right now!"

Hailey's voice startles me. "Can I get an American Girl doll? Ava and Josie have one, but I don't. That's not fair, Mommy."

"Sure, Hailey," I tell her, remembering Grant and how much I adored *fucking* him. Whispering the word, even thinking it, mortifies me. At the same time, I want to drop the kids off, drive to his office, and *fuck* him right on top of his drafting table.

"Oh, my God, Mommy—really? I can really have one? And all the outfits, too?"

Hailey sounds so shocked, I laugh again. For the past six months, the poor kid has been begging me for one of those dumb dolls, and for six months, I've said no. But why shouldn't she have one? Why shouldn't she have two? Why shouldn't we fly to New York and clean out the entire American Girl store? That's how intoxicated I feel, high enough to spend a hundred bucks for a doll that my four-year-old will play with once and never look at again.

For the past three nights, I've been having honeymoon sex with Grant; and for the past three days, I've been reconnecting with Finn. Our phone calls have been short—more like status updates than actual conversations—but each one makes me giddier and giddier. Because I haven't said anything to Grant about Finn, I feel guilty about the calls (and the giddiness), but I tell myself they're harmless. We're just two old friends catching up. There's nothing inappropriate going on, definitely nothing sexual. Finn makes me laugh; he makes me feel young. Why should I feel guilty about that?

"We're here, girls!" I sing out when we drive through the Riverside gates.

Pulling into the lower school parking lot, I don't look for Finn. He's at the dentist, and I know this because I already spoke to him twice this morning—once after my shower, then again while toasting waffles. Because of this, I'm way behind schedule, so I rush Hailey, Ava, and Josie out of the car, into the classroom, and over to the art tables.

"Let's get a move on, girls." I try to hurry them along as they hang up their backpacks and sweaters in their cubbies. "We all have a busy day."

Despite what I told Hailey, I'm not heading to my office. Given the lateness of the hour and the traffic—always the traffic—it makes more sense to go to the library for a few hours, then come back here for pickup. Why drive all the way across town when Emory is so close? Earlier, Finn mentioned that he would try to stop by the library after lunch just to say hi, although he did add that he had a meeting at noon, so it may not happen.

"Don't count on me," he warned just before we hung up.

"I'm probably going to my office anyway," I told him. "It all depends on the traffic."

As I get Hailey situated, I keep turning around, expecting to see Finn standing behind me. Now that he and I are back in touch, I sense his presence everywhere, watching me.

I kiss Hailey good-bye. "I love you, my sweetest pea. I love you so, so much."

"Why are you yelling?" is her moody reply. "You're so loud, Mommy."

"Am I? I'm sorry. I don't mean to be." But then I hear my voice, boisterous and fake, booming through the quiet classroom. Chastened, I kneel by Hailey's side.

"Do you want to color?" I ask softly.

She shakes her head. "I want to be with you. You haven't been with me in a long time."

"That's silly, Hailey. Last night, we spent the entire night together."

"No, you were on the phone with Grandma."

This is true, I did speak to my mother, but briefly; for the next half hour I talked to Finn.

"So, let me get this straight," he said. "You're not married to the guy, but you live together. What's that all about? Do you not love him enough? Or are you living out some weird hippie fantasy?"

"What kind of question is that? Of course I love Grant enough. But I'm with him because I want to be, not because I have to be. Marriage is an obligation, whereas living together is a choice that I—that we—make every day."

"That's *such bullshit*, Eliot. You're a good girl. You shut off the lights when you leave a room, floss regularly, and always say 'please' and 'thank you.' You live to do the right thing. Face it, Eliot: I know you. You're the kind of girl who gets married."

"You *used to* know me, Finn." Talking like this was making me light-headed. I was at my kitchen table, so I couldn't see myself, but I knew I had that same dopey smile on my face.

"I *still* know you. If you really loved the guy, you would marry him."

"Why can't I be in love with him? Oh, my God, you are so arrogant." Maybe I *don't* love Grant enough, I thought suddenly. Is that why I don't press the issue? Or maybe *he* doesn't love *me* enough. If he did, wouldn't he have proposed?

Finn chuckled. "You know I'm just teasing you, right?"

"I don't know. Are you?" *Stop it,* I told myself. Of course you love Grant. And Grant loves you. *Stop it right now.*

"Of course I am. It's obvious you love him. And he sounds like a great guy—anyone who fights for his kids has to be decent. God knows what I would do if Parker walked out. Don't get me wrong—I love my kid—but Parker is the captain of this ship. If she left, we would sink like a stone. So, kudos to Grant for manning up."

"Mommy! I'm talking to you."

Hailey's voice startles me. "Oh, I'm sorry, sweet pea. What's the problem?"

"I hate school, Mommy. I hate it so much. Please let me be with you today."

"Hailey, I don't like the word *hate*. And unfortunately, we can't spend the day together because I have to work. But I'll come back later to pick you up, just like I always do."

"After-school is ending early today," Miss Lulu reminds me. "We have an all-staff meeting, so please plan on picking up Hailey at five instead of six."

"See, Hailey? I'm even coming early." I kiss her good-bye. Then I hold her in my arms and dance her around the room, performing a little two-step for the pleasure of anyone watching.

Chapter Eleven

BACK IN COLLEGE, when Finn kissed me that first time, I thought everything would change. This is it, I told myself. It's finally happening. But as it turned out, that one brief, aborted kiss was all I got.

"I can't do this," he said, pulling away. "I'm sorry, Eliot. I don't want to hurt you."

"You won't hurt me." I was bewildered. "Why would you hurt me?"

"I'm not the guy you want." Finn looked straight at me, right into my eyes. "These are true words. I'm not what you think. You are nice, you are pretty, you are smart, and you deserve better. Someone will love you the way you want to be loved, but it's not me—not now."

My eyes filled with tears. "What does that mean, 'not now'?"

He wouldn't elaborate. All he said was that he cared about me *a lot*, but he was sorry. "If I lost you, I'd never forgive myself. I can't fuck this up, Eliot. I need you too much."

I wanted to ask why we couldn't have both, but I couldn't find my words. All I knew was that he'd kissed me and then rejected me. "What's wrong with me?" was the most I could muster.

"*Nothing*, Eliot. You're amazing. You're my best friend, my true friend. If we hook up, everything will be different. I won't want it to, but it will."

"Maybe it won't," I said sadly.

"Come on, Eliot. Look at my track record." He shook his head. "I'm sorry," he whispered. "I know myself, and I know what I'll do. Please trust me. I can't hurt you."

After that night, Finn never referred to our kiss again, not once, not even as a joke. And as the weeks passed, I began to question if it had actually happened or if I'd just imagined it. Unfortunately, the only person I could ask was Finn, and he wouldn't talk about it. He also began to withdraw, canceling our standing lunch date, calling only when he was sure I wouldn't be around.

I knew I had to make other friends. I also knew I had to have other—real—romances. Still, it was hard to let go. After Finn's kiss, and his promise that we'd eventually be together ("not now" had to mean "someday," I told myself), no one else could measure up, and I was constantly distracted, comparing. During this time—that is, after Finn kissed me—the world became hazy and unfocused. Everyday conversations were muffled; no one made any sense. I felt disconnected from my surroundings, as though I were sleepwalking through a recurring dream. All I cared about, all I thought about, was Finn—Finn, who had kissed me unprompted.

By senior year, Finn had moved off campus and was seeing a girl named Leslie. On the rare occasions we ran into each other, he was friendly but distant. He didn't flirt anymore; he didn't lean in *this close*; he didn't discuss anything personal.

Had I offended him? I wondered. Did I do something wrong? I replayed all our conversations but could never pinpoint an answer.

I began to date, although I didn't enjoy it, largely because no one I went out with was Finn. The guys were all too clean, too predictable—too much like me. But they were pleasant, and as long as we were talking, I was okay. Any unexpected moves, though, and I froze.

"Just relax," my dates would insist, which made me more uptight. "I like you."

"I like you too," I'd say politely as I removed their hands from my arm, my breast, my leg. "But I'm sorry. Not tonight." Not here, not now, not with you.

I couldn't bear it, the way those boys touched me. Although a few were handsome, even desirable, they all touched me anonymously, as if I were just another girl, just another body. That these strangers expected me to take off my clothing and spread my legs was unfathomable to me. My virginity, which had never had much significance before, was suddenly weighted with meaning and consequence.

I'll just wait, I decided. I don't care how long it takes for Finn to come around. I'll wait.

Eight months later, I was alone in the library, bent over my books. I sensed someone moving behind me and lifted my head. The second I felt his breath in my ear, my body went on red alert.

"There you are," Finn said, panting. "I've been looking all over for you."

I studied him carefully. His hair was matted, and his eyes were red, although it wasn't clear why—exhaustion? drinking? I hadn't seen him in a while, so I couldn't be certain.

"Is everything okay?" I asked.

"Leslie and I were skiing in Gatlinburg. She caught me with one of her friends. I think it's over; I mean, I *know* it is. I rode the bus back alone—I'd say it was over, wouldn't you?"

When he wiped his eyes with his sleeve, it hit me: He'd been crying. He was *crying* over *Leslie*? It made absolutely no sense. "What were you doing with her friend?"

Finn laughed. It was a short, tight laugh, more like a moan. "I kissed her."

"Why is that funny?" My voice was terse, but I wasn't angry—not yet. At this point, I was still confused about him being so upset about a girl, about *Leslie*, that he'd actually cry.

"Because it was so ridiculous. It was like I wanted to get caught. Christ, what's wrong with me?" He was shaking. "It's fucking freezing in here. Why isn't the heat on?"

"Where's your jacket?"

"In Leslie's trunk, but she's not speaking to me." A sob escaped, and I averted my eyes, more for my sake than his.

I handed him my puffy coat. The sleeves were too short, and the zipper was tight, but he wrapped himself in it and sat down beside me. Looking as if he were wearing a twelve-year-old's clothing, he seemed so boyish and sorrowful, I wanted to hug him. Instead, I patted his arm.

"She'll get over it, Finn. She'll forgive you." Every word killed me, but what else could I say?

"I'm such an asshole." His eyes flooded with tears. "Last night, Leslie went to sleep early, but a bunch of us stayed up, drinking. At one point I went to the bathroom, and this drunk girl cornered me. Don't get me wrong—I was drunk, too—but this girl was *trashed*. She started saying all this crazy shit about how Leslie wasn't good enough for me, and she'd always liked me. Then she lunged"—Finn raised his hands as if warding off an attack—"and starts kissing me just as Leslie's best friend walks by. She told Leslie about it this morning, Leslie went ballistic, and well…" He shrugged: *Here we are now.*

"No offense, but this sounds pretty juvenile. Why didn't you just tell Leslie that the girl cornered you?" I stared at him, but he didn't look up. "You're leaving something out."

He didn't answer.

"What? You knew this girl beforehand? You'd flirted with her?"

He nodded.

"And you wanted to get caught, so you could date her instead of Leslie?"

"Partly." He stared at his hands. "I didn't want to go out with her, but I did want to want to stop seeing Leslie. I like Leslie—I like her a lot—but she keeps asking me about my plans for after graduation, and what do I think about living together. She deserves an answer, but fuck, Eliot—I don't know what I'm doing tomorrow, much less in three months. It's been eating at me for days, so when this girl cornered me, I just…I let it happen because it was easier than dealing with Leslie's questions. *Fuck, fuck, fuck.* What kind of person does that? It's like I'm morally corrupt or a sociopath or something. I know the way I treat people—well, girls—isn't right, and I don't want to do it, but I can't stop myself. I'm just like my father, except I'm worse—at least he didn't cheat on my mother right in front of her."

"You're not a sociopath, Finn, nor are you like your father. And you didn't cheat on Leslie right in front of her, you kissed someone. It was a dumb thing to do, but people do dumb things all the time."

He shook his head. "This wasn't just dumb—this was *cruel and heartless*."

"It wasn't cruel—"

"Stop it! Stop trying to make me feel better. Leslie is right—it was *cruel and heartless*. I humiliated her. It was an awful thing to do, and you know it. What happened to me, Eliot? Why am I like this?" He looked up expectantly, as if I had the answer.

"You're not a jerk, Finn, or a bad person. You made a bad decision; she'll forgive you." Please God, I thought. Please God, don't let her forgive him. Please let him love me.

This made him smile. "It's so great to see you. I should've called, but I got caught up in . . ." He lifted his hands and then spread them apart, as if to illustrate the enormity of his life.

"Did I say I was upset?" I hadn't asked him to call and didn't want his apology. I changed the subject. "You were looking for me?" I said frostily, meaning, *I'm here; now what?*

"I needed to see you." Sheepish, he raked his hand through his thick blond hair. "Coming back from Gatlinburg, all I could think about was you. You're the only one who gets me, Eliot, the only one I can talk to. I really fucked things up between us, haven't I?"

This bothered me, too. I was tired, I realized, of waiting for Finn, tired of his lack of interest, tired of being his last-resort call. "Finn, I'm right in the middle—"

"Look, I know you're mad I haven't called—"

"I'm not *mad*!" But then I added, "They don't have phones in Gatlinburg?" which wasn't what I meant. I meant: *Please, Finn, please leave me alone. Can't you see I'm not the same girl I used to be? Please let me get on with my life.* "Finn, I'm sorry, but I really have things to do."

I started to leave, but Finn stopped me. "Hear me out? Just for a second? See, I had this epiphany. Leslie was smart to break up with me—Christ, she never should've dated me in the first place. She's not right for me, just like Perry wasn't right for you. I realize now—"

"Perry?" I interrupted, my voice rising an octave. "You remember his name?"

"You think I don't listen, but I do. I listen to everything you say." He leaned closer. "You are so pretty, Eliot. How come you don't know how pretty you are?"

He *had* been drinking, I realized. Bourbon always made him overly emotional. Thinking about Finn coatless on the bus, and drinking out of a brown paper bag like a hobo, made me feel even worse for him.

"Please, Finn." Please what? What did I want him to do?

He was so close now. *Just one more inch . . .*

"You're my person, Eliot. I want us to be the way we used to be. I've missed you so much. Don't you miss me? Don't you miss us hanging out? I've been thinking about you a lot recently, how much I miss talking to you."

"I can't believe you remember Perry," I said, breathless now, a little giddy. He *does* listen. *I need you,* he said. *You're my person—the only one. I've missed you so much.*

"After dating all these idiotic girls, I realize how important you are. Not that Leslie's an idiot—she got, like, a perfect score on the LSATs—but she doesn't know me the way you do. I'd never tell her *half* the shit I've told you."

I shook my head, wondering how high I would score if I took the LSATs. "No, Finn," I agreed. "Leslie doesn't know you like I do. No one does."

"Maybe I'm just feeling sentimental, but . . . I don't know . . . you've always been so good to me. And so much is happening—school's ending, I'm broke, I need a job. I've missed being around someone so . . . so concerned about my life. I'm a lousy friend, I know I am, but I'll change, I swear. I'll do whatever I have to; please give me another chance." He leaned forward.

"There's nothing wrong with you, Finn," I said solemnly.

"Why are you whispering?"

"I don't know." Then I said it. I couldn't help myself, he was just so close. "I love you, Finn. I've always loved you." There was silence—just a beat—but I had to fill it up. "Do you love me?" I quickly revised myself. "I know you love me."

He held my gaze. "Of course I love you, Eliot." Then he reached for me, whether to hug me or kiss me I can't say for sure. But when he put his arms around me, we started to kiss, and it was so much like a stupid romance novel that I began to cry.

⌒

And then, a few hours later—voilà—I was no longer a virgin. It happened fast; faster than I expected, given all the years of waiting.

Finn and I were alone in his room. "Are you sure you want to do this?" he kept asking. "I'm just not... I mean, I don't want... Look, I'm screwed up; you have to know that."

I assured him it was fine, perfectly fine, I was screwed up, too. We could be screwed up together. "But what about Leslie?" I wanted to know. "What happens if she wants you back?"

"She won't. Besides, I'm here with you. That's what matters." Finn pulled me closer and continued to kiss me. "Eliot, do you know how many times I've wanted to do this?"

His question made me weak, but was it rhetorical? "So you thought about me before?"

"Are you kidding? I've thought about you since you kissed me last year. Christ, I can't think about anything *but* you. Why do you think I've stayed away from you? I was afraid I wouldn't be able to control myself."

This, by far, was the greatest thing anyone had ever said to me—except for one thing. "Uh, Finn," I corrected him, "*you* kissed *me*."

I wish you could've seen us, how perfect we were together. We knew each other; we loved each other. At last, after all that waiting, it was love at first sight. My one true soul mate, I thought, relishing the expression, repeating it silently, over and over. In his bed, on my back, I slowly unwound. Finn reached for me, and for the first time ever, I let my whole self go. My mouth and chest, my arms and legs—I opened up like a window.

"It's always been you," Finn told me, his breath sweet and sticky. "You're the only girl I ever wanted. I've been so stupid, haven't I?"

It worked for a few months, the two of us. We fell into a routine—the library, meals, class—that felt like a relationship, like a genuine love affair, although it's true I had nothing to compare it with. It was the same as it always was, but different, better, although as with any relationship, there were downsides. Finn disappeared for hours, sometimes days, and then reappeared with a chip on his shoulder. We didn't talk as much; rather, he didn't talk, nor did he listen. As for me, I was . . . well, I was myself: nervous and insecure, overly solicitous, and preoccupied with his feelings instead of my own. It was obvious he was disengaged, so while before I kept waiting for him to come to me, now I kept waiting for him to leave.

And then in April, he had an announcement: "I have a job interview."

"That's great," I said. "With who?"

He told me the name of the company, which I didn't recognize. "The interview is downtown." He looked away. "But the job is in New York."

"New York?" I was baffled. *"City?"*

"It was Leslie's father, actually, who helped me out. Remember Leslie?"

I nodded. Of course I remembered Leslie, but what about New York?

Apparently, he and Leslie had bumped into each other two weeks before. They got to talking, had a few drinks. He apologized for the way things had ended between them ("fear of commitment," was how he phrased it). And she, in turn, forgave him.

"Just like that?" In my mind, I was turning over his *fear of commitment*.

Finn nodded, just like that. "She's starting Columbia Law this fall. Apparently, her LSAT scores made a difference—well, that and her father, who's a judge on the New York Court of Appeals. Anyway, she offered to introduce me to him and to his squash partner, who is *el jefe*"—he grinned; hear that, Eliot? Spanish!—"at some company in Manhattan. It's called National Brands, and it's a spin-off of American Home Products—who the fuck knows? It's all very confusing— but supposedly the guy runs the place. They have an Atlanta office, but they need an entry-level person in the marketing department, which is based in New York. Trust me, it's nothing glamorous. The company makes bathroom stuff—toothpaste, deodorant, whatever. And I don't know anything about marketing, but I brush my teeth, right?"

All I could think was: But where was I when he ran into Leslie?

Finn aced the first round of interviews and was invited to New York to meet *el jefe*. He came back two days later, offer in hand. At the time, it seemed like a lot of money. "They also said they'd help me find an apartment! I have to get a roommate, but still . . . Isn't that great?"

"I thought you loved Atlanta," I said, which wasn't what I meant. I meant, *I thought you loved me. I thought we were spending the rest of our lives together. I thought you were my one true soul mate.* "I guess I thought wrong."

Of all my regrets about Finn—and there are many—that I never asked, *But what about us?* haunts me the most. Instead, I remembered how he reacted when the Dahlias and Leslies pressed him about the future and kept my mouth shut. I also thought, stupidly, that it would eventually occur to him that he'd forgotten to invite me. *Oh, my God, Eliot,* I kept waiting to hear, *you have to pack!* I realize now that regardless of what I said or didn't say, Finn was leaving without me, but in the years that followed, "if only" became my constant refrain: *If only I'd told him, if only I'd asked him, if only I'd begged him . . . then everything would be different.* I made myself crazy, replaying our alternative history, the one where, at the end of the story, I tell Finn how I feel, Finn tells me how he feels, and we live happily ever after.

At one point, I did mention that I might want to see New York, too, someday, but he didn't bite. "You should do that," he replied, flashing his famous smile.

"I should," I agreed. "Maybe I'll find my own job there."

But rather than move into action, I did what I always do, which is to wait too long to do anything—or rather, long enough to force a decision. In this case, I stayed in Atlanta while Finn left for New York. I sent my résumé to a few places—four, to be exact—but never followed up. Two months later, there were girls giggling in the background when we talked on the phone. Speaking of the phone: Finn and I had only three conversations after he left—and I initiated all of them. One weekend, he flew down for someone's postgraduation party (oh, and to see me, he added). But it wasn't the same. Or rather, it was exactly the same: Finn was distant and sullen, while I chastised myself for everything I didn't say. We didn't have sex; we barely touched. We went to the movies, but I cried the entire time, quietly, in the dark theater, my hands balled into fists. By the time Finn left, I was actually relieved . . . well, devastated but relieved. Deep down, I knew—had always known—that he didn't love me as much as, the same way, I loved him, and yet . . . and yet, having spent so much time praying that someday he might, I still wasn't ready to give up hope.

"I'll call you," he assured me when I dropped him off at the airport.

"Really?" I asked. "True words?"

Finn smacked the top of my car. "True words. See you soon, Eliot."

"Okay, then," was the last thing I ever said to him. "I'll wait."

~

Inside the Emory library, it's impossible to concentrate. Every time I turn around, I see Finn: slouched on a chair, bending over the water fountain, standing by the men's room. I write a press release. I Google Finn. I Google myself. I Google Grant. I Google Parker Montgomery and Humphrey Montgomery. I read Charlotte's blog. I eat a turkey sandwich. I turn my cell phone off. I turn it back on. I turn it off again. On-off, on-off, on-off. I apologize to the girl in the next carrel. I wait. I wait some more. And the next thing I know, the whole day has gone by.

There's no way to calculate the number of hours I've spent waiting for Finn. One minute he's there, and the next—poof—he's gone. When he finally disappeared for good, I fell apart. I couldn't eat, couldn't sleep. I tortured myself over whether I should go to New York and confront him. I tortured my mother and sisters, who eventually got tired of discussing it.

"The guy is gone," Sylvia said. "It's time to change the station."

Desperate to talk to someone, *anyone*, I blurted out my story to whoever would listen. I even called my father, Barney, surprising us both.

"He really left!" I shouted into the receiver. "I didn't think he would, but he did."

Caught off guard, Barney stumbled. "Eliot? Who left?"

"Finn! He moved to New York. How could he do that...uh...?" I almost said *Dad*, but it felt wrong to address him so intimately.

The shock of hearing my voice, my hysteria, my uncharacteristic anger—it was all too much for my father. He was also confused, having, of course, no idea who Finn was. I understand this now. I would've been shocked, too, if someone had called me in distress after so many years. But I wasn't just someone; I was his child, his eldest daughter. And because I was an immature kid, with no patience for his old-man foibles, when he bleated, "I'm sorry, Barbara—uh, *Eliot*...I don't know what to say," like some kind of lost lamb, I hung up, stung by what felt like still more rejection. Then he failed me again by calling my mother, not me, to see if I was okay.

How could he call me *Barbara*? I kept asking myself. Barbara was my mother's sister, my favorite aunt, who had recently died. *See, I knew I couldn't count on him!* At this point, though, reality finally sank in: just like my father, Finn was never coming back.

Months passed. I got up off the floor. I brushed my teeth. I stepped outside. I went out for dinner with my sisters. I took a shower. Then one day I laughed, unself-consciously, at a joke, and slowly but surely Finn began to recede. Soon, I could even forget about him for long stretches of time, although the forgetting never lasted. No matter how far I got or how steady my rhythm, as soon as I spotted a tall, golden boy rake his hands through his hair, Finn would be as present as the day he had left me. Or I'd get an unexpected whiff of Irish Spring soap, and memories would roll in like fog over water. Then I'd have to wait, sometimes days, often weeks, for Finn to fade away, so I could go through the long, painful process of forgetting again.

The thing about my relationship with Finn—and my father, too, I suppose—is that it never really ended. I mean, it ended—of course it ended—but I don't have a specific moment I can point to and say, "Right there, that's when it was over." How could I? When your father moves out, he's still your father, isn't he? If not, what does he become? An ex-father? An unparent? Similarly, when you finally find your one true soul mate, doesn't he always remain yours? According to the literature, it's only one true love per lifetime, so what did my future hold if I had already found and lost mine? This is why, even though a year passed and then two and then three, I held on to the possibility, however remote, that Finn and I might still be together—or if not together, then at least still in love.

"*Are you fucking insane?*" Sylvia would shout. "You have to get over him, Eliot."

Yes, I was insane. It's insane, isn't it, to love a ghost? To obsess about a man who treated you badly, then left you behind without so much as a backward glance? It's insane to wait for him to reappear, even though you saw him vanish with your own two eyes. It's insane to tell yourself that everything would be different *if only*, *if only*. The whole thing was insane, even the idea that he—that they—truly loved me in the first place.

And yet.

I started to see a therapist. I needed someone to explain why this had

happened, how I ended up this way. And although I didn't get a definitive answer, the one that said, *Because of x I am y*, I did find someone
to talk to. And once I told the story—not just the story of Finn, but
also the story of me—I began to understand that he (my father, my boy
friend who wasn't a boyfriend or even a friend) may have left, but life—
my life—was still going on. Whether to live it or not, the therapist
said, was up to me.

Hearing that my life was a choice was a revelation. Until that point,
it hadn't occurred to me that I had any say in what happened next. But
by taking an active role in my fate, I was able to truly put Finn behind
me. And once he was no longer crowding out everything else in my
head, I was finally able to focus on other parts of my life.

Around this time, I was approached by Oliver Morgan Consulting, a
well-known PR agency that was looking for corporate writers to build a
new practice. For the past four years—since graduating from Emory—
I'd worked for a medical device manufacturer doing internal communications. The job was pretty easy, even after a couple of promotions, and
since I'm well organized in general, I had a lot (*a lot*) of time to obsess
about Finn. But when this new company called, I started weighing my
options. At first I was afraid—my only sales experience had been a high
school fund-raiser, where I sold seven chocolate bars to myself—but the
money was great and the people seemed nice. And Oliver Morgan already had established clients; they just needed someone to provide them
with expanded and specialized services.

As it turned out—*who knew?*—I was a natural service provider.
Although it makes sense, right? I mean, who better than me to be a
beck-and-call girl? My new job—excuse me, career—gave me confidence, and it showed, not just in business but also in life. As I traveled,
met with clients, and discussed strategies, I felt truly engaged, even
excited, about what I was doing. I got to know people and let them
get to know me, and thus I developed my first relationships based on
mutual respect and trust. My world burst open with possibility—I
dated, I went to parties, I stayed fixed in the now—but my interior life

remained my own. And my secrets remained secret, no longer currency to be traded, either by me or by anyone else.

When I eventually met Grant, ten years had passed since Finn and I were together. By this point, he was nothing more than a memory, just a bittersweet story about some boy I once loved. Now, in the light of day, I could see clearly: I had a crush, not on a bad guy but on the wrong guy—that is, the wrong guy for me. Now there was Grant, a man with solid character and an equally solid upper body, a man who had showed his mettle when advantage had turned. Now I had, if not a husband, then certainly a partner; a man I loved who loved me back—the same, as much, enough.

Still sitting in the library, I realize I can't do this again. I can't wait for Finn anymore. I have my own people now, people who are waiting for me—Grant and Charlotte and Gail. I also have Hailey, my funny redheaded girl, to whom I owe an American Girl doll, complete with accessories. Seeing Finn would be fun, but it isn't real life. It isn't my life. My life is Grant; my life is the girls; my life is Hailey.

I check my watch. Pickup is early today, and I have to leave soon or else I'll hit traffic. I glance around one last time, and when there's no sign of Finn, I sigh in relief.

"*Dude!* You're still here."

I hear him before I see him. Startled, I turn around. "Dude yourself," I choke out.

So tell me: If Finn Montgomery is nothing more than a long-ago crush, why does the room start to spin the second he appears? Why is the air lighter? My voice higher? Why am I reeling like a drunk, unable to stand? I love Grant; I do. But look at me falling off my own feet. Look at me grabbing the desk, the chair, the walls, for support. Just look at me: red in the face, weak in the knees, bent at the waist, completely off-kilter.

"I'm glad I caught you," I hear Finn say, sounding far away. "I thought you'd be gone."

He's watching me closely. Feeling as though I'm caught in his crosshairs, I'm afraid to move, even to breathe. "No, I'm here." I don't trust myself to say more. It's disorienting, seeing him in front of me. If I glance away, I wonder, will he disappear?

"You're staring," he says.

"You look different."

Finn rakes his hand through his hair. Now that I'm closer, I can see a small patch of scalp on the crown of his head. "Different good, though, right?" he asks.

His need for reassurance helps me loosen up, although not by much. We're stilted together, and the awkward silences make us both uneasy. I think we both expected the same easy repartee we had on the phone; but standing here face-to-face, neither of us has much to say.

"Different good," I answer, nodding.

"Let's walk," Finn says. He takes my arm, and then maneuvers me toward the library doors. By the time I agree, I'm already outside.

In the sun, as we stroll across our old campus, our conversation starts to pick up. Soon we're reminiscing, and the next thing I know, ten minutes pass and then twenty-five.

I check my watch, careful not to fall into Finn time, which is when the universe opens like a wind tunnel and time flashes by at lightning speed: minutes become days, days become months, months become years. A whole life can pass by like time-lapse photography.

"So you're okay?" I ask as if I can sum it up in one single shot. "You're happy?"

"I'm good," he says, stopping to sit on a bench. "But happy? Is anyone really happy?"

"I'm happy." I throw this down like some kind of gauntlet. "Grant's a good guy."

"Parker..." He laughs. "Parker is *very kind* to put up with me. And I thank God every day that her father is loaded. What she spends on shoes alone could make you weep." But then he pats his stomach, like a man after dinner whose belly is full.

"You're rich, though. You got what you wanted." Why am I so pre-occupied with his money? I wonder. I sit beside him, but not too close.

"It's like this, Eliot. Every six months, it's my turn to take the dog to the vet. So Howdy and I—that's the dog's name, *Howdy*, and get this, Howdy is a *teacup Chihuahua*—so anyway, Howdy and I will be rid-ing the elevator together, and it'll suddenly occur to me: How did I— a poor mope from Buffalo—end up toting a dog named *Howdy* around in a fucking *purse*?" He offers up a wry, self-deprecating grin, and that's when I see what I've been looking for: there, in this middle-aged man's face, is a golden teenage boy.

"Why didn't you call me when you came back to Atlanta?" I ask him—not the Finn with me now, but the boy I used to know.

"Honestly? I had every intention of calling, but the more I thought about it, the more I realized you probably didn't want to hear from me, given how I left the last time, which I know was...uh...I know it was unforgivable—" He stops, changes course. "Parker and I were going through a rough patch, and as much as I could've used a sympathetic ear, I wanted to spare you the details of yet another relationship I was in danger of fucking up."

"You thought about calling me?"

"We're friends, aren't we?" He stands up and dusts off his pants. "I'm glad you found someone good, Eliot. I'm glad you're happy."

Like he said, I think, Is anyone really happy?

I stand up, too. "You shouldn't have worried—about calling, I mean. I would've been the same...I would've been..." I search for the right word. "Me."

He leans forward *this close*. When he speaks, I feel his hair on my cheek, his breath on my ear. "Eliot," he says softly, "that's exactly why I didn't call."

Chapter Twelve

I WAS LATE—very late—picking up Hailey. I left Finn on time but mis-judged the traffic. Actually, that's not true. I stayed with him fifteen, uh, twenty minutes longer than I should have, so by the time I got to Riverside, the entire staff was ensconced in a meeting; Hailey, Ava, and Josie were corralled in an office with a frazzled teacher's aide, and every-one was miserable.

Grabbing the girls, I apologized profusely for what was clearly a mis-communication about early dismissal and raced out to my car. So now I have three cranky kids in my backseat, two pissed-off mothers burn-ing up the phone lines, and a concerned husband waiting patiently at home.

"It's no big deal," Grant is saying, offering me kindness I don't de-serve. "These things happen. You're on the road now, and everyone's okay. Right? Is everyone okay?"

"Everyone's fine. The girls are just confused; we're all confused. Miss Lulu told me about the meeting, but I don't remember her saying it *started* at five. I remember something about five, but not that I had to be here by then."

"You keep repeating the same thing, Eliot, and I keep telling you not to worry."

"But I feel awful, especially since you had to deal with Phoebe and Grace. I'm so sorry, Grant." I drive quickly, one hand on the wheel, the other clutching my phone. "You girls okay back there? Ava? Josie? Sweet pea? I'm sorry I was late. Silly Mommy mixed up the times."

"I have to poop," sweet pea announces.

"Grant? *Hold on! I dropped the*—sorry—I dropped the phone." I take a deep breath. "I need to focus, so I'm going to hang up, okay? And like I said, I would've called but my phone ran out of battery."

"How can you have no battery? You're talking to me right now."

"I meant service. I had battery but no service. The good news is that there isn't any traffic, so I won't be home much later than I normally would."

Grant sighs. "Eliot, you're forty minutes late already."

Hearing this makes me want to cry. "You think I don't *know* that? Are you *trying* to make it worse?"

"No," Grant says quietly, "but you need to calm down and get the girls home safely."

Grant doesn't understand. I can't calm down. This is just the beginning. I'll do my best to stave Finn off, but he infiltrates my system the way a virus attacks its host, by attaching himself at the cellular level and hijacking the very machinery designed to resist him. It's a proven scientific fact: I'm doomed.

When I finally get home, I'm still agitated, but I wrap my arms around Grant and tell him, again, that I'm sorry. Hailey runs upstairs to see her sisters, but Grant follows me into the dining room where I toss my keys, to the foot of the stairs where I kick off my heels, and then back to the dining room where I rifle through the mail.

"The kids must be starving." I walk into the empty kitchen. It feels odd to be here, as if I'm on a stage set, auditioning for the lead role in a domestic drama. Everything, including Grant, seems artificial, and the roar in my head only heightens my dislocation. "Did you feed them?"

"They wanted to wait for you." He shrugs, as if to say, *What could I do?* "I'm starving," he adds, watching me fill a pot with water and turn on the stove.

"You should've ordered a pizza or heated up some soup." Enter matriarch, I think. Stage right.

Grant nods as if this is a good idea. There's a sleeve of Oreos on the counter. He takes out four, which he eats quickly, one right after the other. "So, Sylvia called." Mouth full, he swallows. "She told me she's having problems with the pregnancy—something about spotting or bleeding, I didn't catch which—and that you're taking her to the doctor tomorrow. Is that right?"

"Yes—well, she's not having problems. It's just a routine visit, but what about it?" Whipping through the kitchen, I take a box of pasta out of the cabinet, lettuce out of the refrigerator, and plates out of the cabinet.

Grant pops open a beer. "Why is your sister seeing a doctor on Saturday?"

His question surprises me. Does he think I'm lying? "A lot of doctors have weekend hours."

He takes a long gulp, then lets out a body-rocking belch. Normally, we'd both find this hilarious, but I'm too preoccupied to laugh. "Well, I have to go to the office tomorrow, so if you're planning on spending the morning with Sylvia, we have to get someone to watch the kids. Oh, and next Wednesday night I'll be late. Maybe Thursday, too."

"Okay, but that's a week away. Why are you telling me now?"

"It's not a week, Eliot, it's only five days. And if you're going on vacation, I have to get as much work done in advance as I can. Have you forgotten you're going to Wyatt Island in less than two weeks?"

Actually, I had, but I shake my head. "Anyway, remember Dr. Hall? The internist you saw last April? He has office hours on Saturday." I dump the spaghetti into the pot and start washing the lettuce.

"So what?"

"You asked why Sylvia is seeing a doctor on Saturday, so I'm reminding you a lot of doctors have weekend hours. Hey," I add casually as if the thought just occurred to me. "Can you give me a hand with dinner?"

"Sure," Grant replies as if he's a guest. "What do you need me to do?"

Watching him set the table makes me wonder if Finn does chores at his house. Given what I know of him, I'd say it's unlikely. But what if

Parker is caught in traffic? Does he help out then? Or, like Grant, does he sit around eating Oreos until she gets home, even though it's seven thirty and everyone is so famished, they're about to chew off their own arms?

Thinking of Finn makes heat rise to my face. "Guess what?" I blurt out, suddenly needing to say his name. "Finn Montgomery sends his daughter to Riverside. Remember Finn? I went to Emory with Finn."

"You dated him, too, right? How do you know about his daughter?"

"She's in Dylan's class. How weird is that? *Finn Montgomery,*" I say, rolling my tongue over the F, the M, and the y.

"Are you going to call him?"

"Call him?" I stare at Grant blankly. "What could we possibly have to talk about?"

Hours earlier, I had zeroed in on his marriage. "So you and Parker have a lot of problems?" We were walking to the parking lot; time was running out.

Finn looked confused. "What kind of problems?"

"You said that when you first moved back to Atlanta, you went through a rough patch."

"Oh, that. Parker was positive I was in love with this woman at work. We even went to a marriage counselor." He rolled his eyes. "In the end, I stopped talking to her. To Julie, I mean. I wasn't going to risk losing Parker or Humphrey. The two of them—they're my whole life."

The name Humphrey wasn't so ridiculous after all, I decided. Hearing Finn say it, I thought *Humphrey* sounded perfectly lovely. "But you were in love with her? With Julie?"

"Of course not," Finn said, but he started to laugh.

"Why is that funny?" Steering him toward my car, I rooted around in my bag for my keys.

"I laugh when I'm nervous. Parker says it's one of my least appealing qualities, among others. So, no, I didn't *love* Julie; I barely *knew* Julie. It wasn't a sexual thing. I mean, I wasn't sleeping with her. It was…" He squinted into the distance. "I don't know what it was, Eliot. I couldn't describe it to myself or to my wife, which was part of the problem. But I felt relaxed with Julie in a way I don't feel with Parker—with anyone, actually. You know how, when you're on vacation, you breathe differently? It was like that, like getting time off."

Finn's wistful smile made my heart ache. "But things are okay between you and Parker now?" I recalled the icy blonde with the great hair and long, slender legs.

"Yeah, they're fine. This was four years ago, remember. We'd just left Manhattan—which we both loved. Parker grew up here, so it wasn't like Atlanta was a foreign country for either of us, but we moved because of my job."

"National Brands, right? You're still with the same company."

He nodded, surprised. "How did you know?"

Caught, I swallowed hard. "Lucky guess," I mumbled.

"It's actually Global Brands now. But it's hard to believe I've stayed with the same company since graduating from college. I mean, of all people, right?" He shook his head. "Anyway, Parker wasn't working, so all the logistics fell to her and it was a big adjustment. I mean, she still has family here—in fact, I met her through one of her cousins, a guy I knew at Emory—but she had to deal with the house and school and everything else because I was at the office all the time—"

"With *Julie.*"

"Yes, with *Julie.* And Parker has a jealous streak." Finn shrugged. "Net-net, I learned not to give her anything to be jealous about, and our relationship got much better."

"Like telling her you and I were *study pals*?"

"Something like that...I actually did tell her that you and I were good friends, but I didn't elaborate. Look, I'm not trying to hide my past—or you—but I want Parker to feel secure with me; I want her to know I'm a stand-up guy. Trust me, this didn't happen overnight. Eliot, you know better than anyone that I was a mess with women—although by the time I met Parker, I'd already started to change."

"So what happened with Julie?"

"Nothing happened. After we moved here, she helped me get acclimated around the office, but I realized pretty quickly that being around her was dangerous, I backed off—" Stopping midsentence, Finn studied me.

"What?" Self-conscious, I touched my cheek.

"Julie reminded me of you, actually. She was a nice girl too. She had your same..." Finn trailed off. "This is your car?" He peered inside. "Yours, right?"

My same what? I glanced at my watch. "My same what?"

"Eliot, it's not something I can condense in five minutes. I promise, I swear"—he covered his heart with two fingers—"I'll call you."

I didn't move. I had my keys in my hand and my hand on the door, but still, I stayed put. Squinting into his face, I tried to find the old Finn.

"Why did you leave me?" There, I finally said it: *You left me. You loved me and left me but never said why.*

"I didn't *leave you*, Eliot. I took a job. You could've moved too, but you didn't."

"Bullshit, Finn. You didn't want me to go." There, I said that, too: *You didn't want me.*

Finn was quiet, as if debating whether or not to answer. "You've changed, too," he said finally. "You never would've put me on the spot before. You're right, though. I couldn't handle our relationship, but rather than admit it, I acted like an asshole. I was totally self-centered, but I was just a kid."

"That's not an answer," I snapped. Really, what did I have to lose at this point? "That's saying, 'I was immature because I was immature.' Do you have any idea how much you hurt me?"

Head bent, he nodded. "Of course. I realized it then too, but didn't know how not to. You were the closest friend I ever had, but I couldn't be with you—not because I didn't care about you, but because I couldn't give you what you needed."

I blinked back tears. "What makes you think I needed so much?"

"It wasn't 'so much,' Eliot, but it was definitely something—or someone—different than me."

"That's not true! You were exactly what I wanted. You were *every-thing*. I *loved* you, Finn! But maybe *you* didn't love *me*; maybe *I* wasn't what *you* wanted."

"Who knew what I wanted back then? I was so mixed up. We both knew you deserved better, but then we got together—Christ, it happened so fast. On the one hand, I'd never met anyone like you. You were real, you were honest, you were so...I don't know...*good*. And you were so pretty. Jesus, Eliot, you had no idea how pretty you were. But on the other hand..." He didn't finish. Instead, he squeezed my fingers, and then held them for a beat before letting go.

The sun was setting, casting long shadows across the parking lot. After a minute, Finn checked his watch. "Don't you have to go?"

"On the other hand what?"

"*Eliot!*"

Hearing my name, I snap to attention. Grant, I realize, is shouting at me.

"The spaghetti's boiling over!" He lunges for the stove and turns down the heat. "Eliot, where are you?"

"Calm down, Grant." I blink to clear my head. "I'm right here."

⌒

On the other hand what? Finn hadn't said. Instead, he took my car keys and clicked open the locks. "You're gonna be late, Eliot. We'll talk about it tomorrow."

But I can't wait until tomorrow. It's almost midnight, and I'm wide awake. The girls are asleep, Grant is upstairs, and I'm sitting in my darkened office, debating, once again, if I should call him.

I flip my phone open, when it suddenly rings, startling me. When I see that it's Finn, my heart starts to pound.

"What's wrong?" I ask. "Is everything okay?"

"Eliot?" Finn sounds surprised. "I didn't expect you to answer. Sorry to call so late. I thought you'd be asleep. I just planned to leave a message."

"Which was what?"

"Well, now it'll sound stupid."

"So call back and I won't answer."

"No, this is fine..." He clears his throat.

For a few seconds, there's silence.

"You still there? Finn, it's okay if you want to wait until tomorrow to talk about this—"

"No," he says. "I'm good...So, anyway, I called because...See, the thing is— Wow, this would've been so much easier if I had just left a message. Fuck it, here goes: Eliot, I want you to think I'm a stand-up guy, too. I've owed you an apology for fifteen years, and...well, the truth is, I was a coward when I was younger. I'm actually still a coward—"

"Oh, Finn, you're not a coward."

"No, let me finish. I am a coward. I wasn't completely honest with you earlier."

"Let me guess. You lied to Parker. You really *did* have an affair with Julie. You're *still* having an affair with her. In fact, she's there right now."

"How can you say that?" He laughs. "One time, *one time*, I kissed someone else when I was with Leslie, but I wasn't a cheater—and you know it. Maybe I went out with a lot of girls, but I never screwed—"

"Calm down. I'm just kidding. I don't think you're a cheater—well, maybe I think it a little, but who cares what I think? Why, *did* you sleep with Julie?"

"Ha ha. What I was going to tell you before you so rudely disparaged my character, was that this afternoon, when we were talking about our relationship, instead of avoiding the issue, I should've been more direct. And what I should've said was: Yes, *of course* I loved you at Emory. *I've always loved you, Eliot.*"

My breath catches. "You loved me?"

"How could I not? You were the nicest girl I had ever met. You made me feel good about myself, like anything was possible. But you also scared the shit out of me. You had this fixed idea in your mind of how a relationship should work, and given who I was, it was completely unrealistic. I wasn't ready. But more than that, you had such high standards for yourself, for me, for us, and there was no way in hell I could've lived up to them. So I bolted. It was an awful thing to do, and I've always regretted it."

"Finn, all I needed was for you to be honest with me."

"And to love you the way you loved me."

"Yes," I say, "that too."

He sighs. "That's the thing, Eliot. I couldn't—not back then. You were a nice girl who cared too much about everyone else. And I was a selfish prick who only cared about himself. I thought there'd be a hundred more Eliots in my future. Imagine my horror when I found out there was only one." He chuckles but sounds as though he's grieving. "Don't get me wrong—I love Parker. But if I'm truly being honest with myself, I know something's missing between us, some rare spark that makes my life transcendent, or complete, or whatever quality allows you to breathe differently. The only time I ever felt that way was with you, and then later, with Julie. I only hung out with Julie for a couple of weeks—and no, I *absolutely did not* have sex with her—but I knew if I continued to see her, I'd start to question my marriage, and I wasn't prepared to do that. But when I saw you last week...Jesus, Eliot, it was like a fucking tidal wave. It hit me all over again—that same shock of attraction, that same desire. You know?"

I nod, transfixed, even though he can't see me.

"And I'll tell you something else. My mother passed away about eighteen months ago."

"I'm so sorry," I say softly.

"Thanks. It was much harder than I expected. Why I thought it would be any easier, I don't know. After my father walked out, it was just me, my mom, and my brothers. You know that story—we had no money, no nothing. She and I were always close, and after college, when I moved to Manhattan, we got even closer. I used to fly back and forth to Buffalo twice a month to see her, and then later, Humphrey came too. Christ, my mom adored that kid." He sniffles. "She had breast cancer, so her death wasn't a surprise, but it still fucked me up. I never realized how much I depended on her—not financially, but for support... She had this crazy faith in me, even when I was at my worst."

"I'm really sorry," I repeat.

"But here's the weird thing—right after she died, I started thinking about you."

"Me? Why me? We hadn't seen each other in years." Still, his admission is flattering.

"We may not have seen each other, but I still thought about you. You had this crazy faith in me, too. And when my mom died, I became fixated on those long conversations we had at school. Remember? How we used to sit and talk for hours?"

"We were kids, Finn. That's what you do when nothing else is expected of you."

"Still, they were a huge part of my life—*you* were a huge part of my life—and then I lost you. So when you showed up at Riverside, I was literally struck dumb. I hadn't seen you since Emory and then my mother dies and the first person I think to call is you and then suddenly—*no shit*—there you are. All I wanted to do was grab you, and tell you how crazy I was for leaving Atlanta—for leaving *you*— but I could barely open my mouth, much less form coherent sentences. I was in shock. I'm still in shock, actually, at how absolutely idiotic I was. Eliot, you were, by far, the best thing that ever happened to me, and I'm sorry I didn't see it when we were younger. I'm so sorry I hurt you. And I wish—God, I wish—I could go back and do everything differently, but I can't, and I'm sorry about that too."

"Me too." My eyes fill with tears.

"I hope you can forgive me. I'm a different person now, which I realize doesn't help you, but it's the truth."

"Of course I can forgive you, Finn."

"So, friends, then?" he asks, although we both know this is impossible.

"Sure." I wipe my eyes on my sleeve and then whisper good-bye. "Friends forever."

Chapter Thirteen

THE NEXT MORNING, I wake up groggy but looking forward to a day with the kids and then a rare Saturday evening out. Charlotte and Gail have (confirmed) plans to sleep at their mother's tonight, so Grant and I hired a sitter for Hailey. We're going to a swanky restaurant downtown where they don't serve chicken nuggets or macaroni and cheese, but they do serve enormous goblets of wine.

I glance at Grant, who's still asleep. It'll be good to spend time together, I tell myself, shaking off last night's conversation with Finn. I feel as if we haven't connected in days.

A moment later, Hailey toddles in. "Can I sleep with you?" she asks in a tired, plaintive voice. "I don't feel good."

After I pull her up into the bed, I feel her forehead.

"What's going on?" Grant asks, slowly rousing himself.

"She feels warm."

"Are you sure?" A second later, Hailey throws up all over the sheets. Rubbing her back, Grant shrugs. "I'll cancel the sitter," he says wearily.

"I'm sorry, Grant. I was really looking forward to tonight."

"Me too." He scoops up Hailey in his arms. "Let's get you into the bath, pickle. Hey, Eliot, will you be okay if I go to the office? Charlotte and Gail don't have to be at their mother's until six, so they can give you a hand around the house." He stops. "Oh shit. Aren't you supposed to take Sylvia to the doctor today?"

"Maggie can take her this time. We'll be fine here."

I spend the day cleaning the house, cooking meals, doing laundry, paying bills, and taking care of Hailey, who starts to feel better by midafternoon. With so much to do, I'm able to put Finn out of my mind. Not completely, of course, but enough to stay focused; enough (thank God) so that Finn fever wanes.

When Grant gets home, I offer to drive Charlotte and Gail to their mother's. "Sylvia just called. She's home and wants to meet Maggie for dinner, but needs a ride."

Grant is distracted. "She can't drive herself?"

"Of course she can, but she won't. Why do you think someone has to take her to all of her doctor's appointments? Anyway, Maggie is busy until seven, so do you care if I pick Sylvia up and we meet Maggie at the Olive Garden?"

"Nah. Hailey and I will just get a pizza. Right, pickle?"Resplendent in a tiara and beaded necklace, Grant is sitting cross-legged on the floor and trying to help Hailey solve a vexing dilemma. From what I can glean, all six of her Barbies were invited to the castle, but she has only four pairs of high heels. This means at least two Barbies will be forced to meet the prince in flats or, more horrifying, barefoot.

At the moment, Hailey is preoccupied trying to fit Polly Pocket's miniature shoes onto Barbie's Amazonian feet. "It's not working, Daddy." She throws the doll into his lap. "My girl's feet are too big."

Grant hands her a pair of lavender pumps. "Here. These don't go with my girl's dress."

"Eliot, can we please go?" Charlotte says behind me. "Mom's waiting."

"Where are you going?" Hailey asks. "Why are you wearing that?"

"What's wrong with it?" Charlotte snaps, although I wanted to ask the same thing. She has on a very short tutu and sky-high stilettos. From the waist down, she looks like an open umbrella.

"We're having a sleepover at our mom's house," Gail reminds Hailey, tossing her hairbrush on the couch so she can put on her jacket.

"That's not fair! I want a sleepover at your mom's house, too."

"You were sick today, Hailey," I tell her. "Besides, you'll have fun playing with Daddy."

"But I don't want to stay with Daddy! I want to be with Gail's mother."

This Beckett-like exchange continues for another minute, with Hailey demanding to go to the Sculptress's house and me trying to convince her otherwise. Finally, Grant's had enough. "Stop negotiating with her, Eliot. You're the mother—just go . . . Hailey, hand me that brown purse, would you?"

"You didn't say 'please,' Daddy, and besides, that's my girl's bag."

"Please, Hailey? It matches my girl's gown."

Listening to them, I feel a surge of affection for my strapping, sensitive husband. I kneel down. "I love you." I kiss him hard, on the lips, then adjust his tiara. "Your crown is slipping."

He kisses me back. "I love you, too."

"*Gross,*" all three girls say in unison.

Later, after I pick up Sylvia—Wait; allow me to rephrase: After I drive to Sylvia's house, stand in her foyer for fifteen minutes while she searches for her *saddle*-brown jacket ("No, Eliot, *saddle* brown; the jacket in your left hand is *chocolate* brown, and the one in your right is *walnut*"), and then help her shuffle out to my car and s-l-o-w-l-y lower her barely pregnant body into the front seat, we're finally on our way.

I glance at Charlotte and Gail in my rearview mirror. "So, are you guys excited to see your mom?"

"Why can't me and Charlotte go to the beach with you?" is Gail's reply. "Why does Hailey get to go, but not us?"

"*Charlotte and I,*" I say, buying time. "Daddy told you about my trip to Wyatt Island?"

Gail nods.

"Normally I would take you, but you and Charlotte have school."

"So does Hailey."

"Nursery school isn't the same." I ramble for the next ten minutes, explaining that my mother is getting older and needs a hand around the house, so it's not exactly a vacation. At the same time, I chastise myself for buying Hailey the wand she wanted at Target but not buying Gail the detective kit. Granted, the wand was only $4.49, whereas the kit was $59.99, but the money is irrelevant; it's the gesture of doing something for one kid, my daughter, and not her sister, my stepdaughter.

"So you see," I conclude, glancing back again, "it's just a matter of logistics."

"Uh-huh," Gail says, staring out the window.

The girls always get moody around their comings and goings with the Sculptress, but tonight they're both especially cranky.

"Are you doing anything special tonight?" I ask Charlotte, who doesn't reply.

Beside me, Sylvia turns in her seat. "Charlotte, Eliot asked a question. Do you have plans tonight? Maybe going someplace where they don't allow pants?"

"Mom's having a big party. Everyone she knows is coming."

"Tonight?" I blurt out. "She's having a party *tonight*? What about you and Gail?"

Charlotte sighs. "It's a *goddess party*, Eliot. We're *invited*."

"Yeah, *Eliot*," Sylvia says. "It's a *goddess party*. How dumb can you be?"

I swallow my rising frustration. How could the Sculptress do this? All Charlotte and Gail want is their mother's undivided attention, but instead of a quiet evening alone, she invites a houseful of people over for a *goddess party*. What *the fuck* is wrong with her? And what *the fuck* is a goddess party, anyway? However difficult it may be for me to tolerate Beth's behavior, though, it's got to be ten times harder for her children, which is why, when Gail begs me to stop in and say hello to her mother, I agree, even though whenever I'm around the Sculptress, I want to shake her until her kohl-rimmed eyes fall out of her head.

The Sculptress's apartment complex comprises several low-story buildings set around a small pool. We're still on the far end of the courtyard, but I can already hear music blasting from her ground-floor unit. As we get closer, I see that her front door is flung open and several women are standing outside, smoking. I pray it's only cigarettes.

"Are you okay with your mom having a party tonight, Charlotte?" I ask, but she's a few feet ahead of me, wobbling bowlegged on her stupid stilettos. "Charlotte." I grab her sleeve. *"Wait a second."*

Whirling around, Charlotte gives me a dirty look. "What do you want?"

"I just asked if you're comfortable being here with all these people. It's no problem to pick you up after dinner, if you decide you only want to stay for an hour."

"Of course I'm comfortable, *Eliot,"* she says as if I am an idiot, which I must be, because unlike her genius mother, I would never have a party on the one night of the year my kids came to see me.

"Mom?" Charlotte shouts into the house. *"We're here!"*

I turn to Gail to ask if she wants to go, but as soon as I open my mouth, the Sculptress steps outside. Seeing their mother, Charlotte and Gail wrench away from me and fling themselves at her with such force, she's knocked against the wall. Gail is so relieved to see Beth, she bursts into tears. Even Charlotte slumps against her mother as if she can no longer support her own weight. Watching them, I think about Hailey. When my own child is seven, then fourteen, and then all the ages thereafter, will she run to me with such unabashed need, with love so palpable and greedy?

After a while, though, the way Beth and her daughters are touching one another feels too private to watch, but when I turn away I'm surprised to find that, like Charlotte and Gail, I'm blinking back tears.

"So, Beth," I say, composing myself, "I see you're having a party tonight."

She nods coolly, tugging the belt of her thigh-high kimono. The Sculptress is so tiny that even wearing sky-high mules, she barely reaches Charlotte's shoulder. "Do you have to leave straightaway?" she asks in her nutty British accent. "Why don't you stay and have a pint?"

Gail grabs me. "*Please* come inside, Eliot. *Please?* Just for a little while?"

"Some other time," I demur, giving Gail a tight squeeze. "I really have to go."

"You should stay." This is from Charlotte. "Don't you want to meet Mom's friends?"

"Thanks, Charlotte, but Maggie's waiting at the Olive Garden." I turn to the Sculptress, who continues to watch me. Why does it always seem as if she's expecting me to do something? "We love the all-you-can-eat salad. And when you're there, you know . . . you're family." I take a step back. "Sylvia's in the car, so I should probably get going."

"No, I'm not!" Sylvia calls out, speed-walking across the lawn. "I'm right here. I called Maggie, and she said she didn't mind waiting a little longer."

"*I* mind, Sylvia. We made plans."

"But it's a *goddess* party, Eliot." She elbows me aside to peer into Beth's house. "You *love* goddess parties, *remember?*"

⌒

The Atlanta Goddess Network is a philanthropic society created by writers, artists, and activists to help low-income neighborhoods. According to their website, the group raises funds for homeless shelters, rape hotlines, and literacy centers. I was impressed with their services and even considered talking to the Sculptress about volunteering until I remembered that this would require interacting with her.

The AGN is a legitimate organization, but apparently the Sculptress has co-opted the goddess theme for her own bizarre purpose. As I walk through her dimly lit apartment, I'm riveted by what I see. Gauzy pink scarves cover the lampshades, strands of beads hang off every available hook, and fluffy feather boas are strewn all over the furniture. Goddesses are perched everywhere, each wearing some variation of trashy lingerie: slips with low-cut décolletage, sheer nightgowns, lacy pajama shorts with tiny camisoles. Surrounded by so many exposed breasts and asses, I feel overdressed in my Levi's and long sleeves.

Watching the Sculptress twirl her daughters around, I am struck by the realization that this grown-up goddess party is not unlike Hailey's princess party. In fact, the two are almost identical, aside from the rampant cellulite and mulled-wine martinis. Oh, and the eight-foot vagina painting hanging on the wall in the living room.

"What the fuck is this?" Sylvia is tilting her head to one side.

"It's a vagina."

"It's my vagina, actually," the Sculptress says, sidling up to us. "Fantastic, eh?" She throws her arms around a tall woman wearing flowing robes. "Christina held the mirror."

This cracks them up, prompting Sylvia to give me a familiar look. When she opens her mouth, I grab her. "Whatever you're about to say, Sylvia—don't. It's too easy."

"But it's right on the tip of my tongue. Please, Eliot? I'll apologize afterward, I swear."

"McGregor is roasting goat blinis in the kitchen," the Sculptress informs us. "Which I'm sure you'll find more edible than whatever the *Olive Garden* is serving." Still cackling, she and her friend clomp away.

This time, Sylvia is offended. "Can you believe that lunatic dissed the Olive Garden? Who doesn't like the Olive Garden? And why is she talking like Harry Potter?" Surveying the room, she shakes her head. "Someone should beam that crazy fool back to wherever she came from."

I hear a booming laugh and turn to see the Sculptress breaking out some erotic dance moves. Her kimono flies open, revealing her... well, everything, but she just keeps dancing. It continues to open, and I look away, fearful she might decide to just take it off.

Although I know it's true—and Charlotte and Gail are living proof—it is impossible for me to imagine Beth and Grant together. Then again, he says she wasn't always this flighty and provocative, nor was he so grounded and dependable. They met in art school, where she studied portraiture. Her work was traditional, if not conservative (think John Singer Sargent), and her subjects were all fully clothed. In fact, according to Grant, he was the one doing experimental art. Back then he made nonsensical installations out of wood, wire, and plastic, but eventually he moved to graphic design to earn a living. After they got married, Grant stopped making art altogether while the Sculptress became more and more avant-garde.

The music is deafening. "Come on, Sylvia. I can't take any more of this."

"Wait a second." Grabbing my arm, she lowers herself onto a nearby couch. "I need to sit down. My stomach is suddenly *killing me*. I feel like I'm being *stabbed* by *a hacksaw*."

"Okay, but once I say good-bye to the girls, we're leaving."

Behind me, my sister groans.

I make my way slowly through the crowded apartment. In a room at the end of a dark hallway, I spy Charlotte and Gail lounging on a queen-sized bed. The Sculptress is sitting on the floor, surrounded by goddesses.

Stepping inside, I try to get Charlotte's and Gail's attention, but the Sculptress is in the middle of what sounds like an intense story. I catch Gail's eye, and she pats the bed, motioning for me to sit down.

"I can't stay," I whisper. I lean forward to touch Charlotte's arm. "Bye, Charlotte."

Engrossed in her mother's monologue, Charlotte just nods.

I'm almost out the door when something the Sculptress says makes me stop. "So he was never what I'd call *Prince Charming*—I mean, what kind of prince doesn't give head?"

I spin around. All the goddesses are snickering. Even Charlotte is snickering, although I can't tell if she gets the joke. I grab Gail's hand. "You sure you don't want to come home with me?" I plead.

"We did have some *divine* moments," the Sculptress continues, "but our relationship was destined to fail. I told him you can't make great art while working in industry. For God's sake, you dilute the whole creative process. But he refused to listen, and just as I predicted, he started to resent his work, then my work, and then, finally, me. And I was so *repressed* in that marriage. You can see it in my paintings, which were flat, boring, and one-dimensional. My art only became interesting when I was able to reclaim my independence. Of course, the man did give me two beautiful and charming girls. So he was good for something, right?"

He, I realize, *is Grant!* She's talking about *Grant!* I reach out and clamp both my hands over Gail's ears. "*Beth? Hello, Beth?* I just want to say good night to the girls."

"Eliot!" She gives me a loopy smile. "Well, good night, then. I guess I'll see you tomorrow morning."

"Tomorrow? What's happening tomorrow?"

"I got *fabulous* seats at the ballet."

"The ballet?"

"Didn't Grant tell you? God, what is *wrong* with that man? I'm going to a matinee, so it would be great if you could come get the girls by ten."

"I have an even better idea. Why don't I just take them home with me now?"

"Now?" She gives me a strange look. "But then they'll miss the whole party."

I feel Gail tug at my hand. "Eliot? What does it mean to 'give head'?"

Oy vey, I think.

Out in the living room, Sylvia is lying on the couch. Sitting next to her is a woman who looks familiar. Unlike the other goddesses, though, this one is wearing a knee-length tweed skirt, a strand of pearls, and sensible shoes. She looks like a real estate appraiser who has accidentally stumbled into a home for wayward prostitutes. Her only concession to goddess-ness is a plastic tiara on her frosted blond hair.

"Phoebe?" I say, surprised to see her and also to see Grace, who is sitting on the floor. "What are you two doing here?"

"Eliot," Sylvia snaps, "do you mind? I was telling a story...So, anyway, that's the reason we're not friends anymore. The word is 'buffet' with an 'uh' sound, like 'fun'—*buffet*, not *boofay* with an 'oo' sound like 'boom.' *Come over, we're having a boofay?* No, I don't think so." Sylvia shrugs. "It matters; I'm sorry, but it does."

"We have to go." I pull her arm. "And we have to go *now*."

"In a minute, Eliot. I've been telling these guys about my *horrible* spotting. When I went to the bathroom before, there was blood everywhere. It was like *The Shining* in there!"

"But Maggie's waiting."

Sylvia looks at Phoebe. "Can you believe I'm practically having a *miscarriage*, and my sister is concerned about *dinner*?"

"You're not having a miscarriage, Sylvia," I say. "You went to the doctor this morning. According to Maggie—who was there—you're perfectly fine."

Ignoring me, she touches Phoebe's arm. "Would you mind rubbing my feet? I have such a terrible cramp."

"So, how do you know Beth?" Phoebe asks me.

"She's . . ." What is she? My stepdaughters' mother? The Gluckman we support? "She's my husband's ex-wife. How do you know her? Are you a sister-goddess?"

"Oh, Eliot, you are so funny." Phoebe adjusts her crown. "My friend Annette is a trustee—"

"She's *my* friend too, Phoebe," Grace interrupts. "I met her first."

"Please, Grace, not now. So, as I was saying, my very good friend Annette is a Goddess Network trustee. So I mentioned to her that the chapel committee was looking for an artist to help us renovate the Riverside chapel, and she told me about Beth, and, well, here we are."

"You need someone to paint a mural, right?" I point to the Sculptress's large gaping vagina hanging on the wall. "So, you hired *Beth*?"

Phoebe clears her throat. "Of course, the mural will be . . . uh . . . more . . . restrained—"

Sylvia interrupts us. "I just had a thought, Phoebe. It sounds to me like you and Beth have gotten pretty friendly. So you know she's taking a trip to Italy next week, right?"

"She did mention something about Italy," Phoebe replies. "But only that she was going—she didn't give me the details."

"Well, relationships take time. Anyway—"

"Sylvia," I interrupt anxiously, "why are you bringing this up now?"

"Eliot, you're a good mother. You always put Hailey first. But let's face it, you're becoming a very crabby person. I'd even go so far as to call you a bitch. You need a vacation." She smiles. "If your sister can't tell you the truth, then who can?"

"I am taking a vacation," I say. "I'm going to the beach with you in a week and a half."

"A vacation *without* kids, you dope." She turns to Phoebe. "See, we planned this *relaxing* trip to Wyatt Island, but it turns out Eliot has to bring Hailey. Have you met her? Cute kid, but *exhausting*. So my thinking is this: Since you and Beth are such great bff's, you could suggest to her that she postpone her trip for a couple of weeks. That way she'll be in town to take care of Charlotte and Gail (who are, after all, her children), Hailey can stay with Grant, and Eliot can go to the beach alone." Sylvia claps. "Easy peasy lemon squeezy."

I'm mortified. "Sylvia, I told you: *Grant* is perfectly happy with *Charlotte and Gail* staying here, and I'm fine taking *Hailey* with *me*. Beth doesn't have to postpone anything."

"All I'm saying is that if *you* could go to the beach *alone*—"

"But I don't *have* to go *alone*, *Sylvia*."

"Let me finish. If you could go *alone*, then Hailey won't be tagging along with her sippy cups and dirty diapers while *you* and *me* and *Maggie* stroll on the beach, drink margaritas, and get massages. Again, that's all I'm *saying*, Eliot. The three of us *never* get time together, and my *one wish* for this trip is to have you *all to myself*, so I can unwind in *peace and quiet*. And I'm afraid if Hailey is there, *my wish won't come true*."

"That is *so* sweet," Grace says wistfully. "I've always wanted a sister like you, Sylvia."

Sylvia nods. "I know, Grace. Me too. I am *such* a good sister."

I stare at Sylvia, unable to decide whether to laugh, cry, or smack her.

"I can't believe you're mad," she says in the car afterward. "Did you not hear me tell those women that you're a *great mother*, and that you always put Hailey *first*?"

"What the hell is wrong with you, Sylvia? Would you *stop* that?"

"Stop what?" Next to me, she's making monkey faces, trying to get me to laugh. "And how about my fixing it so you can leave Hailey with Grant? Perfect, right?" She pauses. "You could at least *thank me*, Eliot."

"I *like* Hailey, Sylvia. I *like* Grant, Charlotte, and Gail, too. I like being with them; they're my people. In fact, if Mom didn't need the company, I wouldn't even go."

"First of all, Eliot, stop saying Dolores *needs* you. *You* need *her*, and both Maggie and I are sick of you acting like she's an invalid. Once again, the favorite daughter rushes to rescue—"

"This has nothing to do with—"

"Don't cut me off; it's fucking *rude*. Second, all we want is a *fun* weekend, but you're making it into a three-act opera about who can go and who can't. And third, since when is Grant your people? Maggie and I are your people. We'll always be your people. Sisters forever, Eliot— live it, love it, be it."

Chapter Fourteen

Memo To: All Barnett Tech Colleagues
From: Lawrence Barnett, CEO
Re: Barnett Tech's Future Holds Robust Opportunities for YOU!

Dear Colleagues,

After exhaustive analysis, Corporate is pleased to announce that we will be making some minor adjustments to our internal business structure. We believe this action is vital to the Company's ability to sustain our leadership position in this increasingly volatile economy.

Effective October 1, Barnett Tech's nine departments (Accounting, Administration, Call Center, Distribution, Human Resources, Marketing, Legal, R&D and Sales) will be consolidated into two business units (Corporate and Sales), which will henceforth be referred to as "divisions."

What This Action Means for the Company

As you may have heard, OSHA has recalled 500,000 of our D7 Meister computer chips. However, contrary to media reports, only 40% of computers containing a D7 Meister chip spontaneously combusted; the other 60% merely caused system failure. So, we're pleased to report that because no one expired as a result of our D7 chip, there is insufficient basis for a class action suit!* Furthermore, any negative impact on Q3 earnings as a result of the OSHA recall will be mitigated by the reorganization outlined in this memo.

What This Action Means for YOU!

Exciting news for colleagues currently in Corporate and Sales: You will remain in Corporate and Sales, where you can expect to see your job description expanded as you assume many new responsibilities!

Equally exciting news for all our other colleagues: You now have the opportunity to pursue employment elsewhere! (Please see Lindsey in Corporate to drop off your badge and your parking deck permit.)

* Barnett Tech is reviewing individual suits on a case-by-case basis, particularly those brought by customers who were allegedly holding their computers when the D7 Meister chips allegedly malfunctioned. Barnett Tech is also making a sizable donation to the National Registry for Artificial Prostheses. For any Barnett colleagues who experienced digit or limb loss due to the D7 Meister chip, we are pleased to announce that we will be distributing *free* Totes umbrellas! Available in three colors (red, black, or Barnett blue), these umbrellas are embossed with the Barnett~~Avery~~ logo as a reminder that *Barnett's always got you covered.* (Note: Supplies are limited.)

⌒

My mistake, I realize now, is that I've failed to set limits. Although I made it clear to Finn that I'm happily committed to Grant, I haven't restricted how much contact we have. Because of this, our calls have become longer and more frequent. Sometimes, too, I find myself daydreaming about him and how things were back in college, when we were both unencumbered and free.

I have to stop, I tell myself, aware that I'm in the throes of Finn fever. Instead, I agree to meet him at a restaurant on Friday afternoon. When he asked, it sounded innocent: two old friends, a glass of wine, a few laughs. But now it's almost four o'clock, and I'm falling-down drunk, not on wine, though (I had only one glass)—on Finn.

"I considered not coming today," I tell him, eating fries off his plate and then licking my fingers. "Don't you think that seeing each other in person is a bad idea?"

He doesn't respond. He's doing that silent-Injun thing, and it's driving me crazy. He's also wearing his sunglasses.

"Finn, we're inside. You can take these off." I reach for the glasses, but he grabs my hand. "What's the problem? Are you afraid of being seen with me?"

"Don't, Eliot. My eyes are sensitive to light. It's not a coolness thing, I'm getting cataracts."

"Oh." I feel foolish. "I didn't know. If it makes you feel any better, I need reading glasses already. Soon, I'll need bifocals."

Across the table, Finn squeezes my hand. "I'm an old man." He leans forward. "You're right, though. It probably is a bad idea to see each other. You know what's worse, though?"

I shake my head.

"Not seeing you. The idea of spending tomorrow and the next day and the day after that without talking to you, or worse, not looking at you, kills me. I just spent the past fifteen years without you, Eliot. There's no way I will ever do that again."

A line has been crossed, and my entire body lights up. Finn is so close, I can practically taste him. What would happen, I wonder, if he moved forward one more inch?

I sip my water. "I have car pool today." I look at my watch. Wait, where's my watch? Rubbing my naked wrist, I imagine Finn trailing his fingers along my skin, up and down my arm, and then exploring the rest of me. "I have to go soon."

Finn leans forward again, one more inch. This time I lean, too. Our foreheads touch, and I am so aroused, it's all I can do not to kiss him.

"Sorry, Eliot, but you can't get rid of me so easily. Now that we've refound each other, I'm staying." Then he grins—*oh God, that grin*—and I feel myself tingling.

"Who says I want to get rid of you?" The air between us crackles. Reaching out, Finn wipes my lip with his thumb, letting his finger rest a beat longer than he should. When he speaks, his voice is husky. "God, I love your mouth."

Another line; another crossing. This one makes me euphoric. "I love your teeth," I blurt out. "They're so white. Did you use Crest strips or trays? Or did you do that bleach-zap thing?"

I'm flying now. I'm utterly weightless and soaring through space. I'm way too high, I know that, but I don't want this feeling to end. Why would I? Finally, after all these years, after all that waiting, Finn and I are together. Just a few more minutes, and then I'll come down. But I continue to rise, and before I know it, I've slipped into Finn time and lost track of myself. Case in point: One minute it's four thirty, and the next? Across the restaurant, I catch sight of a young mother lifting her son out of his high chair when I suddenly remember that I'm a mother, too. Hocus-pocus: it's ten to six.

"Oh shit! It's almost six o'clock! Why didn't my phone ring?" Grabbing my phone, I see that it's off. "That's so weird. I never turn off my phone." *Hailey! I have to get Hailey!* "Oh, my God, Finn—I have car pool today!* I was supposed to be at school at five thirty."

Panicked, I jump up, and my knee smacks the table. The glasses shake. A saucer hits the floor and shatters. Small porcelain chips fly everywhere. "Oh shit, oh shit, oh shit!"

"What can I do?" Finn reaches into his pocket. "Should I call the school?"

Shouting, "Thank you, but no," I race out to my car, trying to balance my phone, my keys, my sunglasses. As I drive, I listen to all my messages. I have five plus two hang-ups: Miss Lulu, Grant, Phoebe, Grace, Grant again. *Ms. Gordon? It's pickup time. Did something happen? The girls are ready. The girls are waiting. The girls are worried. We're all worried. Where are you? Where are you?*

For one brief—very brief—second, I consider plowing into another car. One simple accident and this could all go away. Instead I drive on, frantic, sweaty, sick with guilt. Mascara stings my eyes, so I wipe them, which makes them sting more. My heart is racing, but my head is foggy, and I have no depth of perception. Cars are whizzing by, and I can't tell if they're right next to me or two lanes over.

"Where are you?" Grant asks when I get him on the phone.

"I forgot I had car pool. I'm on my way to Riverside."

"It's too late." Grant sounds more bewildered than angry. "Phoebe already picked up the girls. Hailey will be home in a half hour."

"Is Phoebe mad?"

"She's concerned." Grant speaks quietly and deliberately, as if I'm a mental patient. "Eliot, why didn't you call? Any one of us could've gotten the girls, but no one heard from you. Where have you been all afternoon?"

"At Emory. One minute it was four thirty and the next...I don't know...I lost an hour. My phone was off, and my watch..." My watch! It's on my nightstand! Remembering this feels like a stroke of good luck. "I forgot my watch this morning, so I had no idea what time it was. I've been out of sorts all day." I pause. "I'm so sorry, Grant. What will you do about dinner?"

"Come on, Eliot." He's exasperated. "Does it really matter at this point?"

A jackknifed truck has traffic backed up for miles, so I don't get home until almost eight. I rush inside and find Grant, Gail, and Hailey watching TV in the living room. Gail jumps up to hug me. Over her head, I glance at Grant.

"I'm so sorry. I really am."

"Don't apologize to me." He puts his hand on Hailey's shoulder.

I get down on my knees. "I'm so sorry, sweet pea," I say quietly. "I should've been there to pick you up."

"It's okay, Mommy." She holds out some pretzels, then tucks one between my lips. "I saved these for your dinner. Don't be sad." Hailey turns to Grant. "Mommy's crying," she tells him, as if our roles have reversed and she's the wife and mother. "You should help her, Daddy."

Yes, Grant nods. Mommy is crying. But he doesn't comfort me. Instead, he scoops Hailey into his arms and carries her upstairs for her bath. Nor does he respond two hours later when we're lying in bed and I apologize again. He just stares ahead at the TV, clicking through the channels. Fortunately for Grant, we have satellite TV; he can keep clicking for hours.

My watch! It's right on my nightstand, just as I said. I slide it on and buckle the clasp. Of everything that's happened today, forgetting my watch is by far the most peculiar. I've been wearing it for how long? Five years? And then to forget it, just like that?

Grant clears his throat. "What's going on with you?" He doesn't look at me, though; he doesn't even shift his eyes.

"I've had a lot on my mind."

"Oh, really? What's so important that you could forget our child at school? That you couldn't call? Eliot, I'm not upset you forgot Hailey. I'm upset because you're not making any fucking sense."

I know, Grant, I want to say. I can hold up my wrist. I've been wearing this watch every day for five years, and then one random morning I forget it? It makes no fucking sense. Instead, I tell him that the afternoon got away from me.

"Eliot, come on. You have to do better than that."

I don't want to lie. But at the same time, I know that telling Grant about Finn is a mistake. Because the Sculptress cheated on him during their marriage, he's very sensitive about the issue. To hurt him the way she did seems doubly—and unnecessarily—wrong. Nothing happened with Finn, so why reopen that wound? Finn is—he was—a harmless

I COULDN'T LOVE YOU MORE

flirtation; he doesn't mean anything. I can walk away anytime. Besides, isn't everyone entitled to something of her own, even a secret, even if she's in a committed relationship? Without personal space, we melt into each other like wet cubes of ice, dripping and dripping until we dissolve into nothing. So I tell Grant something else, something that may not be true at the moment but is certainly true in general. Unfortunately, the conversation veers off in a direction I hadn't foreseen.

"I'm concerned about my mother," is how I start. "She's complaining she doesn't feel well. At her age, she should be slowing down." I stop, unsure where to go next. "She's going to die soon." I stop again, wishing I had mapped this out first.

"What does that have to do with Hailey?"

I feel cornered. I want to protect Grant (and yes, myself, too), but I'm not clever enough to think on my feet. That's Sylvia's department. So I tell him that I was at the library and lost track of time. Trust me, I'm not proud of this, but once I get started, I can't stop. "I was doing research for my mother about different types of illnesses. She thinks... Well, she's afraid she has cancer—"

Grant cuts me off. "Your mother thinks she has *cancer?*"

"She's just going for tests. In fact, she may see the doctor on Saturday, which I know is neither here nor there, but like I said last week, a lot of doctors see patients over the weekend. Anyway, I spent the afternoon researching her symptoms, and guess I lost track of time. I mean, I *know* I did, but I didn't get any messages because I shut off my phone and forgot to turn it back on." This last part is absolutely true. I *did* shut off my phone, which now that I think about it is a lot like my watch. Why, of all days, did I forget to turn my phone back on today?

For some reason, I half expect Grant to stay angry. But he surprises me with his concern. "Eliot," he says softly, "I know you're worried, but have you considered that maybe she's being a little dramatic? I mean, did *she* say it might be cancer, or did the doctor?" He reaches for me. "I don't want to diminish your fears, but let's take a step back, okay? Tell me everything she said."

Why does this surprise me? Grant is a good man, a concerned partner, a loving father. *Of course* he'd be sympathetic. I, on the other hand, am a terrible liar and a terrible person.

"Honestly, Grant? I don't remember. Our conversation was so quick. It never occurred to me to question her, but now that you mention it, you're probably right. My family always overreacts. Remember how I thought the chicks in Hailey's classroom were dead? I went crazy! The same thing happened when my mother said 'cancer.' I lost my shit. I mean, look how scattered I've been! You said yourself I'm all over the place. Grant, *I forgot to pick up Hailey from school*. Can you believe *I* forgot *Hailey?*"

This chokes me up again. *Never again,* I resolve. *Never, ever again.* Repeating this makes me feel stronger, back in control.

I take Grant's hand. "I don't know what I was thinking. I should've told you what was happening, right from the start. You would've given me some perspective." This, too, is absolutely true. "I'm very sorry I didn't."

"So given the circumstances, do you think it's a good idea to take Hailey to the beach next week? Won't that be too much work for your mother? Maybe you should both stay here?"

I consider this. But then I have a better idea. "No, she'll be fine. In fact, I want to take Gail and Charlotte too. They can't stay with Beth since she'll be in Europe, and you have that presentation. They'll be thrilled to miss a couple of days of school." This, I decide, will be my punishment. Instead of a relaxing getaway with my sisters, I'll take all three girls to the beach and make sure they have a good time. "My mother did say she's lonely for company. So what the hell? It'll be fun."

"Then why don't I come too?"

"Because you hate the beach, Grant. Besides, what about the Nike guys?"

"They'll be gone by Friday. I can fly down that night and spend the weekend with you. This way, we can drive back together on Monday."

His kindness breaks my heart. "That sounds great, Grant. It'll be nice for all five of us to go away together."

~

"So everything's okay at home?" Finn asks. It's Monday morning after drop-off, and we're in the parking lot at Riverside. "I was worried when I didn't hear from you."

"Everything's fine. I've just been busy."

We haven't spoken since our coffee date. Although I had a lot to do over the weekend, I also made a concerted effort to cut down our contact. The only reason I agreed to meet him today was that I was going to be here anyway, having offered to drive car pool for Phoebe since she stepped in for me last Friday. "It's the least I can do," I told her after apologizing profusely.

"Walk with me," Finn is saying now. "Walk with me, talk with me, tell me what's new."

"I don't have time." I check my watch, which is right on my wrist. A small thing, but still . . . order has been restored. "I have to go to my office today."

Finn is pulling my arm. "Come on, Eliot. You can't spare ten minutes?"

"Ten minutes," I tell him. "But that's all I have—not one second more."

He leads me down the road toward the chapel. The Sculptress has started outlining her mural; two sides are shrouded in a dark green tarp. According to Phoebe, Beth shared preliminary sketches with the renovations committee. "At first we were skeptical," Phoebe told me, "but she assured us the final product will be stunning. It's certainly . . . um . . . *unusual*."

As Finn and I get closer, I see several cans of paint, a ladder, and two pairs of workman's coveralls scattered around, but there isn't a soul here.

"I love this church," I say. "I'm not really a church person, but there's something special about this one. Don't you think?"

Finn doesn't answer. Instead he asks, "You're leaving for Wyatt Island on Thursday? It's in South Carolina, right? I've been to Hilton Head a couple times, but never Wyatt."

My pulse quickens. "You should see it...I mean, at least once."

"I could meet you there." He pauses. "If you want me to, I mean."

I pretend to study the mural. So far, the Sculptress has outlined three figures, but I can't tell what they are. Trees, maybe? Naked women? Naked men?

"Grant's ex-wife is painting this mural." As I say this, I stumble over the ladder.

Finn catches my arm. "The Sculptress?"

"You remember her name?"

"You don't think I listen, but I do. Why do you still doubt me, Eliot?"

"I don't mean to." Yes, I think. Meet me at Wyatt Island; yes, yes, yes.

Inside the chapel, it's chilly but peaceful. We stand in the back, listening to the quiet. I hear a car pull up outside and then a couple of voices, but they're muffled.

"I'd love for you to come to Wyatt Island," I say as if to acknowledge the voices. "But you can't." This is a public place, so I'm making my position public. "Seeing each other is a bad idea for both of us. We have to stop."

"I know, Eliot," Finn says, but I'm not sure which statement he's referring to.

We walk slowly down the aisle together. When we get to the altar, Finn suddenly drops to one knee. He holds out his hand. "Do you, Eliot, take me, Finn, to—"

"Finn, don't play around." My voice echoes in the cavernous sanctuary.

"Do you, Eliot, take me, Finn, to have and to hold, in sickness and in health, for blah blah blah as long as we both shall live?" He stares at me a few seconds, waiting.

Taking his hand and blinking back tears, I nod.

Finn is crying, too. He's quiet about it, but still, the tears are there. "I'm sorry, Eliot." He stands up. "I never meant to hurt you. I was just dumb and selfish."

"It's okay." I close my eyes. At that moment, there's only him, only Finn; twenty years of his voice in my ear, his breath on my neck. I can feel him moving closer, leaning in. *One more—*

"Eliot?" Someone is calling my name. I hear it again; this time it's shouted. *"Eliot!"*

Startled, I open my eyes. Standing there, wearing too-tight jeans and her favorite Ugg boots, is my stepdaughter, my Charlotte. Seeing her, I drop Finn's hand.

"What are you doing here?" she demands, but she's not looking at me, she's looking at Finn.

"Uh, hi there." Confused, Finn glances at me. "Can we help you?"

Charlotte walks toward us but then stops short, as if ordered to halt. In her hand, she holds a paintbrush, high, like a torch, or in this case a weapon.

I'm still too stunned to speak, so Finn continues. "We were just leaving." He tries to steer me back up the aisle, toward the door.

"Eliot," Charlotte says flatly, just like that: *Eliot.* It's only my name, but the way she says it fills me with despair.

"Finn! Finn, this is Charlotte—Charlotte Delaney—my elder stepdaughter."

He slows down, backtracks. "Oh, hi, Charlotte. It's great to finally meet you. I've heard a lot about you." But then he pulls my hand again, harder this time. "Eliot, we should go."

Seeing him nudge me away, Charlotte looks stricken. *You're leaving? Who is this guy?* She and I stare, first at Finn, then at each other. She has her father's eyes, I notice. Those dark brown eyes; they're Grant's. Gail has them, too. All my girls do.

"I have to get to work," Finn insists. "And so do you. Ten minutes, remember?"

Is he serious? "I can't just leave, Finn." Is he pretending not to understand, or does he really not get it? Charlotte is a child; she's *my* child. I thought I made that clear. I would never abandon my child, even for him.

Charlotte is still watching us, waiting to see what I'll do next. Shamed by how young and fearful she seems, I suddenly realize I can't see Finn anymore. Charlotte's trust in me and her faith that I will always protect her is too important to gamble and, ultimately, more important than he is. *This*, I understand, is the moment when our relationship ends. *This* is the final good-bye. But first I have to take care of my child.

Fully recovered, I turn away from Finn and leave him standing alone at the altar. Then I hustle up the aisle toward Charlotte. "Hey, kiddo." Touching her shoulder, I'm calm and composed, a perfect example of motherly confidence. "Come meet Finn. He's an old friend from college. His daughter goes to school here. Her name is Humphrey, and she's seven."

"Humphrey's a girl?" Charlotte asks.

"She's eight." Finn comes up behind me. "Humphrey is eight."

Flashing him a fuck-you look, she turns back to me. "What are you doing here?"

"I was showing Finn your mother's mural."

"The mural is *outside*, Eliot."

"Do you go to school here, Charlotte?" Finn asks, flashing his famous smile. Although I see the charisma that used to stop women in their tracks, Charlotte is left unfazed.

"No, my *half-sister* does." She glances at me; she knows I dislike that expression. Hailey is your *sister*, I tell her. You don't love her half as much, do you? "I go to Pierce High School. Pierce has the best arts program in Atlanta. I'm a painter like Mom."

"Eliot told me about your mother's mural. We were about to go see it."

"Mom got a million dollars to paint it. It's pretty different from her usual work—she's, like, a hard-core feminist—but she said for that kind of money, she'd be willing to paint anything, even some guy's dick!" Charlotte laughs, but it sounds more like a sob than actual laughter.

I flinch. "You're sure it was a million dollars?"

"That's a lot of money, Charlotte," Finn adds.

Charlotte shrugs as if to say, *What the fuck do you know about it?*

It occurs to me that Charlotte shouldn't be here. "Why aren't you in school?"

"Mom's friend Jacinda asked me to help stretch canvases for this new installation she's working on. Mom said it was okay to skip today, so she picked me up before first period. She was gonna call you and Dad, but I guess she got busy. I can get credit for doing it, if you're so worried about me missing class. And also? Mom's leaving for Italy to study with this painter, so she wanted some alone time with me. He's really famous, and only accepts, like, *one* out of every, like, *twenty thousand* people, so she can't pass up the opportunity."

"That's exciting," I say, completely bewildered. "Tell your mom congratulations for me."

Charlotte shrugs. "Tell her yourself. She'll be back in five minutes from the paint store."

"She's *here?*"

"In five minutes, I said," Charlotte snaps.

Finn clears his throat. "I'm late for work." He holds up a hand. "Well, nice meeting you, Charlotte." He turns to me. "You're staying?" His tone is clipped.

"I want to say hello to Beth."

"Okay, then..." Finn stands for a beat, as if awaiting further direction, but then quickly, almost comically, sprints up the aisle and out of the church.

"Tell Parker we'd love to come over," I call out behind him. "Parker is his wife," I explain to Charlotte. "She wants the whole family to come for dinner. Isn't that nice?"

"I don't know." She glances toward the door, as if unsure whether she should wait for her mother outside or stay in here with me.

"Finn is an old friend. It was funny bumping into him. There's a chapel at Emory that's exactly like this one, which is why we were in here."

"Uh-huh." Charlotte's face is blank. And when her mother appears a few minutes later, neither of us mentions Finn, nor do we bring him up the next day, the day after that, or any other day. I do call Grant on my way to the office and tell him I ran into Charlotte and the Sculptress, and how weird it was, but he's preparing for his Nike meeting and isn't paying attention. On Wednesday night, I make one more reference to Finn—to Charlotte, in passing—but other than that, it's as though the incident—indeed, the past few weeks—never even happened.

Chapter Fifteen

WYATT ISLAND is a tiny beach town off the coast of South Carolina. It's close to Hilton Head—ten minutes by boat, twenty by car—but not nearly as well-known. Wyatt, like Hilton Head, is called an island, but it's actually a peninsula that juts out off the southeastern tip of the state. Also like Hilton Head, it used to be a sleepy mecca for rich southern golfers, a best-kept secret that has since exploded with year-round residents and jacked-up real estate.

I've been coming to Wyatt Island since I was a teenager. After we moved to Atlanta, my mother, sisters, and I vacationed here every year with my aunt Barbara until she got too sick to travel. We always came in late September when tourist season ends and prices fall. We'd miss a week of school, but no one cared—my sisters and I least of all.

Every year, my mother would load up the car in the morning and drive the six hours from our house in Atlanta to a rented scenic-view condo, where we'd spend a week swimming, watching TV, and eating fried seafood. We did this for several years, but I don't remember the vacations themselves; rather, no single week stands out more than any other. However, I do have vivid memories of all the hours we spent on the road driving there and back, with Sylvia providing comic relief. She'd flash her boobs at church buses, taunt truck drivers with "You're So Gay!" signs, hang her ass out the window—anything to amuse us. Once she made a sign that said, "Help! Kidnapped!" and a passing motorist called 911. The state troopers caught up with us and spent twenty minutes questioning my mother. "I'd consider an ass whuppin', ma'am," one trooper suggested, a comment Sylvia still loves to repeat.

Because my sisters and I had so many laughs together, I'm upset that my own girls are having such a lousy time. "Mommy?" Hailey calls out from the back where she's strapped in next to Gail. "When will we be there?"

"Soon, sweet pea." This is the third time she's asked, and we set off only fifteen minutes ago.

A few minutes pass. I don't hear a sound from the back. At first it's pleasant, but soon I get concerned. I glance at Hailey in the rearview mirror. Seeing me, she waves, coughs, moans, coughs again, and then vomits all over herself.

"Mommy!" Hailey bursts into tears. "I threw up. I threw up all over Molly!" Molly, the latest addition to our family, is Hailey's new American Girl doll.

"Gail, what's going on back there?" I try to turn around, but traffic is moving too fast.

"It's *not* vomit," Gail reports. "More like spit-up. But *oh, my God*, she stinks!" Holding her hand over her mouth, she rolls down her window and takes dramatic gulps of air.

Beside her, Hailey is hysterical. "I don't *stink*! *You* stink, not me."

"Calm down, Hailey." I reach for the paper towels and nudge Charlotte beside me. "Please, Charlotte, help your sisters. Hailey, I said *calm down*!"

"Huh?" Charlotte is listening to music. She lifts one earbud. "Did you say something?" When I hand her the paper towel, she uses it to blow her nose.

I was really looking forward to this trip. It was supposed to be my fresh start, my open-road adventure. "Isn't this fun?" I ask, but my question elicits no response. No, wait—Hailey's speaking.

"When will we be there?" she wants to know.

All week, I was optimistic. I envisioned the four of us singing songs,

telling jokes, sharing our hopes, dreams, and desires—all the things I
did with my sisters on this very road, making this very trip. But here
we are, less than a half hour in, and Hailey is covered in vomit, Gail
is nauseated, and Charlotte—poor, caught-in-the-middle Charlotte—
is on the phone with the Sculptress, giving me disdainful glances and
whispering so furtively, she could be selling nuclear launch codes.

Five and a half hours left to go, and each one of us is miserable.

"Mommy! Mommy, guess what? Mommy, I peed!"

⌒

Until today, this trip, this moment, I was perfectly fine. Although I
have had twinges of sorrow, once I made the decision to stop seeing
Finn, I instantly felt better. My life, I exhaled, was my own again. I was
so sure it was the right thing to do, I acted immediately: on that same
morning, minutes after Finn raced out of the chapel, I left him a message.

"I can't speak to you anymore," I said firmly. "I know this is abrupt,
but our relationship is too confusing for me. Grant and the girls are
my whole life, Finn, just like Parker and Humphrey are yours. I can't
do anything to hurt them, or myself, and I know you feel the same.
I'm sorry, but deep down you know this is the right choice, our only
choice."

He tried to reach me several times, but I didn't call him back—not
once. Instead, I wrote him an e-mail explaining my reasons: my commitment to Grant, my love for my children, how fulfilled I am in my
life. "I have everything I need, everything I've always wanted." I also
made it clear that he should refrain from calling me again. "A clean
break," I stressed, "is best."

Over the next few days, I doted on my family. Relishing my new-
found freedom, I packed for our trip, treated the older girls to mani-
cures, saw a movie with Grant, and played Polly Pockets with Hailey.
For the first time in weeks, I could focus, and in doing so, I realized

how much I'd missed—not major life events, of course, but the small, day-to-day details. Hailey, it turned out, could almost write her name. Gail was studying autobiographies and wanted my mother to speak to her class. Charlotte was failing algebra and barely passing English. ("English!" I was incredulous. "But that's your native tongue.") And Grant? Well, Grant was consumed with his Nike ad, but he did say I seemed less distracted. Which is true: I am less distracted and glad—and grateful—to be back.

Now, as we reach Dublin, Georgia—our halfway mark—it hits me: I almost screwed up my family. What the hell was I thinking? *I could've lost everything.* I take a deep breath. Don't get dramatic, I tell myself. You didn't lose anything. You walked away before anything happened.

I glance at Gail and Hailey, happy they're here. Charlotte, too. This weekend will be fun. My sisters and I will sit up late, I'll tell them about the bullet I dodged, and Sylvia will make fun of Finn's gnomes. I don't care that I still have hours of driving left or that we're replaying (over and over) *The Sound of Music* sound track, or that the kids won't stop fighting over the Game Boy. I don't even care that Charlotte is barely speaking to me, although I do try to parse from her clipped responses what, if anything, she saw in the chapel and how much, if anything, she plans to share with her father.

"So, Charlotte," I ask winningly, "did your mother leave for Italy on time?"

"What?" She lifts an earbud.

"I asked about your mom's trip. Didn't she leave yesterday?"

"Mom didn't go. The plane ticket was too expensive." She turns to the window, where there's nothing to see except a few billboards and mile after mile of uncultivated land.

"That's too bad. I thought she got a lot of money for painting the mural."

"She *did*, Eliot, but it's for *living expenses*, not for *plane tickets* to *Roma*." She trills her tongue as she says this, which shouldn't strike me as funny but does.

I wait a few minutes, then say, "Wasn't it weird that I bumped into you and my old friend on the same morning? Remember, at the chapel?" I nudge her. "Charlotte, I'm talking to you."

She turns in her seat. "What?"

"I just said how strange it was to bump into you and Finn on the same day. I hadn't seen him in, like, fifteen years, and boom, there he is, and boom, there you are."

"Not that strange if he's your friend." Fiddling with her iPod, she slumps back in her seat.

I correct her, but she's not listening, so I speak to the empty air. "Finn isn't my friend, Charlotte. I hadn't seen him in years. We lost touch. That's what makes it so strange." I glance at her, but she's turned back to the window with her headphones on, staring vacantly at nothing. Even from behind, I can see how unhappy she is.

"You can always talk to me. I know you feel lousy. And I'm sorry about that. I wish I could make things different." Then I add, "I love you," just in case she's only pretending she can't hear me.

Charlotte doesn't respond. Inside the car, the silence is deafening. Outside, the long, desolate highway rolls on and on.

⌒

When I finally see signs directing us to Wyatt, I get misty-eyed. It's a relief to be so close. The main road is busy but not impossibly backed up. It's the end of September, and most of the tourists left weeks ago. As we drive through the island, I'm filled with both nostalgia and hope.

I find the rental house and pull into the driveway. My mother rushes out to welcome us. "Did you have a good trip?" She leans into the car to look at the girls, all of whom are sleeping.

I stand up and stretch. "A new day has dawned."

"What's that supposed to mean?"

"I'll tell you all about it this weekend."

We move inside, dragging suitcases and backpacks. In the living room, my mother pulls me aside and points to Sylvia, who's lying on the couch, watching TV. "Your sister hasn't moved from that spot in three days," she tells me.

Sylvia rubs her belly. "I heard that, Dolores. The doctor said to stay off my feet." She sits up clumsily, as if she's nine months pregnant, even though she's only six weeks gone. "You were there, Eliot. Tell Dolores what he said. She won't believe me, but she'll certainly believe you."

"That's your hello?"

"Tell her," Sylvia insists.

Maggie is on the floor, eating strawberry ice cream. "I heard the doctor, too, Sylvia." She passes the bowl to her so she can have a bite. "He also told you to get some exercise."

"If I'm *up to it*. And for your information, Dr. Seuss, I'm spotting again. Only this time, it's blood *clots*. The doctor said if I see *any blood at all*, I have to lie *flat* on my back. I'm also in *excruciating* pain. It started this morning, but I didn't tell anyone because I didn't want to make a big deal out of it."

"So what made you change your mind?" Maggie asks.

"You are so *rude*," Sylvia snaps.

Watching them, I smile.

Alone in the kitchen, Maggie tells me that Sylvia went running earlier in the evening. "Don't believe a word she says. She's only in pain when it's time to make dinner."

The girls are exploring the house, and I round them up to get ready for bed. Hailey and Gail don't complain, but Charlotte refuses.

"It's only, like, ten thirty." She's looking at her phone, sending a text. "I'm *fourteen*."

Watching her thumbs twitch reminds me that I have to call Grant and tell him we made it, but first my mother wants to discuss climate conditions. "Eliot, if you're planning to go to the beach tomorrow, you should expect to finish up by noon. The mornings have been fairly mild, but we're getting weather in the afternoons from Cuba—not much rain, but the winds are ferocious."

I remember she came here to write a new book. Because I've been preoccupied, I have no idea how it's going. "How's work?"

She's cryptic. All she'll tell me is that it's been "interesting."

"I want to hear all about it," I say, indicating that I'm here now and ready to make everything right.

Charlotte is still hung up on her bedtime. "It's *too* early. I'm not a *child*!"

She sounds exactly like her mother, and every time I look at her, I see the Sculptress. Charlotte isn't the Sculptress, though. Charlotte is Charlotte, and she *is* just a child.

"That's fine. You can stay up as late as you want." I smile wide to show my sincerity. "You're on vacation, too."

Hailey and Gail are gazing at the TV in a sleepy stupor. All week, I've been lavishing them both with long, tight hugs. Tonight is no different. I grab Hailey and crush her against me. "I love you," I say.

"I love you, too, Mommy." Hailey adores the attention and gives me kisses and more kisses. My mother wants in on the action. She takes Hailey from my arms and hugs her, too.

"Tomorrow, we're going to buy everyone new outfits," my mother announces. She looks at Gail and Charlotte. "Your grandma plans to clean out the stores."

I can see she is expecting me to chastise her for spoiling them, but I don't. Let her indulge them; let them indulge her. *We all need someone to lean on.* Tonight, I'm filled with platitudes: *Hang in there, baby. This too shall pass. 'Tis better to have loved and lost. You're once, twice, three times a lady.*

Because it's off-season, my mother got a great deal on the house, which has six bedrooms, three bathrooms, a working fireplace, and an enormous backyard with a two-tiered deck. The ocean, which is a three-minute walk, is hidden behind a dense row of trees, but when we slide open the glass doors, we hear the waves crashing on the sand. The sound is so loud, it's as though the water is right on the property.

I go through the house, opening all the windows. The beach air wafts in, humid and salty. I hold the fresh air in my lungs before exhaling. I feel a weight being lifted, a clenching released.

My mother says the girls can see the ocean, but I overrule her. "Tomorrow," I promise. "It's too late tonight." I pull pajamas out of suitcases and fling tops and bottoms into the air. Gail catches hers, but Hailey's land on her head, which makes us laugh.

"Look at me!" Hailey shouts. "I'm a ghost. Boo, you guys!"

The house is owned by a rich retiree who lives half the year in Connecticut. "He's a snowbird," my mother explains as we walk down the hall. "He owns a mansion in Greenwich that has fourteen bedrooms and eight bathrooms. It's family money, which a lot of people tend to have in Greenwich. His grandfather made a killing in Houston. Oil money, if I remember correctly. After that, he moved the whole clan from Texas to Greenwich, where they've been ever since."

I don't know whom she's trying to impress, because I'm grabbing sheets from a linen closet and clearly not listening. But I whirl around and see Charlotte is standing there, enraptured.

"It's not only Wall Street money in Greenwich. It's oil money, too."

My mother keeps repeating "Greenwich" the same way I repeated "Finn," as though it's a secret word, a dirty word, and titillating to say out loud. I hate that she's become this way: deferential and humbled, in awe of rich people's ways. She's going to talk about money all weekend, I realize, and I vow not to let it bother me. *Money doesn't equal happiness,* I'll say. *Let me tell you a story . . .*

The rich oilman's bedrooms are divided up: My mother has one, Maggie has one, Grant and I get the third, Hailey and Gail will share the fourth, and Charlotte can have her own room, a small study, in the back. "Sylvia and Roger," my mother says, "can take the sixth."

"*Roger's* coming?" I blurt out.

"He's my *husband*," Sylvia says from her perch on the couch. "*Of course* he's coming."

My sister always invites people without telling us. It used to be girlfriends to dinner, then boyfriends to the movies, and now it's a husband to our sisters-only weekend. Grant's coming, too, but that's not the point. Sylvia's people are always larger than life; when she's around them, she gets boisterous and aggressive—rather, more boisterous and aggressive than she already is. Although I like Roger a lot, again, that's not the point. "Why didn't you tell me?"

"Why does it matter?"

I don't have an answer because it doesn't. I change my tune. "That'll be nice."

"So listen," Sylvia says. "Dolores offered to watch the kids for a few hours tomorrow. Then you and I could go shopping."

"I want to go shopping, too!" Maggie calls out.

It always strikes me as odd how every time we come here, Maggie and Sylvia are anxious to go shopping. We live in Atlanta, where there are thousands of brand-name stores, but when we're at the beach, all they want to do is troll through the mom-and-pop tourist traps. They don't even go to the outlet malls near Hilton Head. They confine themselves to the T-shirt and shot-glass shops in "downtown" Wyatt.

I help the girls get ready for bed, and then, after all the hours on the road, after the Waffle House and McDonald's, after the vomit and the pee, I can lie in bed and relax, relieved to finally be here.

Chapter Sixteen

THAT IT IS really, truly over with Finn hits me hard on Friday morning. I don't regret my decision—I know I did the right thing—but the past few weeks of pent-up emotion have taken their toll, and when I wake up I feel like a hormonal teenager, vacillating between anger and sorrow. Nor are my mother and sisters helping the situation—Sylvia is being lazy and demanding, Maggie won't get off the phone, and my mother is calculating the net worth of everyone she knows. Although I have renewed sympathy for Charlotte and her adolescent moodiness, I'm a mess, bitching at everyone and then choking back tears. I know it will pass, but I'm ashamed to be my age and feeling so out of control.

Luckily, by midmorning I'm finished with anger and settled squarely in sorrow. Actually, it's worse than that: sick of myself and ashamed of my shame, I plunge into despair. I well up at the sight of my mother's smudged, gogglelike glasses and the old-lady way she licks butter off a knife. Historic footage of a bloated, battered Jerry Lewis on *Access Hollywood* fills me with anguish. All those magnificent telethons, I think, and to end up like that?

"What's *wrong* with you?" Sylvia asks from the couch, which has become her territory. Even the kids know it.

"That's Aunt Sylvia's place!" Hailey shrieks whenever I try to sit down.

On the floor beside her, I point to the TV. A team of heavyset women are doing the Macarena on a talk show. "Look at them." I'm crying openly. "There's so much discrimination in the world, especially against obesity." I blow my nose. "Oh, my God, it's just so sad."

"They're fat people dancing!" Sylvia barks. "They're perfectly happy. Is this the new face of menopause?"

I want to explain why I'm like this, but it's neither the time nor the place. Instead, I try to distract myself with a book. But just as I'm about to start a novel I've wanted to read for months, Gail has a few questions.

"Eliot? Who invented the word *soup*? And why is it called *soup*, anyway, and not, like, *fork* or *battery*? Why don't we say, *I'd like some battery and crackers, please?*"

"I don't know, Gail." I turn a page. "We just don't."

"But who were the first people to say, 'That stuff should be called *soup*'? There had to be someone, right? Or a group of people?"

"That's a good question for Daddy." Having lost my place, I flip back. It was your stupid idea to bring all the kids, I remind myself. What did you expect?

"Dead Eye Peter, this weird kid in our class, says he hung upside down on the jungle gym for two hours. All the blood rushed to his head, and his eyeball almost burst in his socket. We used to call him Dead Peter, and now he's Dead Eye Peter. People are weird, aren't they? Weird but cool. Did you notice how many times I said the word *weird*? *Weird* is my word of the day."

"Holy shit," Sylvia hisses in my ear. "Does that kid ever shut up?"

This pisses me off. "Leave her alone. She's only seven."

Later, I lash out at poor Grant. When he calls at two to tell me he's decided not to come until tomorrow, and by the way, his ticket costs five hundred bucks, I snap.

"Five hundred dollars to fly to Savannah? Grant, that's crazy! Did you look at flights to Charleston?"

"Wyatt is much closer to Savannah than Charleston. The flights are cheaper, but not by much."

"But five hundred dollars is ridiculous."

"You *told* me to fly, Eliot. You also told me not to worry about the money."

"What I *told* you, Grant, was to buy the ticket *last week* when it was a *third* of the price."

"I was *busy* last week trying to get all my shit done so *you* could go away."

This is the third argument we've had today. We've been bickering, not like spouses, but like siblings; and every fight is my fault.

"Why are you so angry?" Grant asks. "It's just money."

"It's not 'just money.' It's five hundred dollars, plus a rental car. And now you're not coming until tomorrow? We had a *plan*, Grant, and you *changed* it."

"What's the difference when I come?"

There is no difference. So why am I begging him to fly down earlier when I don't want him here at all? Nor do I want the kids here. I don't even want to be here myself. The rich man's house has six hundred bedrooms and three hundred bathrooms, and I still can't find anywhere to sit. I roam from room to room, trying to get comfortable.

"I'll get there by two," Grant promises. "I miss you, Eliot."

This chokes me up. "I don't know why I'm being so difficult, Grant. I don't mean anything by it. It's not your fault. It's me. I'm really sorry."

"How's your mother?" he asks, and at first I have no idea what he's talking about. Then I remember she's afraid she has cancer. "Oh, she's much better."

"Has she been to the doctor yet?"

"She decided to wait until after we leave."

"But she's feeling okay?"

I just said yes—yes, yes, yes! "She's fine. But don't bring it up, okay? Let's pretend she never said anything." I tell him I have to go. "Have a safe flight. I love you," I add.

I walk into the living room, where Sylvia is still on the couch. The way she clicks through the TV channels reminds me of Grant. *I'm sorry,*

I tell him telepathically. *I'll make it up to you when you get here.* "I'm tak-ing the girls to the beach." I shove towels into a bag. "Want to come?"

"I'm busy."

"Oh. I thought you were just lying there, watching television." I shove more things in the bag: sunscreen, water, pretzels, sunglasses, Hailey's Snow White underwear, hats, more water. Taking three kids to the beach is like packing for six months at Yale or, in our case, clown college. More towels, zinc oxide, a pail and shovel, a sand sifter, a wa-terwheel, a Frisbee.

"Why are you being so mean?" Sylvia wants to know. "Did you for-get I'm pregnant?"

"They're just a lot of work," I reply, referring to her nieces, not one of whom she's spoken to since we walked in last night. Glancing at her, I notice her ears. "Those are *my* earrings, Sylvia!" I can't believe she's had them since Hailey's party! "They're *my* diamonds."

"Relax." She's focused on the TV. "I said I'd give them back."

I walk over to the glass doors to watch Gail and Hailey. They're out-side on the rich oilman's deck, filling up water balloons and throwing them into the rock garden below. Every time one bursts, they howl with laughter. Seeing them together, drenched and having fun, makes me feel better.

Hailey slides open the door. "We had a water balloon fight." She flings her wet body against me. I hug her tight until I'm wet, too.

I throw another pair of shorts into the bag, as well as three oranges, three apples, a couple of plums, bags of pretzels and Gold-fish, apple juice. I consider making sandwiches but then don't, deciding to buy something on the beach. It'll be a treat, something to look forward to. This is how I break up my day, by events yet to come: my first iced coffee, a hot dog on the beach, salty fries with ketchup.

Charlotte walks into the living room, still wearing her night-shirt. Her eyes are ringed with makeup, which means she didn't wash her face last night the way I asked her to. "I don't feel like going to the beach. Grandma said I could work on her computer. She gets the Internet here."

I must look skeptical because she tries to convince me. "It's true. Mom already sent me, like, three e-mails. And there are things online that I need to check out."

We're very tense with each other, tenser in this gigantic house than we were side by side in the car when there was nothing between us but air.

"Do what you want, Charlotte." I kneel down to help Hailey buckle her sandals. "Gail, you too. Put your flip-flops on. We're going to the beach."

⌒

Outside, in the sun, I start to unwind. Hailey and Gail play together for hours, building sand castles and forts. I hover over them, watching their every move. Other mothers read or talk on the phone, but I'm too anxious. Hailey loves the ocean, but she's afraid of the waves and won't go in unless I carry her. Gail's a good swimmer, but she's only seven. When she runs into the water, I demand she stay close. I'm a nervous pain in the ass, there's no denying that, but late in the afternoon, the sky grows overcast and the wind picks up, so I feel I'm justified.

The day wears on. I'm not relaxed—how could I be; every few minutes, I have to jump up, apply sunscreen, fix a strap, get some snacks— but my mood has definitely improved.

"Remember that storm off Cuba?" my mother asks. It's around four, and she's trundled down from the house to see what we're up to. "Now they're saying it might blow over." She motions toward the girls. "I can watch them if you want to do something else."

I tell her thanks, but it's okay. "I like being here with them."

"You don't trust me, do you?"

"Of course I trust you, Mom." But there's this: Two years ago, Hailey and I spent a weekend with my mother at the Hilton Head Marriott.

Hailey was only two; so rather than trudge down to the beach, we paddled around in the kiddie pool. At one point, I had to go to the ladies' room and was telling Hailey to get out when my mother offered to watch her. The pool was so shallow, I didn't think twice about it. But when I turned to say good-bye, I spotted my mother talking on the phone and Hailey, facedown in the water, struggling to stand up.

"Mom, LOOK! Hailey's drowning!"

"You have to watch them every second," I say to her now, starting to panic all over again as I remember the horror in my mother's eyes. Unbeknownst to us, a poorly placed vent had sucked Hailey under the surface, and she was too small to right herself. I jumped in and grabbed her, so she was perfectly fine, but thinking about that moment still fills me with terror.

"I know you have to watch them," my mother snaps, tired of my self-righteousness, my sanctimoniousness, my unrelenting compulsion to do the right thing. She's got to be sick of me because I'm sick of myself. "Believe it or not, Eliot, I raised three kids on my own. I may be an idiot, but somehow I managed."

"You're right," I say, acknowledging this. "I'm sorry. I didn't mean it like that."

"What's wrong with you?" she asks, not unkindly.

"I don't know—just tired, I guess."

The afternoon sun is gone and the air is cool. I put sweatshirts on the girls and hand my mom an extra hoodie. Hugging my knees, I bury my feet under the still-warm sand. The waves are high, and the sound of them crashing again and again comforts me. "It might rain." I squint up at the sky.

My mother shakes her head, then tells me all the reasons why it won't.

As she talks, I stare out at the ocean. "I'm going for a swim. Can you watch the girls?"

I offer this to apologize for my unhappiness, my unpleasantness, my complete lack of interest in everything she says. We're both pleased by my change of heart.

I race out and dive in, the bracing cold a welcome shock to my lousy mood. The current is strong, and I'm rocked vigorously back and forth. It's scary, actually, how fast the water moves. I start to swim, fighting the pull, which is unyielding—in some places dangerously so. Out here, though, I feel alive, powerful, and in control. The water isn't so frigid anymore, and I cut through it quickly. Soon I'm out too far, so I stop and catch my breath. The rush in my head is exhilarating; my heart pounds, hard, in my chest.

I'm okay, I realize. *I will live through this.* I love it out here in the water, so why don't I swim more often? I claim there's no time, but of course there's time, especially when it makes me feel so good. I swear that when I get back to Atlanta I'll start swimming again—three times a week, no excuses.

I paddle back to shore slowly, and my mother and my girls get closer. Lined up in order of age, my mother, Gail, and Hailey spot me all at once and start jumping up and down. Gail and Hailey do a clumsy tango, then my mother cuts in. Alone, Hailey twirls around and around. The wind whips her faster and faster until she collapses on the sand.

Treading water, I lift my head up and shout, *"I love you guys!"* giddy with relief. After all that confusion, I'm clear as crystal: I love my girls; I've done the right thing, the only thing. They are the reason, what matters most. My feet scrape the bottom, and I realize it's not deep at all. I can stand where I am just fine.

Chapter Seventeen

THE NEXT MORNING, Sylvia announces that she's still bleeding—only now it's *really bad*. Once again she's on the couch, watching *The View*. Staring at the TV, she asks, "What do you think this means, Eliot?"

That she could be having complications is concerning, but I'm not sure how serious to take this. Whereas most pregnant women race to the hospital at the first hint of blood, Sylvia is waiting to see a segment on preventing shower stall mildew before she makes any moves. Then again, I'm still glowing from my swim yesterday, so I feel pretty optimistic about everything.

"Sylvia, if you're worried, why don't you call the doctor?"

Behind my sister's head, my mother raises her eyebrows. "If Sylvia is bleeding," she says, starting to get worked up, "then she should absolutely call the doctor." Although it's obvious my mother doesn't really believe that Sylvia is in danger, she's also afraid not to.

Sylvia holds her stomach and moans deeply. "I feel like I'm *dying* here."

Walking into the kitchen, Maggie says she has to go to Target. "I promised Hailey I'd give her a manicure, but I don't have any nail polish."

Sylvia perks up. "I want to go to Target, too."

"I thought you were *dying*," my mother fires off.

"I still need *maxi pads*, Dolores. How else will I absorb the *pints* of *blood* gushing out of my body?"

My mother turns to me. "Why won't she call the doctor?" she asks, as if this is the only problem, the one thing that makes no sense.

"Maybe I'll go to Target, too," I say offhandedly.

This precipitates a discussion about who will go to Target and who will stay behind that could rival the Allied preparations for invading Normandy in complexity and consequence.

"I have to work," my mother reminds me. "I won't be able to watch the kids."

"Can't Charlotte watch them?" Sylvia asks.

She could watch them, sure, but whether she will or not—and whether I'm comfortable with it—is kicked around for the next ten minutes. I need to go to the bathroom, but our debate about Charlotte's babysitting prowess is far too gripping. As we're talking, Charlotte saunters into the room. As soon as she hears about the Target excursion, she wants to go, which of course causes me to rethink my decision. She's locked herself in her room since yesterday, and my tenderness toward her is waning.

"You guys go," I tell my sisters. "You take Charlotte and I'll stay here with Hailey and Gail. This way Mom can do her work."

"But we want *you* to come too," both my sisters crow, as if there's something magical happening at Target that we all have to experience together.

"It's okay, Eliot," my mother says in a tone that suggests she's offering me her only kidney. "I don't mind staying at home with the children."

I take her up on this, deciding that once we're in Target, strolling up and down aisles filled with ketchup, tube socks, duct tape, and double A batteries, I'll tell my sisters all about Finn. Suddenly, I can't wait to get the story out. My only problem, at this point, is Charlotte. How can I talk if she's there? Once again I want to duck out of the trip, but it's too late, I'm committed.

"Who's driving?" Charlotte asks expectantly, as if we might choose her. She's also talking on her cell phone, which, now that I look closer,

I see she's bedazzled with colored rhinestones that sparkle when they catch the light. "I call shotgun!" she shouts, and then, when she sees me staring at the phone, says dramatically, "Mom, I have to call you back."

"You can sit in the back," I say firmly. "I'm driving."

There's a reason my sisters wanted to get me alone, I find out. "We have something for you," Maggie says as she guides me to her car. She opens the trunk and takes out a big box. "We thought you might like to have this."

"You have *no idea* how much trouble we had getting it," Sylvia adds.

"What kind of trouble?" I ask, but then I see what it is. My sisters have gifted me with a used garden gnome. Although muddy and crusted with leaves and pebbles, it's perfectly intact.

"Why would she want *that*?" Charlotte asks.

"Why *wouldn't* she?" Sylvia counters. "Eliot, we got this as a reminder that some people, who shall remain nameless, have disgusting taste, and should be avoided at all cost. Speaking of which, is there anything you'd like to share with the group?"

"There is, as a matter of fact." I glance at Charlotte. "But not right now."

A few minutes later, we're pulling out of the driveway. In the back, Charlotte is once again calling the Sculptress. It's excruciating, the way that poor kid has to work so hard for her mother's attention. On the other hand, would it kill her to put down the phone for a minute?

"So is Mom getting any real work done here?" I ask my sisters.

Next to Charlotte, Maggie nods. "She has fifty pages of a new novel. I'm surprised she didn't tell you."

"I didn't ask." I'm annoyed that she is the youngest daughter and knows this, whereas I am the eldest and don't. "What's it about?"

Beside me, Sylvia is making gagging sounds. "It's the story of a crabby, middle-aged woman who never learned how to drive. Jesus, Eliot. Take your foot off the fucking brake!"

For some reason, this prompts Maggie to ask about Barney. "Do you ever wonder what Dad is doing? Like if he ever thinks about us when he's going through his day?"

Sylvia and I exchange glances: enough is enough already. Maggie is thirty-three years old; she's not a kid anymore. It's time for her to grow up.

"Is that who you've been calling every five minutes?" Sylvia says in an unpleasant tone. "Eliot, she's been talking to Barney behind our backs!"

I look at Maggie. "You've been talking to Barney? About what?"

Maggie shrugs. "Maybe I have, and maybe I haven't. If you're going to be jerks about it, then I'm not going to tell you."

"Why are you so obsessed with that man, anyway? You talk about him every second of every day, and I'm sick of it."

"I'm not *obsessed* with him, Sylvia. Talking about someone all the time is not *obsessing*. It's being interested in a man who is our father, and—in case you've forgotten—Hailey's grandfather. Don't you think they should meet someday?"

"No," Sylvia and I say in unison.

"Jinx!" Laughing, we high-five.

Then Sylvia asks if calling Barney is Dylan's idea, which makes me wonder if Maggie and Dylan are back together, and if so, am I the only one who doesn't know this, too. It's so difficult with three, I think; someone is always left out of something.

"Barney is your dad, right?" Charlotte asks. "How come no one ever talks about him?" But before anyone can answer, she flips open her shiny red phone and for the second time on this ten-minute drive punches in her mother's number. "Hey, Mom, me again. We'll be home Monday night. I can't remember if I told you that or not. Miss you! Love you!" She looks up. "So, why did Barney and your mom get divorced anyway?"

These are thorny questions, so no one replies. "It's complicated," I say eventually.

There's more silence. Charlotte turns up her music so loud, I can hear it through her earbuds. Then she starts to hum along, which makes me want to scream. Rather than tell her to stop, though, I whip the car around and head back to the rich oilman's house.

"Sorry, guys. I have to get back." Another minute in this car, and I'm afraid I'll blow.

"Why?" Sylvia squawks. "Eliot, why can't we go to Target?"

I don't answer, so she keeps repeating, "Why can't we go to Target, why can't we go to Target?" Finally, she blurts out, *"Answer the cockadoodie question, Eliot. Why aren't we going to Target?"* which strikes me as hilarious and I break apart. I mean, I am shattered. My laughter unhinges in my chest and unravels inside me like a long paper dragon. Soon I am so hysterical that I'm doubled over, and I have to slow down because I can barely see the street, much less steer the car. Sylvia and Maggie have joined in, and together we reach a stratum of hilarity previously unknown to mankind. And when a clearly confused Charlotte wants to know what's so funny, none of us can tell her because we are all laughing too hard.

An hour after lunch, Roger pulls into the driveway. Grant arrives at the same time, and they look funny walking in together. Roger is a head taller than Grant and twice as big. Grant's not small, but Roger is immense. Side by side, they look like an old vaudeville routine, a ventriloquist and his dummy, a giant and a dwarf. But where Roger is large and lumbering, Grant is lean and agile. He's also considerate, twisting around to grab the door so that Roger can maneuver his golf clubs and duffel bag into the foyer.

"Thanks, man!" Roger doesn't talk, he hollers, but he's a hale and hearty guy, a true man's man, and despite what I may have implied, he is a pleasure to have around.

"No problem," Grant replies, tossing his own bag onto the floor. Unshaven, wearing a polo shirt and ripped jeans, he looks relaxed and ready for a few days off.

"You're here!" I race over to give him a hug. "You finally made it! I'm so happy to see you."

Laughing, Grant hugs me back. "I'm happy to see you, too."

"Now that's a *hello*, Eliot!" Roger calls out. "You could teach my wife a thing or two about welcoming her husband into his home."

"He's not her husband," Sylvia mutters from the couch. "And it's not your home."

Roger claps. "That's my girl!"

Sylvia and Roger have been together for twelve years and married for five. When they first met, she was focused on her career; and Roger—who at forty-five is nine years older—was a confirmed bachelor. But then Grant and I moved in together, sparking in my sister a (never-before-seen) burning desire to get married as quickly as possible. Although Roger was still on the fence, Sylvia was determined to change his mind, and for the next six months, she called us from restaurants, ladies' rooms, and therapists' offices to narrate her progress. We knew so much about their relationship that when Roger showed up for dinner, we couldn't help noticing that *no*, he *didn't* flinch when Sylvia mentioned ring shopping; and *yes*, *he* was the one who brought up their six-month timetable; and *my God*, that clicking sound he makes when he swallows would drive us insane, too. By the time Sylvia and Roger celebrated their engagement, Maggie and I felt it was our victory as well.

Roger loves sports: football, golf, tennis—hell, put him in a skirt, hand him a stick, and he'll gladly play field hockey. He's like an overgrown shaggy dog always chasing after balls, but at the moment, he's the only one among us who seems to belong in the rich oilman's house. The rest of us are sloppy in ragged T-shirts and shorts. But Roger is wearing madras slacks, a pink cashmere pullover, dark aviator sunglasses, and golf shoes, which he knows enough to take off before he steps on the thick rugs.

"What a *beautiful* day!" He pads around in his argyle socks. "Just *demolished* the back nine on Hilton Head!" Roger is a former football hero, played for Vandy just like his daddy, and now runs the family brokerage firm. Supposedly he had a chance to go pro, which I believe, judging from the size of his hands. They're massive, like upside-down lampshades attached to his wrists.

"Who wants to go for a swim?" He glances around. "It's *gorgeous* out!" When no one answers, he hovers over the couch. "Hey, baby! How's my best girl?"

Playing hard to get, Sylvia rolls her eyes, but she's got a kittenish grin and we can all tell she's glad to see him.

Grant is down on his knees, holding out his arms for Hailey and Gail, who race in from the living room and knock him off his feet. "Hi, guys," he says, hugging one and then the other. "Where's Charlotte?"

"She's in her room, doing her computer," Hailey tells him. "She won't play with me or Gail, so she got yelled at."

As usual, our funny four-year-old is an eager informant, although I'd hardly characterize my conversation with Charlotte as "yelling." All I said was that we were on a family vacation, and I'd appreciate her participating. Charlotte's reply: "Whatever, Eliot."

Grant looks up at me. "Is everything okay?"

"Everything's fine. Don't listen to *Der Führer*. We're having a great time, and now that you're here, it'll be even better."

And it is. The rest of the day passes quickly. Grant changes into shorts, and we sit together on the rich oilman's deck, drinking beer and watching the sunset. We take a stroll around the development before dinner, looking at all the fancy houses, then Roger cooks steaks and we all go to bed full and content. The next day is a whirlwind, but everyone's relaxed, including me, so there's a lot of teasing and laughter. I get so caught up in the beach and the sun and the running around that I barely think about anything else. In fact, after lunch on Sunday, it occurs to me that I haven't thought about Finn all morning.

In the living room, Grant is sitting on the couch with Sylvia. "Eliot, I don't feel like going to the beach this afternoon." They're clicking through the channels, mesmerized by the rich oilman's enormous TV. "Do you care?"

"Nope." I pack up a tote bag. "You can do what you want. You're on vacation."

"You sure you don't mind going alone?"

"Not at all. Stay where you are and relax for a few hours. You look comfortable."

This isn't true. Sylvia is sprawled out along the entire length of the couch, forcing Grant to huddle against the armrest. But if that's where he wants to be, it's fine with me. He can't swim; he hates the sand—why should he be miserable on the beach?

My mother is working, Maggie is at Target, and Roger is golfing, so once again I'm the one who lugs the bags to the sand, carries Hailey into the waves, throws the Frisbee, and fetches snacks and drinks and sunscreen. I start to think about Finn, wondering if he got my e-mail. But when I look at Hailey and Gail playing on the sand, it's impossible to picture him sitting with them and building a fort. It's impossible to imagine him here at all, frankly.

I return from the beach, really tired, really hot, and really sweaty. I spot the back of Grant's head as he pecks at his keyboard.

"Grant?" I say, but get no response, which aggravates me. "Grant? . . . Grant, *Grant*!"

He turns around, squinting as if there's a bright light in his eyes. "Did you need me?"

"Can you help the girls get cleaned up for dinner? I need to . . ." What will justify this request? Brain surgery, maybe; but am I performing it or receiving it? "I'm not feeling so great."

Grant raises his eyebrows. "Does this mean there won't be any *relating* tonight?"

"Let's wait and see." We haven't had sex for a while, since things got so frenzied with Finn, and although I've missed being with Grant, I'm also exhausted.

Hours later, he tries anyway. He rolls over to my side, then reaches under my T-shirt.

"I want you so much, Eliot. I've been thinking about you all day."

He starts massaging my breasts, but seeing I'm not aroused, he asks what's wrong. "Why won't you kiss me?"

"I am kissing you," I say, although I'm stiff and distant, and poor Grant can feel it. "I'm just tired. It's been a long couple of days." I know he deserves a better explanation, but how do I recount everything that's happened over the past few weeks?

"I know something is bothering you, Eliot. Just tell me what it is." He tries kissing me again, but I can't relax.

I wish we could start over, I want to say. *If we could take it slowly, step by step, then I'll find my way back to you, I promise.*

"Did I do something wrong?" He's hurt and confused, and I don't blame him. Two weeks ago, I was whispering, "I want to fuck you," over the phone, and now I'm barely opening my mouth when we kiss.

"Of course not, Grant. You're great."

"Then what is it? Why are you so far away? I want to feel close to you, Eliot. I want to be intimate with my . . . what are you? You're not my wife. My partner? My girlfriend? Last week, we were in love; this week, you're miles away. What is going on? Why is this so complicated?"

I feel a wave of guilty sadness. "It's not complicated." And then I remember why. "I'm just worried about my mother." This reason, however untrue at the moment, is certainly true in general. I happen to worry about my mother all the time—every day, in fact.

"I thought you said she was feeling better."

"Who knows with her? One day she says she has cancer, the next she's perfectly fine. But she is very unhealthy. She doesn't eat right or exercise." Shrugging, I make a mental note to tell my mother about this conversation—specifically, that she's afraid she has cancer, should the subject arise. "I don't want her to be old, Grant. I also worry that when the time comes, and she does need care—any kind of care—she won't be able to afford it. It's always on my mind, which I know is foolish, but she's my mother. How could it not be?"

Grant looks into my eyes. "I'm so sorry, Eliot. I feel awful for you. What can I do?"

"Honestly? I'd really like to talk—not about anything specific necessarily, just about us."

So that's what we do: we prop up our pillows and stretch out on the bed. We talk about everything—the kids, the house, our jobs, the future. It feels good to be here together, shooting the shit. And as we catch up on our shared life, I start to loosen up, and slowly but surely I make my way back.

At one point I tell him that Charlotte and I are at odds. "It's hard to be fourteen, Grant. She needs her mother. It's obvious that she's sick of me telling her what to do. And as much as I love her, I'm not her mother and both she and I know it."

Grant sighs. He doesn't like to talk about this. All he wants is one happy family, and he doesn't understand why there are issues. "I've tried talking to Beth a few times—you know that—but she's totally unreceptive to spending more time with the kids. She only wants them when it's convenient for her. Nor does she care about the minutiae of their lives, especially now that she's been commissioned to do that mural at Riverside. But why does it matter, Eliot? The kids love you—Charlotte, too. What can Beth do for them that you can't?"

"Kids need their mothers, Grant. It's just a fact." I can see he's uncomfortable, so I try to lighten the mood. "Speaking of that mural, Charlotte said Beth is getting *a million dollars* to paint it. I mean, no offense to her artistic vision, but she paints *vaginas* these days."

Grant smiles. "Charlotte told me the same thing. There's no way it's a million, though. More like ten grand, if that."

"Still, it's time to rethink our financial arrangement. Ten grand may not be a million dollars, but it's a nice chunk of change. So why are we still paying Beth's rent? She needs to stand on her own two feet."

"You're right. There's no reason for me—*for us*—to be supplementing her income."

This euphemism, "supplementing her income," amuses me. We're not supplementing anything; before this mural, the Sculptress didn't have an income. Years ago, when she and Grant first got married, he encouraged her to pursue her art as an act of support. He promised her that if she couldn't sell her paintings, she'd always have fallback money, and it's a promise he continued to honor long after they got divorced.

"But how do I tell her?" Grant asks. "I know she's taking advantage, but she's still Charlotte and Gail's mother. No matter how nice I am about cutting her off, she's still going to make me out to be an asshole. Eliot, I don't want the kids thinking about me that way."

"Just tell her the truth, that we're strapped. Grant, listen to me. The girls know you're a good guy; they know you're a *great* guy. And they'll always love you. But if cutting Beth off is too agitating, then don't do it. Just forget we even had this conversation. I'm on your side, no matter what."

He pulls me close. "You're a good guy, too, Eliot. How did I get so lucky?"

By this point, we're wrapped in each other's arms, and I'm feeling so close to him that I almost come clean. But just as I'm about to say Finn's name, I realize I can't, not if it means hurting him or spoiling this moment. Instead, I tell him I don't know what I'd do without him. "I'm the lucky one, Grant."

We kiss each other and promise we'll always be open like this. We keep kissing and kissing, the way we did when we first met, as though we're five years younger and just starting out. And then we make love, and it's really, truly making love. It's slow, uncomplicated, and familiar—the same as it always was, but also different, better even.

Chapter Eighteen

WE WAKE UP on Monday morning to overcast skies and heavy winds. It hasn't started raining yet, but it will; of this my mother is certain. As we stand out on the deck and study the horizon, she describes how atmospheric pressure is strengthening the weather system off Cuba.

"It should hit later—" She stops. "Did you and Grant have a fight? I got up in the middle of the night and heard voices, but wasn't sure if you were laughing or crying. I thought you might be arguing because he hates the beach."

"No, everything's great. In fact, coming here was the best thing we could've done."

"Well, it sounded to me like you were arguing." She shrugs. "But as long as you say everything's fine..." She looks at me closely.

"I swear. We're getting along really well."

The sliding glass door opens, and Grant steps outside holding a cup of coffee. He's barefoot and wearing his same ripped jeans and a tank top.

"Doesn't look much like beach weather," he says hopefully, squinting up at the sky.

"Sorry," I tell him. "It's perfect beach weather. It's windy, but the sun is warm. You don't have to go, though. Feel free to spend the entire day sitting on your ass."

Shielding her eyes, my mother looks up. "Grant's right. It's going to rain." She gives him a conspiratorial wink. "I hate the beach, too. I should've gone to Vermont. It would've been half the cost."

Maggie joins us. "You should've stayed in Atlanta. Then it wouldn't have cost anything." Like my mother, she surveys the horizon. "We *have* to go to the beach. It's our last day."

This surprises me. "You're leaving tomorrow? I thought you were staying through Thursday."

"I wanted to, but I have work ... and ... other things." Although she doesn't elaborate, I suspect she means Dylan.

"Well," my mother says. "If you are going to the beach, you should go soon, before the weather turns." I glance at her, and it occurs to me that I'm supposed to remind her about something, but as hard as I try, I can't remember what it is.

Back inside, I shake out a bag, and begin to pack for the beach. From the kitchen, I hear Roger's boisterous voice and Hailey's and Gail's shrieks of delight. When I check out what's going on, I find Roger lifting Gail over his head and holding her upside down so that she can walk on the ceiling.

"Again, Uncle Roger!" Hailey cries out, weeping from laughter. "It's my turn—my turn now!"

Gail is in Roger's arms, high above his head. She's trying to touch the light fixture with her toe. "I almost got it!" Her long dark hair hangs like a mop, sweeping back and forth across Roger's face. Her cheeks are red, and her eyes are bulging. "I'm like Dead Eye Peter!"

Roger flips her over, stands her upright. "That's enough, Gail. You're wearing me out."

Hailey pouts. "I didn't get my turn." But just as she starts to cry, Roger scoops her up and flips her over, so quickly that she twirls like a pinwheel, as though inside she is nothing but feathers.

"Okay, Roger. Put her down. Let's go, guys! We're going to the beach."

When I try to round everyone up, there's chaos. Charlotte is on the phone and needs another five minutes. The strap on Gail's left flip-flop breaks. Hailey insists on wearing her pink polka-dot suit, the one with the ruffles on the butt, which is MIA until Maggie spots it stuffed into a plastic Barbie purse.

It's almost noon by the time we're ready. The whole gang is assembled, even my mother, even Sylvia, even Grant. "You really don't have to go," I tell him. But he insists; rather, he doesn't want to be the only one left behind.

"It's a family activity. And I'm part of the family."

The wind has whipped up, but the sun is peeking out, and we're all excited. Well, some of us are more excited than others, but everyone's chattering happily as we cross the backyard to the pebbled path that leads through the trees. Once we cut through them, the path resumes and we take it until we reach a parking lot that's adjacent to the beach.

"They advertised this place as oceanfront property," my mother remarks, "but it's not."

"It's a pretty amazing house," I say.

"Amazing, yes. Oceanfront, no."

Sylvia lags behind, complaining, "These pebbles are murder." Taking teeny tiny steps, she stops every few minutes to fix her shoes. Unlike the rest of us in faded bathing suits, Sylvia is decked out for a cruise-wear photo shoot. Her designer sarong covers up an expensive maternity bikini, and her sun hat has a brim so wide, it looks like a cartoon sombrero. She's also wearing platform sandals with four-inch heels and my favorite diamond stud earrings.

"I hope you don't plan to go in the water with those earrings," I tell her.

"I'm *pregnant*, Eliot," she says, holding her hat onto her head so it doesn't fly off.

"Which means what—that you can't swim?"

"How do you walk in those shoes?" Maggie asks. "It looks like someone glued kitchen sponges together and added a strap."

"Aren't they *awesome*? They were six hundred dollars, but worth every penny." She suddenly bends over. "*Oh no!*" Holding her stomach, she huffs and puffs as though she's in labor. "Whew. That was *unbelievable*. I've been getting these *stabbing* pains all morning."

"Are you going to be okay?" my mother asks.

"She'll be fine," Maggie replies.

Sylvia has already turned back. "I need to lie down." She waves. "You guys go ahead."

It is hard to reconcile this grown-up Sylvia with my childhood sister. When we were kids, she was a tomboy who wouldn't have been caught dead in shoes on the beach, much less sponge sandals that cost $600. She was always first in the water, swimming far out to the buoys, taking chances no one else dared. Now she's inching along the beach path like a painted geisha girl.

Grant reaches over to take her arm, but Sylvia shrugs him off. "I'm fine," she snaps.

He holds up his hands. "Just trying to help."

"Sylvia," I say, indignant on his behalf, "you don't have to be nasty."

At that moment, Roger swoops in from behind. "Do not fear, my dear! I'm here to save you!" He lifts Sylvia in his arms, then whirls her around.

Holding her enormous hat, Sylvia tilts her head back and kicks up her sponge shoes. "Roger, I'm pregnant!" But she's laughing. He's laughing, too, her Vandy football hero. They kiss for what seems like forever, and I think about Grant and how we kissed the same way last night.

"Shall I take thee, damsel, back to your castle?" Roger asks in some crazy, made-up accent. "Let us go quickly, my dearest Sylvia, so that I can maketh mine tee time." He starts to rush off, but just before he ferries her away, back to the couch, where I suspect she'll spend the whole afternoon, Sylvia swivels her head and blows Grant a kiss.

"Your sister is impossible sometimes," Grant says, watching them.

"She's just Sylvia. Don't let her get to you." I link my arm through his. "You still have me," I add cheerfully, and together we cross over the blacktop to claim a spot on the sand.

⌒

Wyatt Island is the perfect location for viewing the Atlantic Ocean. The rich oilman's house is at the very tip of the peninsula, where the land rises higher than anywhere else on the coast. The beach near his development is public, and once you pass through the parking lot, it's maybe twenty-five yards down to the edge of the water. But the blacktop sits on the island's highest point, giving you a panoramic view of the sea.

The shoreline off South Carolina is smooth, and the sand is soft. As we trudge down toward the water, I shield my eyes and look out toward the horizon. Miles and miles away, a pocket has formed where the sky and water meet. It's a breathtaking sight, but also humbling, as though I'm looking at the precise spot where the world ends.

It's still overcast and very windy, so the beach is empty. Other than clusters of senior citizens power walking on the sand and a few scattered mothers with young children, we're the only ones here. There's a sign that warns us to swim at our own risk, but it says nothing about not swimming at all, so we shake out our towels and set up camp.

"I don't want to be so close to the water," my mother says, to which Grant agrees, so we split into two groups. Grant and my mother put up their dolphin umbrella as far away from the shore as they can get without sitting in the parking lot. They're both reading the paper, which they've folded into squares like subway commuters. Down by the water, several yards away, the girls and I are hanging out with Maggie.

We're here for an hour before the rain clouds move out. The sky clears up and some blue peeks through, but the wind still snaps, whipping our hair around and blowing sand everywhere. The air is warm, though, so we all stay put. At different times, Charlotte and I go into the water, both of us braving the choppy waves. Maggie dives in, too, but surfaces with her bikini top all knotted up and her bottoms falling off.

"It's rough out there!" she says breathlessly, wiping her face on a towel. "I almost lost my suit! You guys were smart to wear one-pieces."

Hailey looks nervously at the waves. "I only want to go in with you, Mommy."

"I can go in by myself!" Gail declares.

"Maybe." I force myself to stop thinking about Hailey struggling in the Marriott pool. "We'll see."

For the next half hour, Hailey, Gail, and Charlotte crouch on the sand and dig wet holes. Maggie and I sit on towels next to them and stare at the water. I turn to see my mother standing next to the dolphin umbrella, holding her bag. Cupping her hands, she shouts to me, but I can't hear her in the wind. She gestures toward the house. I wave to her and then to Grant. Grant waves back and returns to his paper.

A few minutes later, Gail says she has to go to the bathroom. "My stomach hurts."

"Grant!" I shout. "Gail has to go to the bathroom…Grant!…*Grant!*"

Maggie reaches for Gail's hand. "I'll take her. I need to make a call anyway."

"We'll be here for another hour." I remind Gail to put on her shoes. "There might be glass in the parking lot."

As Maggie and Gail hike up the sand, Grant meets them halfway, then trundles down to where I'm standing. "It's going to rain," he says. "Maybe you and the girls should go inside."

"We won't be out too much longer." I motion to the girls. "They're having fun."

Grant gazes out at the rough water. "I can't believe you swam in those waves. They're huge!"

I follow his gaze. "Actually, seeing them from here, I can't believe it either."

He shouts good-bye to the girls, careful to keep his distance from the water. He doesn't want any part of his body getting wet. "Be good! And you"—he gives me a kiss—"call me so I'll know everyone is okay. Don't stay too late, Eliot."

And then there were three, I think after he leaves, settling on the sand next to Hailey. Charlotte and I help her dig for a while, but then Charlotte jumps up, runs toward the water, and dives into the waves.

I watch her bob up and down. "Don't go too far, Charlotte!" I call out.

She thinks I'm saying hi, so she waves. I lose her for a minute, see her, but then lose her again. Frustrated, I wave her back in. *"Come back! You're out too FAR!"*

I wade into the surf, making sure to keep an eye on Hailey. Absolutely nothing can happen to her; she's nowhere near the water. But seeing her small ruffled butt on the vast stretch of sand frightens me, and I get annoyed at Charlotte for refusing to listen.

"Come out now!" I yell, and slowly, grudgingly, she does.

Back on land, she plops down beside me. "Oh, my God," she pants, toweling herself off. "It's *awesome* out there."

"You have to be careful, Charlotte! Look at those waves! The current is very strong. You were out way too far."

"I was *not* out too far, Eliot. And I swim *great.*" She goes on, listing all the ways I am wrong, but I'm not listening. I'm watching Gail come out of the trees and walk to the blacktop. This time, though, she's with Sylvia, not Maggie, who must've decided to stay at the house. As they trek across the sand up near the dolphin umbrella, I see that Sylvia is still wearing her sponge sandals. Gail is barefoot, which worries me. There were broken bottles all over the parking lot. Why isn't she wearing her shoes? If she cuts her foot, she won't be able to swim.

"Can you stay with Hailey for a second?" I ask Charlotte, who's sitting on a towel, flipping through a book. "I have to tell Sylvia something."

"Yeah, sure." Looking down at her book, she waves me away.

But I'm afraid to move.

"Just go already, Eliot. Hailey is only, like, six inches away. I'm *right here.* Look"—she pokes Hailey—"I'm touching her!"

I'm ridiculous, I know, and race away from the water and up to the umbrella, looking back twice, three times to make sure Hailey is where she's supposed to be. Of course she is, and Charlotte is right there next to her. I chastise myself for being so neurotic but can't stop remembering how easily she went under in the kiddie pool. My mother glanced away for only a second, but that's all it takes for disaster to happen.

"Are you feeling better?" I ask Gail, but Sylvia answers instead.

"Not really."

Gail peels off her T-shirt and races down toward the water, where her sisters are still sitting, peacefully, on their towels.

"Don't go into the water until I get down there!" I call out.

"Be careful, Gail!" Sylvia adds. Then she lowers herself onto a chair. "I'm still woozy, but when Grant came inside, I figured you might need a hand out here. I guess he's tired from all the roughhousing he's been doing. All that running and jumping must've worn him out."

"Leave him alone, Sylvia. It's not like you've been doing much roughhousing yourself."

"I have an excuse, Eliot." She stares at the water. "Did you let the kids go in by themselves? It's intense out there."

Hailey! I whip around, but she's still on the sand, plopping wet mud into a pile. I grab some pretzels, a water bottle, and more sunscreen, then move back down to the water.

"I need to sit with the kids," I say to Sylvia, but she's on the phone, telling Roger that yes, she's okay; she's helping me with the girls so I can get a break. "We practically have the whole place to ourselves."

Back with the kids, I relax. Now Gail is digging, too, and she and Hailey are building a mud pile, which gets bigger by the minute. Charlotte wants to help, and Hailey is thrilled about this, until she asks for the pink shovel with the faded Elmo sticker—the one in Hailey's hand.

"It's my shovel! Mommy, tell her."

"Charlotte, Hailey's been using that shovel all day. There's another one up by Aunt Sylvia." I purposely say *Aunt Sylvia* to remind her that even though I took Hailey's side this time, we're still one happy family.

"Whatever." Charlotte jumps up. "I'm going inside. I have to call Mom."

And then there are three again... well, four, counting Sylvia. We all return to our activities. Gail and Hailey dig their hole, I watch them dig, and Sylvia talks on the phone, kicking up her $600 sponges. Who spends that kind of money on sandals? My sister, apparently.

I glance at Sylvia again, and for a second, I could swear she's smoking a cigarette. Then I realize it's a white umbrella tassel fluttering in the wind. I stand up to stretch my legs and wade into the surf. I think about taking off my shorts and jumping in, but my phone is in my pocket. I told Grant I would call him, but I'm too lazy. How long ago did he leave, anyway? Two hours ago? Four?

A few minutes later—how many...five? ten?—I'm still marveling at the elasticity of beach time when my phone rings. It's Grant.

"We'll be here at least another hour," I tell him. "The kids are having a great time."

The connection is bad, so I have to strain to hear him. "You...okay?" he asks. "I miss you."

The phone goes dead. Seconds later, it rings again. I shout, "We're doing *Great*!"

"Okay," Grant says—or I think he says. It's impossible to hear with the wind blowing. "I love you! I'll talk...soon...maybe later..."

I can't hear the rest of his sentence. I glance up to see Hailey and Gail throwing mud at each other. Hailey's ruffled suit bottom is covered in sand, and it hangs very low, exposing her perfectly white, perfectly round butt. They're both laughing. Grant says something else, but the call is cut off.

I'm about to help the kids get cleaned up, but my phone is ringing again, and I'm anxious to tell Grant that I love him, too. *"I love you!"* I shout. Then I turn in such a way that I catch a good cell, and our connection is perfectly clear. "Hello?...Grant, is that you?"

There's silence, but it's not my reception. Then Finn says, "No, it's me."

My body freezes. "Oh." I try to swallow, but my mouth feels dry.

"I got your e-mail," he is saying.

My heart is pounding; I try to stay calm. "Did you just call before?"

"Yes, but we got cut off."

"I thought it was Grant." *I love you.* Finn said this, not Grant. *I love you; I miss you; I'll love you forever.*

Running in circles, Hailey and Gail are covered in mud from head to toe. They look like black tar creatures. "Girls," I say sternly, "stay away from the water." I turn back to Finn. "So? What did you think?"

"I thought it was very..." The reception is scratchy.

"What?" I twist and turn, trying to find that good cell.

"I thought it was very sad!" he screams. He's perfectly clear. "It was sad," he repeats.

"You don't have to yell," I say, and we both laugh.

Finn is telling me he loves me, he's always loved me; he can't live without me. I'm listening carefully and can hear some of what he says, but my reception goes in and out. I do catch, though, that he doesn't want to lose me again, and if I agreed, he'd be willing to tell Parker—

"Tell her what?" I shout, suddenly frantic. *"What are you going to tell Parker?"*

I hear my name, "Eliot!" but it's very faint and far away. A second later, I hear it again, so I look up and realize—*How did this happen?*—that I'm no longer facing the ocean. I'm turned backward, facing the trees. I'm also several yards away from— *Hailey! Where is Hailey?*

I whip around, and this is what I see: my child, my Hailey, out in the choppy water, tumbling over and over and moving away fast. There's the top of her head, then a flash of pink ruffles, then white skin, then red hair. Is it red? I can't tell; it looks dark, almost black, in the water.

I also see this: Behind her, but much farther out and over—way over—and also moving away fast is my stepchild, my Gail, whose head I spot, then hand, then head, then nothing.

So this is what I do: I scream for them, for both my girls, to hold on because I'm coming; *I swear to God*, I'm coming; and I drop the phone in my hand and dive into the choppy sea.

And this is what I know: I can swim in only one direction, toward one child—toward Hailey or toward Gail—but I must make a choice and I must make it now.

Book Two

After such knowledge, what forgiveness?
—T. S. Eliot, "Gerontion," 1920

Chapter Nineteen

IN THE END, there is no choice. My options aren't one child or the other, Hailey or Gail; they are whether I swim to Hailey or whether I don't. And these aren't true options because there is only one answer. Of course I will save Hailey. To not swim to her never even occurs to me. It's instinctive, this movement. It's not deliberate or even conscious; it's reflexive, like breathing. I see my child go under and I react. It's what mothers do.

So I swim, faster and faster, out, not over, toward my four-year-old daughter.

The waves are fierce, but I'm a strong swimmer. This, too, is reflexive: head down, I cut through the water stroke after stroke after stroke. The current pushes me back, but I keep swimming, gasping for air, and then swimming again. I kick harder and harder, moving faster and faster, until finally, *thank God*, I reach my girl, whom I grab in my arms. Her eyes are closed and her body is cold, not freezing, though, just cold, and her skin is a peculiar gray color, but I believe—yes, there's a pulse. Wait, am I wrong? Is there a pulse or is that my own heartbeat I feel?

I'm trying to tread water, but the waves make it nearly impossible. I have to help Hailey breathe; I have to sustain her pulse. I lift her up, above my head, until I can garner the strength I need to steady her in my arms, force her lips open, breathe into her mouth, and continue to kick, all at the same time.

"Breathe, Hailey, *breathe!*" I take in a salty gulp of water, which makes me gag. Hailey is heavy and slippery in my arms, but I open her mouth again. "Come on pea, *breathe.*" My eyes burn, and I rub them with my knuckles, which only makes the burning worse, but I keep them open. I need to see her face. I need to watch her breathe.

I'm still kicking until I realize, stupidly, that I can stand. The water is only as high as my neck. Up on my toes, I try to find Gail, and when I see—what is that, the top of her head? Yes, that's her head; she's not as far out as I thought—I scream bloody murder: *"I'm coming, Gail! Hold on."* Please, God; please let her hold on.

Adrenaline surges through me, but I still have my wits. Because I am holding my daughter, and because (I believe) there's a pulse, and (I believe) she is breathing, I can be smart and take action.

"Gail!" My voice is hoarse: *"Gail, Gail, Gail!"*

I'm moving now, in the direction I didn't take before, which is over—way over—and out into the waves. I can do this, though. Now that Hailey is safe, I can save Gail, too.

I hold on to Hailey, whose eyes aren't open but who suddenly chokes and sputters. She coughs up water, vomits debris, and then gasps, still choking. She's crying for me to stop, to stay still, but her voice is hoarse, too.

"Mommy, stop, Mommy!" I can barely hear her. She's just a little kid, still only a baby. *Jesus, what have I done?*

You're okay." I try to calm her down while I paddle. "I'm here. I have you. You're okay, you're okay, Hailey."

The longer we're out here, the colder it gets. But I have to reach Gail. I'm Supermom, a mother who hoists cars off her children, jumps in front of bullets, cuts off her own limbs.

As I force my way through the water, the ocean floor drops off, and I am out in the deep with nothing beneath me. But I'm still swimming, still swimming, and still holding Hailey, who is mewling in my arms like a small animal.

Please understand, Hailey, I say, or think I say. *I can't stop. I have to get your sister. She's just a little kid, too.*

I kick harder, hold tighter, and trudge through the waves toward Gail, who is moving farther and farther away. And just as I feel myself fading, just as I see her small head moving too fast out into the wide-open water, I see a figure tearing down the beach, a single moving body that races over the sand, dives into the ocean, and swims out toward the horizon. She's fast, whoever this is, faster than I am, and she's not holding a squirming child, so she can slice through the waves like a champ.

I glance back at the beach, and I see a pair of discarded shoes. From out here, they look like a bunch of sponges stuck together.

"*SYLVIA is coming!*" I scream to Gail, who is still far away. "Sylvia will save you!" I start to cry. My crazy, pregnant sister—*oh God, she's pregnant*—will save my stepchild, my other daughter, the one I didn't go for, the one I left out in the ocean to drown.

~

A crowd has formed on the beach, a few yards to my left. Now that we are out of the water and safe on the sand, I cradle Hailey in my arms and scan the horizon. Squinting, I can see Sylvia closing in on Gail, although they're far off in the distance and look very small. The waves are high, so I'll spot one and then lose one, but—*thank God, thank God*—they always resurface.

Hailey is awake, but her breathing is shallow and erratic. Her eyes are closed. Someone has called an ambulance, and I can hear a siren wailing louder and louder as it gets closer.

"Here, let me hold her." My mother takes Hailey from me and wraps her up in a hoodie. "*Oy vey,*" she gasps quietly. "Eliot, my God, she's freezing cold."

I nod, still surveying the water. How many minutes has Gail been out there? Ten? Twelve? Long enough for Maggie to appear with my mother and Grant, who said they were out on the deck and heard Sylvia screaming. Charlotte is here, too, with her be-dazzled phone. She's only holding it, though, and I'm grateful for this, grateful she's not narrating for her mother what's happening to Gail.

Shielding my eyes, I watch Sylvia closely and realize she's veering off course. "*Left*, Sylvia! Move over, move *LEFT*!" I'm waving and screaming as though she can see and hear me. Oddly, she chooses this moment to lift her head and look around. She spots Gail, bends her head, and keeps swimming.

Grant is beside me, also watching Sylvia. He's breathing hard, and his hands are clenched. "How did this happen, Eliot?"

I'm about to answer when he dashes forward, only to stop short as soon as he hits the water. I know Grant is desperate to do something, but he can't swim. As it is, he's only ankle-deep in the surf, and already his whole body is shaking. After wading out a few feet, I grab his hand and help him shuffle back onto the dry land. I want to put my arms around him, but knowing what I know, I am afraid to hug him. If I do, I might blurt out the whole story, and then he will hate me for the rest of our lives.

"*How did this happen?*" he repeats. His voice is pinched, as though he is being strangled. Grant—whom I love so much right now—is a good man and a great father, but he's a disaster in high-pressure situations. His panic is so palpable that it's infectious, and everyone around him becomes more panicked than they already are. Ironically, or—what's the word? coincidentally?—Grant's father was career military. He was in the army, did tours in Sarajevo and Bosnia and then one in the Gulf before he died of a heart attack, so it's weird that Grant falls apart when he's caught under fire. See, you never know how your kids will turn out.

"*Tell me, Eliot.*" Grant is angry with himself for standing impotently on the sand while his middle daughter, his favorite cheese, drowns in the ocean. He needs an answer, which I understand. If he has an answer, then he'll know where to focus his attention. Unfortunately, I don't have an answer; rather, the one I have isn't one he'll want.

"We were on the beach. The girls were playing...and one minute, they were there, and the next—" I stop, change direction. "Listen to me, Grant. Sylvia will bring her back." I am sure of this, as sure as I've ever been. "She's a fast swimmer, the fastest of anyone we know. She was all-state hundred-meter breaststroke for two years in a row." I grab his face, hold his eyes; I swear to him, swear to God. "Sylvia will save Gail."

Still staring ahead, Grant nods. Yes, Sylvia will save Gail. He believes me. He has to believe me. What other choice does he have?

"Look!" my mother shouts. *"Look at Sylvia!"*

Out in the water, my sister and Gail have become two little specks, but these little specks are no longer yards apart. It's hard to gauge distance from here, but it looks as if Sylvia is closing the gap. A helicopter flies overhead, canvasing the area. I see the pilot wave to two lifeguards who have motored up to the beach on Jet Skis and are preparing to go out. They have rope and netting slung across their chests like ammunition belts and towing boards strapped to their backs. Just as they gun their engines, we see one of them point.

"She got her!" someone else, a woman, calls out.

I follow her finger, watching the two specks moving together. They're not moving this way, but at least they have merged. "Sylvia got her!" I scream. *"She got Gail!"*

⟿

The ambulance has arrived and idles on the sand. I hover over Hailey, who is lying on a gurney underneath a blanket. The EMTs have put an oxygen mask on her face, and as they help her breathe, they check her pulse, her blood pressure, and the rest of her body for broken bones and God knows what else. Occasionally, when they pause, I ask if she's okay.

"We're checking that now, ma'am."

I look up. Out in the water, the lifeguards have reached Sylvia and Gail. The helicopter has dropped a ladder, and a third figure is hanging from it, helping the guards get situated. The wind is still whipping and the waves are rough, so the rope ladder swings in wide arcs, back and forth, over the Jet Skis, as all the men work.

Beside me, Grant is in agony, watching this. He's bent at the knees and hunched over, as if he's been punched in the stomach.

"Are they going to lift them into the helicopter?" I ask one of the EMTs, loudly, so Grant can hear, too.

He shakes his head. "Lancaster is strictly cargo. He's not equipped for medical rescue. The guards will tug the swimmers back, and if necessary, we'll resuscitate in the ambulance."

The word *resuscitate* frightens me. I glance at Grant. He has moved over to Charlotte, who is crying. Along with Maggie and my mother, the four of them huddle together, trying to make sense of what is happening out in the ocean.

There are two EMTs working on Hailey. They're both bruisers, big guys who remind me of Roger but who are also much younger, maybe eighteen at most. One of them notices me staring and gives me a smile. He has piercing blue eyes and sandy blond hair. His name, which is on his breast tag, is Randy Peterman.

"She's breathing, which is a good sign," Randy says, referring to Hailey. "And her color's coming back. But we have to make sure there's no hypoxia or acidosis, which can affect the brain and other organs."

"Okay, great." I nod as if I understand completely. I want Randy and his buddy to feel encouraged, to go the distance, to do whatever it takes to make Hailey perfect, or at least the same as she was before she went into the water.

Randy draws blood. "We do this to measure oxygen levels and determine electrolyte balances." He covers Hailey's finger with a small plastic hood. "With kids coming out of the ocean, ma'am, it's hard to know what we'll find, so we prepare for everything: cardiac arrest, hypothermia, spinal injuries." He pauses, says something to his partner, and then turns to me. "We have to take her to the hospital for a full exam. She'll need to spend the night, mostly as a precaution. It's standard procedure for anyone who's been out in the water a while," he adds.

I get the sense he's telling me this so I'll know what to expect with Gail. I consider this a good sign because it means he believes Gail will be rescued, and when she's rescued, there are actions he can take to make her the same, too—not the same as Hailey; I mean the same as she was before she went in the water.

"She's four, you said? Any history of heart disease? Lung problems? Anything odd when she was born?" Randy reels off a list of questions. The answer to every one is "no."

The EMTs work rapidly and efficiently. For a second, Randy looks up, and I follow his eyes. Out in the water, they're strapping Gail onto a towing board.

"The guards are very well trained, ma'am. They know exactly what to do in these situations." The way he says this makes it sound like a promise.

"Everyone will be okay," I reply as if we're a team, Randy and I—as if together, we can right this horrible wrong. I motion to Hailey. "How is she? How are you, Hailey?"

There's a mask on her mouth. She tries to talk but struggles. I hold her body, her pale little body, and try to soothe her. "It's okay. You're going to be fine." But she starts kicking and crying. "You're okay, my sweetest pea." I get choked up. "You're fine."

My mother sidles up to me and touches Hailey, too. "You'll be fine, kiddo," she says gently, stroking her granddaughter's legs. "Pork chops," my mother likes to call them. She's stroking her granddaughter's pork chops. My mother has tears in her eyes, which she wipes away with the sleeve of her sweatshirt.

Randy is listening to Hailey's heart. "We have to go," he says abruptly. This time, his voice is measured but urgent. He speaks into a radio and I hear a crackle, then a clipped response. "Another ambulance is on its way."

"Why?" I look around wildly. *Where's Grant? They have to go!*

"Your daughter's heartbeat—it's tacky. She needs to see a doctor."

"Grant!" I call out, and then race to him as he lumbers over, refusing to take his eyes off the water. I repeat what Randy told me but do my best to sound confident. "They're taking Hailey to the hospital. It's standard procedure. There's another ambulance coming for Gail."

"Hailey's okay, right?" Grant continues to watch the horizon. By this point, the helicopter has lifted off, and the guards are getting ready to return. Or at least it looks that way. My eyes aren't what they used to be. "I need to see Gail come out," he says softly, which I understand.

I pat his arm. "She'll come out, Grant." Like Randy, I make him this promise.

Behind the ambulance, Randy and his partner are adjusting Hailey's gurney, but just as they whisk her into the back, Maggie grabs Hailey's hand and flashes her million-dollar smile.

"Hi, sweet pea." She turns to me and Grant. "I'll go with her. You stay here and wait for Gail. Don't worry, Eliot. I'll be with her every second. I'll call you as soon as I know something." Then she hikes herself up and moves next to Hailey.

Randy takes me aside. "It's best if a parent travels, too. Everyone else can follow behind."

I nudge Grant gently. "One of us needs to ride with Hailey. But I don't want you to wait for Gail alone. Maybe my mother can go in the ambulance, and I'll stay here with you." It is easy to say this, to be magnanimous, because even though Hailey's heartbeat is tacky, I know she is safe and in good hands. I have already chosen her, so now when it doesn't matter as much, I can offer to stay behind and wait for Gail.

Grant shakes his head. "You go." His voice is raspy.

I'm still wearing my damp bathing suit, so I grab my T-shirt and sandals and sling my bag on my arm. "I will call you the second we get there." Patting my shorts, I suddenly remember something. My phone is in the ocean! I can't call Grant.

"Grant—" I start to say when he cuts me off.

"Eliot, look! They're coming in!" Shouting, he points to the water. "They've got them, and *they're coming in!*"

When I see the lifeguards roaring back through the water, my eyes flood with tears. *Oh God, thank you, thank you.* I race to the driver's side of the ambulance. "Randy! I just need one second, please. I have to check on my other daughter."

Gail comes out of the ocean strapped to a board, her head and body immobilized. The board is attached to a Jet Ski, which the lifeguard maneuvers out of the water and onto the sand. Sylvia comes out on a second Jet Ski, but she's sitting up, with her arms wrapped around her lifeguard's waist. When they hit the beach, the crowd bursts into applause.

As Grant and I race over, I hear the wail of a second ambulance and glance up to see it drive through the parking lot and down the sand to where the lifeguards are waiting. A new group of EMTs jump out, and they cluster around Gail, blocking our access.

Leaning forward, I can see Gail's eyes are closed. Her body is a bluish-white color, and her skin looks waxy. I want to put my hands on her, to see if she's cold, but can't get close enough.

"She's out of the water," I say to Grant, who's slumped against me, weak with relief.

"Thank God." His voice drops even lower. "Is she alive?"

"Of course she's alive, Grant." *Thank God for my sister. Thank God for Sylvia.*

My mother runs over to tell us that Hailey is leaving. "They're not waiting one more second. I'll go with Maggie, so you two can stay here."

I nudge Grant. "You should go instead of my mother. You have your phone and your wallet. You can answer their questions and talk to the insurance company. I'll be right behind you with Gail. She's going to be okay, Grant," I add. "These guys know what they're doing."

I'm afraid now, for Hailey and Gail, but also for Grant. He seems to be in some sort of fugue state and needs looking after. If Gail doesn't wake up soon, I don't know how he'll react. I do know, though, that he's better off at the hospital. Grant doesn't want to go, he doesn't want to leave Gail; but neither is he strong enough at the moment to argue with me.

As I watch him trudge up the beach holding on to my mother, I call out, "Tell Hailey I'll be there as soon as I can!" And when the doors swing shut and the siren starts howling, I exhale in relief, even though my four-year-old's heartbeat is tacky, and my seven-year-old still hasn't opened her eyes. One thing at a time, I tell myself.

⌐

Before Randy left, while he was still working on Hailey, he told me that the first goal will be to stabilize Gail's heart rate and breathing. If possible, he said, the lifeguards will do CPR in the water, but I guess they weren't able to because the EMTs are doing it now.

I lean in to get a better look at Gail's face. Her eyes are still closed, and I'm reminded of the baby chicks in Hailey's class and the way I freaked out when I thought they were dead. Standing here, studying my middle girl, I refuse to make the same mistake twice.

Gail isn't dead, I tell myself. She's just sleeping.

Like Randy and his partner, these new EMTs are barrel-chested and competent. "Come on, kiddo." The taller one, Donaldson, listens to Gail's chest. "Flip said she was breathing before. What the hell happened?"

Donaldson is older than Randy, and although still very young—late twenties at most—he acts as if he's been doing this job for years. His movements are rhythmic and graceful—pinch, breathe, listen, pinch, breathe, listen—and watching him convinces me that he'll have Gail up and on her feet in no time, despite how grim the situation may appear.

"Nothing," he tells his partner. "Trache her, Andrews—fast."

Andrews inserts a tube into Gail's mouth and snakes it down her throat. "I'm in. Let's get her warmed up and inside." He jumps into the ambulance for blankets, which he places gently over Gail's body. He looks up. "Are her parents here?"

I hold up my hand. "I'm her mother." I don't like to lie, so I revise my statement. "Her stepmother, actually."

"We're taking her to Hilton Head," Andrews says. "We have to go *now*."

"I'm ready. I just need to talk to my sister."

Sylvia is lying on a gurney, and as I move toward her, I worry that Andrews is going to ask me the same questions about Gail that Randy had asked about Hailey. Does she have a history of heart problems? Lung problems? Anything odd about her birth? I don't know, I'll have to say; I wasn't there. She had another mother at the time, one who wouldn't have left her out in the ocean.

Sylvia needs oxygen, too, but her eyes are open and she's alert. The EMT is struggling to lower a mask on her face, but she's resisting. "I have...to see...my niece!" she snaps between huffs and puffs. "I have...to...see Gail."

"We need to examine you," the EMT replies firmly. "Your niece is fine. They're taking her to the hospital right now."

"Sylvia," I say, "let them do their job."

She doesn't take no for an answer, my sister, and grabs the hem of the man's shorts to pull herself into a sitting position. Motioning for me to come closer, she puts her hand on my arm. I flinch. Her palm is cold and clammy. Choking back tears, I start to thank her, but she has something urgent to tell me.

"Shut the...fuck up," she gasps, her breathing still labored from her long swim. "What did you...tell Grant?" She digs her fingers into my skin.

I don't understand. "What did I tell Grant about what?"

"About the *kids*...What did you say about the *kids*?" Sylvia is pissed off that I'm so slow. *Snap to it, Eliot, pay attention.* "Did you tell him what *happened*?"

"What happened when?" When I was talking to Finn? "Sylvia, I'm not sure what you mean. I told Grant I was watching the kids and the next thing I knew, they were—"

She cuts me off. "Why didn't you tell him the truth?"

I lower my voice. "About being on the phone, you mean?"

"No!" Her voice rises. "The *truth*—that *I* was the one watching the kids." By this point, she's shouting. "Eliot, *don't cover for me*! We need to tell Grant what really happened."

Now I get it. "Sylvia, stop. I'm serious. Don't do this."

But it's too late; she's already blurting out her story to anyone who'll listen.

"I swear, Dolores," she tells my mother. "Eliot had to go to the bathroom. I only turned away for *one second*. One minute they were there, and the next..." She starts to cry. "I'm so sorry. I can't believe I did this." She cries harder and harder, unleashing wet, guttural sobs from somewhere down deep. And her grief seems so genuine and true, I almost believe her myself.

"We have to go!" The EMTs are insistent. "We're leaving; we can't wait. We can take one family member, preferably a parent. Everyone else rides separately."

All afternoon, my mother has been standing back, quietly watching and waiting. This is not her nature. Ordinarily she is hysterical, carrying on as though she is raising the dead. It's weird to see her so calm, and yet here she is. She steps forward. "Sylvia, it was an accident." But she sounds disappointed, as if she's been waiting for something like this to happen; it was only a question of when. "Sylvia!" She points to my sister's legs. *"Sylvia, look!"*

But Sylvia is in a zone. "Eliot asked me to watch the girls," she keeps repeating. "She had to go to the bathroom. I was on the phone, but I *was* watching, and then—"

"SYLVIA!" my mother interrupts her. *"You're bleeding!"* She still has that same disappointed tone. *What have you done now?* she is asking my sister. "Eliot, look!"

Blood is trickling down Sylvia's legs. It's only a thin stream, but she's pregnant, so any blood at all isn't good. A third EMT, a woman I hadn't noticed until now, rushes over and helps Sylvia into the ambulance.

Following them, I hike myself up. "I'm Gail Delaney's parent," I announce to the EMTs.

My mother tries to hike herself up, too, but stumbles. Both EMTs lean over to help her. "I'm Sylvia Gordon's parent." She looks at me. Each girl has a parent. We're ready.

No, wait—Charlotte is standing on the sand. Somehow we've forgotten about her.

"What about me?" she asks, crying harder, which makes me want to cry, too. It's so difficult with three.

"Mom?" I ask. "Can you stay here with Charlotte—I mean, drive her to the hospital? She can't be alone; she's only fourteen." I tell Charlotte to call Grant. "My phone is gone, so I need you to call Daddy. *Please?* Tell him we're on our way. Tell him Gail is doing much better."

Charlotte doesn't move.

"Just do it, Charlotte!" I lower my voice. "I'm sorry." I close my eyes, count to three. "Please call Daddy. And please tell him Gail is doing much better." How many lies have I told her? How many have I made her tell for me?

My mother moves to the back of the ambulance. Watching her try to find her footing, I'm reminded that she is seventy-eight years old and doesn't need any of this. She only wanted to do her work and spend time with her daughters. Why does everything get so complicated? None of this makes any sense.

"What's going on, guys?" Hearing a familiar voice booming, I watch as Charlotte is scooped up off her feet. It's Roger, our Vandy football hero, our homecoming king. Why is he always lifting people in the air like that?

He targets me, the eldest sister, for details. "I just got back from the golf course. What happened?" He peeks into the ambulance. "How is Sylvia?"

"Roger?" Sylvia calls out weakly from inside the ambulance. "I'm in here."

"We need to get going," the female EMT says. "This little girl needs to see a doctor."

"Sylvia saved Gail's life," I tell him, although I leave out why Gail had to be saved in the first place. "She's bleeding a little, nothing major, but they want to check her out. She'll be okay, Roger, I promise. Everyone is going to be okay." We have to keep our hopes up. Optimism is very important in times of uncertainty.

"Roger?" Sylvia asks. "You'll meet us at the hospital? I don't have my bag."

"Sure, baby, of course. You hang on, okay? Charlotte and I will be right behind you."

The doors close, and the ambulance pulls out. Sylvia is lying next to Gail, who is still sleeping. My mother and I perch on a narrow ledge. It's a bumpy ride, and we hold on tight.

"She looks better," I say, commenting on Gail's color, which isn't as blue.

Neither EMT responds.

"She'll be okay." This isn't a question; it's a statement of fact. Now that Hailey is safe, Gail will be, too. These heaven-sent EMTs, this princely band of brothers, will save my other girl. And once they wake Gail up, we can all go home.

The older guy, Donaldson, is busy. He doesn't acknowledge me. But Andrews, the junior guy, replies: "She was under a long time, ma'am."

Although he's polite, he doesn't look at me. I wonder if this is significant. With my first EMT, Randy, it was different. When he gave me the blow-by-blow, he looked me straight in the eye, but Andrews won't even lift his head. Already, I feel the ground shifting beneath me.

"Thank you for everything." I hope I sound as appreciative as I feel.

Donaldson ticks off numbers, vital signs, blood pressure, just as Randy did for Hailey, only Donaldson is much faster, more serious. I ask a few questions, but neither man answers, except to explain that they have hooked Gail up to a machine that is breathing for her.

As I watch the expert care the men give Gail, I realize I'm not panicked. I'm not calm, certainly, but I'm not as frantic as I was with Hailey. Donaldson and Andrews are professional, and seeing how adeptly they work, I trust they will do all they can for Gail.

On the way to the hospital, I learn several things: How well Gail recovers depends on how long she went without oxygen. Equally important is the condition of her lungs and heart, as well as whether or not her other organs sustained tissue damage.

"Do you have any statistics?" I ask, positive this makes no sense. *Statistics of what, lady?*

The two EMTs glance at each other, and I see a silent message pass between them.

"They'll tell you everything you need to know in the ER," Andrews informs me.

Thankfully, though, he explains what will happen when we get there. First the doctors will determine Gail's body temperature, measure her electrolytes, and do a head CT and complete blood count. They'll also take cultures and do Gram's stains to check for bacteria. At the same time, she'll undergo a rewarming procedure. Then, after a complete assessment, they'll decide whether or not to airlift her to Savannah Memorial, where there's a world-class trauma center.

Hearing about all these tests is heartening. "She won't have to go to Savannah, though."

My mother echoes my sentiments. "That seems a bit extreme."

Andrews shakes his head. "From the way things look, I'm afraid she will, ma'am. They're probably prepping the chopper right now. And once she gets to Savannah, she'll go right into the PICU." The PICU, I find out, is the pediatric intensive care unit.

Still, I remain optimistic. If she were in really awful shape, wouldn't they just go directly to Savannah? Seems to me they're taking a very long detour, which means Gail can't be as bad off as they say. I once read that health care professionals are notorious for giving worst-case scenarios. This makes perfect sense to me. No one wants to backpedal when the patient ends up dying. We do the same thing in corporate communications. In fact, we'll intentionally go all the way to DEFCON 1 (*Due to catastrophic economic conditions, Company X may have to declare bankruptcy*) just to be able to wrap up at DEFCON 3 (*As it turns out, Company X remains solvent; however, to continue to make payroll during these uncertain times, we are freezing salaries indefinitely and reducing bonuses by 30 percent*). This way, employees don't mind getting shafted. On the contrary, they're grateful they still have a job.

I call Grant on my mother's phone. "Gail is much better; they've got her stabilized. She's still sleeping, but her breathing is okay." Because I'm not sure how Grant himself is doing, I leave out the fact that she's on a ventilator.

Thankfully, he sounds stronger and more centered than he did on the beach. "Hailey's heart rate is steadier," he tells me, then recites the numbers. "They think she's fine, but want to keep her overnight." He says something else, something technical I don't catch.

"What about her breathing? Is it still erratic?"

"I'm sorry, Eliot. That's all I know."

"I'm sorry, too," I say before we hang up. *Oh, Grant, I am so, so sorry.*

When I hand back my mother's phone, she says, "Gail's in a coma," and neither Donaldson nor Andrews corrects her. I glance over at Gail, who continues to sleep despite all the tubes and machines, the lights and the noise. "She's *asleep*," I say, and no one corrects me, either.

Sylvia's eyes are closed. "Are you awake?" my mother asks, but my sister doesn't answer. Over her head, my mother raises her eyebrows. "Has anyone called Gail's mother?"

"I'm sure Grant has."

"I'm so sorry I did this, Eliot." Sylvia's eyes are still closed, but tears leak out the sides. She is holding her belly, and I believe she's in pain, if only because she hasn't mentioned it.

"It was *an accident*. There's nothing to be sorry about." I'm so proud of Sylvia—and Maggie and my mother, too. In a time of real crisis, when there is genuine drama, they've all risen to the occasion and done more than their fair share, more than I asked them to, certainly.

"It was *my fault*." Sylvia is firm.

Hearing this, I silently acknowledge something: My sister is a liar.

Sylvia Gordon lies about everything. But that's nothing compared with the real revelation, which is that I am a liar, too.

"It was *my fault*," Sylvia repeats.

I look down at Gail. I consider her and her sisters; and Grant, I consider him, too. They are my family, not my original family, but the one I am raising. As the matriarch of this family, it's my job to protect us. Because of this—because of them—I say nothing.

Chapter Twenty

WE'RE TAKEN TO Hilton Head Medical Center, which is a small, ninety-three-bed hospital near the airport. As soon as we arrive at the ER, Gail and Sylvia are whisked into separate trauma rooms. My mother and I are directed around the corner to the triage area, where Grant and Maggie are sitting with Hailey. Except for the staff, the place is empty. It's Monday, the first of October, so the rest of the world is at work or in school.

In the triage area, there are curtained exam rooms, like cubicles, with a table and two chairs on either side. When I spot Hailey, my eyes fill with tears. *She's okay! My girl is okay!*

"Mommy?" Her voice is weak and she starts to cry. I take her hand and kiss it.

Hailey is definitely better. Her cheeks are pink again and she looks like herself. Sipping apple juice, she's lying on the exam table, hooked up to a machine that is tracking her heart rate.

"I'm here," I tell her, tears spilling down my cheeks. "See? Daddy told you I'd be here, and I came."

As we fill out medical histories and insurance forms for both girls, Grant tells me about Hailey. "She wants to see Gail." This is the third time he's said this and the first thing he said when he saw me. "She's worried about her sister."

"Gail is with the doctors." I keep my voice soft and soothing. "She's getting excellent care." I turn to Hailey. "Your sister will be fine, just like you're fine."

"They want to keep her overnight for observation," Grant says to no one in particular.

"We knew they would." I assume he's referring to Hailey. I haven't told him yet that they're airlifting Gail to Savannah as soon as she's stable. One thing at a time, I remind myself.

Grant leaves to find Gail but has no luck. When he comes back, I sit him down in the chair next to Hailey and hold his hand. Then I describe what will happen next. I tell him everything the EMTs told me, including the tests they'll perform and the different doctors she'll see. Drawing on my long career as a communications specialist, I speak slowly and clearly. I'm gentle, though, and, of course, very positive. I want Grant to feel hopeful because I feel hopeful. I'm frightened, naturally, but determined to stay solid. The worst thing we can do is give in to our fear. Once that happens, we're finished.

"Grant, we're doing everything we can for Gail." I want him to know I am on the case. Now that I'm here, I'll take care of everything and everyone, including him. I lean over and kiss his forehead. "It's going to be okay."

"*Grant? . . .* Grant, can I talk to you?" It's Sylvia. She's being wheeled into her own curtained-off cubicle. My mother is walking beside her, holding her hand.

Grant looks at me. "What does she want?"

I tell him I don't know. "You should talk to her, though." That I can continue to implicate my innocent and heroic sister is crazy. I don't recognize myself. Then again, maybe I never knew myself. Apparently there's a coward as well as a liar underneath my good-girl veneer.

Grant disappears behind the curtain with Sylvia.

My poor little sister, I think. She needs help. I nudge Maggie, my even littler sister. "You go too. She'll want you to be there." That my two kid sisters have to face Grant without me, the eldest, to protect them makes me hate myself. I need to unmix this but don't know how.

"Mommy," Hailey says weakly, "I was in the water." It's exhausting for her to speak. She drifts off for a second, then wakes with a start. She'll be asleep soon; she's just fighting it.

"Yes, but you came out." I'm listening to her, but I'm also trying to hear what Sylvia is telling Grant and Maggie on the other side of the curtain.

"You swimmed to me, didn't you?"

"I sure did, Hailey. I swam and got you and you were safe. And then Aunt Sylvia jumped into the water and got Gail. Aunt Sylvia is a hero. She's a girl hero, which is called a *heroine*."

"I have something for Gail." She unclenches her fist. In her palm, there's a shell. "The doctor gave it to me for being brave, but I want to give it to Gail."

I hear murmuring behind the screen and then Grant's voice. He sounds frantic. "Just *say it*, Sylvia. Just *say it* already." I can tell he's afraid to hear but also desperate to know. "It can't be that bad."

Sylvia is crying. "I'm sorry." Her voice rises. "Eliot had to go to the bathroom, so she asked me to watch the kids. They were playing on the sand and my phone rang, so I picked it up. I turned away for a second—just a second—and when I turned back, both kids were in the water. Thank God Eliot hadn't gone too far. She raced in and grabbed Hailey and I went for Gail."

She's talking abnormally loud, and I know it's for my benefit, so that I'll have the story, too. I wish I could see Grant's face, to see if he believes her. Why wouldn't he believe her? But that's not the question, I realize. The question is why *would* he believe her? Sylvia lies about everything, even the truth.

"It was just for a second," she shouts. "One second, that's it!"

It occurs to me that I'm thinking about this the wrong way—that is, from my point of view. I need to see it from Grant's. Why would Sylvia lie? What she is telling him is so awful, it has to be the truth. That she was distracted while watching the kids is not only plausible, there's historical precedent. The only question Grant will have, the question he's probably asking himself right now, isn't *Why did Sylvia turn away?* It's *How could Eliot allow her crazy sister to watch my kids in the first place?*

I realize Hailey is talking to me. "We were playing monster."

"What did you say, sweet pea?"

"We got covered in sand, so we jumped in the waves to wash our bodies. At first I was afraid, and Gail called me a baby, but then I went in." Hailey looks confused. "The water was fast. I couldn't get up."

"It's okay." I hug her. "I was right there. I grabbed you."

"But I was under a long time, Mommy." She looks around. "Where's Gail?"

"Gail is with the doctors," I say gently, watching her closely.

Hailey yawns. "Is she dead?"

"No, Hailey, of course not. Right now she's just sleeping."

I hear Roger's voice booming across the room. *"She's fourteen,"* he tells the nurses. "She just wants to see her sisters . . . *Hailey?* Someone special is here to see you!"

"Gail!" Hailey yelps, but it takes all her energy, and she has to lie back.

"It's not Gail," I tell her. "It's Charlotte. *Charlotte!* We're over here."

Roger and Charlotte spot us. "Where's Daddy?" she asks.

"He's with Aunt Sylvia and Aunt Maggie." I offer her my seat. "He'll be done in a second." I turn to Roger. "Thank you for bringing her. Sylvia is over there." I point to the curtain, and he moves toward it.

Charlotte is anxious about Gail. "What's going on? When can I see her?"

"Gail is with her doctors; she has a whole team of people taking care of her. As soon as they can, they'll tell us everything."

I hear Sylvia say she's sorry again. Her voice is teary. I don't hear anything for a second, but then Grant yanks open the curtain of her cubicle, steps out, and stomps back to ours.

"I have to call Beth." His jaw is set, and he won't meet my eyes. "She's waiting for news about Gail."

I need this to end right now. "Grant, wait. There's something I have to tell you—"

Sylvia shouts for help. "I'm bleeding! *I need a nurse.* Someone help me!"

A nurse rushes over. Although Sylvia complains to her about being in pain, I know it's all theater. She's creating a distraction so I won't tell Grant the truth.

"What the fuck is wrong with her now?" he spits out.

I'm struck by how angry he sounds. On the one hand, it's Gail and he's frightened, so how else would he react? But Grant is by nature a forgiving man. In his heart, he knows it was an accident, that Sylvia would never intentionally harm Gail. Sylvia loves Gail, and Grant loves Sylvia; she's family. He'll forgive her. Thinking this way gives me hope that no matter how angry he gets, when I explain to him what really happened, he'll be able to forgive me, too.

"I'll be back in a few minutes," he tells me. "I promised Beth an update."

As he walks out of the triage area, I murmur, "I am so, so sorry, Grant."

I don't think he hears me, so I'm surprised when he whips around and announces to the entire ER, "This isn't your fault, Eliot. It's not *your* fault at all."

⌒

We wait and we wait. They continue to work on Gail, but when we ask the nurses what's happening, they can't tell us anything.

"The doctor will speak to you soon as he can," one says, which does nothing to relieve our collective anxiety.

For the first time in my life, I wish I had religion, or if not religion, then at least proper faith. If I had something solid to believe in, maybe I wouldn't feel so nervous. But when it comes to God, I don't know anything about anything. Although I consider myself Jewish, I never went to temple or Hebrew school. When I was sixteen, I did go through a period when I wanted to learn about Judaism. I read a few books and saw some movies. But it was more an intellectual exercise than a spiritual one, so it felt hollow. And when I was finished, I still lacked context for who I am, such as a history or sense of community. Assuming I'd eventually figure it out, I pushed the whole issue aside. But sitting here, waiting for Gail to wake up, I am desperate for something, or someone, to grab hold of, to restore order.

Please God, I pray silently, feeling the emptiest I've ever felt. *Please let her wake up.*

Roger is with Sylvia behind her curtain, and I'm sitting with Hailey, who is sleeping, behind ours. Charlotte is with my mother and Maggie out in the waiting room. There's a sign on the wall prohibiting cell phones, but Grant is beside me, talking to Beth. From what I can gather, she is at the Atlanta airport, waiting to catch the next flight to Savannah.

"Lizzie," he is saying softly, "Lizzie, please stop crying. Gail will be okay, I promise."

He is being sweet to her, gentle, and I'm reminded of what a kind man he is. It's weird, though, to hear him call her *Lizzie*, and the unexpectedness of it fills me with sudden terror.

"As soon as I find out, I'll call you. Just get on the plane, and call me when it lands. Then I'll pick you up at the airport, or you can take a cab to Savannah Memorial."

"You know about Savannah?" I ask him.

He doesn't answer but repeats the directions again to Beth, to *Lizzie*. I bend over, sick to my stomach, imagining how scared she must feel.

"Don't forget to call me when you land," he says as he signs off. "And don't worry about anything. Gail will be—"

His voice breaks. He stands up and shakes his leg, as if that's what caused him to choke up. Then he yanks open our curtain and stomps out of the triage area. Head up, eyes forward, Grant moves with pinpoint precision, squaring off right angles with his arms by his sides, like a cadet marching a punishment tour. Watching this, I see the army in him and realize I was wrong before. Grant is absolutely fine in a crisis.

He secured the required intel, then comforted the women and children, and now he is tracking his daughters' progress, minute by minute. If Fred Delaney were alive, he would be proud of his son.

A few minutes later, he returns, closes our curtain, and sits down. "Beth is on her way."

"How is she holding up?"

"She's devastated." Grant raises his voice. "She can't understand how this happened—how people, how adults, can act so *irresponsibly* with other people's *children*."

"It was an accident, Grant. It could've happened to anyone."

"I understand that, Eliot. I'm just trying to process this, okay?"

I reach for his hand and squeeze it. His loud voice, I'm sure, is for Sylvia. Behind the flimsy fabric, he probably feels fearless, as though he can say anything he wants, no matter how rude or insulting. Behind their own curtain, Roger and Sylvia are quiet. There's some rustling, some shifting of positions, and then they're quiet again.

I open our curtain so Grant won't yell at my sister anymore. I sit in my plastic chair and try to devise a way to undo this. But then I spy the phone in Grant's hands, and I think of Beth, of *Lizzie*, who is alone in Atlanta and can't touch her child, who has no idea, really, if her kid will live or die. I am filled with grief for her, as well as dread, knowing she'll be here in a few hours. And as I feel this grief and this dread, my need to come clean disappears.

"It was an accident, Grant," I repeat, touching his shoulder.

"I know." He quiets down. "Of course it was. I don't mean anything I'm saying. I'm just petrified that Gail is...that she'll..." Unable to finish, he puts his head in his hands. "She's just a little girl." His eyes fill with tears.

A minute later, Roger pulls back his curtain. Seeing him, Grant straightens up, wipes his eyes. As Roger passes, he glances into our area, and his eyes flicker at Grant and then dart away. He stops for a second, then doubles back.

"Hey, Grant. Man, I'm so sorry about all this." He extends his enormous hand. "Let me know what I can do to help. Anything you need—just say the word."

Grant glances at Roger's hand, and I see this as a sign. If he shakes Roger's hand, then everyone will be okay.

I hold my breath.

At first it doesn't look good, but Roger, who towers over Grant, stands firm. I'm afraid Grant will turn away or, worse, spit in Roger's face, when he suddenly reaches out and grabs Roger, not by the hand but around the shoulders. Their clumsy bear hug, complete with affectionate back whacks, is a thing of beauty.

Filled with familial pride, I exhale.

"Eliot?" Sylvia calls out. "They said I'm fine, but I have to stay overnight."

"I should talk to her," I tell Grant, but as I get up from my chair, a doctor walks in. He speaks to a nurse, who points him in our direction.

"Mr. Delaney? I'm Sherman Guthrie, the ER attending. I've been taking care of your daughter."

Grant gets up so quickly that he drops his phone. It hits the floor and bounces. "Yes," he says, scrambling to retrieve it. "I'm Grant Delaney."

The two men shake hands, then the doctor turns to me. "And you're Gail's mother?"

"I'm her stepmother, Eliot Gordon." I hold out my hand, but he doesn't shake it. He doesn't even look in my direction, which is very disconcerting.

"Let's step outside," Dr. Guthrie says.

Grant, Dr. Guthrie, and I move "outside," which is really just ten feet to the left, into a small office adjacent to the triage area. From where I'm standing, I can see Hailey dozing on the exam table. Although she looks peaceful, I feel an urgent need to wake her up and have to restrain myself from rushing over.

Dr. Guthrie speaks first. "Let me start by saying that Gail is doing much better than when she first arrived. We were able to stabilize her breathing and heart rate, her lungs are working, and she doesn't appear to have sustained any external damage to her head or neck. We've also treated her for hypothermia, and her blood-gas results are returning to normal. So far, we're pleased with her progress."

"This is all excellent news," I say firmly.

Dr. Guthrie's beeper goes off. "Excuse me." He turns to pick up a phone. "Guthrie," he says sharply.

I clasp Grant's hand. He moves closer and puts his arm around me. So far, so good, I think.

Dr. Guthrie is around sixty and speaks clearly and confidently, which is also an excellent sign. I was glad that the EMTs were younger in age. The physical jobs—search and rescue, CPR and chest compressions, ambulance driving—require brawn and quick-trigger reflexes, not to mention stamina and heart. But now, seeing Dr. Guthrie's white-tufted hair, the crow's-feet around his eyes, and how he moves with the gravitas of an elder statesman, I'm equally glad that here, in the ER, Gail is in more mature hands.

"Sorry about that." Dr. Guthrie turns back to us. "Where were we?"

"Gail is doing much better. You said she's on the mend."

"Sorry, but unfortunately, Miz...," he falters.

"Gordon," I offer. "Eliot Gordon."

"Sorry, Miz Gordon, but that's not what I said."

Dr. Guthrie isn't smiling anymore. His lips are pursed, and his brow is furled, making him look like a schoolteacher who is disappointed in the way I have misinformed his class. He doesn't like me, and I find this worrisome. I've always gotten along well with authority figures—principals, policemen, movie ushers. I want him to know how famously I meshed with the EMT brothers, that at the end the boys were saying, "Good luck, ma'am," and, "Take care, Eliot." Randy even pecked me on the cheek.

"Let's be clear about one thing, folks: *Gail is in a coma*. As far as we can tell from the CT, she doesn't appear to have sustained any *external* head injuries, but we can't be sure what's going on *inside* her brain."

He looks first at me, then at Grant, as if checking that we've heard and understood him.

"Yes." I nod to illustrate that I comprehend. "Gail is in a coma."

"We don't know how long, exactly, she was submerged, nor do we know how long she went without oxygen, so it's hard to say when she'll recover. She's young, and she's healthy. No history of heart trouble, right? No problems at birth?" He ticks off the questions I was worried about earlier, but Grant is here and answers them all: No, no problems, not a one, healthy kid, healthy birth.

"That's good." Dr. Guthrie takes out a small pad and makes some notes. "So, she's got a strong heart, and from what we were told, she was out there a while, but not under for too long. Apparently, she grabbed some driftwood, and that helped to keep her afloat. She is one lucky little girl. Don't get me wrong, your daughter took in water and debris, but she was pulled out before her lungs flooded. Also, her breathing was reestablished fairly quickly, considering."

I'm buoyed for a second that he referred to Gail as "lucky."

"What are normal recovery times?" Grant asks.

"We don't have any hard and fast rules, Mr. Delaney, but generally, the kids who have the best chances are those who've been underwater less than five minutes, and who get immediate CPR."

"Worst case?"

"Impossible to say. I will tell you, though, that patients who arrive unconscious usually take longer to recover."

"And Gail came in unconscious..." Grant trails off.

Dr. Guthrie looks away.

I rack my brain to come up with smart questions, too, so I can get back into Dr. Guthrie's good graces. This man has to like me. I need him to like me. I know it won't make any difference to Gail's situation; it just feels important.

"Why?" I blurt out, desperate to say something.

Dr. Guthrie turns to me. "Why what?"

I groan. *I don't know.* "Why do some kids wake up sooner than others?"

"A lot of different factors." He raises one finger. "There's submersion time; there's water conditions—temperature, pressure, purity. If the water is contaminated, she could have systemic problems." He raises another. "Does the victim have other symptoms? Is she bleeding internally, for example? Did she hit her head?" He raises a third. "How well did she respond to resuscitation? Does she have any history of heart problems?"

Dr. Guthrie has raised finger four and is starting on five, but I've stopped listening. He probably doesn't think I noticed that he went from calling Gail a *kid* to a *patient* to a *victim* within a two-minute span.

"What we need to do now," he continues, "to rule out hypoxic cerebral injury—that's brain injury resulting from a lack of oxygen—is to get her checked out at a facility capable of providing appropriate intensive care. My suggestion is to helicopter her over to Savannah Memorial, where we'll arrange to have a team meet us."

Grant's face is ashen; he looks petrified. "Yes, Doctor. Do whatever you think is necessary. What time do you anticipate us arriving in Savannah?" He's speaking formally, primly, which tells me he's using everything in his power just to hold himself together.

"If we leave now, it's a ten-minute hop. Just give me the word, and I'll get the chopper."

I can see Dr. Guthrie has concerns, and I understand Gail has a ways to go, but he keeps vacillating between Gail waking up in an hour and needing to prepare the victim for burial. For a doctor, he has a lousy habit of equivocating, which is something I know quite a bit about. Just tell us the story, I want to shout; give us the net-net, the bottom line, the news cycle sound bite.

"Please," I tell him, "please just tell us what you think will happen."

He looks at me. "I don't know what will happen, Miz..."

"*Gordon.*" Christ, if he can't remember my fucking name, how can he accurately assess Gail's condition?

He inhales sharply, which tells me he's annoyed. He's a busy man, this Dr. Guthrie, and doesn't have time for such foolishness. He can't abide these stupid tourists who come to his islands, his beloved Wyatt and Hilton Head, only to abuse their God-given glory. Nor will he put up with any more rich Atlanta folk who refuse to learn about water safety and allow their spoiled children to play unsupervised in the ocean.

Dr. Guthrie turns toward me and stares straight into my eyes. His somberness tells me that I'd better listen closely because he's going to say this only once.

"As I was saying before, Miz Gordon, when children arrive in the ER comatose, permanent neurological damage—even death—is more likely than not. I can't make any predictions about Gail, but statistically, children who require specialized treatment for drowning experience a *thirty percent mortality rate*. An additional thirty percent experience *severe brain damage*. We need to determine the extent of the damage, but I can't do it here, which is why you need to get to Savannah as soon as possible."

It's his use of the modifier "the" that gets me. Dr. Guthrie didn't say "any" brain damage or "possible" brain damage; he said "the" damage, as if it's a foregone conclusion that Gail is in trouble.

Dr. Guthrie continues to list all the other potential complications Gail might suffer, but I can't hear what they are because the air around my head is suddenly too light to breathe. I feel as if I'm in a plane that has lost cabin pressure and is swooping downward.

"Gail has brain damage," I say, but I'm gasping.

Years ago, when my mother's sister, Barbara, was dying of cancer, she moved into our house so we could take care of her. One night at the end, drugged and delusional, she clutched my hand in panic. "I forgot how to sleep, Ellie," she wailed. "I'm lying here and my eyes are closed, but I don't remember what comes next. Go get Dolores. My sister will know what to do."

Listening to Dr. Guthrie, I begin to understand my aunt's terror at forgetting how to sleep because I've forgotten how to breathe.

Inhale slowly, I coach myself, *now exhale. Inhale. Exhale.* My eyes grow cloudy and I begin to sway. I grab Grant's arm for support because if I don't, I'm going to fall off my feet, off the floor, off the very earth. "I understand, Dr. Guthrie." Cold and clammy, I can barely move; all I can do is absorb the net-net. "I understand everything."

"I'm so glad," he says, and turns on his heel to ready his team for travel.

Chapter Twenty-one

THIS IS A FACT: Gail is in grave danger. Another fact: It's my fault. A third fact: Grant has no idea. *What have you done?* I keep asking myself. *What the hell have you done?*

Today started with everyone together on the beach. Now it's evening, and we're all scattered. Gail was taken to Savannah, and Grant and Charlotte went with her. I'm still at the hospital on Hilton Head with my mother and Maggie. Hailey was finally moved to her own room, which is where we are now, helping her settle in. Sylvia was admitted, too, but she's on another floor.

I need to see Sylvia, I decide, unable to sit still. We need to talk this through, make a plan, set everyone straight. I glance at my mother and sister. Maggie is on the bed with Hailey. They're both watching *SpongeBob*, although Maggie is more engrossed in the show than Hailey. My mother is in a chair beside them.

I ask her if she minds staying with Hailey for a few minutes. "I'm going to see Sylvia. I want to find out how she's doing."

She shakes her head. "Of course not."

"And when I get back, you should go home. You and Maggie both look exhausted."

"We're fine," Maggie says, her eyes on the TV. "You're the one who looks exhausted."

On the contrary, I'm racing with adrenaline. Now that I have a mission, I'm anxious to see it through.

Slumped in her chair, my mother is staring off into space. Touching her shoulder, I ask if she's okay. "You look so tired, Mom."

She smiles weakly. "I'm fine, Eliot. And Maggie is right. Don't worry about us. Go see Sylvia. Roger's probably there, too. If he is, could you let him know that Maggie needs a ride back to Wyatt?"

"What about you?" Maggie asks.

"I'd like to sleep here, in the hospital. Eliot, is that okay?"

I'm too agitated to make any decisions. "Let's talk about it when I get back." I lean over to say good-bye to Hailey. "Try to get some sleep, sweet pea. I'm going to go check on Aunt Sylvia, and then I'll come back here to be with you."

Kissing her head, I breathe in her smell. I'm aware that this is a privilege to kiss my child, to smell her smell; a gift denied Grant, whose daughter is lying comatose in a Savannah PICU. Every few minutes I say a small prayer, thanking God or whoever for my daughter's health and well-being. I say a prayer for Gail, too. Although I know it's not much, for the moment it's something.

Hailey is in a TV zone, which is good. Ten minutes ago, she burst into inconsolable tears, which stopped as abruptly as they started. The doctor said it was okay to let her sleep, so she's been dozing on and off since we left the ER. It's clear, though, that she's experiencing some sort of traumatic response to what happened. She'll close her eyes for a few minutes, then suddenly jerk awake, screaming.

"I won't be long," I tell my mother again. I kiss Hailey again, thank Maggie again, thank God again, and race off.

As I make my way through the small hospital, I decide what to do. No more fooling around, I'll tell my sister. Grant has to know the truth. I'll start from the beginning and describe the entire sequence of events, from the moment I saw Finn at Riverside, all the way to that last second on the beach. I won't leave anything out. My only concern is Sylvia. Even if I tell her it's over, that we can't lie anymore, I know she'll do whatever she wants. That's why I have to be firm; I can't let her bulldoze me.

No more games, I tell myself. This is serious.

I get out of the elevator and look for her room. Before I find it, though, I make a quick stop in the ladies' room. I have to throw up, but because I haven't eaten all day, it's more like dry heaving. Still, I feel better afterward. It's also a relief to have a plan and to know that one way or another, the truth will be revealed. Soon, everything will go back to normal.

Ten minutes later, I'm sitting on Sylvia's bed, trying to talk to her— rather, trying to get her to talk to me. Roger is off somewhere making calls, so she and I are alone.

"Why are you doing this?" I ask again.

"What am I doing?" she says, staring at some reality show on TV.

"Come on, Sylvia."

She glances at my feet, which are still caked with sand. "Don't you dare put your disgusting feet on my bed, Eliot. I have to sleep in it tonight."

"Fine, Sylvia, have it your way. But just so you know? I'm calling Grant tonight and telling him what really happened, so you have to stop saying it was your fault. As Gail's father, he deserves to know the truth."

This gets her attention. She turns to me, unblinking. "You may want to rethink that plan," she says quietly, but with just enough menace to shut me up. This scares me. Not because she'll hurt me, but because she's far more confident than I'll ever be. I, for example, am still hung up on whether or not I really will tell Grant, but for Sylvia, this conversation is over. Already turned back to the TV, she increases the volume.

I feel like a fool, not only because my sister won't do what I say, but also because I don't think I want her to. How will Grant ever be able to look at me again once he finds out I was the one with the girls? Oh, and by the way, I wasn't paying attention to them because I was on the phone with my college boyfriend, the one I've been seeing secretly for the past few weeks, the one I somehow failed to mention.

Afraid I'm going to be sick again, I run into the bathroom. Nothing comes up, though, so I crouch for a minute over the toilet, resting my head on my arms.

When I come out, Sylvia is looking at me with concern but doesn't ask if I'm okay. Instead she says, "This place isn't so bad. It's like a hotel. They even have room service." She hands me a pillow. "Relax, Eliot. Get comfortable. I'll ask one of the waitresses to get us a bucket of ice."

"You mean the nurses?"

"*Nurses* sounds so sterile. How about *hospital hostesses*? Or *health care concierges*?"

"Just call them 'nurses,' Sylvia. No one likes a pain in the ass."

She's right, though: the hospital is nice. Her private room has a big picture window with a breathtaking view of the ocean. Paintings of seascapes hang on the walls, and the burgundy wallpaper matches the ruffled curtains. She has free HBO, and there are vending machines down the hall, where I bought three Kit Kats, two packs of Wheat Thins, two bags of pretzels, and a Diet Coke, all of which is piled on Sylvia's blanket like a picnic. If not for the harsh lighting, the steel bars on the bed, and the monitors attached to her stomach, we could be at a Days Inn.

"How do you feel?" I ask.

She shrugs.

According to my mother, there are complications with the baby— something is perforated or torn—and Sylvia has to stay here a few days. When she heard the news, Sylvia didn't cry out or scream. She simply nodded and closed her eyes. "I couldn't believe it," my mom remarked. "I said to myself, Who is this person?"

"You know, Eliot," Sylvia says, "if the waitresses weren't so annoying, I'd stay here all week. But they're constantly bustling in and out. They even have the audacity to talk over the TV." She sighs. "Customer service isn't what it used to be." She settles against the pillows. "Hear anything from Grant?" she asks casually, as though asking what I had for lunch.

I shake my head. Grant hasn't called since he left for the trauma center a couple of hours ago. I suspect Beth has arrived, so now we're divided up the way we were when we first met: he's with Beth, Charlotte, and Gail; I'm with my mother and sisters. When Hailey was born, Grant and I joked about what would happen if we ever did split up. "You would never give up custody like Beth," he said. "You'd never let me take Hailey." My response at the time: "Grant, you would have to find us first." The joke, of course, was that it was ludicrous to imagine us ever being forced to divvy up our child. Thinking about it now, I realize it's no longer so ludicrous.

Surprisingly, Grant didn't want Charlotte to travel to Savannah with him. He was afraid it would be too stressful for her to see her sister in the PICU. "Plus, she doesn't have a toothbrush or a change of clothes." But when he insisted that she stay behind with me, Charlotte got hysterical. She begged him to let her go, threatening to hitchhike if he didn't.

"Mom said I could go wherever Gail goes! Call her *right now*. Call her, Daddy. *She'll tell you.*"

"Your mother isn't here. She's in no position to give you permission." Grant's head was bent and his shoulders were hunched. "Don't do this now, Charlotte. Please, all I ask is *not now*."

"Daddy, please! I'll *die* if I have to stay here with *her*."

Hearing this, I flinched. Her hostility stung like a slap to the face. "Charlotte, please," I said, my voice shaky. "Take it down a notch, okay?" I knew she was angry at me, but until that moment, I hadn't realized just how angry.

"Don't tell me what to do!" she shrieked, her dark eyes flashing.

I felt Grant flinch, too. Leaning against me, he looked so fragile— one more outburst and his legs might collapse. "Let her go," I whispered. "She should be with you and Beth tonight."

Grant finally relented, but when Charlotte climbed into the helicopter, she pulled away as I tried to hug her. Nor did she say good-bye. She just put on the bulky headset and reached for her father's hand, which she cradled in her lap. I blew Grant a kiss, and he nodded, looking dazed and defeated. As I watched them lift off, I waved to them both, willing Grant to get some rest and Charlotte to breathe deeply. Soon the chopper was far above me, way up in the ether, but I could still feel the weight of Grant's exhaustion and the sharp teeth of Charlotte's rage.

Sylvia is still watching TV, but I talk to her anyway.

"Here's the problem, Sylvia. Gail knows what happened—she was *there*—so when she wakes up, the truth will come out. She'll tell Grant I was the one watching them—not you. You weren't even down by the water. So we may as well get everything straightened out now. I appreciate what you're trying to do—believe me, I appreciate it—but I can't lie anymore. It's not only wrong, it's also a tremendous burden to put on Gail."

Rather than respond, Sylvia makes the TV even louder. "Eliot, do you mind? They're about to vote someone off. This is the only part of the show I like."

"Please, Sylvia." I click off the TV, but Sylvia clicks it back on.

"You have your own room," she snaps. "This one's mine. If you want to stay here, then shut the fuck up."

We sit like this for a while: Sylvia watching TV and me watching her watch. Because she's doing me a favor—rather, because I need her to acknowledge both what she's doing and my gratitude for it—all I can do is wait.

Eventually I have to do something. I pick up Sylvia's phone and call my boss, Jared, in Atlanta. The office closed hours ago, but I leave him a message describing what happened and promising to get in touch as soon as I can. Then I call Grant. "Any change? What's happening? How are you holding up?"

He gives me an update. So far Gail's been seen by a pediatrician and a pediatric neurologist, both of whom say the same thing. There's no sign of external injury, and her internal organs seem okay. But because she experienced a near drowning incident, she runs the risk of complications, such as respiratory distress, tissue damage, multiple organ failure, even a heart attack. Meaning just because Gail's organs are functioning now doesn't mean they'll continue to function twelve, eighteen, twenty-four hours from now. There's also the issue of her brain, which is still up for grabs. And along with it, all her other functions... that is, walking, talking, sitting—being Gail, essentially.

"For all we know," Grant concludes sadly, "she could be in a coma for the rest of her life."

"She could also wake up and be fine," I say in his same monotone. I'm not in denial; I understand Gail is in bad shape. I just want Grant to consider an alternative outcome.

"She could. Or she could wake up and have the brain of an infant. It's a fucking crapshoot, Eliot."

"I thought they were performing tests to tell if she's brain—the extent of the damage."

"They are, and according to the results, there's nothing wrong with her. But who gives a shit? The tests can show she's able to perform differential calculus, but it doesn't matter if she's just lying there like a vegetable."

I wince. A few years ago, Grant and I went out for dinner with one of his clients. They were foreign, from Estonia, and their English was terrible. I was on a diet and ordered a salad, which the client's wife noticed. "Are you a vegetable?" she asked, meaning vegetarian. "Sometimes," I answered, which made all the Americans laugh.

"How's Hailey?" Grant asks.

"Much better. She's sleeping now. I'll stay with her tonight. Hopefully, we can leave first thing in the morning. The doctor makes his rounds early. If he says she's okay, we'll check out and then drive to Savannah." Wait, is that right? Do you check out of a hospital the way you check out of a hotel? You don't check into a hospital; you're admitted. But how do you leave? *Check out* sounds wrong, but I can't think of another phrase.

"That sounds good," Grant says. "I'm going to sleep in Gail's room tonight, but Charlotte can't. Visiting hours end at eight thirty, and there are no exceptions. So I have to find a room for Charlotte and Beth for the next few nights. I don't know what's around here."

"Do you want me to make some calls?" I ask.

He doesn't reply. Instead, he asks if, before I come to Savannah tomorrow, I would mind stopping by my mother's rental house and picking up all the luggage—his, Charlotte's, and Gail's—since it doesn't look like any of them will be going back to Wyatt Island. "You may as well return the car too while you're at it."

"Absolutely. Whatever you need—I'm totally here. Grant? I'm really sorry."

I mean I'm sorry in general, but Grant thinks I'm referring to the visiting hours. "It's so frustrating. Security is tighter than the Pentagon. There's a boy on the unit who's very contagious, so we can only see Gail once an hour for twenty minutes. No more than two people can go in at a time, and kids twelve and under can't go in at all, which means as much as I'd love to see Hailey, she probably shouldn't come."

"Whatever you think is best." I glance at Sylvia. "Listen, Grant. I need to tell you something . . . uh, something important." Suddenly nervous, I stop and start again but realize I can't do it. "I really love you."

"Me too, Eliot. Hang on, Beth and Charlotte just walked in." He's back a second later. "I'm sorry. I have to go. I'm down to one bar, and I don't have my charger." He says good night, and we both hang up.

"So?" Sylvia asks.

"No change."

Nodding, she turns back to the TV.

"I can't keep lying like this, Sylvia. You *saved* Gail, and almost *lost your baby* in the process. You had a *placental abruption*. Do you know how serious that is?"

"Of course, Eliot—my phone has Google, too. And in cases where the placental lining separates from the uterus, the fetus dies twenty percent of the time—"

"Twenty to forty percent—"

"Either way, it's less than forty percent, so I'm confident Junior will be fine."

"Grant still needs to know the truth."

"Eliot, let me ask you something: How is Hailey?"

"I told you, she's a mess. She dozes off for ten minutes, then wakes up screaming. The doctor said it will be a while before we know what's going on." Tears burn in my eyes. I can't *believe* this. I can't believe what I've done. "She's only four years old, Sylvia. She's just a little kid." I start to cry.

"But you just told Grant she's 'much better.'"

"Don't twist my words." I wipe my eyes. "You know what I meant. Grant has enough on his mind."

"I understand. I'm saying I agree with you. I would've told him the same thing. Relatively speaking, Hailey *is* better. Instead of drowning in the ocean, she's warm, safe, and dry. In fact, I'd say she's infinitely better." Sylvia shakes her head. "I'm disappointed in you. You're thinking about this all wrong. If Dolores were here, she'd say the same thing."

"Mom? She's not exactly a paragon of honesty. I mean, I love her, but I'm not going to take life lessons from a woman whose claim to fame is two bullshit memoirs. Besides, even she would agree there's a difference between telling Grant that Hailey is making progress and lying to him about who was on the beach. One is meant to be encouraging, and the other is, like, immoral, or unethical, or whatever."

"That's your argument? Come on, Eliot. Dig a little deeper. And don't knock Dolores. That woman rose up from the *ghetto* and published five books."

"She hardly grew up in the *ghetto*, Sylvia. And there were six books, not five—three novels before the memoirs and one novel after. Everyone forgets about the last one."

Sylvia rips open a pack of Wheat Thins. "God, I am *so nauseous*. Carbohydrates are the only thing that helps." She holds out a cracker. "Wheat Thin? They're surprisingly satisfying."

"Sylvia, it's enough! Let's at least admit what we're doing. You're lying for me and I'm letting you. I can't pretend it's not happening. You have to let me thank you."

"You don't have to thank me. You're my sister. If our situations were reversed, you'd do the same thing."

I shake my head. "I'd want to, but I don't know if I could."

"Of course you could. In fact, you did. Remember Coach Coley?"

Years ago, when we first moved to Atlanta, Sylvia had a hard time adjusting. She was in junior high and very gawky—an older version of Hailey, except Sylvia's hair was frizzy, and she had acne and braces. Most of the girls in her class were tan and blond, but there was my sister with her crazy hair and pitted face. Of course now, with her salon-highlighted tresses and overpriced skin treatments, Sylvia has outgrown her adolescent awkwardness. But she always looked different from the pinched, overprocessed southern debs we grew up with, and back then, tan and blond trumped pimpled and frizzy. Poor Sylvia was miserable. For the first few weeks, she complained about everything. She hated our house. She missed New Jersey. She even missed Barney. Then she refused to go to school. My mother, who was distracted as usual, let Sylvia stay home, and my twelve-year-old sister spent entire days staring vacantly at the TV (the same way she's staring at it now, actually). By the third week, it was clear something weird was going on. So I ransacked her desk, where I found a bunch of crude drawings. At first I couldn't tell what they were, but then I realized they were caricatures of Sylvia; and in them she had a bush of orange hair, blacked-out teeth, pus-filled pimples, and an enormous ass. They were also sexually graphic, with boobs and penises coming out all her orifices.

"Some boys in my homeroom drew them," she said, coming up behind me. "I really am ugly, aren't I?"

She sounded matter-of-fact, even amused by the idea, but when I turned around, I saw only sadness in her face.

The boys, it turned out, had been making these disgusting drawings and giving them to her, one per day, since the first week of school.

"When I said something to the teacher," Sylvia told me, "he said to throw them out. He even knows who drew them, but instead of doing something, he just laughed. Can you believe it?" She started to cry, which was startling because Sylvia never cried; she still doesn't. "Why do they have to draw pictures anyway? Do they think I don't know I'm ugly? Like, hello, I have eyes. I can see myself. But you don't *laugh* at people if they're ugly, especially *not* if you're a *teacher*."

At the time, I was experiencing my own shame spiral. My mother's first memoir was out; her essays were on deck. And like Sylvia, I was the new girl—the new *fat* girl. So I understood what it meant to feel your whole life unraveling.

I looked at the pictures again. This was my younger sister. Maybe she wasn't blond and tan, but she certainly wasn't ugly. She was fucking brilliant—ten times more brilliant than anyone I'd ever met. And God help anyone who said otherwise.

I found Coach Coley on the football field. Without introducing myself, I thrust the drawings at him.

He looked at them, then at me. "This is your sister, I take it? Are you as irate as she is?" He had a drawl, and *irate* came out *eye-rate*.

"Of course I'm *eye-rate*," I snapped. "Wouldn't you be?"

"They're just dumb cartoons. Y'all need to let 'em go."

"But you're a teacher…," I faltered. "You're not supposed to be this way."

"I know how boys are, and talkin' to them will only make it worse for your sister. I can promise you that." He turned back to the field.

I started to leave but then remembered the look on my sister's face. "Hey, Coach, you're not going to do anything about those pictures, are you?"

Now he was annoyed. "What would you have me do?"

"Make those boys stop. Teach them a lesson. Do whatever you have to do. What kind of fucking teacher are you? What kind of fucking person?"

"Hey," he said sharply. "I'd watch my mouth, miss."

"I'm not going to watch a fucking thing." I was suddenly overcome. My mother, my father, those boys, this coach—what was the matter with the world? "If you don't punish those boys, I swear to God, I will tell my mother that you pulled down your pants and begged me to blow you. And if you don't think my mother will march down here and get your ass fired, then you are as stupid as everyone says."

Sylvia is watching me. "*If you think my mother won't throw you in jail, then you are as stupid as everyone says.* Every time I think of you on that field, I get a boner, Eliot." She starts to laugh. "That was, like, the greatest moment of your life."

"It's amazing what a teenager will say." I think about Charlotte. *Daddy, please! I'll die if I have to stay here with her.* "That guy should've smacked me."

"No way—you scared him shitless."

"I didn't say anything about jail, though. I just said she'd get him fired." By this point, I'm laughing, too—well, laughing and crying.

"*Poetic license*, Eliot. I'm exercising *poetic license*. See, you were protecting me, and now I'm protecting you. And the seasons, they go round and round, and the painted pony goes up and down. It's the carousel of time." She sounds cheerful, my sister. Or if not cheerful, then at least relishing the moment.

Watching her, though, I get a glimpse of the frizzy-haired twelve-year-old she used to be. No one else can see that face, but Sylvia is my sister, so despite how cleverly she hides it, I see that face all the time. When she's arguing her multimillion-dollar lawsuits, I still see that face. When she's coy, when she's charming, even when she's got me by the balls, I see that face. And it is that face, specifically that twelve-year-old kid's sorrow, that pushes me to do things I normally wouldn't even consider.

"Think about it this way," Sylvia is saying. "Who's a more believable villain in our farcical tableau—me, the pain-in-the-ass hypochondriac, or you, the ideal parent?" She pauses. "You're a great mother, Eliot, and a great stepmother. You've changed those kids' lives for the better—everyone knows that. Imagine what Charlotte and Gail would be like if you hadn't come along. They're lucky to have you, and one split second shouldn't undo all your hard work. It was an accident, a mistake, and if you're not allowed to make a mistake, then I don't know who is."

I start to thank her, but she cuts me off.

"You're my big sister; the good one, the perfect one. All my life, I wanted to be you. For people to think I'm generous and kind. So, stop thanking me. I need this more than you do. Can't you see that, Eliot? *You're doing this for me.* For once in my sad fucking life, let me be the hero." She holds up the Wheat Thins. "Cracker?"

I grab a handful and climb into her bed, careful not to get sand on her sheets. For a long time, neither of us says anything; we just watch TV and chew.

"I wish Maggie and Dylan would get back together," I say at one point.

Sylvia is stunned. "They got back together two weeks ago. Where have you been?"

"Why didn't she tell me?"

"She probably figured you knew. Christ, Eliot, isn't it obvious?" She smiles. "See, that's why we love you—because you're utterly oblivious, and I mean that in the best possible way."

"In other words, I'm clueless."

"*Naïve.* You're also earnest, which is a rare and refreshing quality. You believe what people say simply because they've said it, and then you continue to give them the benefit of the doubt, even after they prove themselves unworthy. I wish I could be like that." She stops. "Actually, no. I think I'd kill myself if I were like you."

"Thank you, Sylvia. That's probably the nicest thing you've ever said to me."

"You want to know what I wonder, Eliot?"

I brace myself. Expecting her to say something else about loving me or something memorable about our relationship, I will myself not to cry again. "What?"

"Why is it that when Dolores sends you e-mails, she writes, 'I love you,' but when she sends me e-mails, she doesn't write anything? Sometimes she writes, 'Love ya.' But don't you think if she *really* loved me, she'd write 'I love you' every time?"

I blink, waiting for more, but that's it. This isn't a joke—my sister is dead serious.

"I don't think it means anything, Sylvia. You know she loves you. I love you, too." I pause. "But since when have you been reading my e-mails?"

"Are you kidding? I've been reading your e-mails for years. Your stupid password is ELIOTG." Then she sighs. "God, I feel so much better. That 'Love ya' thing has been bothering me forever."

⌒

I'd forgotten how lonely it is in the dead of night. Funny, too, because I'm in Hailey's room—in her bed, in fact—so I'm surrounded by people. My mother went back to Wyatt, but Maggie, who stayed here with me, is asleep in a chair. And the hospital is teeming with doctors, nurses, and all kinds of staff, most of whom are awake and bustling through the corridors. But despite all these people, I feel more alone than I ever have in my life.

I can't sleep. Sylvia was right about the nurses coming in and out. Every time I'm about to doze off, someone rushes into the dimly lit room and stands over the bed. Although my body is exhausted, my mind is revved up with a toxic combination of fear and guilt, so I lie here next to Hailey with nothing to do but replay the day's events again and again.

A nurse walks in. "Trouble sleeping?" Without waiting for my response, she picks up Hailey's chart and begins to read.

"I'm fine, thanks." I shift my weight to a more comfortable position. "I'm not used to a bed without my husband, I guess." As soon as I say this, I want to retract it. To call Grant "my husband" feels like a lie—another lie, I mean—and I have to be more careful with my words.

"Try to get some rest." The nurse heads out. "Tomorrow's another day."

Even though I know this is a throwaway line—indeed, that our entire exchange was meaningless—I seize on it, repeating, "Tomorrow's another day," as if it's deep Talmudic wisdom.

Tomorrow will be better, I promise myself. Gail will wake up. Grant and I will straighten everything out. We'll all go home. We'll resume our lives. Everything will go back to the way it was. Tomorrow's another day, which means that this one—and along with it, this horrible nightmare—will finally be over.

Chapter Twenty-two

HAILEY IS PRONOUNCED fit for discharge the next morning. (That's it—you don't *check out* of a hospital, you're *discharged* from it.) She's still too weak for a trip to Savannah (and the PICU doesn't allow children), so after Maggie and I help her get dressed and fill out her paperwork, my mother picks us up from the hospital and takes us back to the rich oilman's house. My sister and mother have offered to watch Hailey for the day so that I can gather up Grant's and the girls' luggage and drive to Savannah to see Gail.

Back at the house, I'm folding Gail's and Charlotte's clothes when my mother steps into the bedroom. "You okay?" She sounds concerned.

I'm kneeling over Charlotte's suitcase on the floor, so my back is to her, but I don't turn around. "I'm fine," I mumble. "Thanks for asking."

What else can I say? That I'm shaking with anxiety? That I'm sick with guilt? That I'm petrified to see Grant? Maybe if I act fine, I'll start to feel fine; or if not fine, at least better. Still, I'm tempted to ask her for a Valium, just to take the edge off, but I'm afraid it will make me too lethargic to face everything ahead of me.

Before I leave, I sit with Hailey. Although the doctor said she's okay, I'm not sure I believe it. In the past twenty-four hours, all the life has drained out of her. Just yesterday, she was screaming with delight as her uncle twirled her in the air. Now she's on the couch, not moving, not speaking. She doesn't want to watch TV, or color, or play Polly Pockets, and she's abandoned Molly, her American Girl doll. She just lies on her back and stares into space.

I take her in my arms. "I love you, Hailey Harper Delaney." The longer I stick around, the harder it will be to leave, so I give her a hug and head out.

An hour later, Maggie and I are walking into the Memorial University Medical Center in Savannah. I would rather she had stuck to our original plan, which was for her to stay in Wyatt and help my mother with Hailey, but Maggie insisted on coming. When I tried to talk her out of it, she got into my car and refused to get out of the driver's seat. I don't like having my little sister chauffeur me around—or, for that matter, my middle sister lie for me—but as we got closer to the hospital, I started to panic and was grateful Maggie was there.

Now, as we ride the elevator up to the PICU, I'm panicking all over again. "Thank you for coming," I say. Breathe in, I remind myself. Now breathe out. "I'm glad you're here."

"Stop thanking me, Eliot. I'm your sister and Gail is my niece; I want to be here."

The PICU is a locked unit. To get in, you have to call a nurse and then wait until she buzzes you in. Maggie and I walk down the hall to the waiting room, which is a glass-enclosed room with vending machines, twenty-odd chairs arranged in rows of threes and fours, and one small window. A sign on the wall limits the use of cell phones. A second sign lists the rules. Quiet, please! demands a third. The TV attached to the wall is on, but muted.

Through the glass, I see Charlotte and her mother sitting across from each other, flipping through magazines. "There they are." I nudge my sister. "That's Beth by the wall."

"She looks different," Maggie says as we walk in.

"Different how?"

She doesn't get a chance to answer because Beth has spied us and is walking across the room, a duffel bag swinging on her hip. As she gets closer, she raises her arms, and instinctively I duck, afraid she's going to hit me. But she only wants to hug me, which some-how feels worse.

"Beth," I say, pushing aside her bag. "How are you holding up?"

"Bloody awful, Eliot." She hooks her arm through mine and leads me to the seat beside Charlotte, who looks up but doesn't say hello. I bend to kiss her cheek, but she turns her head so my lips graze her hair.

Beth plops into her chair. "This is so awful for everyone. I've never seen anything like it." She waves. "Could this place be any more de-pressing?"

In the corner of the room, I spot an older woman wearing dark, silver-rimmed sunglasses. She's staring at the silent TV. Other than her, though, Charlotte and Beth are the only people here.

"Where's Grant?" I ask.

"Off somewhere, making calls." Beth starts to rifle through her duf-fel bag. The bag, which is bulky with a long strap, is slung across her chest and sits in her lap like an unwieldy infant. "It's a travesty, Eliot. That's what it is: a goddamn travesty."

Maggie says hi to Charlotte and then introduces herself to Beth, even though they've met several times. When Beth lifts her head, I see what my sister meant: she does look different. She's not wearing makeup, and without her thick kohl liner and heavy foundation, her eyes are a light, watery gray and her cheeks have patches of acne. Like Charlotte, Beth seems young and defenseless in the stark hospital light.

"It is awful," I agree.

"Bloody awful," Beth says.

I pretend not to hear Beth's Briticism, but Charlotte repeats it, using a weird Cockney accent. "The most bloody awful thing ever," she says loudly, sounding like one of Fagin's orphans. Shifting beside me, Charlotte drapes herself over my shoulder in a theatrical parody of her mother. I pat her shoulder, then sit up straight in my chair, forcing her to sit up, too.

"How's Gail today?" I ask. "I spoke to Grant this morning. He said there's no change."

"No change," Beth confirms. "She's still the same, although I'm a bit more of an optimist than Grant. He always manages to cast himself as the voice of perpetual doom and gloom, doesn't he?"

I want to defend Grant, but instead I ask if he's been in touch with his office.

"Absolutely, and I'll tell you something, Eliot. Stanford is being *absolutely great*. Not only did he tell Grant to take as much time as he needs, but he also offered to charter a plane to fly Gail back to Atlanta. It's *unbelievable* how truly kind and truly decent he is."

Beth's words are punctuated by odd, birdlike hand gestures. I'm equally struck by her body, which seems to have shrunk considerably since her goddess party. Her black jeans and T-shirt hang on her, and she looks lost inside the baggy material. But her neck is what I find most painful. It's as thin and corded as a twig and looks too frail to support her head. Charlotte told me that when Beth was younger, she had anorexia, and I can see it now: her teenager's drawn cheeks and jutting bones; her steadfast refusal to swallow, to admit she is suffering.

Leaning forward in my chair, I whisper gently, "Beth, I doubt there's anything I can say to make this right. But I want you to know that on behalf of my family—on behalf of myself—I'm so sorry."

"It was an accident, Eliot." Beth is searching through her seemingly bottomless bag again. "It was a *horrible, horrible* accident. It's been such an *utterly chaotic time* for me, anyway. Ever since I got the Riverside commission, I've been a bit *whompy*, working till all hours of the night. I don't think I've eaten a decent meal in a month! So when Grant called, I was crazed but immediately dropped everything, of course, and raced straightaway to the airport." She pulls Charlotte toward her. "Come here, baby. Come here and give me a hug."

I have no idea how to respond. "Can I get you anything? A cup of coffee? Some water?"

She shakes her head. "Aren't you a love? I'm fine. By the way, Eliot, Phoebe asked after you. She's hosting the next goddess party and wants to make sure you have all the details."

"Beth, I know what's going on is impossible to comprehend, but..." I'm about to ask if she understands the gravity of the situation and share my own initial denial, when I notice her hands resting on her duffel bag—they're shaking so hard, the nylon fabric is rustling.

Seeing this chokes me up. "I'm so sorry," I tell her again, swallowing hard. I'm sorry for doubting you and for calling you the Sculptress. I'm sorry for everything. You're just a mom like me, trying to get by, and if I ever have the chance—no, the *privilege*—of caring for your children again, I won't take it for granted. "I just want to say..." But I'm too overcome to finish.

"It's just very hard..." Beth trails off, too, her own tears falling.

We sit like this for a few minutes, two moms in a trauma center, weeping. But soon I get scared. She's being too nice to me. This isn't real, I remind myself. Beth hasn't heard the whole story, and when she does, the other shoe—an entirely different kind of shoe—is going to drop.

After a while, when we're both composed, I try again. "So that's the plan, then? To fly back to Atlanta? Did the doctor give you any idea as to when Gail will be able to leave?"

"The plan"—Grant rushes into the waiting room as if he's late—"the plan is to wait and see. Gail will be in the PICU another night, or two, maybe two, maybe three. Then hopefully she'll be moved to a floor where the visiting hours aren't so strict, or rather, as strict as they are here."

He leans over to kiss my cheek, greets Maggie with a hello, and then, apparently reconsidering, leans over to kiss her cheek, too.

I'm about to ask him if he's okay when he cuts me off. "So did you two have any trouble finding this place? God, I was so glad to hear that Hailey's doing better. She's a healthy kid; she'll pull through this just fine. I miss my little pickle, but like I said, Eliot, she's better off spending the day with your mother." He checks his BlackBerry, using his thumb to scroll through his messages. "As much as I wanted to see her," he adds as he pecks at the keys.

"She'll probably sleep most of the day." I watch Grant closely. He seems very agitated; he's even grinding his teeth. "Did you speak to the neurologist?"

"Not yet—this afternoon, probably. At some point, we're supposed to have a conference with all the doctors who've seen Gail since she got here. There's also a trauma specialist, who's out on vacation, but they want him to weigh in, too. According to the nurses, though, she's exactly the same—no better, no worse. Test results are fine, perfect even. Brain stem is intact. Special imaging, MRI, whatever it is—came back clean. It's very, very good news."

"So what's the bad news?" Maggie asks.

"She's in a fucking coma." Distracted by something outside the window, Grant stops to look.

"And?" I prompt.

"And?" He blinks, as if reminding himself who I am. "And what?"

"What happens next?"

"Well, if she wakes up, we can take her home. But if she doesn't, and she's still in this...ah...um...if she's still in this state, she'll stay here in the hospital for another couple of weeks. Then we'll take her to a long-term facility in Atlanta. The Banks Center, most likely—it's the best, I hear, although so is Shepherd and Rusk. Either way, she can't leave yet. I mean, unless she wakes up, of course."

I've never seen Grant this keyed up. Yesterday, when he climbed into the helicopter, he was so sluggish that the pilot had to grab his arm and pull him up. But now he's pacing all over the room—to the window, the door, the vending machines, back to the window, the door, the—

"Grant, can you sit down for a minute?"

"What? Oh sure." But he doesn't. Instead, he stands at the window and continues to describe the tests they're doing, the fascinating technology they have, the statistics they've quoted, and what Gail's chances are, given these and other variables. "They're cautiously optimistic," he concludes, licking his lips, desperate, it seems, for something to drink.

"When is the next visiting hour?" I hand him a bottle of water, which he guzzles down in one long gulp.

"It's supposed to be at eleven," Beth chimes in, "but"—she glances at the clock—"it's twenty after already, and no one's come out. Grant, can you ask them what's going on?"

The lone woman with the silver sunglasses suddenly speaks. We all turn, surprised to see her still there. "They probably canceled the eleven o'clock visit. Sometimes they do that." She gets up. "The next visit will be at noon, most likely. I'm getting coffee. Anyone want anything?"

We all shake our heads no. The woman shrugs and walks out.

Once she leaves, Grant sits down and flips through a magazine. Unable to sit for long, he gets up and walks out of the waiting room, presumably to find out when we can see Gail.

"Does he seem agitated to you?" I whisper to Beth, but before she can answer, Grant is back.

"Twelve," he confirms. "They'll let us see her at twelve. I'd like to go in." He looks around cautiously, as if expecting someone to object.

"You should go too," Beth tells me.

I thank her but decline. "I appreciate it, but I can wait. Gail's your daughter," I add, in case she's feeling territorial.

"Nonsense. You're here, you should see her. I know you're concerned." Beth reaches into her duffel bag again and pulls out a lipstick. Then she beckons to Charlotte, who has moved to a seat near the window, where she's listening to her iPod.

"Come here, baby," she says loudly. "You'll love this."

Sighing, Charlotte adjusts her earbuds and gets up.

"I bought this for myself," Beth says as she applies the lipstick to Charlotte's mouth, "but I think it's more your color than mine." She sits back to appraise her work. "Perfect! I *knew* it would suit you."

Charlotte puckers her lips and kisses the air. "What do you think, Eliot?"

"Nice," I say, although I'm looking not at her, but at her mother, who is moving toward me, still holding the open lipstick. For a second,

I'm afraid she plans to apply it to my lips and I stiffen, prepared to firmly but politely decline. Thankfully, she closes the tube and tucks it into her pocket.

"It's good that you're here, Eliot," Beth says, then rests her fingers on my arm.

As the seconds tick by, her hand gets heavier and heavier. Soon I feel as though I'm bearing a fifty-pound weight. Still, I don't move. Right now, she's experiencing a mother's worst nightmare, and if touching someone—touching me—makes her feel better, then I'll strip off my clothes and lie with her naked. Here's comfort, I tell her by remaining immobile, take what you need.

"Tell me about Hailey," she says, finally, thank God, lifting her hand. "Grant said they only kept her overnight as a precaution. She's with your mother now? How is she feeling?"

"Hailey was much better this morning, thank you for asking. The doctor said she'll probably sleep a lot over the next few weeks, but other than that, he doesn't anticipate any long-term effects. 'Kids are pretty resilient,' were his exact words."

"That's good," Beth says, but I notice she doesn't ask about Sylvia. Nor, it occurs to me, did Grant. Why would they, though, given the circumstances?

I excuse myself to go to the ladies' room, and Maggie comes with me. She checks the stalls to make sure we're alone, then asks how I'm holding up. "This must be so hard for you, Eliot. No one loves Gail as much as you do."

"Come on, Maggie. That's a stupid thing to say. Those three people love Gail as much as—*more than*—I do." I point to the door, which feels silly. I wanted to point to the waiting room, but there's a wall in the way.

"Of course, of course Beth and Grant love Gail. I only meant that I know you love her too. You're a good mother—to her and to Charlotte."

"I'm sorry, I didn't mean to snap. I'm just worried about Gail— and Grant. Did you see how keyed up he is? Everything's all mixed up." I shake my head as if to unmix it. "I don't know how it got this way."

We're standing side by side at the sinks. I glance at the mirror. My sister is studying me. "I'm sorry," I say again. "I don't mean to be a bitch. I'm really grateful you're here."

"Drop it, Eliot."

Maggie looks so pretty, even today. The rest of us are red-eyed and bedraggled with matted hair and dark circles, but my sister looks fresh and clean. Her hair is pulled into two braids, and she's got a blue bandanna holding back her bangs. Her skin is tanned, and her T-shirt has a deep V, revealing her elegant neck and magnificent cleavage. How she manages to look so glamorous in the midst of all this madness is one of the great mysteries of life.

"You've been so great," I continue. "You and Mom both, but I can't stand anyone trying to make me feel better." I speak to her reflection rather than her face because it feels somehow safer. "I fucked up. One minute they were there, and the next...I don't know. They were gone...I keep replaying the scene, over and over, but it's still the same thing."

"I thought Sylvia was with the kids." Maggie has turned away from the mirror and is looking directly at me. "I thought you weren't there."

"I wasn't...I mean, I wasn't down by the water; but I was up by the umbrella so I could see everything. And as soon as I realized the kids were in trouble, I raced down and jumped in."

"Oh," Maggie says.

"I can't imagine what Beth and Grant think. First I let Sylvia watch the kids—which I know isn't a crime, but still—and then I swam out to Hailey, not Gail. It all happened so fast. I could only go one way, Maggie. I had to make a decision." I slump against the sinks. "The whole thing makes me sick."

"Beth and Grant aren't thinking anything, Eliot—and if they are, then they're *wrong*. It doesn't matter who was watching the kids. It was an accident. Besides, Sylvia *saved* Gail. She's *pregnant*, and she swam all the way out to get her. That's, like, miles and miles of swimming. Sylvia is a *hero*; she should get a *parade*."

"I know, Maggie. I really do. Like I said, it just happened so fast."

"Gail and Hailey are *both* Grant's children. And anyone who criticizes you for saving one kid instead of another is *crazy*. No one—not even Beth—would expect you to bypass Hailey to go after Gail."

"Of course not," I say quietly. "But that doesn't mean she wouldn't wish for it."

Neither of us is in a rush to return to the waiting room. Out in the hall, I use Maggie's phone to call my mother and check on Hailey. I call the girls' schools to say they'll be out for a while, although I don't explain why. I click through my messages without listening—home, work—then delete them all. I also call my cell phone, and hearing my own voice, I imagine the phone lying dead somewhere on the ocean floor.

Eventually, Maggie and I go back to the waiting room just as Charlotte announces that she's hungry. "I'll take you to the cafeteria," Beth says, standing up and moving toward the door. "Anyone need anything?"

We both say no but thank her for offering. Although it's nice how we're all trying to feed each another or fetch magazines and coffee, I'd rather we go back to resenting one another if it means Gail will wake up.

Grant, who is pacing in front of the window, shakes his head. "I'll get some coffee later, Lizzie." He checks his watch. "Visiting hours start in five minutes."

Maggie glances at me. It's the pet name, his *Lizzie*, that makes her react. My sister raises her eyebrows: *You okay?*

I nod. *It's nothing,* I tell her silently. *Don't worry. They were married once, remember? Gail is their child, not mine.*

"As long as you're okay," Maggie says aloud, patting my arm. "I'm going to make some calls." She reaches for her phone. "I'll check in with Mom, and see how Hailey's doing."

"I just did." I wonder if Maggie will also be calling Dylan, and if so, why she hasn't said anything about him to me. "Hailey's doing fine."

"Tell Hailey I love her," Grant says absently as Maggie walks out. "I love her very much."

A few minutes later, he and I are standing outside the door that leads to the PICU, waiting to be let in. This is the first time we've been alone since yesterday, when we stood on the beach, watching Sylvia swim out to Gail. I touch his arm. "How are you?"

Although Grant doesn't stiffen or pull away, I can tell he feels the same way I did with Beth: it's too much right now to bear another person's weight. "I'm very worried. I'm worried she's not going to wake up, worried that if she does, she'll be different. All of it worries me." He's grinding his teeth again. "I'm worried about Charlotte; I'm worried about Beth." He pauses. "I'm worried about you."

"What about me? I'm fine." But hearing someone approaching on the other side of the door, I let out a nervous giggle. "I'm scared, Grant," I blurt out. "I'm scared to death to see her."

Grant puts his hands on my shoulders. "It's going to be okay. We're going to be okay." He stares into my eyes. "You know I love you, right? No matter what happens, we're together. We will survive this, all of us—you, me, Gail—we will all be okay."

The door swings open.

A heavy-bottomed nurse with curly hair and a sweet smile ushers us into the unit and down a quiet hallway. Holding hands, Grant and I pass several glass-enclosed, cubbylike rooms. Some have patients in them, most are empty. The rooms are bigger than the cubicles in the ER, although not by much. They have enough space for a bed, two chairs, and a staggering amount of medical equipment, most of which is built right into the walls.

The nurse, whose name tag says LIBBY BAILEY, stops at Gail's room and presses a button. An electronic door slides open. "You have twenty minutes," she says softly. "There's a call button on the wall if you need anything." She turns to Grant. "Dr. Bloom will be here in an hour. He'll be happy to speak to you then."

When she leaves, the electronic door slides closed behind her, and the room is silent except for the pinging of the computers. I step over to the bed. Underneath the white blankets, Gail's face is ashen. If not for her dark hair, she would be lost amid the snowy linen. Her skin looks too delicate to touch, so I arrange her hair, which feels weightless in my hand.

As I rub the strands together, I get a lump in my throat. According to Grant, if the neurosurgeon finds any evidence of physical damage—which he hasn't yet, thank God—Gail may need brain surgery. This means they'll have to cut her beloved hair or, worse still, shave it all off. Imagining her thick waves shorn to peach fuzz makes me want to pick her up and ferry her off so that no one can lay a finger on her small, perfect head.

"I'll tell you one thing," Grant says behind me, "she's getting excellent care. Look at all this equipment. Did you see this?" He points to an enormous monitor that has bright red and green lines snaking across the screen. "This one is measuring her brain wave activity. It's like a camera that takes continuous pictures of her...I don't know...her synapses or something—who the hell can remember? *Hi, Gail!*" he shouts, startling me. *"Look who's here! It's ELIOT! She came to see you!"* He motions for me to get closer. "We're supposed to talk to her."

"Hi, Gail..." I clear my throat. My voice feels hollow, sounds false. "I'm here for a visit."

"Good, Eliot!" Grant pats my back. "That was great. No one is sure how much actually registers, but they say she can hear us, even in her current...uh, even if she's unresponsive. I need to pick up some books so I can read to her. *Right, Gail? You. Love. Books. RIGHT?"*

"Please don't yell, Grant. Please—she's right here." I study him. "Grant, tell me the truth: Are you okay? You've been distracted ever since I got here."

"I already told you. I'm nervous about Gail."

I want to believe him, but because I feel so guilty myself, nothing anyone says is above suspicion. Is it me? I wonder. Does he know the truth? Is he waiting for me to confess?

Leaning over the bed, Grant is listing for Gail all the books he's going to buy. He stands up, nudges me. "Come on, Eliot. Say something to her."

I feel foolish but don't want to let him down. "Let's see . . . Hmmm . . . what's been going on? I guess I'll start with Hailey. She's with Grandma, and right now, I'm sure she's watching *Dora* or *Sesame Street* and asking for you. In fact, you know what she told me? She said, 'I don't like watching TV without Gail,' so you know she really misses you . . . What else? Aunt Maggie is here at the hospital, and later, if there's time, she'll stop in to say hi. Aunt Sylvia is—"

Grant cuts me off. "Don't talk about her," he says roughly.

"Please just let me talk, okay? Aunt Sylvia is fine. She'll be leaving the hospital in a day or two, although she's getting so much attention there, she doesn't want to go. You know how she is. Anyway, she's been asking about you and promised to visit as soon as she can."

This pisses Grant off. "No way, Eliot. There is no way Sylvia is going to see her."

"Grant, give Sylvia a break, okay? It was an accident, you know that."

Just as he's about to reply, the computer suddenly beeps, startling us both.

Grant grabs my arm. "Eliot, look! Look at that line, the red one."

We watch as a red line on the monitor brightens and the needle jumps up and down. Stunned, Grant and I stare at each other.

"Something's happening!" He lunges for the call button and asks for a nurse. "Can we get some help here, please? I think my daughter is waking up!"

I suspect the light means something, although not that Gail's waking up. She hasn't stirred. I put my hand on her head and speak quietly. "Does it bother you when Daddy yells? He isn't angry. He's just frightened and wants you to wake up. He loves you; we all do."

Nurse Bailey appears.

Grant points to the monitor. "That line—the red one—got brighter, and the needle went crazy."

She checks the computer printout. "It's a good sign, Mr. Delaney." The nurse's gaze is kind. "It means she's responding to external stimuli. She knows you're here." She makes a mark on Gail's chart. "Your time is almost up," she says as she walks out. "Five minutes."

Grant is thrilled by this new development. "This is amazing! I've never seen any of those lines light up before. Gail knows you're here, Eliot! That's her way of saying she's happy to see you." Reaching to hug me, Grant almost knocks me over. "*You did this!* You did this just by showing up."

Part of me is excited; another part knows to exercise caution. "It's great news, Grant, it really is. But I think we should take this one step at a time, okay?"

"Okay, sure—one step at a time." But his smile is so wide, I can see all his teeth. "Since she's responding to stimuli, they might move her to another floor tonight. And if they do—why wouldn't they, right? she's totally responsive—then we can both sleep in her room. Did you bring a change of clothes? If you didn't, that's okay." Glancing over at Gail, he nods absently. "You know, I bet she wakes up this afternoon." Elated, he kisses me on the lips. "I am so glad you're here. *You're glad too, aren't you, Gail? Isn't it great to see Eliot?*"

"If Gail is moved to another floor—which may not happen, Grant; let's see what they say—I'm sure Beth will want to spend the night with her." I think about Beth's hands trembling on her nylon duffel bag. "She's her mother, after all."

But Grant isn't paying attention to me. He's focused on the idea of Gail waking up. Hovering over the computers, he searches for more signs.

"If anyone gets to sleep with Gail," I repeat, "it should be Beth."

"What about Beth?" Grant is looking in my direction, but he's not seeing me. He's seeing Gail getting out of bed, going back to school, riding her bike, being every inch the healthy kid she once was. "Beth can't stay with Gail. She's going back to Atlanta tonight. Her flight leaves at five."

"She's *leaving? Tonight?* Are you serious?"

"She has arrangements to make, one of which is coordinating Gail's long-term care. Beth said she wants to do it in person so it's done correctly, although that may not be necessary now, not if Gail is waking up." Grant cups his hands over the monitor to make the red line shine brighter. "She also has to work on her mural. She has a deadline, you know."

I'm still hung up on the idea of Beth getting on a plane and leaving Gail behind. "When will she be back?"

"Maybe she won't have to come back. Maybe we'll just bring Gail to her."

"But let's say we don't, Grant. Will Beth come back?"

"Of course, Eliot," he says, as if I'm insane to think otherwise. "She'll be back on Friday night, Saturday at the latest."

"That's almost a week from now."

"Not a week, more like five days." Grant flicks the monitor, but a loud beep makes him jump, and he backs away. "She said she felt okay about it because you're here."

"Really? It seems like a big deal to leave. I mean, like you said, what if Gail wakes up?"

"That's what we're *hoping for*, Eliot." He glances at Gail, and his eyes fill with tears.

Grant, I know, is suffering and will continue to suffer until Gail opens her eyes and says the word *Dad*. He's been through this before. Six years ago, before he and I met, Gail developed a respiratory infection. She wasn't even a year old, so the doctor admitted her to the hospital, where she ended up staying for four days. Everything turned out okay, but Grant described those days as the worst of his life. "I felt utterly helpless. Gail was just a baby, and all the tubes and machines only reinforced how fragile she was. I kept thinking about the night she was born, how overwhelmed I was. I couldn't believe her seven-pound body had a pancreas, a liver, and a small intestine. She had the same organs I had inside mine, but she weighed seven pounds and I weighed a hundred and seventy. How could that possibly be real? She even had fully formed fingernails. Sure, they were minuscule, but each one was its own separate thing. That night—the night she was born—I made all kinds of vows to protect her. I swore on my life, on everything that mattered, that I would always put her needs ahead of mine. But ten months later, she was back in the hospital. And when I stepped into the room wearing a facial mask and sterile booties, and saw her in an incubator with a tube in her mouth, I knew at that moment that I had failed."

The way Grant is watching Gail makes me think he's remembering that moment. *You didn't fail her,* I want to tell him. *You're a good father, a generous man, a terrific husband—boyfriend, partner, whatever.* "She's going to pull out of this, Grant," I say. "I believe it, and you have to believe it too."

"I'm so glad you're here." Clearly exhausted, he sighs deeply. "I don't know how I would be able to deal with any of this"—he waves at the bed, the monitors, Gail—"if you weren't here." He puts his arms around me. "I love you, Eliot."

Nodding, I murmur that I love him, too. "Grant? I understand you are angry at Sylvia..." I really want to talk to him, but he's moved over to the computers and is fiddling with the dials. "Grant, listen: What happened on the beach was an accident—"

"I know it was an accident. I know Sylvia didn't intend for Gail to get hurt. But right now I'm too angry to look at her, much less talk to her. Every time I think about it, I get crazy. They were on the beach! How could she not pay attention? What the fuck kind of person is she?" Furious, he shakes his head. "Christ, what's going to happen when Sylvia has her own kid? I foresee a lot of emergency room visits, not to mention years of therapy."

"Come on, Grant. She's still my sister." I need to say more, but the words are stuck.

"We wouldn't have to deal with any of this"—he waves again at Gail, the monitors, the bed—"if you'd been the one watching the kids."

"You don't know that. Things happen all the time."

"All I know is I'm lucky to have you. I'm lucky you're the one looking out for my girls."

"But I wasn't, Grant." Tears leak out from the sides of my eyes. "Grant..."

But he's hovering over the monitor again and not listening to me.

I take a step forward, fully prepared to tell him the truth—the whole truth and nothing but the truth, so help me God—when the nurse appears at the door.

"I'm sorry," Libby Bailey says gently, "but your time is up."

Chapter Twenty-three

DR. BLOOM, the chief of neurology, has bad news. "We can't tell you anything for sure," he says gravely an hour and a half later when Beth, Grant, and I assemble in his office. "But it doesn't look good."

Grant refuses to hear this. "I was there when the light got brighter! That nurse, what's-her-name, Libby...Libby *Bailey* said Gail was responding to stimuli."

The doctor straightens his glasses. "I understand how disappointing this is. Given her test results, we expected her to wake up in the first twenty-four hours, but she hasn't."

"But what about the *stimuli?*"

"Like I said, Mr. Delaney, we can't tell you anything for sure. And while Gail does appear to be responding to something, the fact that she hasn't woken up, and that her responses are minor at best, indicates more damage than we initially thought. My recommendation is to wait a day, even two, and then do another battery of tests. I also wouldn't rule out a more invasive examination."

"But her tests are perfect! Her CT, the MRI—they're all clean! You said she isn't showing any signs of damage. You can't just reverse yourself! What kind of medicine are you practicing here?"

"When it comes to the brain, Mr. Delaney, there are so many things we don't know. It's a day-to-day, sometimes hour-by-hour, discipline. But let's not get ahead of ourselves. We'll start retesting Gail and then take it from there." He asks if we have any questions.

Too stunned to speak, Grant, Beth, and I shake our heads.

Standing up, Dr. Bloom holds out his hand. "We'll talk again tomorrow. By then, I will have a more detailed prognosis. In the meantime, you should all try to get some rest."

On the way back to the PICU, Grant turns to me and Beth. "We can't give up hope. I don't care what he says."

"Of course not," we agree.

"That guy is a general neurologist. He doesn't specialize in kids. We still have to talk to the pediatric neurologist, and the trauma specialist, who's not back yet from vacation. Once they look at Gail's films, then we'll know more. Let's see what those guys say before we do anything."

An hour later, the three of us are back in the waiting room, still trying to absorb Dr. Bloom's words, when Grant raises a new, equally complex issue: If the guy is right, and Gail stays in a coma, how the hell will we pay for it?

He looks at me. "Here's the bottom line: At some point in the next year, one of us—or both, depending—may have to declare bankruptcy." He turns to Beth. "Unless someone else has a better idea."

Although I think it is way too soon to discuss this—Grant himself said it's too soon to give up—I keep my mouth shut. The thrill of seeing the red light brighten is gone, the doctor's words have sunk in, and poor Grant is utterly defeated. Maybe by focusing on something he can control, he won't feel so helpless.

He's standing by the windows, staring outside. Maggie is here, and so are Beth and Charlotte, and we're all sitting together, anticipating the next twenty-minute visit. Nothing has changed since Grant and I saw Gail. Although we got some bad news, we're really no worse off than we were before. Gail is still in a coma, Beth is still leaving at five, and Charlotte is still avoiding me. The only difference, as far as I can see, is that once again I have failed to tell Grant the truth; and that's not a difference, that's just more of the same. How can I continue to lie to him? Is this really me? "It makes no fucking sense," I keep telling myself.

"Did you say something, Eliot?" Grant asks.

Yes, I did, Grant. I made a terrible mistake: I was on the beach, not my sister. I was the one who turned away from the kids. I'm the one who's accountable. I think of meeting him for the first time five years ago. In his arms, he is holding an eighteen-month-old Gail. She is healthy, alert. More than that, she is safe.

"No." I check my watch. As usual, it's on my wrist, right where it's supposed to be. "I didn't say anything."

"So, anyway," he continues, "insurance will pick up everything so far, but we have deductibles and coinsurance, both of which will be a lot."

"What's a lot?" Beth wants to know.

I glance at her, wondering how she can just pick up and leave. Gail is her child, for God's sake. Is it fear? Is it denial? Or just plain old narcissism? Who am I to judge? you may ask; but look at me, burning with indignation on my stepdaughter's behalf. Look at me, casting the first stone, bulldozing the glass house, passing wave after wave of self-righteous judgment.

I breathe deeply, trying to calm down. This is the new normal, the new me. One second, I am sick with shame; the next, I'm enraged. I am angry, really, truly angry—at Beth, and the world, at myself. I turn the word *angry* over in my mouth; let it slip between my tongue and teeth. I'm *angry*, and it feels good.

"What's a lot?" Beth repeats. "How much are we talking about?"

"Somewhere in the thousands, at least," Grant replies. "Maybe the tens of thousands. And then we're only covered for two months at a rehab center. After that, we're on our own, and one month in a place like that could wipe us out. We can appeal—which we will—but according to my HR department, we're unlikely to win. I hope it doesn't come to that," he adds. "I mean, I hope Gail wakes up *today*, but we have to prepare ourselves for worst case."

Worse case, worst case, whatever case: I was flirting with another man. I looked away. Because of this, because of me, I deserve to suffer. "I'll do it," I announce. "I'll declare bankruptcy."

Maggie gives me a concerned look.

"It's only money," I tell her.

"I'm getting a lump sum for the mural," Beth says. "It should be close to ten grand, after expenses. I got half already, and I'll get another half when I'm finished."

This disgusts Grant. "Great, that should pay for about a week at the Banks Center. What about the other eighty-odd years of her life, Lizzie?"

Lizzie. The name kills me.

"You honestly think she'll be like this for the rest of her life?" Beth's voice catches.

He backpedals. "Don't listen to me. I'm just talking. I don't know anything." Like me, Grant is all over the place—angry one minute, sheepish the next. Ironically, the only ones holding steady are Charlotte and *Lizzie*. "We don't have to figure it out now."

"I agree." I swallow hard, breathe deeply. "We don't have to figure it out today."

"Eliot?" Maggie has a question. "Mom called. She wants to know what time we're heading back." I must look worried because she adds, "Hailey's okay. She's been sleeping for most of the day. She's just asking about our dinner plans."

"Visiting hours end at what?" I glance at Beth. "Eight-thirty?"

"Normally, yes, but tonight the last one is at seven."

"And you're leaving for the airport? So if I see Gail at six, I'll be home in time to give Hailey a bath and put her to bed." I turn to Maggie. "Tell Mom we'll be home by seven thirty, and that she should eat without us. We can fend for ourselves, if that's okay with you."

"Beth's going to the airport?" Maggie is confused. "Why? What's at the airport?"

"She has to go to Atlanta, but she'll be back in a few days. She has things to take care of. Things for Gail," I add as if that makes a difference.

Looking at Beth, Maggie is wide-eyed. "But don't you want to be here if Gail wakes up?"

"According to her doctor," I say, continuing to defend Beth, "it doesn't look like Gail will be waking up soon. The damage to her brain is more extensive than they thought."

Hearing this, Charlotte snaps. "*Why didn't anyone tell me?* She's my *fucking* sister! Why aren't you telling me *what the fuck is* going on?"

Grant sits down and grabs her hand. "Charlotte, calm down. We just found out ourselves. But the doctor hasn't made his final prognosis yet, and Gail still has more people to see. We're not giving up."

Nodding, Charlotte puts her head on his shoulder. I move to the chair on her other side, but she makes a big show of curling up against her father. Stoically, I stay put, even though it's clear to all of us that she is trying to get as far away from me as possible.

Watching us, Beth blurts out, "I'm not like you, Eliot. My mother was in and out of hospitals my whole life. I can't stand them. I can't stand any of it—sitting around all day, begging for information, waiting and waiting for news. I need to be somewhere else—anywhere else, *doing* something. And then she just died anyway. After all that waiting, just to die . . . That's my child in there—my daughter—" Beth's voice cracks. "I can't . . ."

"What makes you think it's any easier for Eliot?" Maggie asks. "Gail is her daughter, too."

"Maggie, let it go. She doesn't have to explain herself. It's okay," I tell Beth. "Do what you have to do. We'll be here."

"I'm not like you, Eliot," Beth repeats. "You're more comfortable than I am. You're better at this, more natural, I guess. I'm sorry. I just can't stand waiting."

How is this natural for anyone? How can anyone be comfortable? Yet this is what we do, as parents: we reach for our better selves; we swallow the lump; we bear the unbearable. We face the train head-on. What kind of person are you, I want to ask Beth, to shove someone else onto the tracks? Although, perhaps a better question: What kind of person am I?

"I do the best I can." I look at Grant. "I make a lot of mistakes. You know that, right?"

"We all make mistakes," he agrees. "No one is perfect."

⌒

Later, I go to the cafeteria to get a cup of coffee. I'm all the way down the hall, near the elevators, when I hear Charlotte behind me, shouting my name. "Eliot! I have to talk to you."

I turn around. "Is everything all right?"

She's panting. Her long, tangled hair hangs in her face, and I move to brush back her bangs, but she jerks away. "I need you to tell Mom to let me go to Atlanta. She says I have to stay here with Daddy, but I don't want to. I want to be with her."

"I think you should stay here, Charlotte. This is a terrible time for her—and for your dad. It will be helpful to both of them if you just do what they ask."

Charlotte won't hear of it. "You have to do this for me, Eliot. *You have to!*"

"I don't *have* to do anything, Charlotte."

Her cheeks redden. "I know what you did, Eliot! *I saw you!*"

My heart races. "Saw me what?" My first thought is that she means on the beach with her sisters, but that's not it.

"*I saw you with that guy*—in the church at Hailey's school. *I saw what you were doing.* And there's no way I'll stay here with you. *I hate you, Eliot; I hate you!* You're *not* my mother, and *never* will be."

And there it is, the words I've been waiting five years to hear: *I hate you, Eliot. You're not my mother, and never will be.* Finally, someone is telling the truth. I've been dreading this moment for so long, I'm almost relieved it's here. *I'll die if I have to stay with you.*

My response, which I've been practicing, also for five years, is automatic. "You are allowed to hate me, Charlotte. And no, I'm not your mother, but I do love you and wish you felt differently." I turn to leave but not before adding, "That guy you saw? Finn? I already told you he's an old friend. We dated in college, but that was a long time ago. Nothing is going on between us now. I don't know what you think you saw, but whatever it is, it's not that."

"You're a *liar*, Eliot. You're *lying*. I saw you *together*!" From the expression on her face, though, I can tell she isn't sure what she saw.

"Charlotte," I say softly, "I know you're angry with me—"

"I also told Mom that she shouldn't let you be around Gail anymore. It's not right. Mom should be with her—not you. You're not her mother and you should stop trying to be."

"Unfortunately, that's not for you to decide. But I understand how frustrated you are that your mother is going back to Atlanta—"

She cuts me off again. "I'm not frustrated with *Mom*. I'm frustrated with *you*. Gail is my *sister*. You shouldn't be allowed to *touch* her—"

Charlotte's voice breaks, and I move to hug her, but she puts both hands on my chest and pushes me away. "Get off me, Eliot. I don't want you touching *me*, either."

As I did yesterday, I can feel how furious she is, but this time I also feel how scared. Because she knows her father and sister love me—that deep down she loves me, too—I am capable of causing them terrible pain. But it's not, as she says, by sticking around. It's by leaving. Charlotte was only eight when Beth walked out. And I know it was the best thing for everyone, that it would've been worse had she stayed. I also know that Beth left Grant, her husband, not Charlotte, her child; but to an eight-year-old, these are all fine distinctions. By pushing me away, Charlotte is steeling herself for what might happen next. If her own mother, her real mother, could pick up and leave, then why can't I?

"Charlotte, listen to me. I would never do anything to hurt Gail. Nor would I ever do anything to hurt you or your father or Hailey. I'm in your life, and I'm staying."

I'm impressed by the way she's trying to protect her sister. I'm proud too because I taught her this. Knowing you are unable to protect your sister is a horrible feeling, and because I know just how horrible, I promise Charlotte that I will talk to Beth about taking her to Atlanta. Why should she stay here, cooped up in a waiting room with nothing to do, when she can be with her mother or at least back in school?

"I love Gail," I add as Charlotte starts to leave. "I love you and Daddy and Hailey. I love all of you."

Halfway down the hall, she pretends not to hear me, but then she whips around. "Well, you have a fucked-up way of showing it, Eliot."

"That's the funny thing about love, Charlotte," I tell her. "Sometimes it comes out all fucked up."

⌒

During the night, someone calls on the rich oilman's phone. Hearing it in the guest room, where I'm lying in bed, half in and half out of a shallow sleep, I race into the kitchen and grab the receiver before anyone else wakes up.

"Hello?" I'm disoriented, and in my stupor, it occurs to me that it might be Finn. "Who is this?" I ask sharply. "Who's calling? It's the middle of the night!"

"It's just me, Eliot. It's Grant. I didn't mean to call so late. I'm sorry."

When I hear Grant's voice, I exhale in relief. Finn calling here is impossible, I remember. He doesn't have this number. *He can't find me.* "Is everything okay? How's Gail?"

"The same," he says sadly. "How's Hailey?"

"Better," I tell him, then correct myself. "Actually, that's not true. My mother said she slept fine during the day, but I put her to bed at eight, and she's been up, screaming, three times."

"Nightmares?" Grant sounds concerned. "Is this kind of thing normal?"

"I called Dr. Spiegel in Atlanta. He said it was. But really, what's normal? He gave me the name of a pediatrician here—a Dr. Blakely— so I'll call her in the morning. I'm sure Hailey is okay, but I just want to be sure. Spiegel also said that if the nightmares continue, we should take her to a psychologist." I pause. "So, if I can get her in to see Blakely tomorrow, will you be okay without me for a few hours?"

"Of course. But why didn't you tell me this before?"

"I didn't want to worry you. You already have so much on your mind."

"But she's my daughter, Eliot. I need to know how she's doing. Please don't keep things from me. It makes me crazy to find them out after the fact."

"I'm sorry, Grant. From now on, I'll tell you everything, I promise."

Chapter Twenty-four

THE NEXT MORNING, I call Dr. Blakely's office, and they offer us a nine thirty appointment. Hailey clings to me through the entire exam, and when the doctor—an unflappable older woman—tries to look into her eyes, she has a meltdown. Afterward, Dr. Blakely says that although Hailey seems fine from a physical standpoint, it's probably a good idea to get her checked out back in Atlanta. "A psychologist can't hurt either," she adds. "Hailey has been through a significant trauma. And given her sister's situation, it seems the whole family has a long road ahead."

I nod, unable to meet her gaze. "Thank you for fitting us in," I say, but my voice is thick, and it's all I can do to get Hailey out of the office and into the car without melting down myself.

Back at the oilman's house, I feel the need to stay close to Hailey, so I call Grant and tell him that I want to spend a few more hours with her before driving to Savannah. We color for a while and play Polly Pockets, but Hailey isn't interested, although she does perk up when Maggie offers to make mud pies out on the deck.

"Let's put our bathing suits on," Maggie says, taking Hailey's hand. "I bet we get really messy."

While they're outside, I sit on the couch and try to make calls, but I'm too distracted to concentrate.

"So, what's happening with Gail?" my mother asks.

"Still no change—although the neurologist did say we could leave in a few days."

"And take her where? Not home, surely?"

I shake my head. "If she's still in a coma, which is very likely, we'll put her in a long-term facility for a few weeks, or months, depending on how well she responds to treatment. We heard about one called the Banks Center, which is outrageously expensive."

"How expensive?"

We're in the great room, staring at the ocean through the oversize picture windows. The sky is a glorious blue, and the sun is high overhead and beaming. The beauty of the day is deceptive, though. It's windy outside, as windy as it was on Monday when Gail and Hailey were swept away. It's hard to believe that happened only two days ago; the time has gone by so fast. On the other hand, Gail has been in a coma for only two days, and every moment that passes feels like an extra year tacked on to an already interminable prison sentence.

I sigh. "Believe me, you don't want to know."

Through the window, I can see Hailey and Maggie on the deck, playing with sand we brought back from the beach. Hailey is filthy, but seems to be having fun. Earlier, we tried to take her down to the water, but she refused to go near it. She wouldn't even step off the blacktop. Watching her outside reminds me that I'm supposed to tell my mother something, something I should've told her days ago. For a second it's there, right on the tip of my tongue, but just as I form the thought, it's gone, slipped away like a dream in the twilight of sleep. Still staring out at the ocean, I imagine myself on the beach, flirting with Finn. I turn around, and—wait! *Where's Hailey? Where's Gail?* The memory is torture. If only we hadn't stayed out so long; if only I hadn't answered my phone; if only I'd hung up. If only, if only—the possibilities are infinite, and they loop through my mind, endlessly.

"What about your insurance coverage?" my mother asks. "I thought most policies are designed to protect you when something like this happens."

"We max out after a certain point. But don't worry, we'll be okay. I have savings—not a lot, but some. We can also apply for loans. Grant thinks one of us should declare bankruptcy. What do people do when facing catastrophic medical bills? Go on welfare? Become homeless?"

"Grant's a good man," my mother says absently.

"That's funny." I get up from the couch and walk over to the rich man's dining room table, never taking my eyes off of Hailey. "Three weeks ago, you told me to leave him."

My mother gets up, too. "But I'm an idiot, Eliot. You know that."

Outside, Maggie and Hailey are making a sand castle. Hailey is concentrating on packing the sand into a perfect tower and adding just enough water so it doesn't collapse. From where I'm standing, she seems perfect—although I know that, like the weather, looks are deceiving.

"You've worked so hard over the years, Eliot. The idea of declaring bankruptcy must be excruciating for you, particularly since Gail isn't—"

"Don't say it, Mom. I'm responsible for her; she's in my care."

"Eliot, please. Give me a little credit. I was going to say that Gail's not the only thing you have to worry about—you also have your job and Hailey and Charlotte. Regardless, I'll help you out any way I can. I don't have much, but whatever's there is yours."

In the bright light filling the room, my mother looks elderly. The lines around her eyes have deepened, her silver hair is wispy and unkempt, and the skin on her neck and arms hangs loose on her bones. I see her not as Simone Starr the writer, but as Dolores Schneider my mother; and Dolores Schneider has become an old woman. When did this happen? I wonder. It's strange I missed it, particularly since I've been scrutinizing her every move since I was a child. On the other hand, given what's happened, maybe I don't watch as carefully as I think.

"I appreciate the offer, Mom. But I can't take your money."

Yesterday, when Maggie and I were driving back from Savannah, she also offered to help. "You're welcome to whatever I have, Eliot. I'm not kidding."

I tell my mother the same thing I told my sister: "We'll manage.

Thank you, though. That's very nice…" Overwhelmed by their generosity, I choke back tears and change the subject. "Maggie said you started another book. I'm sorry I haven't asked. I've been…" I'm too distraught to finish.

"To be honest, Eliot, I think I'm done. The more I do it, the more I realize that writing is *hard work*." She smiles. I notice her eyes are red-rimmed and glassy, as though she's fighting back tears of her own. "In fact, it's occurred to me that I like the idea of writing rather than the writing itself. To sit on my ass and stare at a computer is a lousy way to live. I'm tired. I'd much rather watch *Law & Order*, which is always on, no matter what time of day. I find that comforting."

I start to protest but realize I'm tired, too. "Sometimes it's okay to stop pushing."

Later that afternoon, en route to Savannah, I call Sylvia. She's still at the hospital in Hilton Head but will be leaving—*discharged*, that is—tomorrow morning. Our past few calls have been mostly transactional: How are you? Fine, how are you? Fine, how is Gail? No change; how's the baby? No change; how is Hailey? Fine; okay; the same; no change.

"I can't stand living like this, Sylvia," I tell her now. "The longer I go without telling Grant the truth, the worse it will be when I finally do. I know I should get it over with—just rip it off like a Band-Aid—but I can't seem to get the words out. I also wonder if maybe it's better just to wait until Gail wakes up, but who knows when that will happen."

Sylvia groans. "We've already discussed this, Eliot. The rules are the rules. I wish I could help you, but it's beyond my control."

"I don't know what to do with myself. I don't know how to *be*. How can I just live with Grant, live in the world, knowing I've—"

"Told a lie? Done something bad? Eliot, get off your high horse. You know, that's another thing that bothers me about you: how you think you're better than everyone else."

"I *do not*, Sylvia. I think I'm *awful*. I just want to do the right thing. I just want to be… I don't know… a good person, I guess, a trustworthy person."

"Here's what would be good—if you got with the program, if you manned the fuck up. Go back to the PICU, go back to Grant, and keep your fat mouth shut. Look, if it'll make you feel any better, I'll keep your diamond earrings. There, now we're even."

As if, I want to say. "Take them, Sylvia. Take anything you want."

"See how easy that was? Easy peasy lemon squeezy."

"It's too easy." But then it occurs to me, how easy it is to be good when your sister is so willing to be wicked.

⌒

"And you are?"

The nurse standing at the reception desk opens a folder and checks a list. She's wearing a yellow sunburst on her lapel that says VIRGINIA.

"My name is Eliot Gordon. I'm here to see Gail Delaney."

I'm back in Savannah. It's Thursday night, three days after the accident. Although Gail's condition hasn't changed, she was moved out of the PICU this afternoon. The good news is that the children on this new floor are less critical, so there are fewer restrictions on visitors.

It certainly seems more cheerful down here, I think, looking around. The walls are painted in primary colors, and stenciled bunnies frolic in cartoon gardens. The staff seems friendly and happy to serve—well, everyone except this woman, this Virginia, who appears to have a chip on her shoulder.

"Who are you again?" she asks.

"Eliot Gordon," I say patiently.

Virginia opens another folder and checks a second list. "Are you the patient's mother?"

"I'm her stepmother."

Virginia turns to the woman next to her whose sunburst says TARA. "Is a stepmother considered immediate family?"

"Of course, Ginny!"

I must look distressed because Tara rushes to explain. "See, at night this floor is like the PICU. During the day, you can have as many visitors as you like, but nighttime is different. Only two visitors are allowed in at once—"

"With preference given to immediate family," Virginia cuts in.

Tara nods. "Of course, a stepmother is immediate family, so you'll get preference—"

"Unless the real mother is here," Virginia says. "Then you have to wait."

"Virginia!" Tara tries to apologize. "It's been a long shift. Everyone is tired. Anyway, parents can stay overnight if the doctor preapproves you, so..." She waves an open hand toward the ward. "I'm sorry," she says again.

It's okay; I understand. Like Gail, Ginny must've been raised by a stepmother, the evil kind who, when given the choice, saved her own kid in the ocean.

A third folder is open, another list is consulted, a room number is given. I can see Gail after all; I can even stay overnight. But Virginia is watching me closely. She'll be stopping by, her narrowed eyes assure me.

Before I see Gail, I stop in the ladies' room to wash my hands. Either everything I touch is filthy or I've developed glandular issues, because my hands always feel grimy. No matter how often I wash them, they still feel as if I've been working underneath a car all day.

At the sink, I stare at my reflection in the mirror. *Man up, Eliot,* I say to myself. *You have to tell him.*

When I walk into Gail's room, Grant rises from his chair. "You're here." He kisses me hello. "It's great to see you."

"You too." I put down my backpack. "You're right, this place is nicer than upstairs."

I'm referring to the room, which is large and airy. There's a cot made up near Gail's bed, and flower arrangements fill the top of the dresser and windowsill. One of the bouquets is from my office; another, larger bouquet is from Grant's. The rest are from our family and friends, including three dozen white roses from Larry Barnett, CEO of Barnett

Tech, along with a card: "I have no words, but you're in my prayers." In addition to the flowers, Larry sent over a stuffed panda and a basket of muffins. Seeing this, I smile. Jared, my boss, was sure Larry would send over Barnett umbrellas.

I walk over to Gail. My sleeping step-princess looks the same—lovely and at peace, if too pale. As I bend to kiss her, I notice a stack of books on the nightstand. "You've been reading to her?" I ask Grant.

"I try to," he says sheepishly, "but I can't get through the first chapter of *Harriet the Spy* without dozing off. How's Hailey?"

"She's doing better. No, really," I add when I see his questioning look. "Spending the day with her was the best thing I could've done. She played with Maggie, and laughed a lot. She also took a nap, and didn't wake up once." I gesture toward Gail. "Any change?"

He shakes his head but then, after studying a screen, changes his mind. "That light there"—he points—"the red one. That line seems brighter than before."

"Than before what?"

"Before you got here."

That he's relying on a line, once red and now bright red, to tell him how his child's brain is faring, how well, if at all, she can think, breaks my heart. "Have you heard from Beth?"

He nods. "We had a long talk yesterday. I told her she needed to get a job, that given what's going on with Gail, I...uh, we...can't afford to carry her anymore."

"How did she take it?"

"She said she couldn't remember why we had the arrangement in the first place." He smiles weakly. "Next time, remind me not to be such a good guy. I'll save myself a fortune."

I manage a weak smile of my own. "Hopefully there won't be a next time, Grant."

He sits in a chair and motions for me to sit down, too. "So, Eliot, I've come up with a few ways we can cut down on our expenses." He picks up a legal pad where he's scribbled a list. "First, we pull Hailey out of Riverside and send her to public school. On the other hand, does it pay to disrupt her life, especially if we won't get this semester's tuition back? Maybe we can get a partial refund. I can't see them refusing us, given the circumstances?"

"Grant, please—we have time to figure this out. Gail's only been here three days. We haven't even talked to the trauma specialist yet. He's supposed to come back tomorrow. Let's hear what he has to say before we start moving everyone around, okay?"

The red line brightens. Grant rushes over to the monitor, but I stay put.

"I don't think that line means anything," I tell him gently.

"You never know."

"Why don't you go back to the hotel? You look exhausted."

"I am exhausted, actually. I also have these shooting pains in my legs." He shakes his foot. "It must be from sitting in these shitty chairs all day." Groaning, he lumbers across the room, dragging his foot behind him in a Frankenstein shuffle. "You sure you don't mind staying tonight?"

"I *want* to stay here."

Grant moves to kiss me good-bye. "Thank you," he whispers. "Thank you for everything."

"I love you," I tell him. But when he leans in to hug me, I feel as if there's a great expanse between us, a distance the size of a western prairie. "Get some sleep."

After he leaves, the only sound in the room is the wheezing and beeping of the medical equipment. Being here reminds me of the night I had Hailey. Of course, it was a different situation, given that Hailey was just born and everyone was celebrating, whereas Gail just had a life-threatening accident and everyone is petrified. But once again, it's just me in a hospital room with a sleeping child—a *comatose* child, I correct myself, looking over at Gail, a possibly *brain-dead* child.

That first night with Hailey, I read to her, too. Despite my discomfort after an eleventh-hour C-section, I heaved my postpartum body into a sitting position. Although Hailey was asleep, I had heard that to be a good mother, I was supposed to start reading to her as soon as possible. So that's what I did, feeling awkward, if not ridiculous. Now, though, having failed Gail so profoundly, I no longer harbor any illusions about the kind of mother I am, and it's only a matter of time before everyone else finds out, too.

I pull a chair next to her bed, put on my glasses, and start *Harriet the Spy*. But after a minute, I stop. Something's not right. I change into my pajamas. Then I wash my hands, brush my teeth, and climb into her bed with her, careful not to disturb the wires and tubes.

"Chapter One..." From the corner of my eye, I can see the computer monitor. Strangely, the red line brightens. "Chapter One," I repeat, louder. This time, the red line is glowing. I start to tremble. "I'm here, Gail! It's me; it's Eliot."

The red line, still ablaze, starts to pulsate. Soon it's so red that I'm sure it will burst through the screen and spray the four walls. Does it mean anything? It doesn't matter. I read anyway—as loudly as I can, from cover to cover. I'm exhausted; I'm hoarse; I'm glassy-eyed and disoriented. But I make it all the way to the end. Because it's important for a child—whether she's yours or someone else's—to know you're still there, telling her you love her, even if she can't hear a single word you're saying.

Chapter Twenty-five

Memo To: Oliver Morgan Consulting Staff
From: Jared Dixon, Principal
Re: Eliot Gordon

Please be advised that due to a family emergency, Eliot Gordon will be out of the office indefinitely. Lucy Torres and I will be overseeing her client work until she returns. Any questions, especially from clients, should be directed to my office, extension 4353.

Eliot has asked me to relay her deep appreciation for the cards and flowers. She said she will keep us apprised of her stepdaughter's condition. In the meantime, we will continue to service her clients so that she will have a seamless transition when she is ready to return to the office.

Thank you,
Jared

Grant wakes me up the next morning with a kiss. "Say hello, sunshine! Hello, hello, hello!"

Yawning, I rub my eyes. "What time is it?"

"Almost eight thirty."

"Really?" When the nurse came by a few hours ago, I moved from Gail's bed to the cot. I had planned to close my eyes for only a few minutes. "I can't believe how late it is."

"Do you have somewhere else to be, Eliot? A hot date, perhaps?" Grant laughs at his own wit. He's upbeat today and fills the room with good news. Apparently, the trauma specialist met with the pediatric neurologist during rounds, and they reviewed Gail's latest MRI together. Although they were careful not to openly contradict Dr. Bloom, they both feel Gail's results are encouraging. "We're cautiously optimistic," is what they told Grant.

"It's *finally* happening, Eliot! She's showing progress! They said her imaging studies reveal *no irregularities*, plus there are areas that have actually *improved* in the past twenty-four hours. This is incredible! This is exactly what we've been waiting for."

He pulls me up from the bed and spins me off my feet.

His excitement is infectious. "That's terrific, Grant. Did they give you any idea as to when she might wake up?"

"Nah, no one wants to be on the hook for an actual time frame. But from the way they were talking, it could be very soon—maybe even *today! Did you hear that, Gail? We know you're in there! We know you're getting better!*"

Seeing Grant so happy fills me with hope—not only for Gail, but also for myself. I'm going to tell him the truth. I'm going to do it today. And he will still love me.

"I feel it, Eliot. Gail's gonna wake up! And once she does, we'll get out of this godforsaken hospital and go home, and everything will be the same as it was before—better, even. Today's the day, Eliot. *Today, it's all gonna change.*"

"Let's not get ahead of ourselves." Although the last thing I want to do is put a damper on Grant's mood, if Gail doesn't wake up and he's flying too high, his fall will be brutal. "Cautious optimism, remember? Isn't that what the doctors said?"

"Yeah, sure." Grant nods. "Cautious optimism."

Still, I can't help being hopeful, too. Yes, I think. Today is the day.

In the bathroom, I scrutinize my face and decide I could use makeup. Nothing special, just mascara and lipstick, but something to give me the confidence I need to make it through the next few hours. "My mother and Maggie are on their way to the hospital," I tell Grant, cracking the door wider so I can see what he's doing. "They're bringing Hailey."

Hovering over Gail, Grant is smoothing her hair. "How *is* your mother? Does she feel like she got lost in the shuffle?"

That Grant is concerned about my mother's feelings strikes me as odd. "She's okay, I guess, although she's talking about giving up the writing life. She may truly be ready to retire."

"Makes sense, doesn't it? Given all she's going through."

"What do you mean?" I step out of the bathroom. "Grant? Where'd you go?"

I look around, but he's moved into the hall, scouting around for more people to tell his good news.

In the shower, I think about how we'll pay for Gail's medical bills. If she doesn't wake up—which she will—but if she doesn't, she'll need round-the-clock care. Even if she does wake up, we have no clue what kind of condition she'll be in. So it's good that Grant is considering public school. I'm also glad he told Beth to get a job. Going forward, I plan to be equally honest and direct. No, it is not acceptable to leave your comatose daughter behind while you gallivant around Atlanta. No, it is not acceptable to ask your new wife—girlfriend, partner, whatever—to pay for your ex-wife's expenses. No, it is not acceptable to be obsessed with another man, to neglect your children, to flirt on the phone while they're swept into the ocean. No, it is not acceptable to lie. I won't accept any of this anymore. Starting *now*.

I'm sitting next to Gail, reading to her, when I hear a noise in the hall. I look up to see Hailey run into the room with Maggie and my mother following behind her.

"Mommy, Mommy, Mommy!" Throwing out her arms, she lunges at me. "I'm here, I'm here, I'm here!"

I scoop her up and hug her tight. Her red hair is a big bush, and as I stroke her curls, my fingers snag on the tangles. "Hey, sweet pea, when was the last time you brushed your hair?"

"How the hell should I know?" Hailey replies, trying to make me laugh.

It works. I hug her again. "You've been spending too much time with your grandmother."

Holding my beloved daughter, I inhale her four-year-old smell. Thank you, God. Thank you for letting Hailey be okay. She seems better today, and I am very grateful.

"Did you say hi to Gail?" I ask, putting her down.

"Silly mommy," Hailey chastises me. "Gail is *sleeping*."

"But we want her to wake up, which is why we have to talk to her. You need to tell her how much you miss her." I turn to the bed. "Hi, Gail! Hailey and Aunt Maggie and Grandma are here. They all stopped by to say hello."

"Have you spoken to Sylvia?" my mother asks me.

"Not since the other day. Why? Is something wrong?"

"She's concerned about Gail. She also said she wants to help you— financially, I mean—since she feels...responsible for the...uh, acci- dent." Leaning over the bed, my mother brushes back Gail's hair. "How is she? She looks pale, don't you think?"

"She's actually doing much better."

My mother's not convinced. "The last time I saw her, she had more color in her face. It also seems like she's losing weight. Are you sure they're feeding her enough?"

I refuse to let anything my mother says bother me. "Gail is getting the best care in the world. In fact, her doctors said she's showing visible signs of improvement."

"So why is she still in a coma?"

"That's the sixty-four-thousand-dollar question. But everyone thinks she's on the verge of waking up—as early as today, even." I shrug. "You never know."

I walk over to the window. There's a single yellow balloon drifting in the otherwise barren air shaft, an oddity that strikes me as a sign. Grant is right, I tell myself, watching the balloon rise up, up, and away. It's all going to change today; I can feel it, too.

"I hope the doctors know what they're doing, Eliot," my mother says.

"Hey, Mom," Maggie warns, "lighten up. Stop questioning everything Eliot says."

"Fine. I'll just listen to Eliot and shut up. So, how is Grant doing?"

"He's optimistic," I tell her. "Of course, this could change, but we're trying to stay hopeful."

"And you and he are doing okay? You're getting along? No problems?"

"Of course, why wouldn't we be doing okay?"

"No reason," my mother says, but I can see her trying to hide a smile behind her hand.

"What's so funny?" I recognize that smile, and it makes me nervous.

"Nothing's funny." But she can't help herself; she cracks up. She even bends over to untie and then retie her sneakers so I can't see how hard she's laughing.

"Then why are you laughing—" Suddenly I know exactly what's funny. I also know why she's so concerned about Grant. *Sylvia told her the truth.* My mother is trying to hide, unsuccessfully, that she knows which one of her daughters was on the beach with the kids and which one wasn't.

"Mommy, catch me!"

I turn to see Hailey standing at the foot of Gail's bed with her arms spread out.

"Mommy, I'm jumping!"

Luckily, I'm already in motion because she leaps into the air just as I shout, "No, Hailey!" I grab her and set her down in a chair. "Here." I click on the TV. "*Sesame Street* is on. You love Elmo."

Loud kids' music fills the room.

"She told you?" I ask my mother, although it's not a question. "Sylvia told you about what happened—" I can't finish my sentence because Maggie is listening.

My mother rolls her eyes. "Of course she told me, Eliot. She told me the moment it happened."

"Told you what?" Maggie wants to know.

Instead of answering, my mother points to the computer screen. The red line has lit up. It's not as bright as it was last night, but it's still very red. "Does that mean anything?"

"We're not sure. The computer is measuring Gail's brain wave functions. Supposedly, when the lines brighten, it means there's definitive activity."

"Told you what?" Maggie repeats. When I don't give her an answer, she touches my shoulder. "I have to tell you something. Remember that conversation we had about the hospital bills? Well, I did something that will really piss you off. So, I can't tell you what it is until you promise, cross your heart, not to get mad."

I sigh. "Just tell me, Maggie."

"I'd rather you promise me first."

I hold up two fingers. "I won't get mad, Maggie. I promise."

"Well, I know you're worried about"—glancing at Gail, she lowers her voice—"money, so I talked to some people, one person, actually, who can help—who *wants* to help. People really do care, Eliot. They want to lend a hand. Anyway, I—"

My mother cuts her off. "What *the hell* are you talking about, Maggie? You're not making any sense."

"Don't yell at her, Mom. She's just trying to help—and I appreciate the thought, Maggie, but this is between me and Grant."

"But what does she mean, Eliot? Who did she call?"

"What are you guys talking about?" Grant walks into the room, holding a package of X-rays. His face is pinched, and he doesn't look nearly as happy as he did before. "What's between us?"

When he spies Hailey, he picks her up and spins her around. This reminds me of Roger, and I wonder how he's faring now that Sylvia is taking the blame for what I did. On the other hand, given that my mother knows the truth, I'm sure Sylvia also told Roger, which means it's only a matter of time before Maggie finds out—

I look at Maggie and want to smack my own head. Maggie already knows! *Of course Maggie knows!* I almost laugh out loud. Sylvia probably told her at the same time she told my mother. And Gail knows, of course, because she was there when it happened, so once she wakes up, she'll remind Hailey, and then Charlotte will find out and she'll tell Beth. After Beth finds out, only Grant will be left. Soon, very soon, he'll be the cheese, the last one standing.

"What's between us?" Grant asks again, and this time his voice is sharp. "What are you guys talking about? What did I miss?"

"We're talking about how we plan to pay for Gail's care," I reply, knowing I have to tell him the truth soon, before he finds out from someone else.

Grant whips around. "Mind your own business, Simone. That's between Eliot and me. We'll figure it out ourselves."

Hearing his tone, which is pretty nasty given the circumstances, I snap, "How *dare* you talk to her like that! She's my *mother*. She and Maggie have offered to gut their savings to help us. How can you be so ungrateful?"

Startled at first, Grant recovers quickly. "If it's okay with you, Eliot, I don't need your family's input right now. Gail is *my* daughter. This is between *you* and *me*. Can't the Gordon gossip girls back off for once?"

Counting to three, I reel myself in. "We know Gail is your daughter, Grant." Breathe, I remind myself. Just breathe. "They only want to give us a hand, that's all."

"Eliot's right," my mother jumps in. "Maggie and I, Sylvia too, we'll do whatever—"

"Let's get one thing clear," Grant cuts her off, his voice tight. "If not for *Sylvia*, *Gail* wouldn't need your help in the first place."

Hearing this, I blurt out, "It was an accident, Grant! No one meant for this to happen."

His voice drops. "I know that." He walks over to the window, sits in a chair, and puts his head in his hands. "Of course it was an accident." His body is drained; his face is ashen. "I'm sorry I got so worked up. It's just too much, Eliot. First your mother, now Gail...how are we going to afford all this?" He takes Gail's X-rays out of the envelope and holds them up to the light. "Why isn't she waking up?"

"What about me?" my mother asks. "Eliot, what is he talking about?"

Grant looks at her. "Eliot told me about your health issues." He turns to me. "We can't take your mother's money, you know that. She's going to need it for herself."

"What health issues?" Maggie and my mother ask at the same time.

In my mind, a memory is taking shape. In it, Grant, my mother, and I are standing on the rich oilman's deck, debating whether or not we should go to the beach. Canvasing the sky, my mother suggests it might rain. Grant agrees. As I listen to them now, I suddenly remember what I was supposed to tell her: *Mom, if Grant asks, you're afraid you have cancer.*

"Eliot told me you're not feeling well," I hear him say. "She said you think it might be cancer, but I wasn't supposed to mention it..." He trails off as if something else has occurred to him. "She was doing research at Emory before we left Atlanta. It's why she forgot to pick up Hailey from school..." He turns slowly to me. "Your mother doesn't have cancer, does she?"

"No," I say, but I'm not looking at him. I'm looking at Hailey, who's been taking all of this in, recording our every move with her 360-degree vision.

"Mommy," she says, "I'm so hungry. Do they have any food in this place?"

"You and Aunt Maggie should go get a snack."

"No." Hailey hops off her chair and runs to my side. "I want to stay here with you."

"So if your mother doesn't have cancer," Grant asks, "then why were you at Emory? And why were you acting so crazy? It was like you were in another world."

Clear and clean, I remind myself, honest and direct. "Sometimes I go to the library after I drop Hailey off at school so I don't have to drive back and forth to my office. You know that."

"But why were you so late picking her up? And why didn't you call?" He pauses. "You're not telling me the whole story, are you?"

I don't answer.

"Were you alone?"

Still nothing.

"Who were you with?"

I'm sweaty and my hands are itching, and I wish Grant would stop asking so many questions. It's hot in this room, blisteringly so. I'm trapped here, in this hospital, in this moment. I close my eyes and let the light streaming in through the window sear my face.

When I open them, Grant is still watching me.

"I was seeing an old friend." I dig my nails into my hands, scratching the skin until it's raw. "You don't know him." But Charlotte does; Charlotte saw us together. Charlotte knows exactly what happened.

"Which old friend, Eliot?"

The man I used to think was my soul mate, I almost say but don't.

"Which old friend?" Grant asks again.

It's over, I realize. I can't do this anymore. I can't have any of my daughters, real or not, keeping secrets for me. I have to protect my child, even if she isn't mine, even if she hates me.

"Charlotte met him," I say. "He and I were together; we saw her at Riverside. Remember I told you that I bumped into Charlotte and Beth at the chapel? It was that same morning."

Grant gets up from his seat and takes two steps toward me. I, in turn, take two steps back. "Charlotte met him?" He is so confused. "What was she doing at Riverside?"

"She skipped school to help Beth with the mural. It was last Monday, a few days before we left for Wyatt Island. I was with my old friend; it was very awkward for all of us."

"When were you going to tell me this, Eliot?"

"I did tell you about Charlotte."

"No, when were you going to tell me about *spending time with your old friend*?"

"Never," I whisper.

"We should go." My mother reaches for Hailey. "Let's let Mommy and Daddy talk."

Hailey refuses. She attaches herself to my leg and lashes out at anyone who tries to take her away.

Grant walks over to the bed and touches Gail's arm. "Did Gail meet him too?"

"Gail is sleeping, Daddy!" Hailey shouts. "Don't touch her! She's my sister and she's sleeping and you're not allowed to touch her."

Hearing this, Grant jerks his hand away. He's watching Hailey cling to me, and I know what he's thinking. Once again, he's been left out of a girls-only club, only this time it's not me and my sisters who have excluded him; it's me and his daughters. His life is overrun by women, women and their gossip and their drama and their dirty little secrets.

"Eliot? What else haven't you told me?"

Hailey's still talking. "No one can touch Gail except Mommy and Aunt Sylvia. Aunt Sylvia was the one who swimmed in the ocean, and bringed her back in."

Grant's retort is robotic. "Sylvia didn't *save* her, Hailey," he snaps as if she's a full-grown adult instead of a four-year-old child. "It's because of *Sylvia* that your sister is here."

"No, Grant. That's not right." I pick up Hailey and hold her tight. Thank you for allowing me to hold her like this, for letting her be okay. "Sylvia didn't do anything wrong. It was me—the accident was my fault."

My mother gasps. Maggie reaches to take Hailey away, but I won't let her. She's *my* child, *mine*. Now that I've told Grant the truth, she may be all I have left.

"Sylvia wasn't with the girls on the beach," I continue. "She wasn't anywhere near the water. Hailey, Gail, and I were down by the shore, playing in the sand. My phone rang, so I answered it. I talked for no more than a minute, maybe two, and when I turned around...one second they were there, and the next"—I look up, beseech him—"they were gone, Grant. Just, I don't know, just gone." Bewildered by the memory, I shake my head.

"You?" That's all he says—one word, no affect—just "you."

"Yes," I say, again clear and direct. "It wasn't Sylvia. It was me."

See, I would rather Hailey know terrible things about me than believe lies about my sister. Of all the lessons I teach my kid about the world, she must understand this: Charlotte and Gail are her sisters. No one else will know her the way they do; no one else will see her true face. "I really am ugly," Sylvia cried to me once, a long time ago, and as her elder sister, it's up to me not only to prove her wrong, but to defend her against anyone who says otherwise.

I hold up my daughter; I look into her eyes. "Hailey, listen to me, okay? The accident was my fault—no one else's. You and Gail were playing in the water, but I wasn't watching. I was talking on the phone. The waves were very rough, and pulled you and Gail away. But as soon as I saw you, I swam as fast as I could to get you, and Aunt Sylvia swam to Gail. She saved your sister. She saved the day. She's a hero. But the accident was my fault." I turn to Grant. "It was an accident, Grant, and I'm sorry."

He's quiet for a long time. Finally he says, "But who were you on the phone with? And if it was an accident, Eliot, why didn't you just tell me the truth? I would've understood."

"Sylvia was trying to protect me, and I...uh, let her. I was afraid to tell you I was on the phone. That's why, really—I was scared. So when Sylvia blurted out that it was her fault, I didn't correct her, and—"

Grant cuts me off. "But who were you on the phone with, Eliot? That's the piece you keep glossing over. Who was so important that you—"

He doesn't finish. Staring at me, he tries to figure it out. I watch as a shadow passes over his face. Then he blinks and the shadow disappears.

He remembers something. He blinks again, and then it all makes sense: a secret friend, Emory, a man so important that I would neglect my own children. He knows all my stories, especially the one about the boy who broke my heart, the one I could never get over—

There's a knock on the door. Everyone freezes. There's another knock, stronger this time and more insistent. For one horrible half second, I'm panic-stricken.

It's Finn, I think, whirling around. How did he find me?

But it's not Finn.

"Oh, my God," my mother sputters. "What the hell are you doing here?"

The stranger speaks, although when he does, I realize he's no stranger. "Maggie called me. She said it was an emergency. I came as quickly as I could."

"Maggie?" my mother asks, but my sister is as astonished as we are to see who it is.

Standing there, back from the dead, is my long-lost father, Bernardo Lorenzo Carmello Giordano, the notorious Gluckman.

But wait; there's more.

"Mommy!" I hear behind me. It's Hailey. "Mommy, turn around! Mommy, look!"

I turn around. I look.

"Mommy!" Hailey can't believe it. "Gail waked up!"

Chapter Twenty-six

"MOMMY, LOOK!" Hailey says. "Gail waked up."

Hearing this, I turn. I look. And there is Gail, dazed, confused, but definitely awake.

"Gail?" Grant asks slowly. "Are you okay?"

"Gail?" I ask softly. "How do you feel?"

She doesn't answer; she just opens her eyes wider and watches us watch her. We are a big crowd, and we are hovering, so it is a lot to take in: Grant, me, Maggie, my mother, Barney, and, finally, Hailey. But when her eyes rest on her little sister and Hailey blurts out, "It's me! It's sweet pea," Gail breaks into the goofy smile we all recognize, and we breathe a collective sigh of relief. Even my father, whom Gail doesn't know and who doesn't know her, beams like a newly minted parent.

None of us have ever felt so blessed before (except maybe Barney, because, really, who knows why he is here, much less how he feels?). Gail isn't talking, nor can she sit up, so although it's immediately clear she isn't quite our same Gail, we are determined to celebrate our good fortune. Bystanders are ushered out, doctors are summoned, Beth is called, tests are arranged, and for a few fleeting moments, I once again allow myself hope.

Maybe this will turn out all right, I think. Maybe everything will go back to normal—or, if not normal, at least back to the way it used to be.

A few minutes later, Dr. Bloom, the neurologist, rushes into the room, holding a clipboard and a fat sheath of papers. "I'd like to speak to Gail's parents—alone, if possible."

"Of course," I say, directing my mother and Hailey toward the door. But when I sidle next to Grant, he puts up his hands.

"He's referring to me and Gail's mother," Grant says. "Not you."

"Of course you and Beth," I realize, taking elongated steps backward—one, two, three, stretch—until I am out in the hallway. "Of course not me."

Gail is *his* child, I remember—not mine—*his* and *Lizzie's*. And there it is, the transformative moment. Unfortunately, it isn't the transformation I had hoped for. On the other hand, I always knew the evil stepmother suffered; until now, I just never understood how.

I go to the cafeteria with my mother, sister, daughter, and Barney. I half expect Grant to summon me back, but he doesn't. Instead, he shuts the door with a curt, "We'll talk later," and this, I fear, is the beginning of the rest of the story.

In the elevator, my father speaks first. "It's good to see you, Eliot. It's been a long time."

"It has been a long time," I agree.

"Why can't we be with Gail?" Hailey demands. "I want to be with her *right now.*"

"Gail is with her doctor, sweet pea. We can be with her soon."

"But that's *not fair!*"

"It may not be fair," I say firmly, "but that's the way it is."

As we get our coffee and find a table, I begin to wonder if maybe all isn't lost. Maybe Barney showed up for a reason. Maybe my father, the Gluckman, will turn out to be my happily-ever-after.

"So, Barney," my mother says, "Maggie called to tell you about Eliot?"

My mother and father are watching each other closely. To anyone else, they appear to be meeting for the first time, as if on a blind date; and it occurs to me that this might all be a ruse. What if Maggie is trying to parent-trap them the way Sylvia once tried to parent-trap me? That this idea could excite me is shocking. After all this time, after all I know, do I secretly hope my parents might fall back in love?

"Yes, Mom," Maggie says. "I told him about Eliot. Why is that so surprising?"

"You know why, Maggie," I snap. "It's *insane* that you would talk to Barney about me. This whole thing is *insane*."

My father breaks in. "Uh, excuse me, Eliot." His voice is so soft that I have to lean in to hear him. "When Maggie called, she said you were in trouble, that you were having...what did she call it? Family issues, I believe...so I figured I'd fly down...to...uh...lend a hand..." He seems as perplexed to be here as we are to see him. "I suppose...uh...it may have been a bit...uh...impulsive...but I figured...well, at that moment, it seemed like a good idea."

Time has been a cruel mistress to Barney Gordon. I last saw him when? Twenty-three years ago? I was fifteen, and he was fifty. It's hard to remember what he looked like at fifty, although I can almost see glimpses of that younger man in his face. His wrinkled skin hangs in soft folds around his neck, and his eyes are rheumy, but they are still sky blue like Maggie's, and he still gestures with his hands when he talks, although slower now than before.

Sitting there, I feel my throat start to close up and my chest start to tighten. Soon I can't swallow or breathe. This is familiar, too. Twenty-three years ago, when my father and I sat on his dumpy couch in New Jersey, and he asked about my new life in Atlanta ("How y'all doin' a-ways down yonder in *Georgia?*" he asked in a hokey drawl), I felt myself shutting down in exactly the same way.

"I'm sorry," Barney says.

"It's okay," Maggie assures him.

Blinking, he looks around, as if realizing he is lost. "I just wanted to help."

Afraid I may suffocate, I stand up and speak. "Why would I want your help?" I gasp. "I don't even know you." Although I know I sound rude, speaking has become a means of survival. If I can get my words out, I can get the air in. My impulse to be the good girl, the nice girl, the what-can-I-get-you girl, is gone, replaced by the need to breathe. "I don't even know you," I repeat, still struggling.

Hailey is eating a doughnut, and her lips are dusted with powdered sugar. "I'm still hungry. Can I have more doughnuts?" She grins at me coyly. "Please, Mommy? I love doughnuts so much. You can have one too if you want."

Without waiting for me to agree, my mother plucks Hailey out of her chair and carries her off.

"Just a small one," I call foolishly, as if anything I say matters at this point.

Barney is watching them go. "Hailey looks exactly like you," he says, and I can swear I see a tear in his eye. "Your little girl is beautiful."

"She's hardly *beautiful*, Barney. She's just a regular kid. And she doesn't look like me; she looks like Mom." It's not a tear, I realize. It's only the reflection of the light in his glasses.

"You're right. It's the hair." He touches his own bald head. "Hailey has Dolores's red. You had that same red too, as a baby, but it darkened by the time you were three. You probably don't remember it." He smiles weakly, first at me and then at Maggie. "You weren't even born yet, Maggie." He thinks for a minute. "Sylvia was only one. Can you imagine that?"

"Barney, listen." Honest and direct, I remind myself. "While I appreciate your intention, I would prefer not to reminisce." I, too, turn to Maggie. "What the hell were you thinking?"

"I wasn't, I guess. But you said you didn't have enough money to take care of Gail, that you might go bankrupt, so I...I just wanted to help, Eliot."

"By asking him to come here? What can he do for me?"

Disappointment dissolves like a bitter wafer on my tongue. Barney's unexpected appearance, I realize, means nothing. On the contrary, his being here is one more burden for me to bear. Anyone can see he wants me to tell him how *great* it was that he came, how *generous*, how *selfless*. That it is *perfectly okay* he blew off the past twenty years. *It's absolutely fine because you're here now and that's all that matters.*

My father points at Maggie and then at himself. "Your sister didn't ask me to come, Eliot. She only asked for my help. I came on my own."

"You can't help me, Barney," I say, unable to stop seeing myself on the beach, flirting with Finn, while my two little girls are swept out to sea. *Turn around! Be a parent! Do your job!* Knowing that this single split second will haunt me for the rest of my life, I begin to understand the terms of my punishment: *a fate worse than death*. Isn't that how the fairy tale goes?

I burn with shame. Even my own father, who doesn't know me as a daughter, as a person, knows I am a bad mother, a worse stepmother. And I still have to face Grant and the consequences of his finding out that I almost killed Gail—*his* child, not mine—while I was on the phone with another man. So tell me: How the hell does Barney Gluckman think he can help?

"Give him a chance, Eliot," Maggie says.

"How could you do this?" How could she allow this stranger to come here and witness my disgrace, to watch from the bleachers as my life falls apart? "We haven't spoken to him in almost twenty years."

"*You* may not have spoken to him."

"And you have?" And here I thought nothing else could shock me. "*You've* been speaking to *Barney*?"

"I *told* you I was going to call him, Eliot. He's my father, too."

"I thought you were *kidding*. I didn't think you would actually *do it*." Feeling like a fool, I turn to my mother, who has returned to the table with Hailey. "Did you know this?"

My mother nods.

"Does Sylvia know too? Does *everyone* know but me?" I pause. "That's the problem with three," I say aloud. "Someone is always left out of something."

"I wasn't trying to hide it from you," Maggie says. "But every time I brought him up, you made it clear you weren't interested, so I tried to respect that. He's still my father, though, and I've always wanted to get to know him, so I called him a couple of months ago, a few days after Dylan proposed—"

"A couple of *months* ago?"

"—and we had some great conversations. So when the accident happened, I called him to let him know. I didn't realize he would come, but I'm glad he did." Maggie thrusts out her chin. "He's not just your father, Eliot," she says again. "He's my father, too."

"Mommy," Hailey says, climbing into my lap, "I want to go see Gail."

"Soon, Hailey," my mother tells her. "We'll see Gail very soon. In the meantime, let's go to the gift shop. Eliot? Hailey and I are taking a walk."

"No!" I wrap my arms around Hailey. "I want *my child* to stay with *me.*" I turn back to Maggie. "Okay, he's your father, too. But this is *my business.*"

"So what if it's your business?" She says this defiantly, so unlike the Maggie I know.

"This is *my business*, Maggie—not *yours*—and you've dragged him down here for something that is *not your concern.*"

"That's the part you're not getting, Eliot—or maybe you're just not listening. *Dad* didn't fly down here just to see *you.*"

As we glare at each other, it strikes me how much I don't know about my little sister; or rather, how much I've underestimated her. Was she always this bold? If so, why didn't I ever notice? Here she is, taking risks I would never even consider, surpassing me in so many ways. Forget that Maggie is thirty-three years old and a full-fledged adult. She's my kid sister, so she was never a real person—that is, someone to be reckoned with. But now I can see all the ways she's outgrown me, which means I have to reconsider her place—and mine—in the Gordon sister lineup. It means I also have to reconsider Hailey, who will one day outgrow me too.

Barney rises, clumsily, to his feet. "All this is my fault," he says, clearly uncomfortable in both body and spirit. "I shouldn't have come. It's just that I've made a lot of mistakes in the past twenty years—mistakes I know I can't undo—but I thought if I came, if I did this one thing, maybe...I don't know...it was silly to think..." He holds up his hands as if to silence himself.

"It wasn't silly." Maggie helps him settle back down. "It was very brave and very nice."

Barney grabs Maggie's hand. Seeing this, I feel my small, fisted heart gripped by rage. I don't care that my idiot sister has been talking to my idiot father or that everyone but me knows about it. I don't even care that she is defending his unannounced, inappropriate visit in the midst of my crisis. But their *intimacy*, that they are *touching* each other like a *father and daughter*, is more than I can tolerate.

"*Shut up*, Maggie," I blurt out. "Just *shut up*. I can't believe you invited him here—"

"I didn't invite him, Eliot. We just told you that."

Nothing anyone says can stop me from plowing forward. Not even Hailey's plaintive, " 'Shut up' isn't a nice word, Mommy." There's a certain freedom in anger, I realize. Having already set fire to the curtains, I may as well watch the whole house burn down.

"In fact," I continue, "of all the *stupid* things you've ever done in your whole *stupid* life, this is, by far, the most *stupid* of all." Still holding Hailey, I get up from my seat. "I have to go."

"Where are you going?" Maggie is concerned. How could she care about me when I just called her *stupid*? How could anyone possibly care about me? "Are you going to see Grant? Here"—she reaches for Hailey—"let me watch her so you can talk."

I yank her away. "Why is everyone trying to take her from me? *She's my daughter, so please take your hands off her.*" I look at my father. "I'm sorry you flew all the way down here. I'm also sorry you didn't get the reception you were hoping for. But it's been too long, Barney. Way too much time has passed, and right now, I have too much to deal with.

I can't worry about making everything better for you. I'm sorry," I say again. "I know this must be very disappointing."

I walk away, cradling Hailey in my arms. "Let's go see Daddy," I tell her, wiping leftover powder off her lips with my fingers.

"I don't want anything from you, Eliot," Barney says loudly. "I just want to help. You're my daughter. You've always been my daughter. I never stopped loving you."

"I'll be fine," I tell him.

"You don't have to do this alone," my father, the stranger, calls out.

I keep walking.

"Who's that man?" Hailey asks.

"For a little girl," I tell her, kissing her cheek, "you sure do ask a lot of questions."

I go back upstairs to see Grant, who, it turns out, has no interest in talking—not to me, not about Gail, "not at the moment," he says, his voice brittle. There is, however, one thing he does want me to know: Now that Gail is awake and can be evaluated properly, it appears the doctors were wrong. She *had* suffered head trauma after all.

"Gail," he says again to make sure it sinks in, "did suffer head trauma. Her cerebral cortex and brain stem were compromised during the accident, and it will be days, maybe weeks, before the doctors can determine the full extent of the damage."

I feel my stomach drop. A second later, as if on time-released delay, my heart starts to race, and it is impossible for me to focus. This, I guess, is what is meant by "unthinkable." What I did to Gail is unthinkable: I truly can't think it. A part of me was still hoping she would be fine, that all she had to do was wake up and she could go back to being Gail. But now...

I start to cry.

We are standing in the hall. Hailey is in Gail's room, and I can hear her recounting to her sister everything she'd missed, most recently (and importantly) the two doughnuts she just ate. ("Two *big* ones, Gail. And they were your favorite, the powder kind. I'll

bring you some, if you want. And then Mommy said 'shut up' to
Aunt Maggie!")

I squeeze my eyes to make the tears stop. "What's the plan, then?" I
say, trying to absorb this new normal and stay in the now.

"The plan?" Grant echoes. In his hand he holds a yellow pamphlet.
"The plan is to keep her here another week, then transfer her to a rehabilitation facility in Atlanta."

I gesture toward the pamphlet, but when he sees me looking, he
folds it into a square and shoves it into his pocket.

"What kind of facility?" My ears are ringing, and my stomach is
woozy, as though I can suddenly feel the earth's spin.

"What kind do you think?"

"I don't know, Grant. That's why I'm asking." The hallway whirls
around me: wall, elevator, wall, door, wall, elevator, wall, door. I am
so dizzy I could topple over even though I'm standing perfectly still.
Grant is silent, so I ask again. "What kind of rehabilitation facility?"

"The kind where they rehabilitate her." He checks his watch. "Excuse me," he says as if we'd just met. "But I have to go check on my
daughter."

"I'm so sorry," I blurt out, the ringing too loud to contain. "I'm sorry
for everything."

For the first time since finding out that I—not Sylvia—was the one
on the beach, Grant looks directly at me, and what I see makes me gasp.
He is Grant, but not Grant. Like Grant, he has thick hair, black and
curly, and his skin is dark and grainy, with several days of stubble on
his chin and jaw. But Grant's eyes are bright, as if lit from within; they
flash with humor and kindness. And these eyes are flat and empty, as if
they were carved out and cauterized, then put back into his skull.

"Can I go in?" I whisper. Having never seen eyes look so dead in a
person still living, I am spooked myself. "Can I see her? Gail?"

He shakes his head. A single tear falls. "Please, Eliot—" His voice
breaks. "Please just let me be."

"Grant? I just want you to know that I will do whatever I can to make this right." How are you going to do that? I ask myself, hearing how meaningless, how altogether irrelevant, everything is in light of Gail's brain damage. "Can't we just talk? Just for a minute?"

"Eliot," he says sadly, his thousand-yard stare focused on a point far beyond me, "right now you are the last person I want to talk to." Then he walks into Gail's room and shuts the door.

Chapter Twenty-seven

SO THAT'S AS FAR as Grant and I have gotten in terms of discussing the accident. In fact, other than exchanging details about Hailey, he and I have barely spoken in the past three days. Beth and Charlotte flew back from Atlanta a few hours after Gail woke up, so he's been preoccupied with them, and with Gail, of course, whose days are busy with evaluations and physical therapy.

Even though Grant won't talk to me, I still come here, to the hospital, every day. I show up in the morning and stay until dinner, but I slink around in the back, like an unwelcome smell. I figure as long as I don't get in the way, I won't be asked to leave. Although I continue to ask Grant if he'd like to get coffee, he always says, "No, thank you, not right now" (always polite, always strained). We both try to appear upbeat, if only to help bolster Gail's spirits. But after visiting hours, when I drive back to the oilman's house and Grant goes to the hotel, I suspect that, like me, he allows himself to break down privately, under the harsh spray of the shower.

It's not unusual for Grant to withdraw when he's wounded, but he's never cut me off before or put up any barriers between me and his girls. Now, though, he won't speak to me at all—not about Gail or Charlotte or himself—he won't even look at me. But rather than trying to push him and risk alienating him further, I've been asking Gail's doctors and nurses for status reports. Surprisingly, they offer information freely, although this is probably because I frame my questions in a way that makes it seem that I know more than I actually do.

"I was speaking to Dr. Bloom about Gail's latest MRI," I might say, tilting my head like a scholar. "He's cautiously optimistic. Do you agree?"

More often than not, I'll get some kind of response, from which I've been able to parse that Gail's prognosis, while precarious, isn't completely bleak. Although she hasn't spoken yet, she's awake and alert and is able to recognize family members, answer simple "yes" and "no" questions, and identify basic shapes and colors. Similarly, she can't walk or feed herself, but she can stand up with help; and as her therapy progresses, it's safe to assume that her motor functioning will (hopefully) return. No one can predict how long it will take her to fully recover, or if she'll recover at all. And while every day brings progress, she'll never be the same Gail. On the other hand, as one of the nurses told me, miracles do happen.

"You just have to have faith," she said.

"In what?" I asked. "In the doctors? In the treatment process? In God?"

"In Gail."

I look at my watch. It's ten thirty, which is later than usual. I like to get here early, when Grant and Beth give Gail her breakfast, but this morning I spent a few hours with Hailey. Because it's too hectic to bring her to the hospital, she's been staying with my mother on Wyatt Island while I travel back and forth. I can't stand being without her all day, but I also can't stand the idea of not being with Gail, so I'm doing my best to split my time between them.

I knock on Gail's door, then let myself in. She's still in bed, but awake and watching TV. Grant glances up, but he doesn't greet me. Nor does he respond when I say hello. He's alone, although I spy Beth's and Charlotte's bags on a chair, which means they're here, too.

I lift my hand and wave. "Hi, Gail." According to the doctors, it's important to gesture as often as possible. Apparently, children relearn to communicate by mimicking what we do as well as what we say.

Gail raises her hand to wave. "Hi," she says. Her hair, unwashed and stringy, hangs in her eyes, and she's drawn and sickly-looking. Tucked into the white sheets, wearing footed pajamas, and mesmerized by cartoons, she seems a lot younger than she did only a week ago.

I hold up a bag of jeans and T-shirts. "Are you ready to get dressed?"

Grant gets up. "Mommy will help you get dressed, Gail," he says, and then pretends to take off a shirt. He turns to me. "Beth will be back in a minute. She and Charlotte went to the cafeteria." He pauses. "Thank you for the clothes. It's time she got out of those pajamas."

We stand for a minute in awkward silence. I put my hand on his arm, hoping that, like Gail, he'll mimic me. Gestures are important, I tell myself, willing him to allow me this small moment of contact. But before he can do anything, Gail suddenly says, "Da."

We both whip around.

"Da." She struggles for a few seconds, as if trying to disentangle a crumb with her tongue. And then, just like that, she pushes out, "Dad." She points to Grant. "Dad-dy." Then she points to me. "El-lie; El-i-ot." She looks around the room. "Mom?" Her lips form a perfect O.

Grant and I start to cheer.

Gail claps, too. "Daddy!" she repeats.

Grant catches my eye. His grin is proud, if somewhat sheepish, and it occurs to me that he's thinking about the last time one of his daughters said her first word. I hold his gaze, and for a second—just a second—it's as though we're connected. But then, as if remembering that this is *Gail* and not *Hailey*, he turns and sprints for the door. "Hold on, okay, Gail? I have to find Mom. I'll be right back."

A minute later, he returns with his arm slung across Beth's shoulders. "*She's talking, Lizzie! She's asking for you.*"

Unfortunately, Gail has nodded off. So they stand there, watching her sleep. I feel sorry for Grant and also for Beth, who more than anyone (more than me, certainly) deserves to hear her girl call her "Mom."

Beth, Charlotte, and Grant sit down together, recounting what just happened. They don't include me in their conversation, and it's obvious (even to me) that I'm in the way. So I lift my hand good-bye, walk out of the hospital, and drive back to Wyatt Island. But I plan to come back here tomorrow and the day after and the day after, as long as it takes, until Gail—Grant's daughter, but also the little girl I love—is our Gail again.

⌒

Ever since the accident, my mother has been extraordinary. In addition to supporting me, she's been a tremendous help with Hailey, in ways I could never have imagined. Like an old married couple, she and my daughter take daily constitutionals, eat their meals together (on trays, in front of a blaring TV), and find never-ending amusement in the size, smell, texture, and frequency of their bowel movements. (The elderly and the young, I have found, are equally obsessed with poop.)

They also share similar passions. When I got home last night, they were perched in front of the Weather Channel, and my mother was describing high- and low-pressure zones along the California coastline. Hailey was captivated. (Although this was more likely due to the multicolored graphics on the weather map, rather than my mother's science lesson.)

"Eliot!" my mother called out. "Guess what! My brilliant granddaughter has decided that when she grows up, she wants to be"—not a doctor or lawyer or best-selling author—"a *meteorologist*."

"Or a princess," Hailey corrected her.

I'm both relieved and grateful that my mother—the same woman who, years ago, called stale saltines with mustard a meal—has assumed the role of grandmother with patience and generosity, and I tell her so every day. Although it embarrasses her, I also think she secretly loves it. "Please," she'll say, waving me away. "It's no big deal."

But it is a big deal, and I tell her that, too. If it weren't for her and Hailey, I would have no one to talk to. Sylvia and Maggie are gone— Sylvia left two days after the accident and Maggie the night Gail woke up. I could call them, of course, but Sylvia is preoccupied with her pregnancy, and I don't want my misery to darken what should be a happy time. Nor do I want to talk to Maggie. I'm angry at her for contacting my father (who is her father, too, I remind myself), and she's taking my refusal of his help as a personal affront. She left me a message and I left her a message, but neither of us is willing to do more. ("I'm sorry I called you stupid," is the message I left. "But I'm not sorry for being mad at you for inviting him. Okay, maybe you didn't 'invite' him, but you did make him feel welcome enough to come.") I don't blame Maggie for not wanting to talk to me; if someone left me a half-assed apology like that, I wouldn't want to talk to her, either. But I feel too sorry for myself to make a full-assed effort. Because of this, though, in addition to Grant and the kids, I feel as though I've lost my sisters.

Barney and Maggie drove back to Atlanta together. Maybe it's odd only to me, but I find it bizarre that she would willingly choose to spend six hours in a car with a man she barely knows. Wouldn't it be awkward having to negotiate bathroom stops with a veritable stranger? (To me, the fact that he's not a complete stranger just makes the whole thing worse.)

According to my mother, Barney plans to stick around a while. "Apparently, he wants to get to know you girls," she said sarcastically. "Seems to me like he's overstaying his welcome."

"What welcome?" I said, as put off by the idea as she was. "I didn't want him here in the first place."

"That's your father, though—always dropping out of sight when you need him the most, then turning up again when you need him the least. He is such a strange man."

I agree with my mother because I've always agreed with her when it comes to Barney, and our mutual disgust has once again united us. It's a feeling I know well, one that goes back decades, and I find it comforting. Our anger toward my father fuels our closeness, which I crave more and more as Grant and the girls drift further out of my reach.

At some point in the past few days, Grant explained to Beth that it was me, not Sylvia, with Gail and Hailey on the beach. At first she seemed unfazed, but as time passed and she began to comprehend just how bad off Gail is, she's become increasingly hostile. While I can certainly see why, to my mind, her reaction seems backward. I always thought that with grief, denial came first, then anger, and then eventually forgiveness. But Beth started out with forgiveness, then moved to denial, and now I think she's finally reached anger—well, rage, actually. Three days ago, she was talking to me, but yesterday, she passed me in the hall without saying a word. Later, when we were alone in Gail's room, she turned her back when I asked her a question; and then last night, she told Grant she didn't want me visiting Gail anymore.

Grant asked to speak to me out in the hall, so I knew something was up.

"Beth isn't comfortable with you coming to the hospital," he said, staring at his hands. "She thinks it's best if you go back to Atlanta." He paused. "I don't disagree."

"Okay," I said slowly. "But don't you think we should talk before I leave?"

"Beth isn't interested in talking to you."

"Not Beth, Grant—you and I. Don't you think you and I should talk?"

"Tomorrow," he told me, already walking away. "I'll talk to you tomorrow."

"Here? At the hospital?" I was confused. Didn't he just ask me to stay away?

"I don't know, Eliot; wherever."

"Why don't you come out to Wyatt tomorrow night? This way you can see Hailey, and we'll be able to talk."

"Fine." Grant's voice was as dead as his eyes. "Wyatt Island. Tomorrow night. We'll talk."

So now it's tomorrow night, and Grant has been here for almost an hour. So far, though, I'm the only one who's done any talking. I screwed up my courage and told him everything: Finn and Emory and being late for pickup and forgetting Hailey on car pool day and lying about my mother's cancer and, finally, the phone call on the beach. Oh, and Sylvia covering for me. I almost forgot about that.

Grant didn't say much. For the most part, he sat patiently and took it all in, right up until the moment I repeated that nothing had happened with Finn. That's when he snapped.

"Stop saying that, Eliot!"

"But nothing did happen between us, Grant."

"*Of course* something happened! You were on the phone with him. You weren't paying attention to the kids, and because of that, one of my daughters has brain damage and the other is so afraid of water, she refuses to take a fucking bath. *That's* what happened."

"I meant nothing...sexual...happened with him," I said quietly.

"I don't believe you. I wish I could—God, I wish I could—but I don't. I can tell, just by the way you talk about him, that you have feelings for him."

"I thought I did, Grant. But I don't. I know for a fact that I don't. Nor have I ever lied to you before...before I ran into him again, I mean."

"Well, I think you're lying to me now."

"I don't know what to say to convince you I'm not."

Neither of us spoke for a few minutes. Then it was Grant's turn. "To tell you the truth, Eliot, I don't give a shit about this guy you were with. I can't even listen to it, and not only because the whole thing sickens me. At this point, I need to move forward so I can focus on Gail. The only thing I care about is helping my daughter get better."

When he said this, I thought he meant we were moving forward *together*; that he and I would focus on Gail *as a team*. However, I realize now, as Grant clears his throat, that I was gravely mistaken.

"I think..." He clears his throat again. "I think we need time apart, Eliot. You can stay in the house and I'll move out; or you can move out and I'll stay. I don't care what we do, but..."

"But you need to get away from me," I finish.

We're sitting in the guest room. Just a few days ago, this was our bedroom. Soon we'll leave and the oilman will return, and it'll revert back to a guest room. It's weird how a room can change its identity depending on who's sleeping in it, the way a kitchen table can be a breakfast or dinner table, depending on what meal is being eaten.

"Moving out isn't just time apart," I say. "It's a real separation."

"Call it whatever you want, Eliot. It just seems...um...necessary for a while, at least for me. You said yourself that being a stepmother is hard work, that the girls need Beth."

"When did I say that?"

"The night before the accident."

"If I did say that—which I don't remember—it was probably in the context of a whole other conversation. I love the girls, you know that."

"You still said it, Eliot, and quite frankly, I think you're right."

He coughs a few times. His cough is deep and raspy, as though he's dredging up gravel from down in his lungs, and then it turns into a hacking spell where he can't catch his breath.

I hand him some water. "Are you okay?"

"Fine," he wheezes. Wiping his eyes, he thumps his chest. He takes a minute to compose himself, then continues. "The way I see it, Gail is brain-damaged. She will never, ever, be the same. Her life is..."

"Destroyed."

"Yes, destroyed. I understand it was an accident—I do understand that—but..." Grant exhales through his nose. He's speaking in a slow, measured monotone, but I can see how tightly he's clenching his teeth, fighting to stay in control. "But you were talking on the fucking phone while the kids were in the fucking ocean! Jesus Christ, Eliot—what *the fuck* were you thinking?" He catches himself. "So right now, I'm *very angry*. I'm trying to forgive you—believe me, I'm trying—but the truth is...well, quite frankly, I can't. So I think it's best if we split up so that I—so that we—can sort out...I don't know...everything that needs to be sorted out."

When did he start saying *frankly*? It's corporate-speak and very unlike him. "I don't know if I'll ever forgive myself, frankly," I tell him.

He nods. He doesn't know how I will either. "So, in light of this, Beth would rather the kids...that they...well, she doesn't want you to see them. When we go back to Atlanta, Charlotte will live with her mother until I'm settled, and then she'll go back and forth between Beth's house and mine. Gail will be at the Banks Center for at least two months, although it'll be probably longer, given her current...whatever, her current condition."

"Beth doesn't want me seeing them at all?"

He clears his throat again.

"Do you agree with her, Grant? That I shouldn't..." I trail off.

He flips his hands over, as if to say, *What can I do? It's out of my hands.* "She's their mother."

"She is," I agree. "You and Beth can stipulate whatever you want. They're your children, obviously—not mine. I'll go along with whatever you say."

That Grant was conferring with his ex-wife, with *Lizzie*, about the dispensation of my relationships is painful, but I don't say this. Nor do I take issue with their decision. If this is what they think is best for their children, then of course I'll accept it. Beth is their mother, and for the girls' sake, I'm happy she's reasserting her maternal rights, stepping up, as it were, for her kids. But it's been only a day and I already miss them.

Again, Grant does the throat-clearing thing. "I also want to talk to you about Hailey."

My heart starts to palpitate. My mouth fills with the metallic taste of fear. "What about her?" I can't breathe. I try to clear my throat and then, like Grant, start to choke. He hands me back the water bottle. "Grant, what about Hailey?"

"I want Hailey to see her sisters, so when I get back to Atlanta, she'll come to my—"

I don't let him finish. "You want Hailey to stay overnight?" I ask stupidly. "Without me?"

"Of course, Eliot. She's my kid, too."

"Of course she is, Grant. I wasn't thinking." I stand up. "Okay, so, it's settled, then. We'll go back to Atlanta and live separately, I'll stay away from your children, and Hailey will go back and forth between us."

Then, because I think we're finished, I grab linen from the closet to make up a bed for Grant in another room, since I'm sure he doesn't want to sleep with me in this one. It doesn't dawn on me until I'm holding a stack of sheets that there's no need for him to sleep in this house at all.

"I'll walk you out," I say stiffly, still holding the sheets.

"Eliot, there's something else." More throat clearing now, some stammering; he turns his hands over again and stares at his palms.

"Say it, Grant." I suddenly know exactly what it is, though: not only must I suffer a fate worse than death, but the suffering I endure has to equal the suffering I caused. "Just say it."

"I don't think Hailey should go back and forth. I think she should...uh...I think she should live with me. Of course, we'll work out an arrangement for you to see her." He must sense my objection because he starts to falter. "Uh...just until you and I decide...um...until you work out things with what's-his-name, with Finn..." He trails off.

"No." Looking directly at him, I repeat myself so that there's no mis-understanding. "No."

I agreed when he called me a *liar*, when he accused me of *negligence*, when he said I *destroyed his daughter's life*. I agreed to all of it, but I absolutely will not agree to this. He can leave me, take Gail and Charlotte, strip me of all the furniture, the books, the plates; he can take every vestige of our five years together. But there is no way in this whole wild world that I will ever let him take Hailey from me.

"I'm a bad *stepmother*," I say again, as clearly as possible. "Not a bad *mother*."

"I could sue you," he says, equally clear. "And I'd win."

"You would sue me for custody of Hailey? On what grounds?"

"Abandonment, adultery, unfit mothering—I believe I have a few, Eliot. In fact, people are saying that you and your boyfriend planned this vacation for months—"

"*People?* What people, Grant?"

"—that you barged into Beth's house and interrupted a business net-working event to persuade her not to go to Italy so she could stay home with Charlotte and Gail."

"That's ridiculous. You knew I was coming here with Hailey. You also knew it was to spend time with my mother."

"Oh, right—to help with her *cancer treatments*."

"And when did I barge into Beth's house during a business event? She doesn't even have a *business*, Grant." What is he talking about? The last time I was at Beth's, she was having a goddess—Holy shit. "That's not true, Grant, I didn't *barge into* her event. You remember that night—I was dropping off Gail and Charlotte and they *begged* me to stay. Beth herself invited me in for a drink."

Grant shrugs. "Someone also heard Sylvia going on and on about how you always put Hailey first, that you didn't even consider the other girls, *my* girls—"

"She meant ahead of *myself*, not *Charlotte and Gail*." I reach out to touch his arm, but he backs away. "Grant, please slow down. Please—listen to me. You're not making any sense. No judge will grant you custody because of some comments overheard at a grown-up princess party."

"What about the affair—"

"It wasn't an affair, Grant—"

"—and how late you were picking up Hailey *and* Ava *and* Josie from school—"

"*One time*, Grant. It happened *once*."

"What about the *other* time you completely forgot about them? And what about the beach? And the coma? And the years of rehab Gail will need just to hold a fucking fork again?"

I'm struggling to contain my rising panic. That Grant might take Hailey never occurred to me, but I can see how in his rage and helplessness, it has a twisted logic: I can't be trusted with his girls, so I shouldn't be trusted with my own. "Grant, please don't

do this. Grant, please talk to me." And then I blurt out, "I'm angry too, you know."

Grant looks at me quizzically, as if I've spoken another language.
"What right do you have to be angry? What did I ever do to you?"

"I mean, I'm angry at myself."

"I can't help you with that right now, Eliot."

"I know. I'm not asking you to. I'm just asking that you slow down
for a second and listen. I love Gail. I love Charlotte. You know that."

"What does that have to do with anything?"

We are speaking different languages, I realize. The accident has
taken me to an entirely foreign country, where I don't know the cus-
toms, the currency, and, worse, the way out.

I'm on the bed again, still holding the linen, and as Grant paces back
and forth, reiterating all the ways I fucked up, he glances my way as
if to make sure I'm listening. This room is small, and Grant's anger
makes him expand and expand until he almost fills it. Seeing his anger,
exposed and raw, is especially terrifying because I know I deserve it. Yet
I can also see signs that he once did, that he may still, have feelings for
me. His eyes are wet and shiny, not blazing with hatred. Now, too, he
sits down beside me. He even puts his hand on my arm. It's a small gesture, and I don't want to endow it with too much significance, but he
seems to be saying that, no, he doesn't hate me. How could he hate me?
He just can't comprehend how all of this happened.

"I get that it was an accident, Eliot," he says, still touching my arm.
"But instead of telling me the truth, you lied *again*. Why did you do
that? I thought we were partners; I thought we were a team." His voice
rises. "How do you expect me to trust you?"

"I don't know." I wish I could describe for him the way Sylvia came
out of the water with the story all ready, how impossible it is for me
to stand up to her. *You know how she is, Grant,* I want to say. Instead, "I
don't know why I did any of it," is what comes out.

As Grant considers this, a car passes outside the window, and a spray
of headlights crosses his face. For a second, he looks vulnerable, beaten,

but then he gets up and starts to repace his same steps, back and forth, back and forth. That I don't have a good answer, that I really don't have any answer, infuriates him all over again.

"Eliot, what am I supposed to do? My daughter can't *speak*! She can't *walk*!" And then, as if unable to contain himself one more second, his anger gives way to a choking sadness, and his voice breaks. Hiding his face in his hands, Grant starts to cry.

His tears are too much for me; it would be too much for anyone. But I forbid myself from turning away. Instead, I take it. I take it and take it and take it. *Please, Grant,* I plead silently. *Please* forgive me. I'll get down on my knees. I'll do anything you want. But I'm begging you, *Grant, please, please, forgive me.*

"Eliot, *you almost killed my child.* You almost *killed* Gail because of *another man.* Look at her, Eliot. Look at what she's become. Look at her!"

I am looking at her, Grant; she is everywhere. I see how bewildered she is, how frightened. Don't ever think, even for a second, that I'm not looking.

"I'm sorry..." I reach for him. *"I am so sorry, Grant."*

We stand there for a minute, each holding the other, desperate for a way to move past this terrible thing I have done.

"Please don't leave me," I whisper. "Please give me a chance to make this right."

"What can you do?" He's still crying. "There's nothing anyone can do for her."

"We'll figure something out—together. We *are* a team, Grant. We *are* partners. I love you, and somewhere inside you, I know you love me too."

"I need to go." He pushes me aside so he can open the door. "I can't talk to you anymore."

"You don't have to do this alone," I call out behind him. He doesn't answer. "Grant?"

Chapter Twenty-eight

TWENTY-FOUR HOURS later, I drag my luggage into the foyer.

"You're leaving?" My mother is standing in the living room. "Why so late?"

"I need to get back. If we go now, Hailey will sleep on the way."

"You don't want to wait until tomorrow? They're predicting terrible weather tonight, and I'd feel much better about you being on the road if—"

"Stop, Mom. Just stop."

She studies my face. "Will you at least tell me what happened with Grant?"

"I told you this morning. We're taking some time to figure things out. We're fine; everything is fine."

"You don't speak, you don't eat. You just sit there, staring into space. How is that fine, Eliot?"

Instead of answering, I call out to Hailey, who's playing by herself in one of the bedrooms. "We're leaving in ten minutes, pea. Ten minutes, okay? Please clean up the Pollys."

"Okay, Mommy. I will."

Her earnestness is so childlike and sweet, my eyes get misty. When I peek in that bedroom in ten minutes, twenty minutes, even an hour, her Polly Pockets will be strewn all over the room, and she'll be blissfully dug in amid the wreckage. I, by contrast, am utterly lost. I've been wandering around the rich man's house all day, drifting from room to room like a rudderless dinghy. The most basic tasks—brushing my teeth, stacking the dishwasher, tying my laces—require herculean effort, and I have to force myself to zero in just to remember how to complete them. I'm so hollowed out and disoriented that I don't even have the wherewithal to cry.

At four o'clock this morning, I left a rambling message on Grant's phone, begging him to reconsider. "Please don't take Hailey," I pleaded. "I deserve to lose you and Gail and Charlotte, but do I really deserve to lose her too?" Although he called back a few hours later, he only asked to speak to Hailey and didn't mention my message at all.

Seeing my luggage in the foyer reminds me that I am about to head back to Atlanta. "We're leaving in a few minutes," I tell my mother. "This way, Hailey will sleep on the road."

"Eliot, you just said that. Are you sure you're okay to drive?"

I walk into the kitchen to pack food for our trip. "Why wouldn't I be okay? I already told you: I'm fine. Everything is going to be fine."

My mother follows behind me and sits down. She tries to lighten the mood. "Sylvia called this morning. She said she got really fat."

I'm too distracted to discuss Sylvia but make the effort for my mother. "We just saw her a week ago. How fat could she have gotten?"

"According to her, she's as *big as a barn*. 'You can see me from space,' she said."

I smile. "And the baby? Any news?"

"Apparently, the rupture resolved itself, thank God. Sylvia lost a lot of blood, but they gave her multiple transfusions, so of course now all she talks about is having AIDS, which is ridiculous, but that's your sister." My mother shakes her head. "As far as the baby, we won't know anything until it's born. They'll keep doing tests to see if the baby suffered from a lack of oxygen—"

"In which case, he or she will be born brain-damaged," I say, knowing this was a possibility but horrified all the same. "Just like Gail."

"We have to wait and see, Eliot." She murmurs something else under her breath that I can't hear, and I turn away, wondering if I should pack ice. Hailey will want juice, although I should probably limit how much she drinks so we don't have to stop as much.

I pull a lunch box down from the cabinet. "Do you mind if I take this with me? I'll send it back as soon as I get home."

"I hate that you're leaving like this, Eliot."

"Like what?" I hold up a roll of paper towels. "I just need a few squares; I won't take the whole thing." Standing on my tiptoes, I peer into the pantry. "Although you have, like, nine more of them. So I am going to take it, okay?"

"Eliot, please wait a day or two. I need to know that you're okay. Please talk to me."

Please, please, please—everyone's begging for something. I don't want Grant to leave, my mother doesn't want me to leave, and yet in the end, we all go.

I promise to call her as soon as I get on the road. "We can talk for the entire six-hour drive." I cut up an apple and offer her a piece, which she declines. My own bite tastes like cardboard, and I spit it out.

"Talking on the phone isn't the same as talking face-to-face," she says.

I think of her as a younger woman, fixated on her typewriter, her red ponytail swinging. How many times did I beg her to turn around and speak to me face-to-face? How many? Frustrated, I shake pretzels into little plastic bags, cut pears into cubes, wrap turkey and cheese inside tinfoil. The repetitive activity is soothing, and I consider packing up everything in the house just to maintain this rare feeling of Zen.

I'm stashing napkins in my backpack when my mother comes up behind me and puts her hands on my shoulders. She isn't a physical person, and having her *this close*—and touching me—feels so weird, I stop what I'm doing and stand there. For a minute, there's no sound in the room but the hum of the refrigerator and the two of us breathing.

"No matter what happens, Eliot," my mother says, "I love you. I'll do anything to help you, but you have to tell me how. And taking care of Hailey doesn't count. Tell me what I can do for you, just you."

Except for last week when she offered me money, I can't remember my mother asking me if I needed help before, although I'm sure she must have. Of course she has; every mother offers to help her daughter. But why can't I remember? It's such a nice thing for her to do, to offer to help. Why does it hurt so much?

"What do you need, Eliot?"

My throat is burning, and my eyes are wet. My mother is squeezing my shoulders and stroking my hair, and the feel of her hands is so kind, so loving, that I break down.

"Grant left me," I blurt out, and then start to cry. I cry the way Hailey does, the way Grant did last night, with utter abandon, as if the whole world is ending. "He's taking Charlotte and Gail, and he's threatening to take Hailey."

"That's *insane*! Why would he take Hailey?"

Unable to speak, I just shake my head. Taking my hand, my mother leads me to the kitchen table. "Eliot," she says quietly, "Grant can't take Hailey. He wouldn't do that."

I blow my nose. "I'm only telling you what he told me."

"Well, he doesn't mean it. Grant isn't cruel, he's just upset. Give him a few days."

"Maybe he means it and maybe he doesn't. It still doesn't change the fact that I almost killed Gail. I almost killed a seven-year-old child and her four-year-old sister. And then I lied about it."

"It was an *accident*, Eliot. Grant knows this. He also knows that you were very good to her for many years. You were good to Charlotte, too."

"Mom, Gail is *brain-damaged*. We don't know if she'll ever get better. Imagine if it was Grant and Hailey—if Grant was on the phone, and Hailey was brain-damaged. How forgiving would you be then?"

"I hope I'd remember that he would never intentionally harm his own child."

"That's the thing: Gail isn't my child."

We both let that sink in. Then I tell my mother the whole story. I start at the very beginning, all the way back to meeting Finn at Emory, and work my way up to his call on the beach and that one split second when everything changed. When I finish, my mother is still unfazed.

"I know you believe that what you've done is horrible, that *you* are horrible," she says. "But you made a mistake. What parent hasn't? You don't think I kick myself all the time for the mistakes I made raising you and your sisters?"

"Actually, no, Mom. I thought you felt pretty good."

"Please, Eliot. There are countless things I would've done differently. In fact, watching you this past week, I realized just how significant my mistakes were. I put you in an awful position when you were growing up, and for that, I'm truly sorry."

"Oh?" Although I feign nonchalance, I'm on high alert. This is it, the moment I've been waiting for, the moment she finally apologizes. "Because of the memoirs, you mean?" I ask softly. I want her to know that it's okay, I'm not angry. The past is the past; it's troubled water under the bridge, lazy dogs asleep in the sun. *I forgave you a long time ago,* I say without saying.

"*My* memoirs?" She looks baffled. "Why would I apologize for them?"

On the other hand, maybe not.

"You wrote about my private life without my permission. You exploited me when I was too young to defend myself. Don't you think some of my problems stem from that?"

"Of course not." Her laugh tells me she thinks this is ridiculous. "You're a grown woman, Eliot. Your problems are your problems." She laughs again at how absurd it is. "Don't you think it's a little late to blame who you are on what I did or didn't do almost thirty years ago?"

"You *just said* you made a lot of mistakes."

"I did make mistakes, but writing a few books wasn't one of them."

I don't like this, the way she's dismissing me. I didn't like the way she laughed at me, either. I know I should keep my mouth shut, that I'm risking the only person I can talk to. But I don't. Why should I? The whole house is ablaze; I might as well jump in, too. "Did it ever occur to you that what you wrote may have had an impact on my life? You told the whole world I ate *dog food*, Mom. It was *excruciating* being your daughter." Despite myself, I grin. It's absurd, and yet it's my life.

"Eliot, it's hard to be anyone's daughter. You think you're the first kid who was ever embarrassed by her mother? Talk to me in ten years when Hailey makes a case against those pants you're wearing."

My hand flies to my jeans. "What's wrong with my pants?"

"I can see how someone—not me, necessarily, but someone— might find those particular pants a little tight in the ass, but if you're okay with them, who am I to judge?" She raises her hands. "And as far as my work, I have to say I'm shocked. I thought you understood me, or my writing, rather. My writing is how I exist; it's who I am. Maybe I didn't have the career I aspired to. Maybe I didn't publish my most sophisticated books, or my most beloved. But the ones I *did* publish were ones I *could* publish. Why would I apologize for that? I earned a living, Eliot. And you may not appreciate me—as a parent or as an author—but I didn't write my books for you. I wrote them for me. Being your mother doesn't make me any less my own person. I existed for forty years before you came along, and while I owe you a fair amount of myself, I don't owe you everything."

"There are a lot of ways to earn a living, Mom. You could've gotten a normal nine-to-five job. What makes you so great that you don't have to live like everyone else?"

"I did what I was good at—at least I tried to—and what I loved. That I didn't get paid enough is an entirely different discussion. What would you rather I write, Eliot? Romance novels? Books about vampires?"

"Well, you didn't have to write about me and my sisters. Don't you think my life would've been easier if you kept our private lives *private*?"

"You would've had a different life, Eliot, not necessarily an easier one. If I were an accountant or a lawyer, we'd still be having this same conversation. You're the product of a lousy divorce, which has nothing to do with me being a writer."

"Well, I think you're wrong. As my mother you owed me respect and discretion. Instead you used me. You can call it *art* or *literature* or *earning a living*, but it still isn't right. It's *disgusting*, the way you dredged up every dirty detail of my life. You wrote that I peed in my bed! I was eleven years old. I had *anxiety*, Mom—even the doctor said so! But you made it seem like I did it to spite you because—how did you put it? 'Given the choice between washing my kid's urine-soaked sheets and editing an undergraduate's six-hundred-page manuscript, I'll take the editing job every time,' or something equally obnoxious. I realize it was funny, and you needed the money, or however you rationalized your decision, but it was a problem—it was *my problem*. Did you ever think people might read that article and laugh, not with you but *at me? How the hell is that art?*" Realizing I'm shouting, I stop. "Sorry, I don't mean to yell."

She shrugs. "It's obviously something you feel strongly about." But her expression is inscrutable. Then she gets up and walks out of the kitchen. Unsure what to do, I follow her.

"Mom?"

Nothing.

She stands at the picture window, staring out at the backyard. The sun is setting, and the trees cast long shadows across the lawn. Minutes pass, but she still doesn't speak.

I caught her off guard, I think. It's not often that I voice an actual opinion, particularly one that is contrary to hers. Nor have I criticized her before—to her face, I mean. "Mom, I'm sorry if I was out of line."

"You don't have to apologize," she says eventually. "You're entitled to your feelings."

Now she's caught me off guard. I was expecting more of a reaction, something more Lear-like, with thunder, lightning, and threats of disinheritance. Instead I hear, "And I can see your point. All I can say is that those books came out a long time ago. Had I understood then what I understand now—not just about you, but about the world and my work and myself, I might not have written them the same way. Maybe

I would have, though. It's hard to know. Still, as I said, you're entitled to your opinion. And I'm sorry if I hurt you. It was never intentional." She pauses. "Don't look so surprised, Eliot. You're allowed to disagree with me."

This too is absurd: that disagreeing with my mother out loud and face-to-face never occurred to me before. "I don't like to disagree with anyone, certainly not you."

"What am I going to do? Revoke your daughter's license?" My mother smiles at me, but it's a sad, wistful smile. "You, Sylvia, Maggie, Hailey—you girls are the full extent of my reach these days. My God, how the world has shrunk." She pushes her glasses up the bridge of her nose and wipes her eyes. "Eliot, it has been so painful to watch you go through all this. I keep thinking about how vulnerable you were—how vulnerable all three of you were—when you were Gail's age. What I was saying before, about the mistakes I made? I was referring to your father. I never should've discouraged you from having a relationship with him."

"You said yourself he was immature and self-absorbed."

"Eliot, out of everyone Maggie could have called for help, your sister picked your father, and lo and behold, the guy shows up. He didn't even think twice about it."

"So what? I called him for help when Finn moved to New York, but he did nothing for me. He stopped trying to be a father years ago. Don't romanticize him now."

"It's more complicated than that. When you called him, he didn't know what to do, not because he stopped trying but because he'd gotten rusty. And that was my fault. In fact, since we're being honest here—*I'm* the one who was immature and self-absorbed. I was so angry at your father that I ran away to Atlanta and took you girls with me. I didn't consider him at all. Nor did I consider you or Sylvia or Maggie. It's hard to admit, but it's the truth; and seeing him again has made me realize that the three of you needed us both. Had he been around all these years, then yes, in that case, your life might've been easier."

I picture him now, an old man, flagging me down for help. "He would've been just one more person to take care of."

"No, he would've been one more person to take care of you. Look, I don't know if he's changed. Maybe he's still a selfish Gluckman. On the other hand, maybe I believe this because it makes my own selfishness easier to swallow. By freezing Barney in time for thirty years, he will be the same stupid schmuck he always was; and if he's the same stupid schmuck, then I never have to consider that I was—that I am—a stupid schmuck too."

"Why are you telling me this?"

"Because your stupid schmuck of a father has made an honest attempt to get to know you, and even though this seems like the worst possible time to introduce, or reintroduce, someone new into your life, I think you should call him."

I hoist my backpack onto my shoulder. "I'll think about it." But in my mind, I'm already on the road. I tick off everything I've packed: snacks, paper towels, extra napkins, garbage bags. What else do I need? Ice—did I pack ice?

"Eliot, just give him a chance. That's all I'm asking. He's still your father."

Yes, I remember, I did pack ice. My mother wants an answer, but I'm halfway down the hall. "Hailey?" I call out. "We're leaving. It's time to go home."

Chapter Twenty-nine

Hi Eliot,

  Glad to hear that you're back at work! Hope Gail continues to improve. Please review the following draft and give me your comments. Thanks, Larry (and Brandi).

Memo To: All Barnett Tech Colleagues
From: Lawrence Barnett, CEO
Re: More Robust News from Your CEO!

Dear Colleagues,

   Due to our recent merger windfall, and the subsequent D7 Meister chip settlement, financial challenges continue to beseech Barnett Tech. In the spirit of the thriftiness of our forebears and ancestors who lived through the Great Depression years of this, our great nation, Corporate is requesting that all our colleagues tighten our "belts" once again.

Office Space Consolidation: What It Means for YOU!

In the spirit of "collaboration" and to further strengthen "collegial" relations, we are consolidating our office space. Going forward, from now on, all remaining Barnett Tech colleagues will share their office-ettes with a partner, so that we may sublease space to Brandi Barnett, Lawrence Barnett's wife, and the official authoress of this memorandum.

The Brandi Barnett Story

Barnett Tech is pleased to announce the launch of Brandi Barnett Eyes On Design. An industry insider, Brandi has a degree in Interior Design, and five years of life skills as a stay-at-home mom. Her boots-on-the-ground experience and up-to-the-minute know-how includes:

- Overseeing a complete "floorboard to roof beam" renovation of the Barnett family home—her "Kountry Kookin' Kitchen" was ranked five out of five stars on HGTV's "Rate My Space" website!
- Advising numerous Facebook friends on paint chips and fabric swatches.
- Facilitating EyesOnDesignHour—a weekly Twitter webinar devoted to everything new in the Interior Design world. Join us for home makeovers, staging tips, recipes, gossip, and my personal observations on the events of the day! #Eyesondesignhour

To celebrate the launch of Brandi Barnett Eyes On Design, Barnett Tech is pleased to provide you and your eligible dependents with a *free* Totes umbrella! Available in three colors (red, black, or Barnett blue), these umbrellas are embossed with the Barnett-~~Avery~~ logo as a reminder that *Barnett's always got you covered*. (Note: Supplies are limited.)

Next Steps

Corporate understands that each colleague will need an appropriate work space in which to perform their job. This is why, going forward, from now on, we are allowing each of you to retain your own personal chair. We know you will enjoy this company "perk."

To all our Barnett family colleagues, thank you, most "sincerely," for your continued "hard work" and "dedication." And to Brandi Barnett, we wish you Godspeed and good luck.

P.S.—Thinking about "sprucing up" your home? Brandi Barnett Eyes On Design is now located on the second floor! To make an appointment, call (404) 555-3342, or just tell Larry, and he'll let her know.

⌐⌐

I wish Grant would call. I've been in Atlanta for three weeks, and it's strange to be here, at home, without him. I'm on my bed, which used to be our bed, holding the phone, which used to be our phone, waiting to hear from him. I doubt I will—it's very late—but I might. At least, I hope I do. I miss him very much. I could call him, but he's made it clear he has no interest in speaking to me. So except to exchange details about Hailey, we haven't had a meaningful conversation in weeks. I've barely even seen him. He got back with Charlotte and Gail a few days after Hailey and I did, but they went right into a new apartment that Beth must have found, so the only time our paths cross is at the mall where we pick up or drop off Hailey. Sometimes, three or four days will go by before I hear from him, but tonight it's been five. Five days! That's almost a whole week. But rather than push him, I just wait. It's not easy. Although this kind of waiting is familiar, and I happen to be very good at it, each day that passes makes it harder and harder not to just pick up the phone and dial, if only to hear his voice.

Sleeping beside me, Hailey repositions herself against the pillows. I lean over and brush a single red curl off her forehead.

Hailey sleeps in my bed every night—rather, Hailey and Molly, her American Girl doll. Not that I'm complaining. I love it. Without Grant and the girls here, this house feels too big, so Hailey, Molly, and I confine ourselves to my bedroom and the kitchen, but mostly my bedroom—I mean, the bedroom I used to share with Grant. Together, in my bed, the three of us sleep, watch TV, read, color, and play Pollys. We even eat in it. For someone who always prided herself on her superior parenting skills, it's humbling to be living out of a bed with my four-year-old daughter and an overpriced doll, but these days I'm operating solely on instinct. So if eating cold pizza in crumb-laden sheets like two bereft bachelors is what comforts us, then that's what we do. In my mind, it's only temporary. Eventually Grant and the girls will come home. They have to come home. Don't they? (These are the kinds of questions that throw me. At one time I would've answered an unequivocal yes; now I'm not so sure.)

I touch Hailey's face, but she doesn't stir. Still holding the phone, still waiting for Grant, I turn on the TV. I don't sleep very well, if at all. I stay up until two, three o'clock in the morning, holding my phone and watching the clock. Sometimes I stare at the TV; sometimes I stare at Hailey; and other times, just to mix things up, I wander from room to room.

The house looks different. One morning while I was at work, Grant swooped in and packed up the whole place and then swooped back out. I assume he hired help because as strong as he is, there's no way he could've moved the computers, clothes, books, toys, and furniture all by himself. With the exception of our bed, a TV, and a couple of lamps, Grant stripped this house down to its bones. When I first walked in, I was sure he had cleaned out Hailey's room, too. But I did a quick inventory and was relieved to find that most of her things, including her lonesome bottom bunk, were present and accounted for.

"Mommy?" Hailey blinks a few times, then opens her eyes. "The TV is too loud."

"I'm sorry," I whisper. "Go back to sleep."

As she settles back down, I snap off the set. So I'm still on my bed, still holding the phone, only now I'm waiting in the dark.

At first it was comforting that Grant left behind Hailey's things, but now it's been a few weeks, and I'm beginning to worry. Given his new apartment, his job, and getting Gail settled, Grant claims he has too much going on to have Hailey stay overnight, so she's spent only a few hours with him. We never did finish discussing where she would live, so I don't know if he has reconsidered his demand for permanent custody or if he's just getting situated before he hires the most vindictive lawyer in town. What I do know is that Grant avoids any chore that requires an extra flight of stairs, being put on hold, or speaking to someone's supervisor. So there's that.

I could call my mother, who is still on Wyatt Island. She doesn't sleep, either. In fact, right now, I bet she's lying in her bed, watching back-to-back episodes of *Law & Order*. I speak to her every day, sometimes a few times a day. I don't speak to anyone else, though. I feel too guilty to call Sylvia, and I won't call Maggie, and the seasons, they go round and round, and the painted pony goes up and down. As Sylvia said, it's the carousel of time.

I wonder if Grant would call me if we were married. During our last argument, he accused me of being more committed to my mother, sisters, and Hailey than I was to him and his girls. "If you really loved me and my kids," was how he put it, "you would've married me years ago."

"If you really wanted me to marry you," I countered, "you would've asked."

Ever since he said it, though, I've been thinking that maybe he was right. Maybe I was afraid that by marrying him, I would lose something with my mother and sisters. But it wasn't because I loved anyone less; it's because choices like that are impossible. It is true, though, that before the accident, a part of me was uncertain about my relationship with

Charlotte and Gail. They were less than real daughters, which made me less than a real mother; so together we felt like less than a real family. Having lost them, though, I realize this was wrong. Loving Charlotte and Gail is no less meaningful than loving Hailey. It may not have felt as natural, but it wasn't any less real. On the contrary, because my love for them was learned instead of instinctive, it's as true and as deep as my love for Hailey—maybe even deeper, because I worked so hard at it. It's just a different kind of love, that's all.

If Grant calls, I'll explain all that I've figured out and apologize for how foolish I've been. Although a second chance may be too much to hope for, I would like to tell him that I'm sorry. For a former good girl, someone who always derived her self-worth from the judgment of others, not to be given a shot at redemption is especially punishing.

It's twelve forty-five.

There's no way he will call now. He's never called after midnight before. So what I usually do next is run through my finances, mentally adding and subtracting all my expenses. Living with Grant was expensive, but living without him is more expensive. Wherever there's a credit, there's an equal, often higher, debit. I suppose we will separate our bank accounts at some point, but until then we are carrying two rents. Only a portion of Gail's rehab is covered by insurance, so we both contribute to that, although I insist on paying a greater percentage. Beth took a job at a gallery in midtown, so Grant no longer supports her, but Charlotte started seeing a therapist, and I've made an appointment to see one myself. Hailey has been seeing a therapist, too, although not the same one as Charlotte. All of this costs money, money, money. Luckily, my company has been supportive when I need to take time off, and now that the girls aren't here anymore, I can take on freelance work, although there is no upside to this trade-off. Whatever money I make is diminished by how lonely Hailey and I feel without them here. At least we have Molly and all her accessories. She's the American Girl from 1944, the one on the home front during World War II, so there is a lot of history there. Unfortunately, Hailey is too young to care about soldiers and victory gardens. All she wants is a pair of glasses like Molly, which is better, I suppose, than another tiara.

It's twelve forty-eight.

I should probably stop watching the clock. Maybe I can put myself on some kind of clock-watching regimen. I've always done better with a structured life, after all. Going forward, I'll let myself look only once every fifteen minutes. On the other hand, if I can't check the clock, how will I know when fifteen minutes have passed? In the dead of night, these conundrums make for compelling thinking.

It's twelve forty-nine.

Come home, I will say when he finally calls. *I'm here in our house, in our bed, on our phone. I'm here, Grant; I'm waiting.*

⌒

"When will we be there?" Hailey asks from her car seat behind me.

"We're ten minutes away, sweet pea."

Today is Hailey's fourth day at school. I didn't think she was ready to go back, or rather, I wasn't ready, so I kept her home longer than necessary. I had hoped she would have playdates with some of her friends, but when I tried to solicit their mothers, there were no takers. We don't even have car pool anymore. Clearly uncomfortable, Phoebe and Grace never reestablished a schedule, so it's just me, Hailey, and Molly riding back and forth to Riverside every day, and then just me and Molly while Hailey is in school. When Hailey climbs out of the back, she'll position the doll in her car seat, so at least I have someone to talk to even if Molly can't respond.

As we drive through the school gates, neither Hailey nor I look out the windows. She is preoccupied with her waffle, and as for me—what is there to see? Since I've come back, Riverside Country Day has lost its luster. The buildings look dark and small; the topiary gardens, once lush and green, are shriveled and brown; and the castlelike chapel, the exterior of which is shrouded in plastic, looks creepy and uninviting.

The warm, woodsy feeling is gone, but because there are no tuition refunds, Grant and I decided to keep Hailey here, at least for now. If pressed, the administration would make an exception, I suspect, but ultimately it seemed best to keep her in the same school since everything else in her life is different.

As I drive up the hill, past the barn, and up to the lower school, I keep my eyes on the road. The other day, I spotted Finn's car headed toward me in the opposite direction, and my first instinct was to wave hello. It was totally reflexive—my hand shot up before my brain registered who it was—but when he motioned for me to pull over, instead of excitement, I felt panic. I saw his face through the windshield, first his smile of surprise and then narrow-eyed confusion as I shook my head and sped off, but I didn't want to stop. Luckily, I haven't seen him since.

I glance in my rearview mirror and catch Hailey's eye. She smiles and waves her waffle.

"Hailey?" I ask. "Do you remember what we talked about last night? That today is a special day? Daddy has a surprise for you after school."

"Is it candy?" she asks, smacking her lips.

"Actually, yes. He probably will have candy. But he's also taking you to see Gail."

"At our house?" Hailey is puzzled. "I thought Gail was sick."

"She is, but tonight Daddy's taking you and Charlotte to visit her at the hospital, and then you'll both sleep at his new house. Doesn't that sound fun?"

Earlier this week, Grant called to ask if Hailey could spend the weekend with him. "Of course," I had said. "She'll love that." But when I realized this meant not seeing her until Monday afternoon, I got anxious, picturing three long days—and three long nights—without her.

"I don't want to go to Daddy's house, Mommy," Hailey whines. "I want to be with you."

"I want to be with you, too. But Daddy and Charlotte and Gail miss you so much."

"It's not fair!"

It would be so easy to tell Hailey that she's right and if it were up to me, she'd never leave my sight, but I don't. "You'll have a good time. I pinky-swear promise."

"But why can't we be together, with Charlotte and Gail and Daddy?"

"We just can't, Hailey," I say sadly.

A month ago, when she and I were driving back from Wyatt Island, I had tried to explain what was happening to our family. Although it made sense to her that Grant and I slept in different places while Gail was in Savannah, Hailey couldn't understand why we would remain apart when we returned to Atlanta.

"Are you and Daddy in a fight?" she asked.

"No, not really."

"So why can't you live in the same house?"

"Well, sometimes grown-ups get angry at each other, just like you and your friends. But since grown-ups have more problems, it takes us a little longer to make up. Right now, Daddy and I...Daddy is angry with me, and wants to be alone to think about things—sort of like a time-out. But you'll still see him—and Charlotte and Gail, too. They're your sisters. Sisters are forever. You just won't live with them all the time. You'll see Charlotte when you're at Daddy's new house, and you'll visit Gail at her new hospital. Then once she gets better, she'll go to Daddy's house, too."

"But why won't they live with you?"

"Because they're not my daughters. They're Daddy and Beth's daughters."

"When I live in Daddy's new house, will I stop being your daughter, too?"

This flattened me. "Of course not. You will always be my daughter. No matter what happens—you will always be my daughter and I will always be your mother."

Ever since she asked this, though, I've been wondering about my relationship to Charlotte and Gail. If I was their stepmother once, then what am I now? Their ex-stepmother? A former friend? I'm afraid they'll think I've forgotten them or that I've stopped caring. Worse, what if my ex-stepchildren perceive me the way I've always perceived my father—that is, as an unparent, someone who gave up?

To prove this isn't the case, I've been writing them letters in which I reminisce about our old life together. I held on to the letters for a while but eventually started mailing them to Beth's house, with the hope that someday she will let the girls read them. I keep them light and funny, re-telling their favorite stories about their younger selves: Charlotte, age eight, getting her first pedicure; Gail, three, pulling packs of gum off supermarket shelves and hiding them in her stroller; Charlotte, nine, reading *From the Mixed-up Files of Mrs. Basil E. Frankweiler* for our first stepmother-stepdaughter book club; Charlotte and Gail, ten and three, holding a newborn Hailey. These unremarkable stories, of no interest to anyone but us, are evidence of our shared history, proof that I was once there, that I did care.

As I pull into the lower school parking lot, I glance at Hailey in my rearview mirror.

"Hailey Delaney! Why haven't you finished your waffle?"

"I hate waffles, Mommy. Here"—she leans forward—"you finish it."

Sighing, I do as she says, swallowing it in two bites. Then I help her out of the car, and we walk up the path to her class.

"Walk faster, Mommy! It's almost circle time."

Although I'm relieved to see she's resilient, it's also bittersweet. At the art table, when she announces that she is seeing her sisters after school, my eyes get misty.

"Isn't that exciting," says Miss Lulu, who turns to me. "How is Gail?"

"She's moving forward, thank you."

I can see she's expecting more, but that's all I've got. I know only what Grant tells me, which is that Gail has a long road ahead. "She has the mental capacity of a two-year-old," he said. "She's starting over from the beginning."

"Actually," I say to Miss Lulu, remembering my vows (clean and clear, honest and direct), "recovering from a brain injury is a very long, very difficult process. Although Gail is moving forward, it's extremely slow going, and there are a lot of setbacks. She's with her father these days, so I don't see her much...I mean, I don't see her at all. But thank you for asking."

Miss Lulu gives me a motherly squeeze. "Hang in there, Ms. Gordon. We're all pulling for her."

Hailey pats my hand; she's ready for me to leave. "It's okay, Mom. You can go to work."

This chokes me up. *Mom?* Since when am I *Mom?* Only five minutes ago, I was *Mommy.* "Have a good day." I hug her tight once, twice, three times before I head out. *My girl, my girl,* I say silently, hugging her again. *Oh, how I love my little girl.*

I see a group of mothers lingering near the cubbies and nod hello. Although a few of them nod back, none speak to me or invite me over. Embarrassed, I bend my head and keep moving. "I'll miss you, big girl," I murmur under my breath.

"Don't worry, Mommy," my four-year-old suddenly calls out behind me. "I'll miss you, too."

⌒

That night, I have nightmares. In all of them, I'm in the ocean, swimming to Gail, who is caught in a current and drifting away. "Left!" she calls out. "Left, left, left."

In the dream I know it's my fault she's out there. I also know I won't reach her. Still, I force myself to swim faster. My mouth is open, and I swallow gallons of water, far more than I can take in. My body starts to expand, and I grow bigger and bigger until I'm too heavy to move. Cursing myself for being so greedy, I try to keep swimming, but it's impossible. My feet drag along the ocean floor, which is thick with sea-weed. "This water isn't yours," I hear myself say. "It was never yours to begin with."

I spy the top of Gail's head, then a pale belly, then her pink suit with the ruffles. *Oh, my God.* My heart starts to race. *That's Hailey's suit!* I try to paddle out to her, but she's so far away, and I'm starting to fade.

"You said!" she calls out. "You said." It's Gail voice. Or is it Hailey's? Her voice booms in my ear as if she is right beside me. "You said, you said." It sounds like Gail; I'm sure it's Gail.

"What did I say?" I shout as loud as I can, but my words are lost in the wind. I'm afraid how this dream will end, so I force myself to keep sleeping. If I'm sleeping, I'm still swimming; if I'm still swimming, I have a chance.

"You said," she keeps repeating. "You said, you said, you said."

"What did I say?" I'm screaming, but there's no answer, and suddenly the girl is gone, and it's me, not my daughter, who's too far out in the ocean. It's me who's tumbling in the waves, head over heels over head. It's me out here, cold and alone. I am the one drowning.

Of course, I think, of course. It was me all along.

I'm relieved, knowing my daughter is safe. But the water is already up to my neck and rising fast. I thrust out my arms and kick my legs, desperate to feel sand, a wall, anything solid, but there's nothing around me except endless sky and endless sea.

"It's okay," a man says. Although the voice is familiar, I can't place it. "Be patient. You'll get there." His voice is deep and soothing, a celebrity voice, one I'd trust completely with my long-distance service.

"You're sure?" I'm tired of swimming, and the current is starting to ferry me off.

"Of course I'm sure." His voice is firm but insistent. Hearing it warms me all over.

"Are you sure you're sure?" That my neuroses aren't suspended simply because I'm sleeping strikes me as comical, and I chuckle in my dream. I am okay; everything will be okay.

A piercing scream fills the air. It's Hailey. "Mommy, Mommy! Help me!" *Mommy, Mommy, Mommy!*

I wake up with a jolt. I reach over. Hailey's gone.

Mommy, Mommy, Mommy! Help me, Mommy, help me.
Where is she? Where's Hailey?

I remember that she's at Grant's. She's okay. I'm drenched in sweat and overwhelmed by a feeling of defeat, sick with the knowledge that I have forsaken my child, my children. How will they ever forgive me? How could anyone forgive me?

I get out of bed and lumber to the bathroom. I'm about to turn on the light when I recognize the voice. It was my father; it was Barney. And then it hits me, the realization that what my mother said is true: I am his daughter. He has always loved me.

Chapter Thirty

I'M STANDING IN the kitchen when I hear knocking at my front door. It's weird, not only because it's nine o'clock on Saturday morning, but also because I can't remember the last time anyone came into the house that way.

Thinking it might be Hailey, I start to get excited, but when I open the door, no one's there. I'm about to go back inside when I see a plain brown box by my foot. I open the card.

> *Dear Eliot,*
>
> *I bought these for you from Tiffany's, and they're very expensive. I hope you treasure them forever as proof that I love you. You're very lucky to have a sister like me, but I'm also lucky to have a sister like you. Sometimes we forget that (well, I don't, but I think you do).*
>
> *Signed, Princess Petunia*

I open the box. Nestled in delicate tissue paper are my diamond stud earrings, the same ones I paid Sylvia to mortgage what I thought would be a lifetime of lies.

A cell phone rings. It rings two more times until I realize, stupidly, that it's mine. "Hello?" I say.

It's Sylvia. "Don't you know the sound of your own phone?"

"It's new." I still think about my old phone occasionally, dead somewhere on the ocean floor.

"Aren't you going to thank me for the earrings? You knew you'd get them back eventually."

I smile. "Actually, Sylvia, I really wasn't sure."

"Oh, so now you don't trust me? Like I would really keep your *microscopic, cheap-ass* earrings, like I don't have *fifty* other pairs of my own."

"If they're that offensive, why did you take them in the first place?"

"First of all, I didn't *take* them. You *loaned* them to me so I could *liven up* what was probably the *worst* princess party I ever attended. I saved the day, Eliot, in case you forgot. And second, I have no idea what *the fuck* you did to your hair, but you may want to consider a *hat*."

My hair! My hand flies to my head. I forgot about my hair! A week ago, in a last-ditch attempt to rouse my spirits, I decided to dye it. Mousy no more, I am now an audacious redhead.

"You don't like it? Wait a second." I look around. "You're here?"

"At your hut? Maybe... Are we okay? I mean, do you forgive me? I forgive you."

"What do I have to forgive you for? You saved the day. I'm the one who screwed up."

She sighs. "Oh, Eliot, lighten *up*. It's just an *expression*."

It is impossible to tally up all the ways our sisters exasperate us. Our memories are too long; our grievances go back too far—some back even to before we were born. Sisters hurt each other in ways they would never hurt anyone else; ways that are too painful, too humiliating, to discuss outside the family. That's *unforgivable*, other people would say. *I'd never put up with that.* Yet when I consider all the things Sylvia and I have done to—and for—each other, each one is trumped by the sight of her racing down the sand, diving into the ocean, and swimming all the way to nowhere to save someone else's child. I will never be able to give my sister even a modicum of what she has given me, but in some ways, it doesn't matter. Love is not a zero-sum game; there is no even-steven. There are only acts of grace, large and small, through which we reveal who we are.

"Yeah," I tell her, fiddling with my earrings. "We're okay."

Sylvia steps out from behind my house. As she walks toward me, she flutters her fingers like a parade queen. "Holy shit! It's redder than I thought."

"I was sick of the brown. The colorist called it 'bold and brazen,' which I know isn't me, but maybe it's not not me, either. Does it really look awful?"

As Sylvia studies my head, I realize that my hair is the same color as hers, although because she's pregnant and hasn't colored it in a while, my red is even brighter.

"Well," she says finally, "it's certainly bold. But brazen? I don't think so. And I'm not saying you *stole* it from me, but it was *my* color first—"

She's interrupted by someone shouting, "Shut up, Sylvia! She looks *great*."

Sylvia whips around. "*You* shut up, Maggie! I didn't say she looked *bad*."

Maggie? "You're here too?" My voice lifts. "I can't believe it!"

But it's true—Maggie's here, too. She steps out from behind my house, and I race across the lawn to meet her.

"Hey," Sylvia snaps, "you didn't sound that happy to see me! And FYI? This was *all my idea*."

"I'm so sorry," I tell Maggie. "I was such a jerk."

She stares at me for a second, most likely tallying up all the ways I've hurt her, too. "Yeah," she agrees. "You were." Then she shrugs.

The three of us stand together, appraising one another. We don't hug—that would be too weird—but we do nod at one another, acknowledging that if we were different people, this is when a hug would be appropriate.

"I really like your hair," Maggie says, twisting a strand. "You look...I don't know...different."

"Different in a good way?"

"Yeah." She nods. "Definitely in a good way."

By this point, Sylvia is fed up. "Can we stop talking about Eliot's hair? Let's go inside, get some food, and talk about me." Then she leads us into my house, but not before snatching the diamond earrings out of my hand. "Finders keepers," she says.

⌒

Maybe it's the hair, but I really do feel different.

The following Friday, I am walking out of Hailey's classroom when I hear someone say my name. I turn around, but no one's there. Hearing it again, I realize the voice is behind the wall of cubbies next to the door.

"...well, I heard Eliot was having an *affair* with another parent in this school..."

"...the poor kid will *never* be the same...poor father, too."

"...you can't judge. I mean, I'm sure it was an accident, but still: *brain damage?*"

At first, I'm struck dumb. But then I glance over at Hailey, who is watching me with her 360-degree vision, and something inside me shifts.

"It was an accident!" I shout. "I *loved* Gail—I *love* her. She's my *child*."

On the other side of the cubbies, there's dead silence.

"She's my child," I repeat. "I'm her stepmother—" Here, my voice breaks. And although no one responds, I press on. "I will regret what happened for the rest of my life. But it was an accident. It's also a family matter, and you should respect our privacy, if not for my sake, then at least for Hailey's."

A few people cough, someone shifts her position. That's it, though. There's no regretful stammering, no one apologizes. Apparently, everyone is expecting me to slink away in shame. But I won't.

"I'm not a bad mother. I just made a bad decision."

As much as I've grown to love Riverside Country Day, I don't belong here, which is why I walk around the cubbies to where the mothers are standing and grab Hailey's backpack and sweater. The mothers are staring, not at me, but at one another.

"You should be ashamed of yourselves," I tell them all.

There's another long pause, and then Grace takes a step forward. "I'm sorry, Eliot." She holds out her hand. "Please don't go." The other mothers nod their apologies. "What happened with Gail—"

"Could've happened to any of us," Phoebe finishes. "Well, maybe not to *me*—"

"Yes, Phoebe." Grace rolls her eyes. "It could've happened to you, too. You were the one who gave Josie a *hot dog* when she was two years old. You *never* give a two-year-old a hot dog. It's practically a *law*—"

"For God's sake, *Grace*, that was *years ago*. When will you get over it already?"

"I'm *never* going to get over it, *Phoebe, never, never*—"

"Excuse me," I cut in. "But I have to go."

"Come back to our car pool," Grace offers. "It was Phoebe's idea to kick you out—"

"It was not! Grace, *you* were the one who said—"

"Thank you, Grace, but no. It's lovely here, but we can't afford it. I should've made that clear from the beginning."

When Grant first raised the idea of sending Hailey to an exclusive private school, instead of capitulating, I should've said, Our daughter is funny, she is smart, and she is kind. She has curly red hair, and it's usually very messy. She is, by turns, stubborn, cranky, silly, cunning, and spoiled. She is deeply loved. She is not a conventional beauty and refuses to wipe herself when she poops.

By the time she turns five, Hailey will not have read *War and Peace*, either in English or in its original Russian. Nor will she play Beethoven, Bach, or the Beatles on the piano, the violin, the recorder, or any other instrument. She will not solve any theorems related to vector integral calculus, nor will she advance our understanding of quantum mechanics. She will, however, be able to count to twenty using her fingers (and mine).

Hailey Harper Delaney is four years old, and she can write her own name.

"Where are we going?" Hailey asks as we head out of her classroom.

"Public school."

My daughter, like me, is a run-of-the-mill kid. She's average. She's ordinary. Her breathtaking beauty and exceptional intelligence are visible only to me, to Grant, to her grandmother and aunts, and to her sisters (and to them, only on occasion). Sure, I'd be proud if Hailey discovered new methods of gene mapping this year, but I'll be just as proud when she realizes that the name Beff does not, in fact, start with an "F."

A few days later, restless with pent-up energy, I decide to go swimming. Our neighborhood YMCA has an indoor pool, so I drive over and renew my membership. Because of my recent experience in the water, I'm nervous but also feel the need to do something physical.

As I walk to the dark basement, I'm hit by the pungent smell of chlorine. It's also very humid down here—the pool is overheated, so the air is warm and swampy. There's only one window in the cavernous space, and the dim yellow light casts murky shadows on the walls and ceiling.

There's a free lane, so I slip into the pool, adjust my goggles, and kick off. My relief is instantaneous, and I wonder again why I don't swim more often. I allow the water to buoy me and then start to swim, slowly at first, but then I start to gain speed. The repetitive motion is soothing, and the buzzing in my ears fades. For the first time in weeks, I'm able to think. In my mind as I swim, I'm back on the beach. The kids and I are together again, and everyone's laughing. But when I turn away for a second—just one second—an enormous wave crashes onto the sand and carries them off. This time, however, I'm ready.

I'm coming! Gail and Hailey are in two separate directions, but I swim faster than the current moves. Hailey is closer. I see her head, then her ruffled butt, then her head again. *I'm coming! Hold on.*

There's no wind, so I reach her in record time. Hailey is slippery, but I hold on tight, and I know I can get Gail, too, if I just keep going. *Hold on! I'm almost there.*

She's far away, but every stroke brings me closer. I see her head, then her feet, then her head, then nothing. She's picking up speed, but so am I. Gail is there; I can see her now—she's *right there*, I can almost touch her. So I bend my head and swim toward her, cutting across the water, moving through the waves, swimming faster, faster still.

⌒

The Banks Center is a nondescript two-story building set back from the road behind a cluster of trees. Thinking it was the DMV, I drove past it twice. It wasn't until the third time, when I noticed a small sign lost amid the overgrown shrubbery, that it occurred to me to slow down.

My heart is racing. I'm nervous but excited, too. Today I'm visiting Gail after how many weeks? Nine? Ten? I can't believe it's been almost two and a half months since I last saw her, but at least I'm getting the chance today. As far as Grant is concerned, I'm here only because Beth had to work. But it makes no difference to me why—I'm just happy he asked. Happy, but nervous, too, which I think I said already.

"Eliot?" Grant asked last night when I picked up the phone.

His voice startled me. We're communicating more regularly, but mostly through e-mail, so it's been a while since I'd heard it. Nor have I seen him. Now that Hailey stays overnight at his place twice a week, he picks her up directly from school, then drops her off the next morning.

"Is everything okay?" I asked.

"Fine, thanks." As always, Grant and I were polite. (We may be stilted and distant, but we're always polite.) "How is everything with you?"

How is everything with me? My life, once packed with people-pleasing activity, has been pared down considerably. I go to work, I take Hailey (and Molly) to public school, I see my mother and sisters, I play Pollys, and I swim. Prior to the accident, I would've scoffed at the idea that exercise could make a difference in my temperament, but it has. Four times a week—five if there's time—I go to the pool and swim laps. It's neither ambitious nor profound, but it is wholly my own and fills me with peace.

My mother is back from Wyatt Island, but I don't know if she is writing anymore because we don't discuss it. She talks about the weather and other people's money and sees Hailey and my sisters. Mostly, she says, she's relaxing. We're both coming to grips with what this means and trying to enjoy things the way they are, rather than the way we wish they could be. She says that like optimism, contentment is a choice, and she's choosing to be content. I'm choosing to believe her, which makes me content, too.

"I'm doing better," I told Grant. "I'm okay, actually."

There was a long pause.

"So," he said.

"So," I repeated.

"I'm calling because I...um...need a favor. Beth and I have arranged our schedules so one of us can be with Gail every day, but...well, tomorrow we both have meetings...I know this is last minute, and it's really no big deal if you can't make it, but—"

"I'd love to. I'd love it more than anything. Thank you for asking."

Grant filled me in on Gail's progress. She doesn't talk very much and can't walk without help, but she recognizes people and makes speaking sounds. Her memory is gone, though, both short- and long-term, and she's still not quite the Gail she once was.

"She doesn't remember anything?" I asked.

"Not really. She has mentioned school a few times. And her bunk bed—that was weird. All of a sudden, she said the word *bunk*. But that's about it. On the other hand, the doctors say it's easier to treat kids whose speech, motor skills, and cognitive abilities all fall in the same age range. These kids also tend to get better faster, although in Gail's case, that doesn't seem to be happening."

"But she only woke up a few weeks ago. We were afraid she had no brain function at all, so isn't the fact that she's able to do anything considered progress?"

"Sure. And they're not saying she is progressing too slowly; she's just progressing at a rate that's inconsistent with her test results. Her brain appears intact, so she should be further along than she is."

"I guess it takes time." I was referring not just to Gail, but to everything.

"It does," Grant agreed. "It takes a lot of time."

"I colored my hair," I blurted out. "I'm a real redhead now."

"Well, that's random." But he sounded amused. "I always did like redheads." He paused. "Well, thanks a lot for tomorrow. I appreciate it."

We both waited a beat, neither of us ready to hang up.

"Hey, Grant. Can I ask you something?" I wanted to know if he ever thought about me, if he missed me at all. Instead I went with, "Do you think Gail will remember me?" (Bold—yes; but brazen? Not very.)

"It's hard to say. We've been reading her your letters, though, so she does know who you are. That was Charlotte's idea; she reads them to Gail all the time. She really...um...both girls really love your letters, Eliot. She...and I—and Beth, too—we all think it's great you've been writing them. So...thank you for doing that." After clearing his throat, he went back to business. "It would be helpful if you show up between ten and two. How's that?"

Perfect, I told him. And now, as I step into the reception area, I take a few deep breaths, trying to calm my nerves. Surprisingly, the Banks Center is as unimpressive on the inside as it is outside, which helps. Given its reputation, I expected a space age EPCOT Center with doctors in white jumpsuits and goggles discussing neuron-magnetic brain mapping. Instead, there's one bored bleached blonde sitting at a desk eating a Whopper and thumbing through *People* magazine. As I introduce myself, a clump of pickles falls onto her desk.

"Name?" She picks them up with a napkin.

"My name? Eliot Gordon. I'm here to see Gail Delaney. I'm her...she's my...I'm a family friend."

"Seventh floor," she says, flicking a spot of ketchup with her tongue. "Room 554."

Outside Gail's room, I hesitate. I've wanted to see her for so long, but now that I'm here I'm afraid to go in. And honestly? I don't have to be here; Gail is no longer my responsibility. I can walk away at any time. That this is my choice is the point, though. Gail is neither Grant's appendage nor his burden, and I'm not here out of obligation to him—or to her. It's not why I love Gail, either. I love her because I love her, because you can't choose who you love. And when you consider what you risk by loving a child, particularly one who's not yours, it's easy to understand why some people don't, or can't, or try not to. It's not because they're selfish or because the child is unlovable; it's because to invest that kind of emotional capital with no guarantee of return is petrifying.

And yet.

I have known Gail Delaney almost the whole of her life. I held her when she was a baby, I raised her into childhood, and if I'm allowed, I want to see her grow up. Being here is my *choice*; stepping inside is my *choice*. I am choosing to be here for Gail, regardless of what comes next. But equally important, I am also choosing to be here for me. I open the door. I see her, and when I do, I'm stunned by the love—the true love—that wells up inside me.

"Eliot!" she shouts, recognizing me immediately.

"Gail!"

As we both laugh, I take a quick inventory. Her dark hair has grown longer and touches her shoulders. Her cheeks have color again; her eyes are clear. She looks so much like Gail—the old Gail, the real Gail—that when she reaches for me, I instinctively move closer. Just before I hug her, though, I see how thin she is and how frail. Concerned, I jerk back.

This upsets her. "Eliot..." She thrusts her hands forward. *"Come, Eliot!"*

Although I want to touch her, I'm paralyzed. I look around for a nurse, someone who can observe us, who'll make sure nothing unexpected happens.

"I'm sorry, Gail." My hand is so close to her hair that static electricity attaches a single strand to my finger. When I lift it, a few more strands rise. Holding my breath, I let my hand drop. I stroke her head once, twice, but just as I pull away, she grabs my fingers and won't let go.

Thank you for letting her be okay; thank you for giving me this moment.

Shifting her weight, Gail makes room on her bed. I sit beside her, and the next thing I know, my ex–middle child, my un-stepdaughter, rolls on top of me and curls up on my chest. Two minutes later, she's sound asleep.

Pinned underneath her, I fumble for my phone. I think of the one person who would truly appreciate my predicament—someone who, like me, has been waiting for a glass slipper moment to transform his life.

"Dad?" Struck by how naturally, how comfortably, the word feels in my mouth, I repeat it. "Dad, it's me. It's Eliot. Is this an okay time?...Dad, I think we should talk."

Chapter Thirty-one

IN MY MOTHER'S last novel—the one no one remembers—she wrote about a Jewish family who fled from Poland to Palestine during World War II. Throughout the book, the family experiences setbacks and separations, but their unwavering faith sustains them until they're finally reunited. At the heart of the novel is the issue of dispossession, specifically what it means to lose everything you have and start over. It's called *We Went Missing*, and although only about twenty people ever read it, critics hailed the book as a small masterpiece.

Gail's accident and her slow but steady recovery have stirred within me feelings of hope, which to me is what religion—and God, I suppose—inspires. This afternoon, wanting to remind myself how Judaism works, I reread *We Went Missing*. It's only two hundred pages, so it didn't take long, but when I finished, I was so impressed I decided to reread all my mother's other books, too. Hailey is with Grant until Monday, so I sat down and plowed through them, one after the other. Now it is many hours later, and I'm still here on the couch, stunned.

My mother's books, I can honestly say, are genius. Not having looked at them since I was a teenager, I had an altogether different experience reading them as an adult. For one thing, the novels aren't as boring as I remembered; neither are the memoirs as salacious. Compared with what's being published today, they actually seem tame, even quaint. But the bigger shock was realizing that my sisters and I appear in them only briefly—and as minor players. In my memory of these books, I'm front and center, but in fact I'm barely there at all. Similarly, the brilliantly distilled anecdotes of my mother's life are rich and eloquent—hardly the effort of someone out to make a quick buck. Her memoirs reveal a true working artist, a writer who made tremendous sacrifices—not just for financial reasons, but also to sustain herself over the long haul.

My mother is the daughter of assimilated immigrants who came to America from Germany right before the war. Growing up, she always felt like an outsider, caught between her parents'—my grandparents'—longing to return to their beloved Berlin and her own desire to embrace the country where she was born. Writing, then, gave her a way to make sense of a life that felt sprung from nowhere and tethered to nothing. Although her novels were marketed as political dramas, they're actually multilayered meditations on the meaning of family and how, through these relationships, we're able to whittle down an infinite, chaotic world to find our own place within it. I understand now, having read them again, that her novels, her memoirs, and her essays are wholly about her, and I can see why she's so proud of them.

Although it's after ten, I call her. "I get it," I say when she picks up.

"You get what?" It's prime-time viewing for *Law & Order* reruns, and my mother is distracted.

"The whole book thing—your book thing."

This gets her attention. "What about it?"

"Remember the last conversation we had on Wyatt Island? When I was packing up to leave? I said something about you discussing me in your books?"

"When you called me *disgusting* for exploiting you? That conversation?"

I cringe. "Well, I've rethought my position. I reread your books. They're better than I remembered."

"Well, thanks, Eliot. That's a load off my mind."

"No, really. They're incredible. The last time I read your memoirs— well, skimmed—I was so young that it was hard for me to absorb them.

I also resented them. Not the books, necessarily, but how much time you spent working. I felt like your writing was a way for you to escape us, but in fact, you were always right there at your desk, day after day."

"I told you it sucks to be a writer." But I can tell from her tone that she's pleased.

It's true, though. For all her vast reaching, my mother's life was very small. After my father, she never fell in love again; she rarely dated, never traveled. She didn't do much of anything but work and go to work. I always accused her of abandoning us, but it wasn't that way at all.

"So I just wanted to tell you I appreciate what you did for me—what you do. You're a great mother," I add, sheepish to be admitting this so late in the game.

"You're welcome—" Her voice breaks. "That's nice to hear, Eliot."

There's a short pause as we acknowledge each other, not just as a mother and her daughter, but as two adult women who have worked hard to reach this point.

"So that's it? You're quitting? After all these years, you're just walking away?"

She sighs. "If only I could. Believe me, I've tried. But each time I decide I'm done, I'll read some idiot's overpraised book, or see some crazy story in the news, and I have to react, to have my say. Unfortunately, this compulsive need to write often blinds me to everyone and everything around me, and the only way I can satisfy it is to sit down and work." She pauses. "You know what's funny, though. What I remember about our conversation is how you asked what made me so great that I didn't have to live like everyone else. Inherent in your question is the idea that I believe I'm better than other people, or entitled to more because I'm a writer, or rather, *choose to be* a writer—"

"That's not what I meant—"

"Let me finish. You have to understand something, Eliot. While I do believe that we're each entitled to as much as we can get from this life, I don't think I'm better than anyone. In fact, my sense of unworthiness is what fuels my need to write in the first place. In my mind, I'm not talented enough, or talented in the right way, and for every book I do write, there's another, better book I didn't. My whole life has been spent chasing down that other book, the one that will prove my value as an author, an artist, a human being. So even though part of me knows no matter how hard I work, that book will never materialize—it can't, because then what?—I still have to go after it…rather, I can't not. The greater irony, of course, is that from my publisher's point of view—which is measured in units sold—I'm a failure, thus validating my unworthiness and perpetuating the cycle. So do I give up? Work nine to five? Pretend it doesn't matter?"

"I don't know. At some point, don't you have to cut your losses?"

"Eliot, I would rather be a failed writer than a successful accountant. And it's not like I had a choice—if I did, do you think this is the life I would've chosen for myself? For you and your sisters? Being an author, writing books, is what I was destined to do from the day I was born. I didn't have a choice at all."

That sounds like a contradiction, doesn't it, a writer who believes in fate? You'd think that after decades of dreaming up stories, of laboring over the "and then, and then, and then" of fiction, a writer would be the last person to believe in fate. On the other hand, haven't you read a story that when you're finished feels exactly right? As though there were no other way it could've unfolded, even if the ending is completely different from how you first envisioned it? This is because there's encoding in fiction, just as in life; and very often a story will assume its own predetermined form with its own internal logic despite a writer's best efforts to shape it otherwise. And in life, just as in fiction, we are each the sum total of all the stories that have preceded us, stories that are in us and of us, however unique our DNA.

Unlike my mother, however, I'm not an artist. I don't have a passion or a unique talent of my own. I have no calling or larger purpose. I'm just a mom. I go to work. I love my kids. Eventually I'll die. Occasionally, I might come up with a clever phrase for a client. (It was my idea, for instance, to call an underwear manufacturer's newsletter *The Bottom Line*.) But that's the extent of my legacy. Because of this, I've always felt lacking, especially when compared with the one and only Simone Starr. Yet hearing her describe the relentless albatross of art, I actually feel relief in my own ordinariness.

"When you put it that way," I tell her, "I'm happy just to be another bozo."

"Oh, Eliot, we're all a bunch of bozos. Every single one of us is just fumbling around in the dark, trying to find the answer."

"You just said for you it was writing."

"Writing is *how* I live, Eliot—it's not *why*."

"So there's no overarching plan, no all-knowing, all-seeing God?"

"Of course not. How many times have we talked about this? The whole thing is a crapshoot—God or no God, plan or no plan. When it comes to religion, to the plan, to the why, *no one knows anything*, especially those who claim to know best."

I've been thinking about this for a week now, and I'm not so sure my mother is right. In fact, I'm continuing to read about Judaism and Christianity because I want to introduce Hailey to religion. She's only four, so I want to talk to her about faith in a way she can grasp. I also want to provide her with community, as well as context for who she is. Although she may never find out all the answers, at least I can give her a place to start.

I asked Grant what he thinks, but he has no idea. Right now, he said, he's too overwhelmed with Gail's rehab, Charlotte's anger, his job, and our finances to care if his four-year-old believes in God. Although I understand this, I don't think the two issues—that is, the quotidian details of life and the question of faith—are mutually exclusive. Believe it or not, my father has been helping with my research. He wasn't raised with much religion, but he has very solid ideas about faith.

"I always knew I'd see you again," he told me recently on the phone. "I never stopped thinking about you and Sylvia and Maggie. I knew someday I'd get the chance to tell you how much I loved you, and I did."

"How could you know that? I gave up on you years ago."

"I just knew, Eliot. I knew in my heart that when I saw you again, it would be beautiful, and it was."

This is really how he talks, as if he's sloshed and reciting lyrics to old torch songs. I find it touching, though. Who knew that Barney Gordon believed in true love, magical moments, and the transformative power of faith? He's a starry-eyed dreamer, which makes him sweet and harmless, albeit absolutely maddening. In his memory of my mother, for instance, they were always happy, so it shocked him when she filed for divorce.

"You broke up and got back together five times," I reminded him. "How could you be shocked?"

"We were young and foolish," is how he described it.

"You weren't that young. And you fought all the time. You said you hated each other."

"We were passionate. Dolores was the love of my life."

"If you loved her so much, then why did you let her go? Why didn't you fight for her?"

"Isn't a better question: If I loved *you* so much, why did I let *you* go?"

"Either-or," I said, feeling exposed but also protected. There's a difference, I've come to see, in being exposed and being known. My father isn't ignorant, despite all the rumors I've heard to the contrary. He isn't abusive or a leech or desperate, and he doesn't have broccoli breath. He has flaws, sure, but he's no monster. He's just a man.

"Your mother and I made a lot of mistakes," he said, which made me wonder if he'd been speaking to her lately. Part of me was curious, but another, larger part was satisfied with having no idea. I like that my mother and father might be having private conversations. It makes me feel as though we're all young again and have a lot of time left.

"What kind of mistakes?"

"Her mistake was to tell me that you and your sisters would be better off without me, and my mistake was to believe her. We were both wrong, but too dumb to know better. Look at all the years we wasted, not forgiving each other, or ourselves. Neither of us would take the first step, and then a lifetime went by—several lifetimes. Not only did I lose Dolores, but I also lost you and your sisters. The pitiful thing is, had I not been so afraid, we could've had a whole different life."

He was referring to himself, but I also felt he was talking about Grant. "I can't force Grant to forgive me, Dad. I've tried to apologize, but he's not interested." There it was again: *Dad*. This guy was *my dad*, *my father*. I had a whole new vocabulary.

"I'm not talking about *him* forgiving *you*, Eliot. I'm talking about *you* forgiving *yourself*."

I was silent.

"Listen to me, because I'm not playing games here. I'll always wish I had done things differently with you. But I've forgiven myself. To do otherwise, to wallow in the past, would've made me bitter and sad. *Bitter and sad*," he repeats. "You should think about that the next time you see Grant."

So now every time I see Grant, I think about that, mainly because my father told me to, and it's nice to have a father around to tell me what to do, even if he's not here to watch me. Or maybe he is here. I've always said I don't believe in magic, and I don't know for sure if I believe in God, but seeing Barney again has restored my faith. Think about it: One day my father appeared, and the next he was gone, but suddenly, I truly feel free to imagine a future beyond today.

⌒

Hi, Larry: Here's the announcement letter we discussed. As you'll see, I think it's time we moved in a new direction. Hope you're well. Best, Eliot

Memo To: All Members of the Barnett Technology Community
From: Larry Barnett, CEO
Re: Barnett Technology Is Bankrupt

Dear Colleagues,

Barnett Technology's failed attempt to merge with Avery Electronics, coupled with our recent legal issues, has forced us to file Chapter 11. This means we have no money for health care or any other benefits. However, I will continue to pay your salary for as long as you wish to work here, and as long as I am able. In fact, I will be grateful to every employee who stays on, and promise to do whatever I can to help you find affordable medical and dental coverage. (The four-dollar parking deck permit is as cheap as it's ever going to get, so I suggest you take advantage of this while it's still available.)

Next Steps

Going forward, I will no longer refer to you as a "tool." Nor will I call you a "resource," "asset," or, collectively, "human capital." You are an employee, but you're also a person; and I will refer to you, and treat you, as such.

In the next few years, Barnett Technology will work hard to pay off its debts, develop new and safe products, and provide a healthy working environment. I will be holding employee meetings to discuss our strategy, and we're implementing a 24-hour, toll-free hotline for you, should you awaken in the dead of night in a cold sweat with concerns about your future. In addition, I plan to meet with you individually so that you may share with me your short- and long-term hopes, dreams, and desires. I want you to be happy working here, and am interested in your ideas about how the Company can help, including what I can do personally to make this happen.

To demonstrate my appreciation, I am pleased to offer you and your eligible dependents *free* Totes umbrellas! Available in three colors (red, black, or Barnett blue), these umbrellas are embossed with the Barnett-Avery logo. as a reminder that *Barnett's always got you covered.* (Note: Supplies are limited.) (Note: we have 9,900 in stock, so please take as many as you can carry.)

Again, I appreciate your ongoing commitment, hard
work and dedication, and sincerely hope you will be part
of Barnett Technology's future. I expect it to be very
bright indeed.

Best regards,
Larry

⌒

Gail continues to make progress. For the past month, I've been visiting
her every day at the Banks Center while Beth finishes her mural. I arrive
in the morning, give Gail a snack, work on my laptop while she's in her
various therapies, and stay until it's time to pick up Hailey. I usually
bring Hailey back here after school so she can spend time with her father and sisters. There is a marked improvement in Gail's mood when
Charlotte and Hailey are here, even if they're bickering. Since waking
up, she's had dark moments, but little by little, our old Gail is returning.

Surprisingly, it's Charlotte who seems the most changed by the accident. Before we went to Wyatt Island, she was polite, although distant
and insincere. But these days, she's depressed and visibly angry, mostly
with me.

"Hi, Charlotte," I'll say when I see her. "How are you? How was
school?"

She shrugs. Or else she's silent. She doesn't look at me, and when I
try to hug her, she stiffens, as if ticking off seconds until she's released.
Yet she's also relieved that I'm here. Although she hasn't said anything to indicate this, an ex-stepmother can intuit things about her
ex-stepchildren.

Like me, Grant comes every day. In the beginning, he pretended
I wasn't here, but as one week passed, then another and another, he
started talking to me only because no one else was around. Our con-

versations were stilted, like two people from AA who see each other outside the rooms: unless we were rehashing the way we bottomed out in the gutter, we had no clue what to say. Slowly, though, we moved from our work and the weather to the kids, ourselves, and the dumpiness of this supposedly superior medical facility.

"The hole in that wall is as big as my fist," Grant pointed out. "It has to be a safety violation."

"And what about the exposed wires in the bathroom?"

"And the buckling floor tiles? How can this place pass an inspection?"

I get the impression that Beth's continued absence bothers him. Yesterday, in a rare, unguarded moment, he revealed that the real reason she doesn't visit has more to do with her frustration over the slow pace of Gail's recovery than needing to finish the Riverside mural. I was so surprised Grant was confiding in me that I didn't respond, but five minutes ago he raised the subject again, and now he's asking me questions.

"I understand it's hard. But why is it harder for her than for anyone else?"

I hedge, afraid of saying the wrong thing. "Harder for who to do what?"

"For Beth to come to the hospital, Eliot—who the hell else are we talking about? Don't get me wrong, I'm not judging her, but what did she expect? That Gail would wake up from a coma, and be exactly the same?"

"I don't know."

He looks at me. "Well, what do you think?"

"Grant, even if Beth didn't expect Gail to be the same, I'm sure it's what she hoped for. So maybe she finds her progress discouraging. Maybe watching the day-to-day makes her feel like she failed, or continues to fail, or...I don't know...something like that..."

"How did she fail? It wasn't her fault."

"I didn't say it was, but maybe she feels she should be doing more, and since she can't, it's too hard for her to sit here all day and do nothing."

"Everyone feels like they should do more. But isn't that the point, as a parent? To be around for the day-to-day, to do what's right for Gail, regardless of how hard it is? I know it's tedious. We sit here, hour after hour, and clap while the poor kid learns how to pick up a fork and put down the fork and pick up the fork and put it back down. That's the part Beth always ran away from." Grant snorts. "I guess 'ran away' does sound judgmental, but I don't mean it like that. It's just when the girls were babies, I wasn't around for the day-to-day. I mean, I was *there* but not *there*. Now I am totally *here*; I'm here when Gail picks up the fork and puts down the fork. And man, it's *fucking tedious*. But when she finally spears that pea, it's like...I don't know...it's *epic*. And I can't believe Beth would miss it. Look, I know she's trying, but Gail is her kid, and this is a major life event, and it still feels like she's abandoning her. Gail is in there, Eliot. I know she is. I just don't get how Beth can blow this off. She did it when Gail was born, and she's doing it again now."

"But you and I are here. We're here every day, watching her. It's okay if Beth is somewhere else. Gail is fine." I think about what my mother said about the demands of art, how it pulls at her in ways that are impossible to resist. "We're all good at some things, Grant, and not so good at others. I think Beth is doing the best she can. She loves Gail the way she loves her."

"She's the kid's *mother*."

"She's also an artist. I'm not making excuses for her, I'm just stating a fact."

After this, we sit for a few minutes, not speaking. Then I turn to my computer and Grant turns to his, and the only sounds in the room are the clicking of our keyboards and the clanking of the lousy pipes. I'm about to comment on this, how maybe we should consider moving to a better facility, when Gail suddenly speaks.

"Guys..." She rubs her eyes. "I have to pee. Can someone help me?"

Grant and I jerk our heads up. "Gail?" I ask gently. "Did you just say something?"

"I said I have to pee. And I need help getting up." The words flow out of her mouth like a song. Every vowel is pronounced, every syllable accounted for.

Grant starts to laugh. "Say it again. Please, Gail, say it again."

"I need to pee," she says: simply, clearly, precisely.

Grant jumps to his feet. "Gail needs to *pee*. And she told *me*!" He guides her to the bathroom, dancing around on his toes. "Gail needs to *pee* and she told *me*." He sings this over and over, helping Gail finish up and wash her hands. Then he twirls her across the room, and I clap for them both.

It's been a while since I've seen Grant happy. So when he flashes me a smile, I'm startled again by how handsome he is. *Of course*, I think, suddenly a little breathless, a little giddy. *Of course*; how could I have forgotten?

Grant catches me staring, and I feel a familiar pull, a frisson of heat between two people seeing each other in a brand-new light. "She's talking," he says, holding my eyes. "I heard it."

"I heard it, too," I agree, wanting to hold on to this feeling for as long as I can. "It's happening, Grant. She's coming back to us."

Since then, Gail's recovery has sped up considerably. She speaks regularly and constantly, which, as any new parent can attest, is both remarkable and exhausting. She can feed herself, hold a pencil, and recite the alphabet. She is able to walk, but the drowning left her with vertigo, so she's a little off balance. She's getting there, though, and Grant and I are both here to applaud every single step.

According to her doctors, recovery can happen this way—a patient regains her mental and physical abilities spontaneously, seemingly overnight. What's more, it has nothing to do with cutting-edge technology or sophisticated science—"which is good," Grant noted, "since this place has neither"—and everything to do with how the people around her interact with one another.

"However strange the phenomenon," Gail's neurologist explained, "we've seen cases where patients improve dramatically once family members shift their focus away from themselves and over to their child.

When we mapped brain function in these kids, we saw pronounced activity in cell production, as well as increases in serotonin and dopamine levels. We know reduced stress can stimulate functionality, but the results we've seen are off the charts. There's no science behind it—we don't alter treatment protocols—it's just a simple shift in family dynamics. That these shifts can reverse documented neural damage is nothing short of phenomenal."

But Gail isn't the only one making progress. Grant and I are getting to know each other again. This may be an odd thing to say about two people who lived together for five years, but in the past six weeks, Grant and I have become friendly. Actually, we're more than friendly—we've become friends.

It's painfully boring at the Banks Center. If Gail is in her room, Grant and I read to her or play games, but when she's off with her doctors, he and I aren't needed. I still write letters to Gail and Charlotte, but now I also write to Hailey—nothing long or elaborate, just quick notes to recap the day's highlights. Sometimes I'll read the funny parts to Grant, but that's about it, activity-wise. For the most part, we work or read. But we also talk, and we're learning things about each other that are truly astonishing.

Grant Delaney, for instance, loves self-help books. Five years together in the same house, in the same bed, and I had no idea. But one day I walked in and saw Grant slyly slip the book he was reading behind a copy of *The Economist*.

I pointed to the magazine. "What's that?"

"Business reading." He furrowed his brow. "This guy's discussing how debt financing can provide large amounts of liquidity quickly in moments of economic crisis." He looked up. "It's quite fascinating."

"I bet, Sparky." Bending over, I grabbed the book he was hiding: *Heaving Bosoms and Reckless Rogues: How to Make Money Writing Romance Novels*. I winked and gave him an atta-boy thump.

"It's an investment opportunity," he said defensively.

Grant doesn't read just creative-writing handbooks. He reads every

do-it-yourself book he can find. In the past two months, he's learned
how to build a backyard deck, debone a bluefish, start his own Pizza
Hut franchise, and play the banjo. "How do you think I learned how
to juggle, Eliot? It was part of a Time/Life series." All these years I've
been nagging him to take up a hobby, and it turns out he's a Renais-
sance man.

"Why didn't you ever read these books when we were together?" I
asked.

"Who had the time?"

Now time is all we have. Although we both don't need to come every
day, neither of us wants to miss anything, no matter how trivial. So we
both show up. And we both sit. We sit and read. We sit and work. We
sit and reminisce, eat, tell stories, eat, solve crossword puzzles, eat, and
eat some more. We also engage in deep philosophical discourse.

Grant: If the Apocalypse came and everyone was obliterated, would
you be willing to have sex with Benito Mussolini if it meant saving the
entire human race?

Me: He's dead.

Grant: Use your imagination, and think carefully before you answer,
Eliot. We're talking about the future of civilization as we know it.

Me: Of course not.

Grant: If you say no, there won't be any more people—ever. Human-
ity will be gone. Are you going to finish that ice-cream sandwich?

Me: Here, take it. And my answer is still no. So, if the Apocalypse
came, would you be willing to have sex with...um...I don't know,
Grant; you ask me this all the time. Okay, if the Apocalypse came,
would you be willing to have sex with...I don't know...my mother?

Grant, nodding: If the choice is between having sex with your
mother and never having sex again, then I would, absolutely. Hell, I'd
fuck Mussolini if that was my only option.

Over time, I learn that in addition to his willingness to have sexual
congress with some unlikely partners, Grant once ate monkey brains,
believes the animal he most resembles is an armadillo, would rather be

buried alive than burned at the stake, and thinks spinach tastes like wet paper towels.

At the moment, I'm whipping his ass in Candy Land, a game I play with world-class proficiency. Gail is sitting on her bed, playing with Hailey's Polly Pockets. "Can I have a glass of water?"

I pour her a cup of water, and as I hand it to her, she says, "I was in the ocean."

My breath catches. I look at Grant, but he's looking at Gail.

"When, Gail?" he asks. "When were you in the ocean?"

"A long time ago. I lost all my air. I couldn't breathe."

"Was Hailey there?"

She shakes her head. "I'm tired," she says, then closes her eyes.

Grant and I abandon our game. The memory of the accident clouds the air between us, making it hard to focus. Neither of us speaks, not wanting to bring up the subject we've both been avoiding. Eventually, I break the silence.

"Grant, I've been thinking. And I just want you to know once and for all that I am truly sorry this happened, and if I could—"

He holds up his hand. "Stop, Eliot. I know what you're going to say, and it's okay. I've learned a lot seeing you here every day. I never realized how much you did for the kids—and for me, too. I don't think I ever understood how hard it was, not just to take care of them, but to be a stepmother. Anyway, what happened to Gail and Hailey was an accident. I know that."

I think about this. "It was an accident," I echo, and I can feel the idea click into place. "I made a mistake." I want to say more but can't because something strange is happening. I'm experiencing weightlessness, a buoyancy I haven't felt before. My chest is expanding, and all five of my senses are sharpening. The light is brighter, the air is cleaner—it even smells sweeter—and as I breathe, the buzzing in my head disappears for good.

"Eliot?" Grant is watching me.

"It was just an accident." My father was right. I don't have to end up bitter and sad. This is all new, this lightness, and I'm waiting for it to reverse, for my heart to shrivel and my head to fog up, but my head remains unfettered, and my heart—my bruised, battered heart—actually flutters. "I'd like us to be friends, Grant. You're a good man and a genuinely kind person. I like you a lot." I hold out my hand.

Grant considers this. "I like you too, Eliot." Then he leans forward, and for a second I'm sure he's going to kiss me, but instead he makes a megaphone with his fingers and shouts, *"Erin go Bragh!"* into my ear.

Chapter Thirty-two

"I AM *SO NAUSEOUS*," Sylvia says for the third time. She is bent over beside me, her head pressed between her knees. "Eliot, face facts: You. Are. A. Shitty. Driver. Period. End of story."

"We know, Sylvia," Maggie calls out from the backseat. "You said that already."

"You didn't have to come," I remind her, also for the third time.

"That is so *rude*." She turns around to look at Hailey. "Don't you think your mother is *rude*? I'd *never* talk to her the way she talks to me."

In her car seat behind us, Hailey yawns, bored stiff of her aunt. "When will we be there, Mommy?"

Tonight is the unveiling of Beth's mural at Riverside, and although both my sisters are here, my mother opted out. "The last thing I need to see," she said, "is an artistic rendering of the Sculptress's vagina." Sylvia had said the same thing but then agreed to go as long as I picked her up and dropped her off. Oh, I also had to pay for dinner.

"Why should I pay for dinner?" I asked her.

"Because it's a nice thing to do when someone is putting herself out for you."

"But Maggie is going, and we're meeting Grant and the girls at the school. It's okay if you want to stay home, Sylvia. There will be more than enough people there."

"Oh, so now you want everyone else to go but me? You *always* do *this*, Eliot. You *always* leave me out." Which is how I ended up paying for dinner *and* buying her an expensive maternity tunic. Lest anyone accuse me of having no spine, I did refuse the $300 matching pants.

I drive along the winding road, past the soccer fields and lower school building. Outside, the sky is pitch black, but the chapel is lit up like opening night at Grauman's Chinese Theatre, circa 1950. Klieg lights are positioned on the lawn, and billows of smoke waft off the glass, bathing the castlelike church in a dreamy mist. Hundreds of soft white bulbs are strung along the branches of the surrounding trees and flicker in the leaves like fallen stars.

Sylvia taps on her window. "It's bright out there. What'll happen when the Sculptress throws back that tarp? Will our eyes melt in their sockets?"

I pull into the visitors' parking lot and shut off the car. "Beth had to show preliminary sketches to the board. They're pretty uptight; they would've vetoed anything inappropriate."

"What if she did a last-minute switcheroo?"

This makes Hailey laugh. "That's a funny word." She repeats it a few times, cracking herself up.

"Even if Beth did paint her vagina," Maggie says diplomatically, "I'm sure it will be tasteful."

"Will you guys please shut up?" I say. "Beth is a serious *artist*. Riverside paid her for *serious* art."

To which Hailey says, " 'Shut up' isn't a nice word, Mommy."

Sylvia agrees. "See, Hailey? I told you your mother is rude. She's getting defensive over nothing. Do you really care about Beth's painting? I don't, that's for sure. I'm only here because your mother begged me to come. By the way, isn't this outfit *so* cute? I *love* it; don't you *love* it? But do you think it makes me look fat—" She stops. " 'Not pretty,' I mean?"

A still-bored Hailey yawns for the second time in Sylvia's face. "I'm hungry, Mommy."

"I'm hungry, too, *Hailey*. I'm *starving*."

"I'm more hungry than you, *Aunt Sylvia*."

"You are not, *Hailey*. I'm the *most starving* person in the *whole world*, the *hungriest* person who ever existed in *time*, *space*, and *all eternity*. Hailey, I'm hungrier than *God*."

When Hailey starts to cry, Maggie gives Sylvia a wry look. "You're gonna be a *great* mother."

Contrary to what Sylvia thinks, I'm not being defensive. I'm just concerned. For all I know, Beth painted a ten-foot rendering of her vagina as a statement on female oppression, which will serve as a backdrop when she and her goddess gals castrate some guy who dared to hold the door open for them. All I can say is that for Charlotte's and Gail's sakes—for all our sakes—I hope not.

To be honest, I had no intention of coming tonight. When Grant told me about it, I mumbled something about the lateness of the hour and hoped he got the point. But a few days ago, Charlotte and I were visiting Gail, and she asked if I would be here. Touched by her invitation, I couldn't decline.

"I helped Mom paint the mural," she said proudly. "And the night's gonna be, like, a major event. All the Atlanta senators will be there, and maybe even Elton John."

"That's great, Charlotte. It sounds very exciting. Although, just so you know, Georgia has two U.S. senators, who may or may not come from Atlanta. Do you mean state senators, or are you talking about congressmen?"

"You're wrong, Eliot. Atlanta has two U.S. senators and Georgia has four. We just spent a whole month studying how the government works. So, anyway, if you want to come, that would be great. I mean, it would make Dad happy, and I know Mom would appreciate it...and...uh...so would I...that is, if you want to, I mean. But if you don't, that's okay too. Still, it would be good if you could."

"Thanks, Charlotte. I appreciate the invitation." But come on—an *entire month* studying government and she still thinks Atlanta has two U.S. senators? "I'll definitely try to make it."

So here I am, helping Maggie set up Sylvia's all-terrain wheelchair on the dirt path that leads to the chapel. The wheelchair is the latest development in what must surely be the most complex and expensive pregnancy ever to occur in the history of propagation. Convinced she's at risk for eclampsia—which occurs in about only one out of every three thousand pregnancies, mostly in African American women with a history of diabetes—Sylvia has confined herself to the chair "as a precautionary measure."

"You don't have diabetes," I reminded her. "Nor are you black."

"You are *so racist*, Eliot," Sylvia snapped.

My sister, for the record, is perfectly healthy. If there are any complications with her delivery, they will be accident related. So I'm awaiting the arrival of my first niece with excitement and fear, but mostly fear. If not for me, her baby would almost certainly be fine, which is a fact I'm still learning to live with. Whatever happens, though, I'm sure Sylvia will respond accordingly, that is, she'll shock—and awe—us all.

Settling into her wheelchair, she tucks a blanket around her knees. "It's chilly out here, Eliot," she complains as though the unseasonable cold, like everything else, is my fault.

"Please, Aunt Sylvia, please let me ride on your lap," Hailey begs.

"Hailey," she says as if the kid just asked her to lug a four-hundred-pound sofa up eleven flights of stairs. "I'm *pregnant*." She points to the back of her wheelchair, to a cardboard triangle that says *Baby on Board* in luminescent pink script.

And we're off.

On the way to the chapel, I see clusters of people milling around, although far fewer than I had envisioned. Given Charlotte's buildup, I expected a Wembley Arena–sized turnout with bodyguards and crowd control, but there are fewer than thirty people here. Nor is there a politician or pop star among them. It's your average PTA-sized school function.

"Pregnant lady coming through!" Sylvia shouts as she motors along. "Make way for lady and baby." Everyone steps aside, which thrills her. "Why do crippled people—excuse me, *the disabled*—complain about wheelchairs? I'm like a queen on her throne! I should've gotten one of these things *years* ago."

There's a man standing a few feet away, but he has his back to me. Behind him, there are rows of blinking lights, which shine through his cotton shirt, illuminating the perfect V of his back. I'm staring at him when Hailey shouts, "Look, Mommy. Daddy's here!"

Glancing around, I don't see him at first, but then the man turns, and I realize—how *embarrassing*—that it's *Grant*.

He spots me and waves. "Hey!" he says, walking over. Flanked by Charlotte on one side and Gail on the other, he looks centered and solid. Hailey runs to him, and he gives her a big squeeze. "Pickle!" Then he reaches over and gives me a hug. "Eliot, you came after all."

Feeling his arms around me, I get a little light-headed. "I wanted to see you—and the girls...everyone, I mean. I wanted to see everyone. And the mural, of course. How could I miss the fabulous mural? I'm sure it'll be, uh...fabulous..." I blather on until Sylvia interrupts me.

"I'm down here, Grant! It's *rude* to ignore someone in a wheelchair."

"Wait your turn, Sylvia. I'm saying hello to your sister." He brushes my hair off my face. "I like this color more and more every time I see it. It really suits you."

My cheeks get hot. "You don't think it's too much?"

"I think you look great," he says softly, then turns to Sylvia. "Hi, Sylvia. It's *so nice* to see you."

Looking up at him, she grins. "Of course it is, Grant." Both she and Maggie have been to the Banks Center to visit Gail, so Sylvia and Grant have spoken several times since the accident. Although she apologized for lying about what happened on the beach, when she offered an explanation—"Eliot is my sister; what choice did I have?"—she made it clear that, given similar circumstances, she'd do it again. Grant, in turn, accepted her apology, and while he doesn't like this aspect of our relationship, he does understand it. In this way, they've managed to broker their own peace.

I feel someone tugging on my sleeve. It's Gail. "I'm glad you came."

"Me too." Pulling her against me, I hold her tight. In the bright lights, she looks so much like herself again, so much like my old Gail, that I get choked up.

"Come on, Gail!" her sisters call, holding out their hands. "We want to get closer." As I watch her stumble toward them, I again acknowledge my unbelievably good fortune.

I hear someone blow into a microphone and glance up to see Phoebe and Beth standing in front of the chapel. Phoebe holds up her hands, waiting for the crowd to quiet down. "I appreciate everyone coming out to this unveiling," she says, "especially on this very cold night. We're going to start in five minutes, but if you need to warm up, please step inside. None of us realized it would be so *freezing* out!"

"Phoebe, *please*," someone calls out. "It's not *that* cold."

I'm a few yards back, and from where I'm standing, the white klieg lights shine through Phoebe's even whiter hair, making her look like a dandelion. Beside her, Beth's black-on-black ensemble is lost in the darkness, and her disembodied head hovers in the air. She looks happy, though—proud, too, as she makes last-minute adjustments to the tarp covering the chapel wall.

I don't know why I'm so nervous; it's not my vagina she's about to unveil. But lately, I've become oddly protective of Beth. I just don't want her to feel bad about her mural, especially given how hard she worked on it.

Grant and the girls have edged their way to the front, waving to Beth and wishing her good luck. Then they move even farther away, to an open spot on the lawn next to the chapel, where a bunch of kids are playing tag.

Charlotte is unusually animated tonight. She does a cartwheel on the grass and then lifts Gail under her arms and starts to spin her around. Watching them, I call out nervously to Grant, "Grant, please tell Charlotte to be careful!"

He can't hear me, but he steps in anyway, motioning for Charlotte to slow down. Hailey clamors for a turn, so Charlotte picks her up and spins her around, but once isn't enough—Hailey wants more. This time, Grant picks up Hailey, but he swings her by her hands, not her arms, and her whole body whirls in the air. He's swinging her too fast, and I'm afraid he's going to drop her or dislocate her shoulder, or something else will happen, something horrendous—

"Grant, stop!"

I feel someone come up behind me, but before I can turn around, a pair of man's hands cover my eyes, cutting off my view. "What are you doing?" Panicking, I claw at the hands, desperate to make sure Hailey is okay. "Let me go!" I can't take my eyes off my daughter—not even for a second, especially when she's in a compromised state. "Please, this isn't funny."

"Guess who?" Hearing this, I freeze. "It's me."

I stand there, electrified. "It's you." Of course, I think. Who else could it be?

"Finn, let me go. I can't see." That I'm calm as I say this—that I say it at all—is an unexpected twist. Once upon a time, asking Finn to let me go would have been unthinkable, impossible. *You,* I would've said, falling into space; *it's you.*

He hears me, though. He lets me go, and when he does, I scan the crowd for Grant and Hailey. I spot them standing together, both rooted firmly to the ground. Next to me, Finn is talking, but I'm preoccupied with getting back to my girl and her father.

"I figured you'd be here tonight," he is saying.

"What?" Turning to him, I'm blinded by the lights from a bulb-heavy tree. "I can't see you. The glare is too bright."

Finn takes two steps to the left. "That better?"

Shielding my eyes, I study his face. He's still Finn. He still has the same shock of blond hair, the same reckless smile, but seeing this no longer knocks me off balance. For the first time ever, I am steady. I am clear. I am totally in my person.

Finn is studying me, too. "You look different."

"I'm a real redhead. You probably can't tell in this light."

"No, it's not the hair. It's something else..." He shrugs. "So like I said, I thought you would be here tonight."

"You were right. I'm here." I hold out my arms and twirl. "But I can't stay." I motion to Grant and Hailey. "I have people waiting."

"Two minutes? Just so I can tell you I'm sorry I haven't called."

"I told you not to," I assure him. "It's actually better that you didn't."

"Still, I should've checked in to see how you were. I just felt...the truth is I'm not very good in a crisis. But your stepdaughter is doing okay?"

"She's coming along."

"And you're happy?" His voice is hopeful. *Happy?* he said once. *Is anyone really happy?*

Grant and the girls are looking around. Like me, they're getting anxious I'm not there. "I'm sorry, Finn. I have to go." Before I leave, though, I close my eyes and lean forward. "Yes, I'm happy," I whisper into his ear. "Some people really are."

He pulls me closer. "Don't go, Eliot. Stay with me."

A chill passes through me. "It's too late." Stepping back quickly, I'm five, ten, fifteen paces away. "I'm already gone." Then I turn and run, back to Grant, back to Hailey, back to Charlotte and Gail—back to my family.

⌒

The moment is upon us.

Standing in front of the tarp, Phoebe says a few words, thanking the artist, Beth Delaney, the board, and everyone else who helped with the chapel renovation. She talks for a long time, boring us all, and the only thing I take away from her speech is that she failed to thank Grace.

Sitting in her wheelchair, Sylvia is wearing the biggest, blackest sunglasses I've ever seen. They're not just sunglasses, they're protective eye goggles designed for miners who toil in the deepest crevices of Chile.

My crazy sister is equipped not to view an art exhibit, but to witness some sort of mythological, cornea-lacerating solar eclipse.

"What? No hazmat suit?"

"One can never be too careful, Eliot, particularly when one is pregnant."

Maggie is giving my mother the blow-by-blow over the phone. Now that everyone else is here, she feels left out, so we're taking turns narrating.

"Phoebe is handing the microphone to the Sculptress. The Sculptress is thanking her children and Riverside and Grant and... *Wait a second...hold on a minute...*it appears the Sculptress just thanked *Eliot*... Yes, *I know*! She *thanked Eliot*... Mom? You still there?... Okay, she's finishing up, blah-blah-blah... Here"—Maggie thrusts the phone at me—"she wants to know how you feel."

"About what?" I ask my mother.

"Being acknowledged in front of all those people! She's come a long way, that Sculptress. Still doesn't take her kids to the dentist, but a long way nonetheless. What's happening now?"

"She's done speaking. She's about to unveil the painting. We'll call you when it's over."

"Stand back!" Sylvia shouts, adjusting her goggles. "It's time for the money shot!"

Beth waves at the crowd. She raises the tarp. For a second, there's silence.

"Oh, my God," someone gasps.

"Look, Mommy, look!" Hailey calls out.

Holding my breath, I look.

There are, I'm relieved to say, no vaginas here. Instead, there is this: three girls on a beach. Two have dark brown hair and tanned bodies. The third is younger, and unlike the others, she's fair with fiery red hair. The three children are playing on the sand, half facing the horizon and half facing a group of adults. There are six adults: a muscular, olive-skinned man with curly black hair; a small woman with wild gray hair; and a third, very pale woman with bold but not brazen red hair. Behind them are three more women. One—a true beauty—has golden-red hair and blue eyes, and the other has the same rich red as the smallest girl. The third, silver-haired woman is surveying the scene, looking proud and defiant. Although none of these women look alike, you can tell they're all related.

"Mommy, look! It's us!"

At first I say no; it can't be, that's crazy. But as I continue to look, the full painting takes shape. Hailey is right—it is us, and we're on the beach, which I know from the details: the pink polka-dot suit with ruffles on the butt, the platform sandals that look like glued kitchen sponges, the dolphin umbrella. On closer inspection, I recognize even more: a pair of diamond earrings, a cast-off glittery necklace, a pair of plastic heels fit for a princess. The details are painted with the same painstaking care as the people—generously, respectfully, with heart.

"What do you think?" Charlotte asks, leading me over to her mother.

"What do I think?" I can't take my eyes off the painting. What do I think?

I think this is what it means to have your dignity restored, to get a shot at redemption. I think this is my worst nightmare wholly reimagined. What do I think?

"Yes, Eliot," Beth says. "What do you think?"

I turn, first to her and then back to the painting. "I think you really love your daughters. I think sometimes it's braver to let your kids go than to hold on to them. I think they're lucky to have you for a mother."

She smiles. "I think you also love my daughters, Eliot. And I think they're lucky to have you . . . too. They're lucky to have you, too."

Lucky to have you for a mother, too, she almost said but didn't. That's because I'm not Gail and Charlotte's mother—Beth Delaney is, always was, and always will be their mother.

Our moment is punctuated by the sound of Sylvia's angry voice. "What *I* want to know is who signed off on this shit?"

Startled, Beth turns around.

"My *hair*," Sylvia moans. "You ruined my hair. The *color* is *completely* wrong. Can you fix it? Please say you can fix it."

Charlotte catches my eye. "It's called *Three Sisters and Three Sisters, Swimming*. That's why I wanted you to come, so you could see it."

"Thank you, Charlotte. It's an unbelievable painting, and I can tell you had a lot to do with it. There's no way your mom knew about those details. Because of you, it's a true work of art." I'm so moved that without thinking, I reach out and grab her, my long-lost ex-stepdaughter, my beloved un-child, and pull her against me.

"I love you," I say, and then tell my ex-stepdaughter Gail and my four-year-old, Hailey, the same thing. I look at my own sisters. "I'm so lucky to have all of you in my life."

Maggie and Sylvia wave me away. "We know," they say, and return to their debate, which is over what Sylvia should wear to Maggie's wedding. Maggie hasn't told a soul yet (other than Sylvia, my mother, my dad, the kids, Grant, Roger, and me) that she plans to marry Dylan. She hasn't even told Dylan yet. Still, Sylvia is extremely concerned about her outfit.

"Of course it's your day," I hear her tell Maggie, "but as your favorite older sister, it's kind of my day, too." This, as you must know by now, is absolutely true, too. It may be Maggie's wedding, but somehow it will end up being Sylvia's day. Just watch.

I realize Grant is looking at me.

"Can you believe that painting?" I ask him over and over. "Can you believe what she did?" I'm rambling, oblivious to the fact that Grant, my ex-whatever, is inching closer and closer.

"You never stop talking, do you?" And the next thing I know, his arms are around me, his mouth is pressed against mine, and he's *kissing* me. *Grant* is kissing *me*, and I'm kissing him back. It's like a familiar dream, this kiss, and as I lose myself in this strange déjà vu, something dormant inside me is roused and brought back to life. Around us, the crowd is going wild, and I know they're cheering for the painting, but I also think it's for us—for the ordinary, average girl who, when kissed by the everyday, run-of-the-mill prince, is suddenly awakened from a long, deep sleep.

Ever After

"YOU'VE DESCENDED INTO darkness, Eliot," Grant says as he walks into my house, which was once his house, too.

The electrical wiring in this place is lousy. So in the three months he's been gone, almost all the lights have burned out, and I have yet to replace a single one. Luckily, he put long-lasting bulbs in a few rooms—the expensive kind that cost five bucks each—which means that as long as Hailey and I confine ourselves to the kitchen, the bathroom, and the master bedroom, we can see just fine.

"It is a little dark," I admit.

"How the hell can you live like this?"

How? How does anyone live in the dark? I squint, I use flashlights; I gave up reading. It's funny, isn't it, how we learn to adapt, even to the most uncomfortable situations? Although I go to absurd lengths to stay with my familiar, it just seems easier to light a few candles than to find a ladder, drag it through the house, prop it up, and so on. This could be because I'm lazy or stubborn. Or maybe, deep down, I think changing light bulbs is a man's domain.

"That is sexist and shallow," Sylvia would say if she heard this.

"So sue me."

"If only I could." She'd shake her head. "If only I could."

Tonight Grant is here, having dinner with me and Hailey. Charlotte and Gail are here, too. There's no special occasion; it's just a random

Tuesday evening. But he called me this afternoon and suggested we get together.

"Is this a date?" I asked.

Yes, he affirmed. It was a date. He even offered to cook but then added, "But not at my house because I don't have pots, pans, utensils, or food."

I wanted to ask what he's been feeding Gail, who's been living there for two weeks, and Charlotte, who's been there even longer, but I didn't. Instead I said, "Sure. I'd love to." And now he's back in our house, dragging a ladder from one room to another, replacing every single burned-out bulb.

After a few minutes, the house is ablaze.

"Oh, my God," I shout from the living room. "I always thought that couch was green."

"Ha ha," he says, but he's laughing, not because my joke is especially funny, but because he's especially happy. "Tonight," he keeps saying, "I have all my girls back."

While Grant makes dinner in the kitchen, I'm in my office, writing my daily letters, which I'll give to each girl when I finish. I can't help but wonder, though, if years from now all these letters will be saved or if they'll turn up at an estate sale somewhere, weather-beaten and illegible, to be picked over by strangers. If they're not thrown out, I suspect they'll end up in the hands of people who have, at best, a cursory interest in their contents. But such is the fate of our personal histories. My hope, of course, is that over time the girls will reread my words and, in doing so, return to this particular place and this particular time. But it's also fine if they don't—as sisters, they always have one another to remember who they are and where they come from.

Grant yells that dinner is ready, and we all convene in the kitchen. Gail has to be asked three times to wash her hands and Hailey twice to turn off the TV. Gail is tired tonight, but that's normal for a kid who just came out of a coma. It's normal for any kid to be tired, I remind myself, knowing I watch her too closely. Despite my fears, her speech is fluid, her physical self intact, and she's reading and problem solving almost at grade level. All of this, her doctors declare, is nothing short of miraculous.

"She's a remarkable kid," they keep saying, as if this is news to us.

If you didn't know that Gail had been in an accident, you wouldn't see anything wrong with her. But we do know, so we notice everything: her hesitancy when she tries to recall a word, the slight limp when she walks, the way she slurs her *s*'s. There is also the larger question of what might happen later on. Will she grow up with seizure disorders, brain complications, mental health issues—or nothing at all? All these concerns bind us together; they're reminders of what we once survived, of what we will continue to survive, as a family.

Gail sees a physical therapist three times a week and spends Saturday and the occasional Sunday at the Banks Center. She told us she loves it there and that one day she wants to work with kids like herself who have suffered some kind of head trauma. "Maybe I'll be a doctor," she said recently. "Or even a brain surgeon. Did you know that an elephant brain weighs six thousand grams and a cat brain weighs thirty grams? How much is a gram, anyway?" She looked straight at me.

I shrugged. "Like a little less than an ounce, maybe?" I couldn't say for sure; I went to public school, too. "Medicine is a great career, Gail. So is nursing."

Grant, on the other hand, encouraged her to think big. "Look into hedge funds, Gail. With a few billion dollars in the bank, you can afford to help anyone."

"Banking no longer guarantees billions," I remind him.

"I keep telling you, Eliot: Money is cyclical."

Since the accident, Grant has become much more practical, largely because Gail is his only hope for early retirement. Charlotte plans to go to art school like her mother, so there's no money there. Nor can we count on Hailey, our quirky, flame-haired clown child. "All I want," she said solemnly, "is to live in a castle and watch TV all day forever."

"What happened to meteorology?" I asked.

"Oh, Mom." Behind her fake American Girl glasses, she rolled her eyes. (There it was again: *Mom*. And where did she pick up that eye roll?) "I *told* you: I want to be a princess."

We each have our dreams, I suppose.

"What's for dinner?" she asks now, sliding into her seat.

"Waffles," Grant says, plunking one on her plate. "We're having waffles and strawberries."

"But waffles and strawberries are for breakfast, silly Daddy."

"Tonight is opposite night, pickle."

This intrigues her, and she and her sisters discuss what they'd do if it really were morning. Charlotte would go back to bed, Gail would play the Sims, and Hailey would watch TV. (What is it with that kid and the TV?) It's silly, illogical banter—your basic family dinner conversation—and I could listen to it every night for the rest of my life.

I get up to grab the water pitcher; and when I sit back down, I hear Grant tell Charlotte and Gail that after dinner, they have to leave. "Tomorrow's a school day," he reminds them.

Gail grabs my hand. "No, I want to stay here."

"It's not up to you, honey. You live with me."

"This is my house. I'm not going." She is unusually defiant. Unlike my own middle sister, Gail never makes demands; she's the peacemaker, my "go along to get along" girl. But at the moment, she's asserting herself, taking control, rearranging our lives. Look at her growing up right in front of our eyes!

Grant is caught off guard. "Gail, you can't stay here. Your mom, Eliot, and I have an arrangement. We decided it's better if you stay with me for right now."

"But it's not better for me. I live here." She bangs her hand on the table, then leaves it there, as if marking her territory. "This is my real house."

I can see Charlotte watching her, trying to learn from her younger sister in a way I'm learning from mine. She is unsure at first, but then she drops her hand on top of Gail's.

"I live here, too, Dad," she says. "I'm not leaving either."

"I'm not leaving either," Hailey says, dropping her hand on her sisters'. "I want to stay here too."

"You live here already, dopey," Gail says, sighing like Sylvia.

"Don't call her dopey," Charlotte says, sounding like me.

"I'm *not* dopey," Hailey insists, sounding like Maggie.

"Well, then." Grant covers the pile of hands with his own, and when he looks at his girls, I know what he's about to say. After so much time together, we understand each other, maybe too well. We know that we love our children, that we do our best, that we make mistakes. We know we can be generous and kind, but also selfish and cruel, and that in the end, neither of us is too good to be true. We know all this about each other, and so what? In real life, unlike in fairy tales, your happy endings are qualified.

"I guess we're staying," Grant says. He sounds relieved.

Something occurs to me. I clear my throat. "Grant, I...I..."

He's amused. "You what? You love me?"

"No." I try to swallow, but my throat is thick.

"You don't love me?"

"No, Grant, I do, but it's more than love. You're the one. I finally understand what it means to believe in something bigger than I am. It's...I don't know...it's..." I look at them all—Grant, Charlotte, Gail, and my precious Hailey. "It's my life; all of you, together. You're my life." I know I'm not making sense, but I'm about to do something I've never done before. See, here's the thing about change: It's not enough to step up to the edge. You also have to be willing to jump.

I get down on one knee. "Grant—" Choked up, I start over. "Grant Delaney, will you"—the words are there, but, but, but—"Grant Delaney, will you marry me?"

I'm expecting his big rush of "yes," so it's deflating when there's dead silence. He won't even look at me. Panic sets in. He's going to say no, I think. He's going to say no, and I'll be left here, alone and in the dark, on the cold, buckling floor of my small, shabby kitchen. And just as I am about to pick myself up, dust myself off, and somehow find the will to live, he bends down to meet me at eye level.

"Erin go Bragh!" he shouts, then pulls me in for another long kiss.

So that's how the story ends: with *"Erin go Bragh,"* my fiancé's nonsensical mating call. (Love how I slipped in *fiancé?*) I could tell you what happens next—how Grant and I promise to love, honor, and cherish; how we *mow the lawn* and seal the deal—but frankly, some things are too personal to share, even between sisters, even between confidantes, even between best friends, like you and me.

⌒

Later, much later, I wake up in a cold sweat.

Gail is shouting in her sleep. "Eliot, Eliot! Help me, please! Please come, Eliot!"

Grant is up too and racing to the girls' room, where Gail is on the floor in a sleeping bag. By the time I get there, he is already holding her. "It's okay," he says over and over. "You're okay."

"Help me! Save me, Eliot!"

Eventually, she calms down. Soon, all we hear is Hailey's steady breathing. I'm about to go back up to bed when Gail calls out my name: *Eliot, wait!* Although she is still in her father's arms, Grant doesn't move, and I realize it's because Gail isn't speaking out loud.

You said, Eliot. You said.

What did I say, Gail?

You said you would save me.

We speak telepathically, as families often do. It's nighttime language, whispered in the dark, between people who know each other intimately and yet love each other anyway. In this way, we're able to reveal all the embarrassing, private things we can't say face-to-face; the secrets we've stored up for days, for years, for lifetimes.

Why didn't you save me? Gail is drowsy; her eyes are closing, her voice drags.

Because I can't, I tell her, watching and listening as she drifts away. *I can't save you, Gail. I can't save any of you. But look at me. Look at me, my sweet girl—I'm here.*

Reading Group Guide

This is a True Story: An Essay from the Author

As a novelist, the one question I am asked all the time is if my books are based on my own experiences. I suppose this is because the novels I have published (although not all the novels I have written) are narrated in a first-person female voice, so they feel more intimate, and thus more likely to have been drawn directly from real life. Or maybe it's because conceptually, the imagination is slippery, and it's easier to grasp where stories come from if you know they are based on actual events. Whatever the reason, readers are always curious to find out which parts of my novels are real versus which parts I've made up.

Here is the short answer: none of the events that occur in *I Couldn't Love You More* actually happened. However, within this invented, self-contained universe, everything in this story is true. In other words, I personally have never experienced the *Sophie's Choice* moment[1] that occurs at the book's halfway point, nor do I know anyone who has. However, if I have done my job correctly, every detail in this novel, including how the characters look, feel, act, and react will be consistent; that is, true to the way I, the writer, envisioned them and you, the reader, ex-

---

1   Spoiler alert.

perience them. Furthermore, I am none of these characters, and I am all of them. Like Eliot, I have one daughter and two stepdaughters. Like Dolores, I am a writer who has seen her share of rejection. Like Sylvia, I can be bossy. Like Maggie, I often say dumb things. But I live and work in New York, not Atlanta. All three of my daughters attend public school, as did I. My girls are nothing like Eliot's girls, physically or temperamentally, nor is their father (my real-life husband) anything like Grant. I did have a big love in college, but he didn't love me back.[2] In the press, reviewers have referred to the autobiographical thrust of my novels, which both is and isn't accurate. Maybe, like Eliot, I am both a mother and stepmother. Maybe my sometimes-red hair is very thin and getting thinner. Maybe I do work hard to protect my daughters and to ensure that each feels as loved as the others do. But *I Couldn't Love You More* is an extended "what if?" and how well it succeeds as a novel depends on how much of it you believe. So, if you believe the whole book, then I have in fact written a true story.

I Couldn't Love You More, like all of my novels, was born of rage and frustration. Although the reasons for my rage differ from book to book, the underlying motivation is always the same: to have my say, usually about someone who has wronged me.[3] In this case, I was bitterly angry that my career as a published novelist was over, and more important, that it wasn't my choice. Prior to this book, I spent six years on a novel that I deemed The Masterpiece. It was the book that Dolores refers to in Chapter 31, the one that was supposed to prove my worth as a writer of serious literary fiction. It had multiple points of view. It went back and forth in time. It revealed unspoken truths about the human con-

---

2   Well, he did, but not publicly, which is a whole other, different kind of book.
3   To clarify: nine times out of ten, the people who wrong me have no idea. Although I burn with the heat of ten thousand suns, I do this silently. Most people will tell you that I am painfully shy and overly nice (too nice, sometimes), but only my closest friends (and now you) know that I can also be opinionated, competitive, and when it comes to writing, very critical of myself and others. However, because I rarely articulate my truest thoughts (not out of fear but because it's not nice), I need some way to express them.

dition. Seriously, though, I believed in the book so deeply, I genuinely thought it would change my life. Unfortunately, despite several editors "admiring"[4] it, no one wanted to buy[5] it, and now the book sits, dead, on my hard drive. Although my work had been rejected countless times before, this particular rejection flattened me. For weeks, I couldn't stop crying.[6] I couldn't write; I could barely read. I was ashamed of my failure, of my sorrow—it was just a book, after all—and my hubris. A few weeks passed, during which I contracted *E. coli* and spent a week in the hospital.[7] It was time, I decided, to quit the writing life for good.

The truth about writing fiction is that no one asks you to write, and no one cares if you do. In fact, very often it feels as though people are actively arguing against it. As an artist, then, your challenge is to create despite (or in my case, because of) the world's indifference and opposition. To make art is a very lonely, very isolating enterprise. Believe me, I would much rather watch crime shows and British period dramas[8] than stare at a computer all day. But I am a writer, which means that even if I have just spent five years working on a dead book that no one wants to read, much less buy, I will sit down and do it again, and again, and again. Why? Because the world is an absurd, chaotic place, and my books help me make sense of it. Writing is what keeps me tethered. When I'm not engaged in a novel, ambient sounds become deafening. There are too many sharp corners. Time moves at a dull, languid pace. I feel too present, too large and ungainly. But when I'm working, the

---

4   An editor "admiring" your book is very different from him or her lobbying their publisher to purchase it.

5   "Buy" and "publish" are used synonymously. In general, when an author says she "sold" her book, she means sold to a publisher (versus to a reader).

6   I always wanted to say I "couldn't get out of bed" because it's much more dramatic than "I cried," but I've held a corporate job since college, so not only did I get out of bed, I also took my kids to school, went to work, made dinner, and everything else a working mother does in the course of a day. I was very sad, though—just also very busy.

7   This detail has no bearing whatsoever on this story. I just think it's interesting. PS—to this day, I have no idea how I got it.

8   Have you seen *The Wire, The Killing,* and *Downton Abbey*? I loved them all, as well as every episode of every version ever taped of *Law & Order*.

loud noises are muffled, the edges smoothed out, and everything is cast in soft focus. Writing well feels like moving through water. It's easy, endlessly satisfying, often exhilarating, and I can lose eight, ten, twelve hours at a clip.[9] Writing novels is like having a conversation with every person who has ever burned you, except you are the only one talking, so you can finally express all that built-up resentment and sorrow. For someone who rarely had her say growing up, this is a very heady, very powerful feeling.[10]

I am the eldest daughter of a traveling salesman who moved his family seventeen times by the time I was seventeen. At the end of the tenth grade, we ended up in Atlanta, where this novel is set.[11] After high school, I studied writing on scholarship at a fancy private college[12], and then struggled to pay for a top MFA program while working full-time. In graduate school, I discovered I was a terrible editor, and had to first relearn how to read before I could then relearn how to write. Most of the writers I went to school with were talented, many far more talented than I, but talent, we all found out, was the easy part. To actually succeed as a writer (and everyone defines "succeed" differently), you have to be able to sit down and write even when you think you suck, even when you're told you suck.[13] Back then, I doubted myself at every turn, but to not try to succeed seemed worse somehow than failing. At first, I was shredded every week, but I burned with righteous indignation, and wrote and rewrote, read and reread, edited and reedited, and graduated with a thesis (my first real novel) that I sold two years

---

9 Conversely, when my work isn't going well, it's like living with a caged animal that hasn't eaten in days.

10 Again, conversely, when you write a book that doesn't sell (see paragraph three: The Masterpiece), it's as if you just had your say but no one was listening, so your words are forever left hanging in the air, like a cartoon balloon.

11 Spoiler alert.

12 This is only partially true. My parents were able to pay for a portion of my first two years of college. However, this detracts from the inspirational poetry of my personal history.

13 On the other hand, what do I know? Maybe you do suck. In that case, you should probably quit.

later to a high-flying editor for a lot of money. There was a feature-film deal, trips to California, book parties, movie premieres, invitations to write for TV, dinners with celebrities. Most of all, though, there was the promise of a grand life ahead—a real writer's life—which makes what happened next even more poignant: My agent couldn't sell my second book. My third book sold and promptly tanked. I couldn't sell my fourth, and I spent the next ten years writing novels and submitting, getting turned down, trying again, failing again. I was exhausted, bitter, resentful and then finally, finished. The irony, of course, is that throughout these painful, punishing years, it turned out I had been living a real writer's life, after all.

Here is another truth about writing: you are rejected, in one way or another, every single day. I graduated from college in 1985, and since then, as I said, I have worked (almost) full-time at an anonymous, old-fashioned, nine-to-five corporate job.[14],[15] So for the whole of my writing life, I worked and went to work. While my friends went to bars, hooked up, got married, and had children, I worked and went to work. Eventually, I had children and got married, too, but I continued to work and go to work—and I continued to get rejected Every. Single. Day. Despite all the rejection, though, the idea that anyone—agent, publisher, reviewer—could say anything that would make me stop is beyond my comprehension. I may never be considered a literary icon, but my art is my art and I work hard at it constantly, trying to understand why some novels succeed and others end up, dead, on a hard drive.

A few months after I put The Masterpiece away, I briefly considered

---

14 For the record, it is not the same job that Eliot has. Therefore, none of the policies or practices of the companies for which I've worked over the years are reflected in this book. (This disclaimer just cracked me up.)

15 One more point about my corporate career: after college, I made the conscious decision to have a stable job, so I wouldn't have to rely on my fiction to pay my rent. This was largely out of fear but also practicality. Now, though, I spend countless hours wondering if I would be more successful if I wrote full-time, or if I would just fritter that time away, watching crime shows, chewing Klonopin, and trolling the Internet for celebrity mug shots. Hard to say.

writing an autobiographical essay for an anthology about dating.[16] Around this time, there was a proliferation of memoirs and anthologies on the market, and writing a simple, short memoir-like piece seemed like a relatively painless way to, if not make money (it wouldn't pay much), then at least to get published. In the end, I decided against it, particularly after I read several essays that focused not just on the writers but also on their children. Some topics were mundane—behavior issues, picky eating habits. Others, though, were bombshells—ultra-feminine boys who dressed up in girl's clothing, ten-year-olds confronted with their mother's suicidal impulses. Still more were blatantly exploitative—daily blogs that chronicled an unknowing child's every movement. As I read these deeply intimate stories, I was distracted, wondering how these children reacted, or would react, when they realized the extent to which their mothers (and fathers, although mostly mothers) had mined their young lives for material. Would they feel powerful or powerless? How might it affect them later on? Were certain details too personal to include? If so, what details were left out? I admit that I also felt dirty, as though by reading these pieces, I had colluded with these writers in some unhealthy, even irrevocably destructive way.[17] So, for-

---

16 When I say "briefly," I mean I considered this for maybe sixty seconds. Although I have no problem with other people revealing intimate details about themselves in print (and God knows I love to read them—the more intimate and twisted, the better), I am extremely uncomfortable revealing my own (this essay is no exception). Furthermore, I don't like to call attention to myself (it's one reason I didn't have a wedding), and despite what may happen in my fiction, I am not a particularly interesting person, nor is my actual day-to-day life worth writing about.

17 To clarify: This is not a value judgment. As a writer, I believe everything—and everyone— I come in contact with is material, and I will use whatever strikes me with absolutely no remorse. (The other question I'm always asked is where I get my ideas. The truth? At the dinner table, during family vacations, and eavesdropping on other people's conversations.) However, I'm a novelist not a memoirist, so I reweave real life into a tangle of fiction. I also have very puritanical ideas about protecting my own children's privacy. My writing is my choice, not my daughters', and I owe them respect and discretion as long as they are still young and defenseless (or at least until they really piss me off). So reading these essays and blogs about real-life children written by their real-life parents stopped me in my tracks. I was infinitely curious about the backstory behind each essay as well as the larger implications of being raised by a writer in the age of compulsive over-sharing. And in the absence of any real answers, I felt compelled to start writing again.

getting that I had just quit the writing life, I sat down and wrote a scene in which the adult daughter of a memoirist describes how it felt to be the subject of her mother's books: "When your mother is a writer, you are more than just a daughter; you're an endless source of material." This was the beginning of what would eventually become *I Couldn't Love You More*, the novel you are now holding in your hand.[18] And *voila*, just like that, I had un-quit. And *voila*, just like that, here we are.[19]

Despite my perpetual self-doubt and self-criticism, I am proud of *I Couldn't Love You More*, largely because it isn't only a fictitious story about fictitious people. This novel, like all novels, also carries with it every second of the honest-to-God, real-life events that led up to its publication—books written, books published, books sitting, dead, on a hard drive. That I have recounted these events, however, is a departure for me. I have been taught, and thus, always believed that my personal history is superfluous, that the artist's life should remain separate from the art. But times have changed, and maybe now that you know the history of this novel, your experience of reading it will be a richer, deeper, more resonant one. If nothing else, I promise you that all my stories are true. I sincerely hope you believe them.

June 2011

---

18 Weird, isn't it, how ideas originate? At first glance, it would seem that this novel started with Eliot and her children, but it actually grew out of her relationship with her mother. In fact, Dolores was the very first character, and the book's central conflict revolved around her college-age daughter's inability to express anger at what she felt was her mother's betrayal of her privacy. After a solid eighteen months of crafting endlessly boring scenes, I realized this conflict wasn't enough to drive an entire novel. So I took a different tack, which was to make the daughter older and a mother herself. My own daughters were growing up (quickly, quickly), and since two of them also have another mother whose ideas about raising children differ greatly from mine, it made sense to put Eliot in a similar situation so that I could explore these very complicated issues fictively. Eventually, as I wrote about Eliot's inherent goodness, a new central conflict—a mother being forced to choose between two children—slowly evolved, organically, from her need to be all things to all people. What if she couldn't? I wondered. What if she really had to choose?

19 Five years after I wrote that first scene, ten years after my second book came out, but yes, here we are.

Discussion Questions

1. One of the many themes in *I Couldn't Love You More* is the idea that the choices we make have consequences that reverberate long into the future. How do each of the characters' choices impact what happens in the book? Do you think the consequences of their choices will have a long-term effect? Have any of the choices you've made in your own life had long-term consequences? Did you ever make a decision you wished you could undo?

2. Eliot is the eldest of three sisters, each of whom has her own distinct personality. Do you think their personalities are a result of their birth order? How do their personalities change over the course of the book? When you were growing up, how did birth order affect you and your siblings?

3. At the beginning of the book, Eliot refers to herself as a "good girl." Given what happens in the novel, is she a reliable narrator? What does it mean to be "good" in the context of the story? Is Eliot a "good" mother? Is Beth? Is Dolores? Conversely, is Sylvia a "bad" girl? Do you think she will be a "bad" mother?

4. When Finn shows up in Eliot's life, she is left very unsettled. Do you think their relationship was as unresolved for him as it was for her? In general, do you think women pine for men more than men pine for women, or is it mutual? Do you wonder about anyone from your own past? What do you think would happen if he/she showed up?

5. Early in the book, Eliot discusses the concept of having a favorite child. When you were growing up, did you feel there was a favored child in your family? How was this manifested? If you have children of your own, do you find it hard not to play favorites?

6. In the first half of this novel, the story focuses on Eliot's relationships with her sisters, her husband Grant, and her ex-boyfriend Finn. By the midpoint, the story veers off in a different direction. Did the book's climax catch you off-guard, or were you expecting

it? In what other ways did the novel overturn your original expectations?

7. The central conflict of this novel revolves around Eliot having to make an unfathomable choice between two children. Can you imagine making a similar choice or is this simply unimaginable?

8. In most of the stories we read, stepmothers are depicted as selfish women who resent their stepchildren. In *I Couldn't Love You More,* the author introduces a stepmother who genuinely loves her stepchildren and does her best to care for them. Is this a realistic portrait of a family, or is it idealized? Are you a stepparent? If not, do you know any blended families? Do blended families have the same types of issues as regular families? In what ways do they differ?

9. The narrator uses humor throughout the book, even in very dramatic scenes. Does this enhance or detract from the story? Do you prefer books that are either very funny or very sad, or do you like a combination of both?

10. Eliot's mother, Dolores, is a memoirist. In this novel, Eliot discusses how ashamed she felt as an adolescent knowing that her mother wrote about her family's personal lives. Have you read any memoirs in which an author discusses his or her living family members? What do you think about this? Does a memoirist have a responsibility to tell the truth, regardless if the person he or she is writing about gets hurt, or are some details better left unsaid?

11. In this novel, the author explores the idea of personal privacy. At one point, Eliot and her stepdaughter Charlotte argue about Charlotte's Internet usage. Eliot believes that posting personal details on the Internet is dangerous and destructive, whereas Charlotte simply sees it as a means of communicating with her friends. Do you think Eliot is overreacting, or do you think she is justified? Do you and/or your children use social networking sites? Why or why not?

12. Late in the novel, when Eliot rereads her mother's memoirs, she

says the experience of reading them as an adult was entirely different than reading them as an adolescent. Why do you think this is? As an adult, have you reexperienced any of your favorite childhood books or movies? Did they seem different from when you read/saw them years ago?

Acknowledgments

Tracy Agerton, Tami Ephross, Carolyn Fireside, Bryan Goluboff, Sharon Guskin, Ann Hamilton, Dr. Karen Hopenwasser, Dr. Nan Jones, Jeff Masarek, Nell Mermin, Erica Moore, Mickey Pearlman, Lara Shapiro, Kim Schefler and Levin, Plotkin LLC, Rebecca Reilly, Caryn Karmatz Rudy, Nick Tarrant, Robin Tuverson.

Naomi Medoff, Lewis Medoff, Mara Medoff, Kim Medoff Worth, Jeff Worth, David Crombie, Joy Dawson, Steve Nakata, M. Dawson, O. Dawson, S. Dawson.

Jen Gates, my beloved agent, again and always.

Todd Lane, who reads all my lousy drafts, never fails to take my side, and cracks me up Every. Single. Day.

Keith Dawson, for depth, wit, clarity, faith, an encyclopedic grasp of how the world works, and without whom this life would be impossible, meaningless.

The Writers Room, Fundación Valpairaíso, Hachette Book Group, particularly Alana Levinson, Tareth Mitch, Brad Thomas Parsons, Sona Vogel, and my editor, Emily Griffin, for her unflinching suggestions, herculean work ethic, unflagging support, and all-around genius.

Finally, special thanks and much love to Jackie Cantor, who, just as I was about to slip under, threw me a line. *Don't give up,* she said.

About the Author

Jillian Medoff is the acclaimed author of the novels *Hunger Point* and *Good Girls Gone Bad*. *Hunger Point* was the basis for an original Lifetime movie starring Barbara Hershey and Christina Hendricks. Both novels have been translated into many languages, including Spanish, French, Hebrew, Japanese, Polish, and Hungarian. A former fellow at the MacDowell Colony, Blue Mountain Center, VCCA, and Fundación Valparaíso in Almeria, Spain, Jillian now lives in New York.

You can read more about her novels at www.jillianmedoff.com.